13·08·16

A SUMME

Victoria Connelly was brought up in Norfolk and studied English literature at Worcester University before becoming a teacher in North Yorkshire. After getting married in a medieval castle in the Yorkshire Dales, she moved to London where she lives with her artist husband and a mad springer spaniel. She has had three novels published in Germany – the first of which was made into a film.

To find out more about Victoria please visit www.victoriaconnelly.com

By the same author

A Weekend with Mr Darcy
The Perfect Hero
The Runaway Actress
Wish You Were Here

VICTORIA CONNELLY

A Summer to Remember

AVON

A division of HarperCollins*Publishers*
77–85 Fulham Palace Road,
London W6 8JB

www.harpercollins.co.uk

A Paperback Original 2014

1

First published in Great Britain by
HarperCollins*Publishers* 2014

A catalogue record for this book is
available from the British Library

ISBN-13: 978-1-84756-284-5

Set in Minion by Palimpsest Book Production Limited,
Falkirk, Stirlingshire

Printed and bound in Great Britain by
Clays Ltd, St Ives plc

MIX
Paper from
responsible sources
FSC™ C007454

FSC™ is a non-profit international organisation established to promote
the responsible management of the world's forests. Products carrying the
FSC label are independently certified to assure consumers that they come
from forests that are managed to meet the social, economic and
ecological needs of present and future generations,
and other controlled sources.

Find out more about HarperCollins and the environment at
www.harpercollins.co.uk/green

Acknowledgements

To my agents Annette Green and David Smith whose support is very much appreciated.

To all the team at Avon, especially Helen Bolton who helped me to find the heart of this story. To Bridget Myhill who read a really *really* early version – remember? To my lovely friends on Facebook and Twitter and to Judy Bourner – my 'Fairacre friend'. To Bronagh McAteer from Handwrittengirl.com. And – as ever – to my husband Roy.

I'd like to dedicate this book to Jill Saint and to take this opportunity to remember her wonderful mother, the writer Dora Saint (1913–2012), whose 'Miss Read' books are a constant source of joy and inspiration to me.

Chapter One

Nina Elliot glanced at the clock on the wall above the filing cabinet, willing the hands to turn a little quicker. The tiny office was so hot. The air-conditioning had broken yet again and the warm spring weather had sent indoor temperatures soaring. Or perhaps it was just Nina's inner rage that was making her feel decidedly uncomfortable.

She looked across her paper-strewn desk towards her boss on the other side of the room.

'No, I've told you that's not good enough!' she was yelling into the telephone. 'Listen to me – why does nobody *listen* to me?'

Nina zoned out as the person on the other end of the line got their ear chewed off. She'd been working for Hilary Jackson in the marketing department of a doctors' locum agency for ten months now and, as far as she was concerned, it was ten months too long. Her previous boss had been a sweet woman called Melanie Philips, who'd worn pink chiffon scarves and rose-scented perfume, and had never batted a blue-shaded eyelid if her staff were running late after their lunch break. The work would get done eventually, she reasoned, but let's have a nice cup of Earl Grey first, shall we?

Melanie Philips was one of those people who seemed lit from within, Nina had often thought, but motherhood had called and the dark shadow of Hilary Jackson had descended.

Hilary Jackson was a tall, thin, rake-like woman with a pale face devoid of both make-up and humanity. She dressed in sombre-coloured clothing, which usually consisted of a navy trouser suit or, if she was in a more buoyant mood, pale grey. Today, it was the turn of the navy trouser suit.

Nina sighed and then gulped as Hilary put down the phone.

'Have you got hold of Keith Maltby yet?' she barked across the room.

'I spoke to his assistant ten minutes ago,' Nina told her.

'Well, why hasn't he called me back?' Hilary said. 'This is very important, Nina, or don't you understand that? I *have* to speak to him now!'

'I've left three messages for him,' Nina explained. 'His assistant said that he—'

'Honestly! I sometimes think you're trying to ruin this company, I really do! You can't seem to do anything right. I always end up having to do *everything* myself. And where's my tea? I asked you hours—'

'It's on your desk,' Nina said, deciding it was her turn to interrupt.

'Oh,' Hilary said, momentarily floored. 'Well, it's stone cold now, isn't it? Get me another and be careful not to add too much sugar. I'm sure you do it on purpose sometimes.'

'Yes, your majesty,' Nina whispered under her breath as she left the office and went into the tiny communal kitchen to make yet another cup of tea for her boss. Her hazel eyes felt dry and gritty, her shoulders felt tense and she knew she had knots in her back the size of golf balls.

This is no way to live, a little voice inside her said, the thought occurring to her for the first time. *You've got to do something. You can't stay here or you'll go mad!*

Her mind spiralled across the long, weary months of working for Hilary Jackson and the countless infuriating things she'd been made to do. Like when she'd worked through an entire weekend whilst her boss sauntered off to some holistic retreat. Or the way Hilary gave her impossible deadlines to meet whilst screaming at her so much that Nina would invariably leave for home in tears.

She looked at her watch now. It was lunchtime. She'd deliver Hilary's fourth cup of tea and then she'd get out of there. She'd feel better once she was outside.

Stepping out into the street five minutes later, Nina breathed deeply as she forced herself to calm down.

Count to ten. Empty your mind. Calm down.

The mantra only occasionally worked around Hilary Jackson, but it was worth trying.

Her foot had just left the pavement when she heard the car horn. Startled out of her trance, she turned around, her fair hair swinging about her face as she glared at the offending driver.

For a moment, everything seemed to happen in slow motion. Standing as if rooted to the spot, Nina looked into the window of the white car and thought she recognised the man at the wheel. Dark hair, dark eyes, dark mood. He didn't smile, and the ensuing blasts from angry drivers urged her to make her mind up quickly.

Nina's heart raced as she jumped back onto the pavement, just as the car swerved to avoid her. That, she thought,

3

was a close call. She shook her head at her stupidity, cursing herself at the danger she'd put herself in because of her inner turmoil.

Taking a deep breath, she crossed the road safely and, once she was on the other side, glanced back over her shoulder to get another look at the driver, but the car had moved on.

'Calm down,' she told herself again. 'You've *got* to calm down, otherwise you'll have a heart attack before you reach thirty.'

She took another deep breath and cursed herself silently, knowing that, on top of her problems at work, she was still shaken from the night before and what had happened with her boyfriend Matt. They'd been together for four years but, as far as Nina was concerned, it was over. She could still see his face now, ashen and furious, his eyes burning with anger as she'd told him how she felt and how she couldn't go on in a relationship with him.

'I *won't* let you do this to me, Nina,' he'd told her as she'd stood in his flat, desperate to leave.

But the thing was, Nina wasn't going to allow him to do—

She paused. Allow him to do what? She didn't have the words to explain it, even to herself. All she knew was that this man made her feel miserable. Perhaps it was a kind of abuse she experienced with him – an emotional abuse. One thing was for sure – he made her feel worthless and deeply unhappy by the things that he did and the things that he said to her. A romantic relationship wasn't meant to be like that, was it? She was pretty sure that she was an average woman, without too many unrealistic expectations when it came to the opposite sex, but surely she should at least feel happy with her chosen

4

partner and not live in dread of what he might do or say next.

She swallowed hard as she remembered all the times he'd made her cry with his belittling comments. He always had to be in control of her – making her say and do things to please him, and she went along with it just to keep the peace and to placate him. But she'd been living a lie. For all those years, she'd been living a lie. Well, she'd finally vowed to herself that it was over and that she'd never let something like that happen to her again. Not ever. She was free from the hold he'd had over her, and she was going to put him out of her mind for good now. In fact, she'd rather not think about men at all at the moment. She had enough on her plate as it was.

'Talk to Janey,' Nina told herself, thinking of the dear friend she'd arranged to meet for lunch. Janey had an answer to every question and a solution to every problem. Walking through the main door of The Black Horse, she saw her perched on a barstool, and let out a loud sigh of relief.

'Was that you being tooted at?' Janey asked through a mouthful of salt and vinegar crisps.

'Some idiot almost crashed at the traffic lights,' Nina rolled her eyes, not wishing to acknowledge the fact that it had been her fault. 'It's been one of those days,' she said, sitting down heavily on the barstool next to her friend.

Janey stared at her with undisguised horror. 'God, *Nina!* You could plant potatoes in that forehead of yours. Are you okay?'

Nina gave a smile that only just began to unfurrow her brow. 'Actually, it's not just been one of those days – it's been one of those months. Still, I shouldn't be doing this, you know.'

5

'Doing what exactly?'

'Drinking during my lunch hour,' she said with a little laugh.

'Oh, it's only one,' Janey encouraged. 'I've ordered our lunch to help soak it up, so it won't do you any real harm. Anyway, you look as if you need it.'

'I certainly do,' Nina said, her eyes widening until she looked positively possum-like.

'So, what is it? Why the phone call at that ungodly hour this morning?'

'I'm so sorry about that,' Nina said. 'I just needed to see you today.'

'You don't have to apologise,' Janey said sweetly. 'I'm not blaming the bags under my eyes on you.' Janey grinned but Nina didn't respond. 'Tell me,' she prompted, obviously wondering what it was that had cost Nina her smile.

Their drinks arrived and Nina took a sip of her white wine, letting the sweet liquid flow into her system, her bright eyes seeming to focus on something that wasn't quite present.

'I've broken up with Matt,' she said at last.

'What?' Janey almost choked at the impact of her words.

Nina shifted her weight on the stool. 'It's been building up for some time now and it just wasn't working.'

'Are you kidding? You two were *brilliant* together! Matt was – well, he was so charming and handsome and—' Janey paused to find the right word, 'perfect.'

Nina visibly flinched. 'No,' she said quietly, 'not perfect.' For a moment, she thought of her first few magical dates with Matt, when he had completely swept her off her feet with his good looks, his wit and his charm. Like Janey, she'd sincerely thought he'd been perfect, but she soon realised that nobody was perfect and it had been only a few weeks later that she'd seen the true Matt.

He'd been the sort of person who found it so easy to make friends because he had an uncanny ability to charm anybody he liked, but that charm would evaporate in private to reveal the real him – the cruel, controlling Matt that most of the world never saw.

'Well, what then? Was he seeing someone else?' Janey tucked a strand of blonde hair behind her ear and looked closely at her. 'You two have been together for longer than I can remember. I think I've worked my way through half a dozen relationships in the time you've been a couple and I always thought—' she paused.

'What?' Nina asked softly.

'I don't know,' Janey said, a wistful expression on her face, 'just that I'd be throwing confetti over the pair of you before too long.'

Nina suddenly felt guilty for never having confided in her friend before, and suddenly wondered why that was. But, deep down, she knew why she'd kept quiet – because she'd blamed herself for the problems with Matt and had stupidly gone on believing that things would get better. Only they hadn't, and she'd finally realised that she had to put a stop to things.

Nina blinked hard, trying to prevent her tears from spilling. She'd promised herself that she wasn't going to cry because she'd wanted this to happen; she'd *made* it happen by instigating the break-up with Matt, and yet the huge swelling of unhappiness that filled her shocked her to the core.

'Do you mind if we change the subject?' She looked at Janey and, for a moment, neither said anything.

'Okay,' Janey whispered, sensing her friend's discomfort. 'But that's not all that's bugging you, is it?'

Nina shook her head. 'Like I said last night – my whole life's a mess.'

'Come on then – let's hear it,' Janey took a sip of wine, as if she needed fortifying before hearing Nina's next confession.

'Work,' Nina said, making the word sound as if it were some newly discovered disease.

'Well, that makes a change,' Janey said with a tut.

'I nearly walked out this morning,' Nina confessed, closing her eyes and reliving the nightmare again.

'Why didn't you, then?' Janey asked, having long been aware of Nina's ability to aspire to something rather than to act.

'But where would I walk *to*?'

'God – you're always so practical!' Janey chided. 'You spend far too much time thinking, and not enough time doing. Sometimes you should just go for it.'

Nina sighed. 'That's easy for you to say. You've got a great job. But not everyone's dad owns a travel agency and sends his daughter to Greece every other week.'

'Hey – that's research for our new brochure!'

'You're the only person I know who hasn't experienced a British winter for the past ten years,' Nina said good-naturedly.

Janey giggled. 'I know. I've been lucky.'

'Yes, you have,' Nina smiled, 'but you deserve it. The most exotic place I get to visit is the local sandwich bar whenever her ladyship wants a BLT. Other than that, it's the photocopy room or, on a good day, the stock cupboard. I wouldn't mind so much if she was civil to me.'

'She's a cow!' Janey stated with a frown.

'Janey!' Nina said in a reprimanding tone, although she was laughing, too.

'Oh, you're *such* a saint, Nina, but Hilary Jackson would even make a saint swear. Why don't you admit it – she's a complete bitch who doesn't value you a jot!'

'Oh, Janey!' Nina couldn't help giggling at her friend's passionate defence of her.

'What about when she made you take that enormous file home to put all those invoices into date order?'

'I know, but I guess it was a job that had to be done,' Nina said with a shrug, before taking the biggest sip of wine she could.

'Yes, but in company time – not when you had a girls' night out planned. I bet she didn't pay you overtime for it either, did she?'

Nina shook her head. 'No, she didn't,' she said, realising that she had been trampled on for so long that even her friend had noticed. Why oh why hadn't she done anything about it before, she wondered? But perhaps the time was now. After all, she had taken control and ended things with Matt, so surely she could do the same with Hilary, she reasoned. This, she realised, could be a whole new beginning for her.

'And remember when she swore at you for sending that letter to the wrong director – which was her fault anyway because she couldn't ever get her facts straight.'

Nina sighed. 'I know, I *know*!'

'And there's no need for her to be so rude to you all the time. That woman's got more hard edges than a Neolithic flint! It's not on.' Janey shook her head in despair. 'So what are we going to do about it?'

'I don't know – *something*,' Nina said, suddenly hiccupping.

'Oh, no, Nina – not hiccups again! That's another thing too. I never knew you to hiccup before you took that dreadful job.'

'Of course I hiccupped! Everyone hiccups.'

'Yes, but not like that. Not with nervous tension.'

'It's not nervous tension. It's probably just wine,' Nina said, giving her loudest hiccup yet.

'You know what you should do, of course? You should just tell Hilary Jackson where she can stick her job and leave,' Janey advised, getting into her stride as agony aunt.

'You think so?' Nina said, a tiny smile emerging at last.

'Yes I do.'

'Just like that?'

'Just like that. Clear your desk out, tell her what you really think of her and go. Easy. You're far too good to be stuck in that box with Hilary forever. You're intelligent, attractive—'

'Soon-to-be unemployed—' Nina hiccupped again.

'No! You've got to be positive about this. Employers will be trampling over each other to get you on board.' Janey smiled encouragingly, not happy at seeing her friend so down. 'Come on, Nina! You've been depressed about this for months now. Something's got to change, hasn't it? What's happened to the old girl I know and love – eh? The girl whose picture is in the dictionary under "vivacious"?'

Nina rolled her eyes in disbelief.

'Well, obviously not today,' Janey agreed, and a moment's silence elapsed. 'Okay,' Janey began again, 'let me put it this way. In an ideal world – what would you do? If you could do anything – what would it be?'

Nina looked into her wine glass. What did she want? What did she *truly* want? She knew it had nothing to do with the present life she was leading, but was an alternative life waiting out there for her? One in which she was truly valued for whom she was? She looked up at Janey.

'I'd like to go back to the office and press Hilary's delete button.'

Janey laughed, not really expecting Nina to come out with such an answer. 'Then do it!'

'I don't know. I've always been taught not to throw too much caution to the wind in case it changes direction and slaps you in your face.'

'Look,' Janey said, placing a tanned hand on Nina's right shoulder, 'I think you've already made up your mind about this, haven't you?'

'Have I?'

'Yes – you *have*,' Janey said, giving her friend's shoulder a squeeze. 'So, you might as well try and have a bit of fun. Just repeat after me: "I'm going to tell Hilary where she can stick her job." Go on!'

'I'm going to tell Hilary where she can stick her job,' Nina repeated obediently, suppressing a particularly large hiccup.

Janey smiled. 'But first, we're going to have another drink.'

Chapter Two

Dominic Milton had almost crashed the car at the traffic lights. It *had* been her, hadn't it, dancing through the traffic like a ballerina? The same Sahara-blonde bob, swinging neat as a pendulum. The same lovely face with eyes wide and inquisitive. The face he remembered with such affection from over a decade ago. Nina Elliot.

He arrived home, parking his old Volkswagen in the last available space. It was a large driveway by normal standards, but now that both he and Alex had cars as well as their parents, parking was in pecking order, which meant that Dominic was often forced to park further down the lane.

He turned the engine off and sat looking over the dashboard for a moment, remembering the way that Nina had looked at him, accusingly, unknowingly. She hadn't recognised him, had she?

He sighed and got out of his car. His mother was home. She'd remember Nina. Ambling up the driveway, shopping bag in hand, he fished for his key and opened the front door.

'Dom, is that you? Dominic?' his mother's voice sang through from the kitchen above the sound of a dog barking.

'Yes.'

'Did you get my hairspray?'

'Yes,' he replied, reaching into the carrier bag for the golden can. He looked at the price sticker and grimaced, wondering if there was such a thing as a drying-out clinic for cosmetic addicts.

'You're an angel,' Olivia Milton said as she walked into the hallway, kissing her son on the cheek. She smelt wonderful, she always did. It was like nothing he'd ever smelt anywhere else; a sort of condensed talcum powder mixed with old roses. Intoxicating, and as much a part of Olivia as her pearl accessories and high heels.

'I've had *such* a morning – you wouldn't believe it! Firstly, Andrea Giles phoned telling me there's been a crisis and that we've lost the speaker for the fundraising dinner we've got next week, so I've been telephoning everyone in my phone book trying to find somebody else who's both suitable *and* available. Then I was trying to make a list of everything we need to organise for this anniversary party and my head was spinning at the enormity of it when your father blasts into the room, accusing me of having moved part of his manuscript. "I haven't been anywhere near your manuscript!" I told him. I wouldn't dare, Dommie! He bites my head off if I so much as knock on his study door. Honestly, he really needs a secretary or something. He's quite impossible!'

Dominic grinned, knowing just how difficult his father could be when he was writing his novel and just how melodramatic his mother could be when trying to deal with him.

'I'm sure everything will work itself out,' he told her.

It was then that a large fluffy dog tore out of the kitchen, launching itself into the air and crashing into Dominic in his own doggy greeting.

'Oh, Ziggy!' Dominic cried, pushing the dog down.

'He'd absolutely *love* a walk, Dom!' Olivia said.

'You mean you haven't walked him yet?'

'I took him out in the garden but you know how he is in the fields. He just drags me along behind him like a ragdoll!' Olivia said with a sigh.

'I don't know why you got him, Mum,' Dominic said. 'He's completely crazy.'

She ruffled the dog's head. 'I just couldn't say no to that face, could I?' she said in the kind of voice she reserved for animals and small children.

'You've got to get him trained,' Dominic said, remembering the day five months ago when his mother had arrived home with the out-of-control puppy.

'I know, I know,' Olivia said, removing the portion of skirt that had found its way into Ziggy's mouth before pushing him away from her and turning her attention to her son once more. 'You all right, Dom?' she asked, breaking his train of thought.

Dominic looked at his mother. 'Do you remember Nina?'

'Nina?' Olivia walked over to the hall mirror, shook her head upside down and applied a heavy mist of hairspray to her thick red hair.

'Our babysitter from years ago,' he added.

'Oh – Neee-na!' she stood back up to full height. 'Well, of *course* I remember her! She was that lovely girl who looked after you and Alex for – let me see – it must have been at least four years.'

Dominic nodded. 'That's right.'

'Gosh, you were such a cute little boy,' Olivia said, patting his cheek.

'I wish you wouldn't do that, Mum,' Dominic complained. 'I'm twenty-one, for goodness' sake.'

'Never too old for a bit of motherly affection!' she said. 'Anyway, what's all this about Nina?'

'I just saw her in town,' Dominic said.

'Really? How is she?'

'No, I didn't speak to her. I nearly ran her over.'

'*WHAT*?' Olivia shrieked. 'Is she all right?'

'Yes, of course she's all right,' Dominic said, but felt a pang of guilt as he realised that perhaps he should have stopped the car to find out. Too late now, though. 'Anyway, I thought you might want to invite her to the anniversary party in August.'

'That's a lovely idea. The more the merrier,' Olivia smiled. 'And we used to all get on so well with Nina, didn't we? Gosh, remember that time she came with us to the theatre and you were horribly sick into your bag of popcorn?'

'Oh, Mum! Don't remind me.'

'And the time she stayed over and we all went to that stately home the next day and Alex fell in the moat, silly boy!'

Dominic couldn't help but grin as he remembered his brother's misfortune. 'And Nina waded in after him.'

'Yes! She was priceless – absolutely priceless,' Olivia said. 'I don't know what we would have done without her. I've often wondered what became of her. She was like a member of the family. Gosh, Dommie, I'm *so* pleased she's back in touch. Give me her address and we'll send her an invite for the party. I can't wait to see her again.'

Dominic almost visibly jumped. He hadn't thought about that, had he? He hadn't even known where she'd lived twelve years ago, let alone now. She might not even be living in Norwich at all – she might just have been visiting friends before moving on. She could live absolutely anywhere.

He suddenly felt sick. What if he'd missed his one opportunity of finding her again?

Nina walked slowly back to the office. As she arrived, she surreptitiously cupped her hands over her mouth, checking for signs of alcohol. She couldn't smell anything that would give her away but she certainly felt light-headed. She tried to banish the smile that was threatening to stretch across her whole face. She'd poured three glasses of wine down her throat. She felt so naughty. She'd never had anything stronger than an espresso during her lunch hour before today. What on earth had got into her? Was it really the spirit of rebellion? Was she really about to assert her true self after months of being nothing more than Hilary Jackson's doormat?

She opened the door into the airless room where Hilary was inspecting a mound of papers on her desk, which looked as if they'd multiplied threefold since Nina had left. It was Hilary's usual mean trick. Whenever Nina dared to leave her desk, she would invariably find that her workload had increased out of all recognition when she returned. Well, not any more, she determined. She'd had enough.

'Ah! There you are,' Hilary said, making it sound as if Nina had been away on an expedition rather than on her lunch hour. 'Didn't you leave me that letter like I asked you?'

'Yes – it's on your desk,' Nina said, indicating as she tried to keep calm.

'*Where*?' Hilary's voice rose a decibel in disbelief as

16

she raked her hands through her short, spiky hair in agitation.

'It was right in the centre – where you could find it,' Nina bit her tongue before she swore. The temporary numbing effect of the wine was fast evaporating.

'Well, I can't see it, can I?' Hilary pushed the papers to one side. 'Oh – *there*!' she said, holding the letter up. Nina breathed a sigh of relief and sat down at her own desk, already desperate for another glass of wine.

'Well, it's creased now. You'll have to print it out again.'

Nina opened the document up on her screen. This, she vowed, would be the last order she'd take from Hilary Jackson.

'Not yet – wait,' Hilary said. 'There's probably something I need to correct first.'

Nina sighed. Just bide your time, she said to herself. See the day out first and *then* tell her exactly what you think of her. Goodness only knew that she needed that length of time to build her courage up.

At four o'clock, Nina left her desk to make the tea. In the relative sanctuary of the kitchen, she stretched her arms high above her head and yawned loudly. She felt exhausted – as if, quite suddenly, all the hours of tedium, frustration and anger of working with her boss had snowballed into one gigantic mass of mutiny. It was time, wasn't it?

The kettle boiled, and Nina poured the hot water into the mugs and stirred vigorously. She put an extra-large sugar into her own mug and the usual half a teaspoon into Hilary's.

Hilary didn't bother looking up from her papers as Nina re-entered the office and placed her mug on her desk. She sat down again, sipping her tea and glancing at her watch for the tenth time in as many minutes.

17

'For God's sake!' Hilary's voice suddenly rose from behind her computer. 'Did you put the bloody sugar in with a shovel?' It was Hilary's usual comment when Nina accidentally put a couple of extra grains in her tea. But Nina didn't say anything. She was waiting. Just waiting.

Half-past five came and went and Nina's computer remained on. Her eyes were sore from staring at its bright face all day and her cream blouse was damp with perspiration. She watched Hilary's face as she proofread the latest copy of the same letter she'd printed out half a dozen times already that day. Hilary. Sounded a bit like horrible, didn't it? Started with an h, same number of consonants. Horrible Hilary. Hilary the Horrible.

Nina shook her head, feeling as if she was fast sinking into insanity, her foot tapping against the desk leg as she looked at her watch, willing precious minutes of her life away before she could make her escape.

A smile curved the corner of her mouth as she recalled her friend's voice in the pub.

'Just clear your desk out, tell Hilary to take a hike and go.'

I will, Janey. I will, Nina said to herself.

'Right!' Hilary exclaimed, making Nina jump. 'That'll do for today.'

Nina got up from her chair before Hilary had a chance to change her mind.

'But I'll need you here for eight tomorrow to start work on the end-of-month reports. First, though, I've got a few items you need to pick up from the dry cleaners. They open at seven so you'll be able to get them en route to the office but don't – *whatever you do* – crease them like you did last time. Honestly, Nina – the state of my jacket when you brought it in! You really don't think sometimes!'

Nina blinked in disbelief. There was no please, no asking if that was all right with Nina – it was just an order that demanded to be obeyed. And that's when the stirring began – a strange bubbling inside her stomach. It felt like nothing she'd ever felt before. Anxiety, apprehension perhaps, urging her forward because, at last, the time had come.

'I won't be here at eight,' Nina said, her voice unusually clear and calm. 'And I won't be here at nine either.' As she spoke, she opened her desk drawer and took out her little pot of lip balm, before reaching to the side of her computer where a framed photo of her childhood pet dog, Bertie, had lived for the past two years.

Hilary looked at her, not quite comprehending. 'I'm afraid it's necessary to work extra hours in order to get the job done. And if you don't value that—'

'No,' Nina said, blowing the light covering of dust from Bertie's frame, causing Hilary to blink. 'Quite frankly, I don't value it because *you* don't value *me* and so I'm leaving. It's something I've been meaning to do for some time now and I really don't know why it's taken me so long.' Nina's eyebrows rose as assuredly as her confidence. 'You are rude, unreasonable and uncaring, and I've had enough.' She looked at her boss briefly, noting the gaping mouth.

'How *dare* you talk to me like that!' Hilary Jackson said, her eyes narrowed into two mean slits.

'This is something I should have done months ago,' Nina told her, staring right back at her and, for the first time since she'd taken the job, unafraid of her boss. 'The very day after you arrived, in fact, because you've made my life a complete misery. We're meant to be work colleagues, but you treat me like your own personal slave. You never ask my opinion about anything. You bulldoze over any suggestions I dare to make or else claim them for yourself and take all the credit for them with the management team. You swear at me. You set unreasonable deadlines and expect me to do hours of overtime without any extra pay whilst you slink off to your holistic retreat! Well, it's over, Hilary! I'm not going to be treated like this anymore!'

'*What*?' Hilary barked.

'I believe I'm owed my notice in annual leave, which I've been unable to take for some time, owing to your ridiculous deadlines as well as the volume of work you've put my way.' Nina swung her handbag over her shoulder and, after one last look around the room, walked slowly away from her desk.

'Nina Elliot – you just stop and think about what—'

'Goodbye, Hilary,' she interrupted before opening the door. 'And good luck finding a replacement,' she continued, 'because you'll need it.'

When Nina got home, she kicked her shoes off and watched them hit the skirting boards with a satisfying thump. She'd done it; *really* done it this time, and not just acted out a scene in her head with a thousand witty retorts to each one of Hilary's nasty instructions. It had felt wonderful. She'd felt free and full of all the possibilities that the future now held for her. She just had to decide what she wanted to do with it.

Chapter Three

When one door closes, somewhere a window is opened. At least, that's how the saying went. But, Nina couldn't help wondering the next morning if it had been wise to close a door before even knowing where to look for a window. Maybe not, but it had certainly been liberating.

Janey had sounded delighted when Nina told her.

'Well done, you!' she cheered down the phone. 'Now don't go walking into another nasty little job again. Have a break – enjoy yourself,' she advised. That was all very well, but what was she going to enjoy herself with? Fun always seemed to come with a pretty hefty price tag. And, finding herself out of teabags as well as T-shirts, Nina thought she should at least start to look for another position.

The local recruitment agency wasn't exactly what Nina had hoped for on the first day of her new-found freedom. The stark walls and bland office furniture looked like a 'before' room on a television makeover programme, and the jobs the city had to offer were just as uninspiring. Nina tutted, rolled her eyes, bit her lip and then walked back out into the sunshine. Janey was right. There was absolutely no point in summoning up the courage to jack in your job only to leap into another job that you didn't totally love. She was worth more than that, and this was going to be a new start for her – not just in terms of a job but in her personal life, too. She was leaving behind the old Nina with the bad boyfriend and the bad job. Who knew what the future held in store for her? All she had to do was to remain optimistic and keep smiling.

She held her face up to the early summer sunshine, rejoicing in the fact that she'd never have to face Hilary Jackson again in that tiny, airless office. She'd never forget her boss's face as she'd said goodbye. Like Munch's 'The Scream' with a touch of Lady Macbeth. It had been quite scary, and Nina began to feel sorry for the next poor soul to be taken on by her old boss. But that wasn't her concern. She'd done her time and now she was free.

It was a bright Wednesday morning at the end of May and she didn't have to work; the city was her oyster. She could do what she wanted – visit all the places she never had time to when she was working. She could go to an afternoon matinee at the cinema, amble up the cobbled back streets and poke around the galleries and antique shops. She could browse around the bookshops or sip a cappuccino overlooking the rainbow array of the market. It was all there for the taking.

Nina chose the market.

The scent of fresh fruit and vegetables filled her nostrils and she walked without any real direction between the stalls. Cards for every occasion, cushions, CDs, casual coats, courgettes and chips – it was all there, and Nina ambled happily amongst the shoppers, smiling at everything yet nothing in particular, losing herself in the living labyrinth.

When she finally tunnelled her way out, she had to shade her eyes against the sun and, as she did so, she noticed a small boy crying and pointing up to the sky. She followed his gaze and saw a bright red balloon drifting high above the shops towards the heavens. His mother grabbed his wrist and dragged him away.

For a few moments, Nina stood transfixed, watching the red balloon until it became nothing more than a scarlet pinprick against the sky. Best go shopping for some food, she thought. It would be a new experience to go shopping on a weekday and the very thought of it made her smile. Even the simplest task was beginning to seem like an adventure.

Dominic wasn't having any luck at all. First of all his mother and brother, Alex, had blocked his car in – again – and then he'd found he was out of petrol. He'd had to beg twenty pounds from his dad in return for a promise to trim the yew hedges at the back of the house, which was a task worth at least fifty pounds of anyone's money.

And things didn't get any better when he reached Norwich. Just what was he doing? It was madness, sheer madness to be driving around, getting caught up in the one-way system in the desperate hope of spotting her again. And the lunch hour traffic was hell. But on he drove, narrowly avoiding several careless workers who thought they could cross safely in front of him after having one too many at the pub. But not once did he run into Nina.

Where was she?

Since nearly running her over, he hadn't been able to stop thinking about the old days, when he and Alex had been growing up. He had so many fond memories of his childhood and the reappearance of Nina had woken them all up. And his mother was very keen to see her again. If only there'd been more time. If only he'd got her number.

After an honorary lap around the one-way system, he parked his car. He might as well make the most of finding himself in the centre of town, he thought, so he walked around the market, breathing in the scent of fresh flowers and fruit, the salt tang from the fish counter and the glorious smell of hot chips. He wandered about, turning left here, right there, until he surfaced once more into the dazzling light.

It was then that something caught his eye: a small boy was crying and pointing towards the sky. Dominic looked up and saw a red balloon floating away. Poor little mite, he thought and then sighed. Like the little boy, he wasn't quite sure what he should do next.

He loved the city and often wandered around without a particular direction in mind, and today was no exception because he really didn't have a direction to follow.

It might be worth going back to the zebra crossing, he thought, but it wasn't very likely that she'd be there. He was just wasting his time. She was but one person in a city of thousands. But he had to try, didn't he?

Olivia Milton clinked a second bottle of wine into her shopping trolley and searched her pockets for the list she'd made earlier that morning. It wasn't there of course. She knew she'd left it on the kitchen table. She also knew that there'd definitely been more on the list than parmesan cheese, olives and Pinot Noir.

She pushed her trolley into the next aisle hoping that, by scanning the shelves, her memory would be jogged and that they'd all actually be able to eat that night.

Olivia always did her shopping on a Wednesday. Nina, on the other hand, had never experienced the pleasure of a supermarket when one was able to move freely through it and not spend longer in a queue than you had spent actually choosing your items. And, also unlike Olivia, Nina had her list with her.

It was the strangest feeling being in a supermarket when she should have had her feet tucked firmly under a desk and her ear glued to a telephone, having orders barked at her by Hilary Jackson. However, now she was unemployed, she became acutely aware of the cost of things and had to make sure that she only got the absolute essentials.

As she turned into the next aisle in the hope of finding a jar of pesto sauce for under a pound, she almost crashed into a trolley that had been left at right angles for all and sundry to trip over and into.

Nina grinned as she saw the contents: two bottles of wine, a slab of parmesan and copies of *Hello!* and *Country Life*. She could just imagine the sort of person who'd own such a trolley. Barbour and pearls, she thought. Land Rover and Labrador sort. This woman wouldn't have to hunt for three-for-two offers or dented tins that had been reduced. Oh, no.

Nina looked down the aisle and gasped. It was her: no Barbour today – it was far too warm – but little pearl earrings, an old-fashioned piecrust blouse and a long loose skirt in a Liberty fabric, which might have made her look terribly middle-aged and dowdy but which, in fact, looked wonderfully regal on her and marked her out as part of the country set. Her red hair was cut sharply and blow-dried to perfection, and her flawless skin was made up with the absolute minimum of make-up.

She watched the woman bend down to reach for a bottle of tomato sauce. It was the next item on her own list and she walked towards the shelf. Leaning forward, the strangest sensation hit Nina – via the nostrils. The most heavenly scent enveloped her and instantly transported her back to her past. An image of a beautiful white Georgian mill house by a river in the heart of the Norfolk countryside. A house that had been hung with heavy printed curtains and filled with huge log-like pieces of furniture in oak. And the two young boys she'd looked after.

It was Mrs Milton.

Nina watched for a moment, just to be sure, smiling at the memories that were resurfacing, before summoning up the courage to speak.

'Mrs Milton?' Nina's voice was quiet, but obviously startled the woman.

'Yes?' she said, turning around in surprise.

Nina cleared her throat. 'I don't know if you'll remember, but I used to babysit for you. I'm Nina Elliot.' Nina watched in amazement as the woman's face beamed, her eyes crinkling at the edges.

'*Neena!* Gracious! I don't believe it. Are you all right?'

'Yes, very well, thank you.'

'No – I mean – after what happened.'

'Pardon?' Nina was puzzled. How on earth could Mrs Milton have heard that she'd walked out of her job?

'Dominic – the car – he told me all about it.'

'Car? But I don't have a car,' she said.

'No – *his* car. You know – he nearly ran you over. I was terribly worried. Silly boy.'

Nina's expression remained one of complete bafflement but then the cogs of her memory slowly turned, releasing

26

the image of the stern face at the traffic lights, the car horns, the panic, the half-recognition.

It had been Dominic. Little Dommie Milton whom she'd once tucked up into bed; the little boy who'd once woken her up because of a nightmare involving giant sunflowers. This same little boy had nearly run her over.

'Oh, yes!' Nina exclaimed, 'But I didn't know it was him. I mean, I thought I recognised him, but—'

'But you're okay?'

'Yes! Absolutely fine. It was my fault really,' Nina said. 'I just wasn't thinking straight, but I'm fine, thank you.'

'What a relief. Honestly. He goes around in a dream, that boy. He really shouldn't be behind a wheel at all. Well, other than a potter's wheel.'

'Gosh, how is everyone?' Nina asked with a smile, trying to imagine the young boys who would all be grown men now.

'Oh, very well – very well,' Olivia enthused. 'Billy's working in London as a pilot and taking off all over the place. Alex has had about twenty different jobs since graduating and can't seem to settle to any one of them, and Dommie's just graduated from art school and is preparing for his first art show in Norwich.'

Nina beamed a smile. 'You must be so proud of them all.'

'Oh, I am!' Olivia said. 'And you wouldn't *believe* it but Dudley and I have our twenty-fifth wedding anniversary this summer,' she said, as if not quite believing it herself.

'Oh, congratulations!'

'Thank you,' Olivia paused and then her forehead crinkled, 'only there's so much to organise! We've never thrown such a big party before. We're having a marquee set up in the garden and a band and balloons and flowers – the works! It's almost as much fuss as our wedding day.'

'It sounds like it's going to be a lot of fun,' Nina said, remembering the times she'd joined the Miltons for lunches and dinners at the mill and how splendid they'd made even the simplest of meals, with the great table set with silver, glass and fine china. She couldn't imagine how splendid an anniversary party was going to be.

'And you *must* come along, Nina! We'd love to have you as our guest,' Olivia said. 'Now, would you mind *awfully* if I looked in your basket? I've come out without my shopping list and I've gone completely blank. I can't remember a *single* thing we need.'

'Of course I don't mind,' Nina said, trying not to grin as she remembered the wonderful forgetfulness of her former employer.

Olivia looked thoughtful. Milk, bread, a tub of margarine, a small box of nasty-looking soap powder, bananas and an economy pack of tissues.

'See – I haven't got any of those. TOILET PAPER!' Olivia shouted, startling a passer-by before taking off into the next aisle, leaving Nina to stand guard over her trolley. She really was a case. Nina had never managed to work out how she could host a dinner party for twelve and bring up three boys, but never know where to find her lipstick.

'Here!' Olivia said, returning with two bumper-sized packs of toilet paper. 'Thank goodness I ran into you. My head is spinning so much with everything at the moment that the simplest things seem to elude me. Anyway, I simply can't believe how many years it is since we all saw you. There's *so* much to catch up on.'

'Yes,' Nina said, trying to remember exactly how many

years it had been since she'd last visited the mill. She'd stopped babysitting for the Miltons after going to university, and that was ten years ago now.

'So, what are you doing with yourself these days?' Olivia asked her.

Nina bit her lower lip. It was the question bound to be asked sooner or later, but she hadn't had time to prepare an adequate answer, not thinking she'd ever meet anyone she knew during a weekday trip to the supermarket.

'Secretarial work,' she said. 'Actually, I've just finished a job that was – well,' she paused, 'it wasn't right for me and I'm trying to find something that fits, you know? Something where I can really make a difference and feel valued.'

Olivia nodded. 'Well, you were always valued at the mill. You were our favourite babysitter. You had *such* a way with our boys. You deserve nothing but the best,' Olivia said, smiling kindly and then her eyes seemed to glaze over for a moment. 'Goodness,' she said. 'I've had the most wonderful idea. You said you're looking for a job?'

Nina nodded. 'Yes,' she said warily.

'Then I might just have the very thing for you,' she continued, her eyes widening. 'How about popping over to the mill tomorrow morning. Are you free?'

'I am,' Nina said.

'Excellent!' Olivia said. 'Oh, how exciting this is. I can't believe it. First, Dommie nearly runs you over and then I run *into* you! I tell you, this is fate, Nina. It really is. Now, don't forget about tomorrow – mid-morning?'

Nina nodded, wondering what on earth Olivia had in mind for her.

'Oh, God! I've forgotten the mince!' Olivia suddenly exclaimed, grabbing her trolley and executing a quick three-point turn, narrowly avoiding the tins of custard. 'See you tomorrow, Nina!'

'Goodbye, Mrs Milton,' Nina called after her, watching Olivia waltz away with her errant trolley.

Grabbing a bottle of tomato sauce in a brand she'd never heard of, but that was offering twenty per cent free, Nina felt a definite skip in her step as she headed towards the check-out. She was going to visit The Old Mill House. With the river rushing by it and buttercup fields and bluebell woods on the doorstep, it was a little piece of paradise in the heart of the Norfolk countryside. It had been years since she'd been there, years since she'd even thought about it, but it had always held a special place in her heart. It would be wonderful to see it again – wonderful to see the boys again. Perhaps, Nina thought, this was the very door she'd been looking to open.

Chapter Four

Olivia couldn't wait to get home. For once in her life, she'd managed to leave the supermarket with more than a carrier bag filled with magazines and what her husband referred to as 'entertaining food'. No, this time she had real, edible food that would fill bellies and, what was more, a piece of news she couldn't wait to tell Dominic.

The narrow winding Norfolk lanes almost shook as she drove home and the thick hawthorn hedges seemed to tremble as Olivia took a corner a little too fast here and braked a little too hard there. She knew she was the perfect picture of the sort of woman men cursed to see behind a wheel, and it had only been a few minutes since she'd been telling Nina that it was Dominic who shouldn't be driving. If there was such a thing as driving genes, Dominic had certainly inherited his from his mother.

Turning into the unmade lane that led to The Old Mill House, Olivia heard the bottles of wine clinking on the back seat and slowed her speed, winding her window down to inhale the sweet perfume of the hedgerows. It really was the most perfect place, she thought, and that was saying something for the girl who'd seen the world as a cruise director on The Sea Queen.

That was how she'd met Dudley, of course. He'd been accompanying his elderly mother on holiday and, after playing Cupid on behalf of her shy son, Delia Milton had had the pleasure of welcoming Olivia to the quiet corner of Norfolk that the Miltons had owned for decades. Olivia had known that her voyaging days were over, but she had happily settled into the role of wife and mother, dedicating herself to her husband and three boys, and throwing herself into every committee going, organising charity events and jumble sales for the local church as well as the village horticultural show.

Even though her three boys were now all grown-up and independent, her time was still wonderfully full, she thought, as the car bumped down the lane. She shook her head. Ever since her arrival as Dudley's bride, he had said he'd get the overgrown and pothole-filled lane into some sort of order, but Olivia rather liked it. It added to the overall charm of the place and she adored the feeling of leaving the tarmac and venturing onto the bare earth.

She bounced along, her eyes darting about the hedgerows, which were a froth of white cow parsley, as her nails drummed a pink tattoo on the steering wheel. Since the meeting in the supermarket, her mind had been working overtime.

'Secretarial work . . . I'm trying to find something that fits,' Nina had said. It seemed almost *too* perfect, what with the organisation of the anniversary party and her husband's current helplessness. Olivia knew that, as a struggling author, Dudley really couldn't operate without a secretary and, since 'Teri with an i' had walked out, his mind, as well as his study, had been in dire need of organisation. He'd been driving everyone potty lately, wandering around the house, looking for someone, anyone, to drag back into his study and help him clear up the mess.

'How am I expected to do *everything*?' he'd rail, as if he really had lost the plot completely. Honestly, Olivia had always been under the impression that writing a novel was a nice, relaxing sort of a pastime, but Dudley made the whole experience sound horribly painful. She often wondered why he didn't give it all up and just play golf instead. It would have been much simpler.

She shook her head in despair as she thought of her husband. She'd never washed so many dishes in her life as recently, quickly learning that, as soon as his footsteps were heard on the hallway tiles, a quick dip in the sink gave her the perfect pardon from the dreaded typing duties. But that was no answer to the problem. 'Teri with an i' hadn't been perfect, but at least she'd been present. However, Dudley's terrible temper had obviously been too much for the poor girl to handle – although Olivia had her suspicions that her middle son, Alex, might also have had something to do with Teri leaving so suddenly, without an explanation. Alex was usually at the root of any problems to do with young ladies and, with him planning to come home for part of the summer, The Old Mill House would no doubt become one giant light-bulb, with the county's female population playing moths.

Honestly, she despaired of her sons sometimes. Alex, with half of Norfolk's girls after him as if he were some sort of Pied Piper of passion, and Dominic, dreaming his life away into his paintings. Then there was Billy – her beloved eldest – who seemed to work all the hours God gave him, but still hadn't sorted himself out in the girl department. Olivia rolled her eyes. Sometimes she felt as if she was a modern-day Mrs Bennet, only with sons instead of daughters to marry off.

Crunching her car into a position that wasn't quite straight and that would be testily commented on later by her husband, she grabbed the bags of shopping and practically ran into the house.

'Dommie? Dud? Anyone at home?' she called into the echoing hallway.

The house was quiet apart from the excited barks of Ziggy. She walked through to the kitchen, gave Ziggy a dog treat to shut him up and sat on one of the stools, shopping bags surrounding her, looking at the antique clock on the wall that was always set ten minutes fast and knowing that she should really make a start on lunch. But it was too late; her eyes had caught sight of one of the bottles of wine. Not too early for a drink, was it? She'd just make it a quick one, give herself a chance to flip through the magazines and catch up on the celebrity gossip.

Nina sighed as she picked up the telephone. Her eyes ached as she read the tiny print of the local newspaper. Situations Vacant. Nina knew why they were vacant, too. Badly paid, badly run companies with no perks and definitely no prospects – but she nevertheless felt compelled to find out what her options were on the job front. But would this one be any different from the others she'd circled?

'Hello, can I speak to Mrs Anne Conti, please?'

There was a pause as the receptionist transferred her call to the human resources department via a blast of Vivaldi.

'Hello? Is that Mrs Conti? My name's Nina Elliot. I've just seen your advertisement for a secretary and was wondering if you could send me an . . . oh, really? So quickly? Okay. Thank you for your time.'

Nina hung up and drew another neat red line across the paper. Internal applicant no doubt, she thought, realising she'd been through half the paper without any success.

She got up and crossed the room, looking out of her flat window and up into a sky the colour of forget-me-nots. It was a lovely day again, and she was looking forward to visiting Olivia. Images as pretty as a Monet painting filled her mind. The Old Mill House. Green fields stretching to the horizon, a garden overflowing with flowers, the river – rushing and rousing – the perfect restorative. She hadn't thought much about Olivia's mention of a job the day before. She hadn't dared to. Remembering Olivia from her time at the mill, it was probably something like arranging the flowers on her hallway table or helping out with the weekly shop. Anyway, it was nothing that was likely to add up to a living wage, Nina thought with a sigh. Besides, the idea of returning to the mill and actually working there was just too good to be true.

She'd always been made so welcome there. In the four years she'd been the Miltons' babysitter, The Old Mill House had been like a second home. Well, a first home, if Nina was really honest with herself. She'd always been so happy there. It had been a little sanctuary away from her own home when her parents had been fighting about who should move out and what belonged to whom in the run-up to their divorce. It had been tough being an only child and Nina had been secretly jealous of the Milton family, with their three young boys and inexhaustible number of cousins, aunts and uncles who were always popping over. The house was never empty and Nina couldn't help

35

wondering what it would be like now. Would it still be the happy drop-in centre that she remembered – or had the boys and the cousins all found places of their own and no longer felt the need to return to the family home?

All the same, Nina thought, how comforting it must be to have a family home to come back to, even if you chose to live on the other side of the world. It was a rare thing nowadays to have your parents still together and still living in the same home where the family had been brought up, and she couldn't help envying the Milton boys that security, because she'd never had it in her own life.

Olivia anxiously buzzed around the house like a mad wasp. She straightened the hemline of a curtain, adjusted a vase on the mantelpiece, picked a few dead leaves from her house plants and plumped a few cushions. She wanted everything to be absolutely perfect for Nina's visit.

She hadn't spoken to Dudley about the possibility of a new secretary – not yet – she wanted to tell Dominic first. Wouldn't he be surprised? She couldn't wait to see the look on his face. At least it might replace his current demeanour. He'd been a little brooding of late and she was worried about him. Olivia was used to worrying about her youngest, of course. It had always been the same, she thought, picking up a silver-framed photo of the boys.

Billy, the eldest, was the brains of the brothers, always ready with the answers for Trivial Pursuit; Alex was the playboy, and had been chasing girls as soon as he'd been able to walk. Then there was Dominic. Olivia's finger traced the face in the photograph. A mother wasn't supposed to have favourites, but Dominic had always had a special place in her heart; he was the introvert, the artistic one, who'd spend his evenings painting a canvas whilst his brothers would be painting the town.

Not that he'd been short of admirers. The lovely Faye had been around almost as long as there'd been a Dominic, and the relationship had been quite serious throughout their teenage years. But, since Dominic had been away at university at one end of the country and Faye had been studying horticulture at the other, they seemed to have forgotten about their burgeoning relationship. However, since Olivia had employed Faye to give their garden a makeover, she now realised that the young girl was still very much in love with her son.

Olivia's mind drifted back to the past and some of the family occasions when, as far as she was concerned, Dominic and Faye had been Norfolk's sweetest couple. Birthdays, Christmases, New Years and countless afternoon teas and evening suppers had always included Faye. She had been an honorary member of the Milton family and Olivia couldn't bear the thought of her not being a part of their family's future, which was why she was, in her own unsubtle way, trying to get Faye and her son back together again.

Dominic was having none of it, of course.

'Mum! Just stop!' he'd insisted. 'It isn't going to happen. We've broken up. End of story.'

'But Dommie—'

'And don't call me that. I'm not a child any more.'

No, Olivia thought, he wasn't. He was a twenty-one-year-old graduate. A young, single man who really would benefit from the love of a good woman.

But where on earth was Dominic?, Olivia wondered, as

she waited for Nina to arrive. It wasn't just Faye he was avoiding lately, but everybody.

Nina couldn't help but smile at the reflection that greeted her. The dress she'd pulled out of the wardrobe was old but pretty, and was certainly an improvement on her jeans.

She rubbed her hands over the goose bumps on her arms, that were fast turning into goose-mountains, and rummaged around on the floor of the wardrobe for her cotton jumper. She grinned. Not exactly the height of fashion, but she was a practical girl and refused to freeze just in case she ran into an old boyfriend she didn't even want to impress any more.

For a moment, she thought about Matt, looking at the answer phone that was telling her she had five messages from him. He wasn't going to give up that easily, was he? The first message had been the Matt she'd fallen in love with – the charming young man who had wooed her with his words as well as his good looks.

'I miss you so much!' he'd told her. 'Call me. I can't bear not seeing you. You're everything to me.' Her hand had hovered dangerously over the phone. The second message was similar but his voice sounded more anxious and, by the third message, the anxiety had turned to anger.

'Where *are* you, Nina? What's so important in your life that you can't call me back? Who do you think you are, anyway? You can't do this to me. I won't let you!'

Nina's hands had begun to quake in the way that was all too familiar from the past when Matt's moods turned, and she'd listened to the fifth and final message with trepidation. It had been horrible. He'd sworn, called her names, said he never wanted to see her again – *never, never, never* – and then hung up. It was a pattern that she had come to know well.

Throughout their relationship, she'd often thought that she'd prefer him to physically hit her rather than inflict so much emotional abuse on her. It might, she thought, have been less painful in the long run.

Now, looking at her reflection, she knew she'd done the right thing in breaking up with him. Friends like Janey might be shocked by the split, but they'd only ever seen one side of Matt. They never saw the other man because he was an expert at hiding him to everybody but her.

She took a deep breath. She wasn't going to think about Matt now. He was her past, and she was determined to make the very best of the present. She grabbed her hairbrush and decided to put a bit of make-up on in the hope that it might ward off the possibility of freckles. She'd once naively thought that freckles were like spots and that you grew out of them, but hers seemed to be getting more prominent as she charged through her twenties.

She glanced at the contents of her bathroom cabinet and pulled out a likely looking tube of foundation. Oil-free, retouch-free, perfume-free, high SPF, enduring and moisturising. That was all very well, but did it prevent freckles? Nina squirted a small amount onto her fingertips and got to work, and then, finally, she was ready to go, leaving her small flat for the bus and the short ride back into her past.

Dominic hadn't been hiding, not consciously anyway. He'd just been busy. Busy thinking. It was summer, and that usually meant that it was summer project time.

It had begun five years ago during the sixth-form holidays. He'd set himself the challenge to create some huge canvas; some monstrously large painting that would occupy the whole length of the summer holidays. The last two efforts had even impressed his parents enough into hanging them in their hallway where they accosted unsuspecting visitors.

The first had been a view of the mill house from across the river, but its primitive style suggested more of a great white palace standing at the top of Niagara Falls. It was stunning, and any visitors who hadn't seen it before were shocked into instant silence.

'That's one of Dominic's,' Olivia would explain with the pride peculiar to mothers. She'd then hand them a thick embossed card with her son's details on, which she'd had made up in the hope of creating an initial customer list.

The other canvas was of Burgh Castle out on the Norfolk coast; a hauntingly isolated place with great icy flint walls that stretched to infinity. The foreground, which was dominated by the castle's walls, was spiky, and shown in great flashes of white paint, but the distance softened into pale reed beds, gentle as feathers, and a windmill could just be spied, extending its sails into the vast sky.

This year though, Dominic was steering away from landscapes. He was after something special, something a little more human. After all, it was his parents' twenty-fifth wedding anniversary and he wanted to create something special for them. He also had his mind on his own future, teaming up with a group of his artist friends to put on an exhibition at the end of August at a gallery they were hiring in Norwich's Tombland – a beautiful part of the city where medieval buildings jostled with Georgian ones, and tourists congregated along the cobbled streets in wide-eyed wonder. Dominic only hoped that wallets as well as eyes would be wide open when the time came for their show, and that such exposure would help him to get his name out there.

He also had another goal to fulfil – to get a London gallery to take him on. He'd had interest from a number of galleries around the Norfolk and Suffolk coasts, whose owners had fallen under the spell of his large breezy canvases that captured the East Anglian light so perfectly, but Dominic was ambitious and wouldn't rest until his paintings were hanging in the capital. He'd been making approaches on the quiet, keeping the rejections a secret from his friends and family, and trying desperately to remain optimistic whilst jostling for attention in an overcrowded field.

But he couldn't think about it just now, not on an empty stomach. He'd been walking around the fields for what seemed like hours in search of inspiration, resulting in only a few brief sketches, and his hunger had made him gravitate towards the mill where he was sure there'd be something tasty to cook.

For a moment, he thought about Nina and the foolishness of his wild goose chase around Norwich the day before. He couldn't help feeling sad that he'd never see her again, but there were other things to think about right now.

Crossing the old brick and flint bridge, he gazed up at the three-storey mill house and smiled. The sight of the imposing white house never failed to fill him with joy, and he couldn't imagine living anywhere else. It was a characteristic of so many of his friends, too. Sure, university had beckoned, sending him away, and gap years with travels across Himalayan mountains and South American deserts had enticed many of his friends, but Norfolk had a strange pull on a person and, one by one, each of them had returned.

For an artist, it was a hard place to beat, with the lucidity of its light and the domineering sky. There was always something new to see. A field, for example, would be an arctic-white wilderness one minute and a green paradise

41

the next, and a hedgerow would be a bristly tangle of thorns one season and a perfect lacy froth of flowers soon after. Each season was a gift and Dominic never stopped feeling grateful for that.

He glanced up into the chaste blue sky. Even his brothers Alex and Billy weren't immune to the charm of the place and both would be spending more time at the mill now that the summer was here. Long weekends would be taken away from their lives in London and, of course, they would both be back for the big party in August.

Dominic shook his head as he thought about his brothers. Alex would never admit to it, but he loved the mill as much as anyone. The only thing was, he loved the city just as much and got the heady thrill he needed from the bright lights and night-long parties that his new job in advertising allowed him. Still, Dominic saw the look of pure content-ment on his brother's face whenever he returned home to sink into the sofa and be waited on hand and foot by their mum.

And Billy? At twenty-four, Billy was only three years Dominic's senior, but he seemed to have lived a lifetime in that age gap and had a worldly wise look about him that made him seem much older than he was. He'd been working in London as a pilot, but he was spending more time in the Norfolk countryside and Dominic had a suspicion that he might be thinking about moving out of the city. Still, Billy played his cards pretty close to his chest and usually stayed with friends in the next village when he came back to Norfolk because he liked being able to come and go without the well-intentioned interference of their mother, so they never really got to the bottom of things with him.

At least, Dominic thought, he was here and he had no plans on packing up and leaving. The furthest he ever got was the North Norfolk coast or the great stretches of water in the Broads. There, he would stand away from the crowds, his paintbrush in his hand as he silently surveyed the scene around him.

He smiled. It was an artist's lot to live on the outskirts of society, but he wouldn't have it any other way.

The bus dropped Nina off at the end of the lane. She'd nearly missed her stop, not quite recognising the bend in the road and the avenue of trees after so many years. She breathed in the warm June air and rolled the arms of her jumper up above her elbows as she began walking down the potholed lane that would take her to The Old Mill House.

It was beautiful. A perfect little corner of Norfolk, tucked away from prying eyes. Everything was so still and quiet, too, after the noise of the city, and Nina listened to the hum of insects as she walked, each footfall audible as she crossed the road.

White campion was growing on the verges, their flowers luminous amongst the deep green of the grass and, as she walked by a little cottage to her left, she noticed the great towers of hollyhocks shooting skywards, their blooms yet to open.

Nina took her time, looking about her as she walked and humming lightly. This is what summers were about, she thought. Not sweating it out in some paperwork prison with a boss that didn't appreciate you.

For a moment, she flung her arms out wide as if she were about to fly, but thought better of it when she heard a tractor in the field on the other side of the hedge, and continued walking.

In all her years of babysitting, she hadn't realised that

the house was set so far back from the road because she'd always been chauffeured there and back by Mr Milton, and her first glimpse of it made her gasp. The first thing to catch her eye was the driveway packed with cars. It looked like the parking lot of a sales garage. Perhaps the Miltons had visitors, she thought, or perhaps they were the boys' cars. She looked at each one in turn, half-recognising the white Volkswagen from the incident at the traffic lights. At least that meant someone was at home.

She turned her attention to the house, its splendid Georgian facade gleaming white in the summer morning. Eight windows, spanning three storeys, winked invitingly in the sunlight, and an enormous climbing rose shot up over the door, its deep red blooms swaying seductively in the light breeze, scenting the air with its perfume and lending the house a softness which winter didn't know.

It was all just as beautiful as she remembered it – its understated elegance as timeless as a pearl. And it all looked so familiar: the same curtains at the windows, billowing and blowing; the old rocking horse in the living room, dappled and damaged. It had always been a house full of laughter, and Nina remembered that the very walls seemed to shake at times, its seams almost splitting with the mirth they contained. It was so close to the road and the city, and yet so close to Nina's idea of rural heaven; seeing it again felt as if she was coming home.

She listened as her feet crunched up the driveway, the roar of water reminding her of the closeness of the river. Would Olivia be there to welcome her or would she have forgotten she'd even invited her? She walked up to the pale blue door. Just as it had always been, there was no bell and you needed reinforced knuckles in order to be heard.

Nina knocked as loudly as she could and waited, taking a step backwards to see if anyone was at the windows, but she couldn't see anyone. Strange then, that she felt as if somebody was watching her.

Dominic had just emerged from the walled garden where he'd done a quick sketch, when he had a vision. He stopped and, for a moment, thought he'd been out in the sunshine too long and was hallucinating. My God, it was Nina. What was she doing here? How had she got here?

He watched in amazement as she knocked at the front door. She was visiting, but why? She hadn't been in touch for years and then, in the space of a few days, he'd almost run her over and now she was visiting his family's home. Perhaps she'd recognised him at the traffic lights and was about to sue him for negligent driving and leaving the scene of an accident.

Dominic panicked. She'd tracked him down and, more importantly, she'd see him with mud on his trousers, paint in his hair and stubble on his chin. This wasn't good. This wasn't how he'd imagined it at all. Not exactly the scene he'd pictured, with Nina sitting in the living room, sipping tea with his mother and then him striding confidently into the room.

'Ah – Nina,' his mother would say, 'you remember Dominic, don't you?'

Nina would look up from her china cup and their eyes would meet, as surely as their hearts would.

He shook his head in exasperation. He was such a fool. That wasn't going to happen at all, was it?

Chapter Five

Nina knocked on the door again and waited. Three cars in the driveway and nobody at home? It didn't seem very likely. She looked up again at the windows, half-expecting to see a curtain twitch, but there was no sign of life other than a faint barking coming from somewhere deep inside the house.

A sudden turning of the latch brought a smile to her face but, when the front door opened, she was greeted not by Olivia but by a little boy with a drink carton in his hand and a straw stuck in his mouth.

'Hello!' Nina smiled. 'Is Mrs Milton at home?'

The boy merely looked at her by way of response.

'Can I come in?' Nina tried, bending down to his height so as not to appear quite so grown-up.

The little boy opened the door wider, took the straw out of his mouth and burped. Nina blinked in amusement and watched as he turned around and ran down the passage into one of the rooms, leaving her standing alone in the hall with the sound of barking louder than ever.

It was funny but, being in the hall again, even after so many years, Nina half-expected to see her two dear young boys come running towards her to grab her hands and drag her into the playroom, and was quite disappointed when they didn't. Instead she'd been faced with one little boy running away from her. Nina wondered whom he belonged to and, looking around, imagined that somebody would be along at any moment. Nobody would have left such a young boy at home on his own with just a mad dog somewhere in the house for company. Perhaps he was Billy's little boy, or Alex's? Or maybe even Dominic's? Who was to say that the Milton boys weren't all married now with families of their own? Just because her own love life was a disaster, it didn't mean that the Milton boys weren't all happily settled. She'd not seen them all for years. Anything could have happened in that time.

Her eyes scanned the walls absently until they caught sight of something quite extraordinary; a huge painting of a white mansion standing by the most incredible waterfall. It took a few seconds for Nina to register that it was actually The Old Mill House. It was the most amazing painting she'd ever seen. She could feel the energy in the bold brushwork and taste the spray from the wild rush of water.

'Hello?' A woman's voice floated down the hall from one of the rooms, breaking Nina's concentration.

'Hello?' Nina echoed.

'Hello?' the woman's voice came again, before the owner of it actually appeared. 'Oh! *Nina*! How *wonderful* to see you!' Olivia said, talking in her familiar italics as she walked forward and gave her a hug. Nina was instantly enveloped in a waft of rosy perfume and time seemed to spiral out of all recognition as if a portal to her past had just opened up to her.

'It's so kind of you to invite me,' Nina said with a smile as Olivia finally released her.

'Not at all! I was just telling Benji all about you.'

47

Nina looked down and saw the burping boy half-hidden by Olivia's skirt.

'Hello, Benji,' Nina said, bending down to his level again, but her movement only encouraged him to hide further in the paisley pleats.

'He's the cleaner's boy,' Olivia explained. 'She's upstairs tackling a mountain of ironing. She's *much* more efficient than I am. I always end up with more creases than when I started when I attempt the ironing, and I once managed to burn an entire cuff off one of Dudley's Thomas Pink shirts.' She laughed, and Nina couldn't help smiling at the confession.

'Come on through and sit down.' Olivia said, leading the way to the living room at the front of the house, a bright airy room with walls the colour of a summer sky and honey-coloured floorboards. 'Now, I'll just release poor Ziggy before he bursts a blood vessel in excitement.' Olivia took a deep breath. 'I should warn you, he's a bit lively and he'll probably jump up, but he's very friendly.'

Before Nina could protest or even ask what exactly Ziggy was, Olivia had left the room and a dreadful scraping and whining could be heard from further along the hallway.

'*No* – you'll be nice and calm now, won't you? Ziggy? Ziggy! Nina – he's on his waaaay!' Olivia called. Benji got up from where he'd flopped down on the rug in front of the fireplace and dived behind a chair in the corner of the room as an enormous hairy dog came hurtling in and launched itself at Nina.

'Oh!' she cried, as the apricot-coloured face pushed itself towards her in instant adoration. '*Oh!*'

'Nina! Are you all right in there?' Olivia's voice came from the hallway.

'He's a bit—' Nina couldn't speak because her mouth was full of fur.

'Ziggy – down! DOWN! Oh, *why* doesn't he do what I say? I'm having *such* problems with him.'

'I've never seen a dog quite like him,' Nina said. 'What is he?'

'One of these Labradoodles,' Olivia said. 'He was *so* cute as a puppy – like a little teddy bear. I didn't realise he'd grow to be quite so huge!'

'Oh, but he's wonderful.'

Olivia smiled. 'He is. I know. But if *only* he'd do what he's told!'

Nina patted the soft apricot head and smiled at the flappy ears and the lolling tongue. 'He's gorgeous!'

As if knowing he was being admired, Ziggy let out a volley of barks and bounced up on his hind legs again.

'Okay – that's enough, Ziggy!' Olivia cried, pulling the dog off Nina and dragging him out of the room.

Nina brushed herself down and sat on one of the huge sofas and felt herself sinking back into a kingdom of cushions.

'I'll get us some tea,' Olivia shouted from the hallway.

It was only then that Benji emerged, obviously realising that it was safe to come out from behind the chair.

'And how old are you, Benji?' Nina asked, her voice quiet and non-threatening. He didn't reply but continued to stare at her in the most unnerving way. 'I bet you like this house, don't you?' Nina continued, undeterred. 'Especially Prince Caspian?' she said, pointing to the rocking horse by the window. 'Isn't he wonderful? I bet you like riding him?'

Benji's small grey eyes stared at her as if she were quite mad.

Nina looked over at the rocking horse. Poor old Prince Caspian. He didn't look so regal these days. What was left of his mane looked limp and wiry and, if Benji were indeed to use him as a plaything, he would very soon be completely bald.

'Have you finished your drink?' she asked, rapidly running out of things to say to the boy, and wishing Olivia would hurry up with the tea things. She'd always adored children, and usually got on well with them, but it seemed that she didn't have the knack with this particular little boy. Perhaps, she thought, she should just pick up one of the magazines on the table in front and ignore him completely.

'Yes!' his small voice suddenly piped.

'What?' she asked in surprise.

'Finish drink.'

'Oh, I see.'

Conversation completed, he turned around and bombed out of the room to his own soundtrack of an aeroplane.

'Benji!' Olivia shrieked from the hallway before entering with a small tray. 'It's like having the boys all over again with him.'

Nina smiled. 'I thought he might actually belong to one of yours.'

'Good gracious, no!' Olivia gasped as she pushed the magazines off the table and put the tray down. 'My lot haven't even got as far as the altar yet.'

'Oh, really?' For some reason, Nina found this a comfort. It was hard to imagine any of the boys grown-up and married off, especially Alex and Dominic, whom Nina had always thought of as hers in a maternal sort of way. They had always been her special boys and, as an only child, they'd filled the gap that Sindy dolls couldn't possibly have filled. It didn't seem possible that they were handsome young men, ripe for marriage.

'Between you and me, I can't *wait* for the right women to take them off my hands,' Olivia confessed, pouring the tea and offering Nina the milk and sugar. 'The trouble is, they don't seem in any rush at all. I mean, Billy's had his fair share of girlfriends, but he seems more concerned about his career at the moment, and Alex – well – he's certainly had his share, too, but he never spends long enough with any particular girl for me to think about booking the church.' Olivia sighed and stared wistfully into the sugar bowl.

'And what about Dominic?' Nina asked, wondering what the youngest son was up to, but finding the image of Dommie as she remembered him – aged nine, in his football kit – hard to shake from her mind.

'Dominic?' Olivia half laughed, 'Dominic's no nearer than his brothers. There's Faye of course. She'd marry him tomorrow, I'm quite sure of that.'

'Faye?' Was little Dominic Milton really old enough to have a girlfriend, Nina wondered, and then remembered the young man who'd stared so darkly at her from his car.

'Dominic's old flame from high school. She's such a sweetheart. They kind of broke up a few years ago,' Olivia paused and then whispered, 'but she's still a great friend of the family and I think she's definitely still holding a candle for him. She's helping me out with the garden here and is working wonders on it. Honestly, she's such a lovely girl and Dommie really doesn't deserve her, but he won't listen to the reasoning of his old mother, will he?'

Nina sipped her tea and smiled sympathetically.

'And what about you, Nina? Anyone on *your* horizon?'

Nina gulped a mouthful of tea a little too quickly and coughed. 'Er – no. Not at the moment,' she said.

'But there has been, hasn't there? A pretty girl like you!'

Nina blushed, thinking it strange that she should still be thought of as a girl at the ripe age of twenty-eight. 'There has been,' she confirmed, not wishing to open up that particular wound, 'but not anymore.'

'Well, I'm sure there'll be plenty more,' Olivia said in the comforting way that other people's mothers had.

'I'm *so* glad you came,' Olivia said, her smile filling her face. She really was a beautiful woman, Nina thought, and absolutely impossible to pin an age on. Nina looked at her shiny red hair in a gloriously thick bob, and the vivid green eyes smiling out of a face that was round in the prettiest sense of the word.

'So, you're not working at the moment?' Olivia probed gently.

'N— no,' Nina replied, suddenly remembering her position in the world; unemployed. She'd almost forgotten. In her delight in being a free, if rather poor, spirit, she'd forgotten that it was actually a weekday and that she should be working. But then, she mused philosophically, it was rather hard to keep track of exactly which day it was when you didn't have a job to decide it for you.

'Not babysitting?' Olivia prompted.

'Oh, I haven't done that for years,' she said.

'You know, you were the only one the boys would have? Gosh! The trouble we had with them before you arrived on the scene!' Olivia laughed in remembrance. 'They were little terrors. How on earth did you manage to tame them?'

'Tame them?' Nina queried. 'I don't think I did anything to tame them.'

'Then you don't know your own magic!' Olivia said.

'I really don't think there was any magic,' Nina said honestly.

'Ah, I miss those days,' Olivia confessed. 'My darling boys. Of course, it wasn't the same when Billy went off to boarding school. That was the beginning of the end really, but Dudley insisted that it was the right thing to do and Alex and Dommie followed in their turn.'

'But you missed them?'

'Of *course*!' Olivia said. 'I drifted around this big old house like a lost thing, but then I began to fill my days with charities and local functions. Plus, looking after Dudley has always been a full-time occupation.'

There was a pause and Nina could hear the distant sound of a vacuum cleaner upstairs and the continuing soundtrack of Benji, who had transformed himself from an aeroplane to a train.

Olivia took a deep breath. 'And it was secretarial work you said you did, wasn't it?'

'Yes,' Nina said, biting her lip, and wondering what Olivia was leading up to. 'But I've done a bit of everything really,' she added quickly, trying to inject a little bit of colour into a rather bland CV. 'Receptionist, sales, human resources, civil servant.' She winced. That sounded anything but colourful. It was downright fickle and foolish; as if she'd never spent enough time mastering anything in particular.

'That's marvellous!' Olivia enthused.

'Is it?' Nina's eyes widened. Marvellous wasn't exactly the word she would have chosen for her patchwork career. Dull, tedious, boring, monotonous, and every other word in the thesaurus, but never anything as grandiose as marvellous.

'I have a proposition for you,' Olivia said enigmatically, leaning forward in an eager manner, 'and I *do* hope you'll say yes.'

Dominic had almost tripped over in his Wellingtons when he'd seen Nina coming up the driveway, and it had been a stroke of luck that she hadn't turned to see him standing in the middle of the garden like a scarecrow.

Somehow, he'd managed to manoeuvre himself to the back of the house without being seen, and had quickly extricated himself from the offensive boots before opening the back door into the kitchen, thinking that, if he was lucky, he'd have time to shower and change into one of Alex's shirts. His brother, unlike himself, always had racks of immaculate shirts and never noticed if the odd one went AWOL.

Dominic felt sure that the little scene he'd created in his head was about to be enacted for real. He would walk into the living room with quiet confidence and greet Nina with a firm handshake and a smile that would begin the rest of his life. Goodness, he still couldn't believe she was here. How many years had it been since he'd last seen her? He'd been so young, but he still remembered that great big crush he'd had on her.

Dominic took a deep breath to steady his nerves, knowing that he was ready to meet her once again.

'What on *earth* is that racket?' Olivia sprung out of her chair in alarm. 'Benji? What's the matter?' She placed her hands around the boy's scarlet face as he charged into the room and crashed into her legs.

'Dom hit me,' he wailed, his nose running.

'Dominic?' Olivia exclaimed. 'Not on purpose, I'm sure?'

'Hit me,' the boy repeated, wiping his nose on Olivia's skirt and putting Nina off her chocolate digestive.

'*Dominic*?' Olivia called. 'Is that you? Come on through.'

Dominic stood stock-still in the kitchen. It was just his luck that Benji had been playing with the coloured letters on the fridge door. Just his luck that the 'Q' had taken flight from a grubby hand and had landed by the back door. And of course it was typical that Benji had gone to rescue the errant letter the minute Dominic had opened the door.

'Dominic? Come and see who's here,' his mother's voice called above Benji's exaggerated howls and the echoing howls of sympathy that were now coming from Ziggy in the playroom.

Dominic sighed, tripping over the army of Wellington boots by the back door as he raked his hands through his hair, which he knew was sitting on his head like an overgrown gorse bush. He cleared his throat nervously and noisily. Nina Elliot was really here and she was about to get an eyeful of his best scarecrow impression ever.

Chapter Six

'Nina – you remember Dominic?' Olivia smiled enthusiastically as her youngest son entered the room. 'Dominic, isn't it *lovely* to be back in touch with Nina? I ran into her in the supermarket yesterday. What terrific luck and *such* an amazing coincidence after you spotting her in town the other day, too!'

Dominic looked at his mother and then at Nina, and a shy smile escaped him as Nina stood up and shook his hand.

'Hello, Dominic,' she said, noticing how tall he was and how his dark hair fell about his face in disorganised skeins. She looked at his eyes; as dark as conkers. 'How are you?' she asked.

'Fine, thank you,' he said, in his characteristically quiet voice, raised just enough for him to be heard. Nina couldn't help but smile. She couldn't believe the transformation from gauche schoolboy into handsome young man. But did he remember her? It had been so long since their last meeting.

'Well, aren't you going to apologise?' Olivia said, interrupting Nina's train of thought.

'Apologise?' Nina asked, surprised.

'Not *you*, dear Nina,' Olivia said.

'What?' Dominic turned to face his mother.

'For the other day, silly! When you almost ploughed Nina down.'

'Oh! Yes!' Dominic stumbled, averting his eyes in obvious embarrassment. 'I, er—' he looked up hesitantly at Nina, 'I'm sorry for the other day.' His eyes widened very slightly. 'I wasn't looking where I was going.'

'He shouldn't be on the roads,' Olivia butted in again, shaking her head in despair.

'But it was *me* that wasn't looking!' Nina said, perplexed. 'It's me who shouldn't be on the roads, I'm afraid.'

'Nonsense!' Olivia said in her defence, Benji's head still hiding in the depths of her now rather damp skirt.

'No, really!' Nina assured them, 'My head's been somewhere else lately and it's a wonder I haven't found myself under a car long before now.' She smiled lightly at Olivia and then at Dominic. 'So it's me who should apologise.' Dominic frowned in confusion. 'You see, I'd had a bit of a bad day at work and was trying to forget about it all by going to the pub during my lunch hour.'

'But I thought you said you were between jobs?' Olivia said, her face clouding with a sudden frown.

'I am now, but I was working that day. That was my last day, in fact. My boss and I parted company, so to speak.' Nina shrugged her shoulders, not really wanting to divulge any more about the whole unfortunate incident.

'Then you *are* still looking for work?' Olivia continued. Nina nodded. 'Good. Then I think I've got the solution to all our problems.'

Dominic looked across at his mother as she caressed Benji's reddened cheek.

'Why don't you go and play with Ziggy?' she said to the boy, turning him around by the shoulders and patting his bottom until he ran out of the room. 'And why don't we all sit down?'

Nina sat back down on the sofa and was instantly engulfed by the cushions again. Dominic took up a position in the chair opposite. He looked rather awkward, but he obviously wanted to hear what his mother had to say.

'Nina,' Olivia began, 'Ever since Dudley took early retirement eighteen months ago, he's been hanging around the house like a lost thing. Of course, doctor's orders were that he should take things easier these days. All those years as a city banker have taken their toll, I'm afraid, and he has to take care of himself now.' She fiddled with a gold bracelet she was wearing, her index finger rolling around inside it as if she was building up to something important. 'He's got his country club, of course, and spends a fair bit of time up there when the weather is good, but he's also had this mad notion about writing a novel. Can you believe it?'

'Really?' Nina said, her eyes wide with surprise.

'Mad fool that he is. But little be it for me to try to stop him. Who knows, he might actually have a real bestseller in his head. But, unfortunately, that's where it will remain if he doesn't get someone to help him.' Olivia looked across at her son and tilted her head to the left. 'Are you all right, Dominic?'

'What?' he said, his eyes rising from his jeans.

'You look as though you're waiting for the world to end.'

'I'm fine,' he said, looking awkward under her scrutiny and shifting in his seat.

'Good. Anyway,' Olivia said, turning her attention back to Nina, 'Dudley's been in a bit of a state recently. You see, our last secretary, Teri, left us all of a sudden and we've never heard from the girl since.'

Dominic cleared his throat, causing his mother to look across at him, but he merely shifted in the chair again, eyes fixed to the floor.

'And with this anniversary party to organise, you could say that we're in a bit of a pickle and could do with a helping hand.'

Nina nodded in sympathy, wondering what the punch line was going to be, not daring to hope that it might involve her.

'Well, I've been thinking and it seems to me that we'd both be doing each other a huge favour if you'd agree to work as Dudley's secretary and research assistant – for the summer period at least.' Olivia paused, allowing her words to sink in for a moment as she tugged on the gold bracelet. 'We could even let you stay in your old room – if you wanted to – it has an en suite, if you remember?'

Nina nodded, remembering the numerous occasions she had slept over at the mill when Mr and Mrs Milton had had a particularly late night or if they'd invited her to stay so she could join them for lunch the next day.

'We had it all replaced just last year. I'm sure you'd be very comfy. You *will* say yes, won't you?' Again, the vivid green eyes had set into an expression that made it hard for anyone to say no.

For a moment, Nina sat absolutely stunned. It wasn't that she didn't want the job; it was just that she hadn't expected to be handed such a lovely one on a plate.

'*Do* say yes!' Olivia pleaded, leaning forward in her chair until she practically fell out of it.

Nina thought of the comfortable bedroom at the top of

The Old Mill House. She thought of roaming around the fields and woods with the boys, collecting little branches of wood for the fire and making giant snowmen in the winter. She thought of the buttercup meadow in the summer and of the long hot days when they would dip their toes into the shallows of the river. She thought of how she'd always longed to be part of a family like the Miltons; how growing up as an only child had led to the belief that being part of a clan was better than being alone.

She took a deep breath. 'I'd *love* to work here,' she said, and laughed as Olivia flew across the room to embrace her.

Chapter Seven

'I think it best if you see the study first, don't you?' Olivia asked, leading the way out of the living room. Nina turned to look at Dominic, whose face was now quite red.

'Wish me luck!' she whispered excitedly.

'Good luck,' he said with a tiny smile.

Olivia marched Nina along the corridor. The study was at the front of the house and, when Olivia opened the door, Nina had to stop herself from laughing out loud at the sight that greeted her.

Up until then, Nina had believed that Hilary Jackson was the most disorganised person to be put in charge of an office, but that was before she'd seen this room. In her four years of babysitting at the mill, she'd never ventured into this part of the house, and she could now understand why nobody had encouraged her to do so.

The room had one floor-skimming window overlooking the sweep of driveway, and patio doors on the other side that looked out over a lawn as immaculate as a billiard table. But it was what lay in between that made Nina nervous.

Two large wooden desks lay like felled oaks at right angles to one another, and a yellow sofa stretched alongside the biggest bookcase Nina had ever clapped eyes on. Every available surface, though, was completely covered with great mounds of paper and files that threatened to topple and cascade onto the carpet, which itself had its fair share of papers stacked in precarious piles. It was as if a whole army of Hilary Jacksons had been let loose in the room.

Nina's eyes widened as she tried to take in the scene, desperately searching for some sort of filing cabinet or stack of in-trays: any sign that order could be restored to the room. She looked at Olivia who smiled a very tiny smile and shrugged her shoulders.

'You see what I mean – chaos! *Absolute* chaos.' She'd started up with the bracelet-twiddling again. 'I *know* it's a lot to ask, but you would get a good hourly rate and you could stay here if you want. I mean, I'm sure you've got your own place, but you'd be very welcome here. But I should mention that Dudley probably wouldn't agree to more than a couple of months – to begin with. Just until you both find a routine with each other. He obviously needs help getting everything into some sort of order and keeping it that way. Then there'll be the typing duties for the book he's writing, and he's been making noises about help with his research, too. I don't think it'll be anything too onerous – just a bit of reading and note-taking really,' Olivia said, chewing her glossy lips anxiously.

Nina nodded. It sounded absolutely blissful to her. A bit of tidying, a bit of typing and a little light reading. She scoured the room again, noticing the coating of dust on the backs of the chairs and along the pictures that lined the walls. A sorry-looking Swiss cheese plant slouched in a dark corner, in dire need of a drink, and dozens of empty envelopes were scattered like dead leaves on the floor. A computer sat on the floor under the far window, its screen turned away from onlookers as though trying to avoid attention.

Then there was the paperwork: great mountains of the stuff, untouched by human hands for what looked like decades. This was more a job for a large team of archaeologists rather than a solitary secretary.

It was certainly different – but wasn't that just what she was after, Nina reasoned?

'I should warn you, though,' Olivia said, 'my husband can be—' she paused, 'erm, a little difficult to work with.' Her face twisted into a strange expression.

'Difficult?' Nina said. 'I've done difficult before – believe me.'

'But I'm sure you'd be able to cope with Dudley's little ways. It's just part of the creative temperament, you see, and we'd all be *so* grateful. We've always felt so comfy with you, Nina,' Olivia said warmly. 'It would be lovely to have you here again.'

Nina smiled. She wasn't used to such flattery. It would be hard work, but not impossible, and surely Dudley couldn't possibly be worse to work with than Hilary Jackson. She remembered him from the days when she used to babysit. Sure, he had a bit of a temper, but she didn't think it was anything she couldn't handle and besides, she needed to be occupied at the moment; she needed to find an escape. After being with the wrong man and the wrong boss for an inexcusable length of time, she needed a change, and it looked as if she just might have found it.

'I'd be happy to help in any way I can,' Nina said. She held out her hand and Olivia beamed, taking it in hers and shaking it vigorously.

'Oh, Nina! That is wonderful. *Really* wonderful!' Olivia enthused.

'I just have one question,' Nina said.

'Yes?' Olivia sounded a little nervous.

'When do I start?'

Dominic scratched his head as he looked down at Nina's teacup. If the blue and white china hadn't been sporting a smudge of pink lipstick, he might well have believed that he'd just invented an entire scene in which his mother had asked Nina to stay at the mill. But there it was. Pink lipstick; as bright as the Norfolk Broads' daylight.

Dominic smiled as he remembered the tickle of her hair as she'd bent over him to help him with his homework that time. He'd been eleven years old and she'd spent twenty minutes reading through a comprehension and helping him to answer the questions, but he hadn't heard a single word. Well, he'd heard her; the soft lilt in her voice, the way it rose so beautifully in the middle of a question and the melancholy tenderness with which she read the story; he just hadn't heard any of the answers.

His teacher had given him two out of ten.

But, as with most childhood crushes, she'd been placed, very firmly, in the back of his mind as he'd grown up – the image of her fading over time, along with those intense boyhood feelings he'd had for her.

So why then did he now feel as if he'd swallowed a snake? His insides were wriggling about in a most disconcerting way. Ten long years separated him from those feelings – yet he could still recall them, and that made him uncomfortable. He couldn't still harbour feelings for her, could he? He didn't even know Nina. He had *never* really known her.

But that, in its own way, had been part of her appeal. She'd always been rather elusive; like a movie star whom you can dream about, but whom you'll never meet. It would be completely irrational to think he was in love with her. It would be utterly insane to suggest that the old feelings could just bob back up to the surface in the space of a smile and a hello.

Wouldn't it?

He took a glance in the mirror and his eyes widened with horror. He'd suspected he might look like an extra from a low-budget horror film, but it didn't prepare him for the reality. No wonder Nina had been smiling at him so much. He looked hilarious. Like Groucho Marx after an electric shock.

He shook his head in despair and left the mill before Nina could clap eyes on him again.

When Nina finally got home, she looked around her flat and smiled at the peeling wallpaper with the damp patch in the shape of Italy. She'd wasted many fruitless hours trying to cover it up with a succession of posters and cheap prints in frames, but the thing had merely spread to enormous proportions.

She smiled down at the ancient carpet that was so hard underfoot that you could grate cheese on it. She smiled as she heard her neighbour revving up the motorbike he'd been fixing in his kitchen for the last four months, and she grinned widely as she smelt the familiar waft of curry, courtesy of her other neighbours, through the air vent in the open-plan kitchen. This had been her home for the last two years, and she was smiling because she was leaving it forever.

She knew it would be reckless to give up her little place, but she meant to continue as she'd started – if she really wanted to get her life back on track she was going to throw caution to the wind and leave it for good anyway. Determination fuelled her, and a sudden sense of calm and purpose filled her. She was getting good at leaving things recently. This could very well be the new Nina, the new direction, the new way forward that she'd been looking for, she thought.

The flat had come fully furnished, so Nina only had a few personal belongings to pack up and, if at the end of the summer she couldn't find a new place to rent, she could always make do with Janey's futon until she got on her feet again.

'Goodbye mouldy wallpaper!' she yelled as her neighbour revved his motorbike. 'Good riddance crumbling window-sill!' And, just for old times' sake, she pressed a finger into the woodwork and the paint flaked away under her touch.

'Farewell clanging pipes!' she sang, deciding to put the radio on; it was one of the few things in the flat that actually belonged to her. She'd pack her things, tidy around and get out of there, taking her keys to her landlord the very next morning, and then she'd take the bus out to The Old Mill House, walking down the potholed lane to a place where she felt truly welcome.

Olivia was absolutely delighted. She was also rather anxious. It had been a great shock losing 'Teri with an i', and Olivia had no intention whatsoever of losing Nina – although she doubted she would, as she remembered how well Nina and her husband had got on in the past. Still, she'd have a word with Dudley about the situation and make sure he behaved himself and that he was especially nice to Nina. She knew all too well that he could be brusque once the creative mood took hold, but he had to be warned that it would be at his own peril. Poor Teri used to surface from the study positively shaking after her encounters with Dudley – her face pale and her eyes wide in terror.

'I can take dictation, but I *won't* take being dictated to!' she'd once cried, before grabbing her bag and leaving. Olivia had been left to sort the mess out, appeasing Teri by telling her that the creative muse could take many a strange form and that it took a special sort of person to handle it, and that Teri was obviously one in a million. And the flattery had worked. Well, for two further weeks anyway, before the next verbal volcano had erupted. Dudley, of course, had denied all knowledge of why Teri had left, although Olivia believed that there was more to it than just her husband's temperamental nature.

Anyway, she wasn't going to let it happen again. She wandered back into her husband's secret domain and trailed a finger over one of the few empty spaces on the desk before inspecting it. Just as she thought: it was as if she'd dipped it into a sack of flour. Dudley hated having anyone invade his special place, but Olivia was quite determined that she'd get Marie in with the vacuum and dusters before Nina started work the next day. Anything to help make Nina's job easier. After all, Nina would have Dudley's mood swings to cope with, a study that looked as if a tornado had passed through it, plus the three boys hanging around the house for most of the summer. There was no guarantee that she'd like it, let alone actually stay. But then again, miracles were known to happen.

Chapter Eight

Nina handed the keys to her flat to a bemused Mr Briggs, who said he'd have to keep her bond because she hadn't served out her period of notice. But she didn't care about that. She was free – free of her job and free of her flat. Free to start again. After the last few dark weeks, she felt as if she was on the edge of a great adventure and, right there and then, she made a promise to herself – to steer clear of men. The recent months with Matt had left her scarred and scared, and she felt that it would be a long time indeed before she would even want to think about entering into another relationship.

No, Nina thought, she was going to focus solely on herself for a while.

She arrived at The Old Mill House at ten o'clock the very next day, as agreed, and Olivia was ready to greet her.

'Nina! I was so worried in case you'd changed your mind,' she said, ushering her into the hall. 'I'm glad you didn't,' she added with a smile. 'Gracious – is that all you've brought with you?' Olivia said as she saw Nina's modest suitcase and her portable radio.

'It's all I need,' Nina smiled, thinking of the humble wardrobe and miniature library of books she'd packed.

'Oh, *do* be quiet, Ziggy!' Olivia said, addressing her command to the closed kitchen door, which was being pounded from the other side. Then, turning to Nina, she said, 'Do you remember where your old room is?'

'Oh, yes.' Nina nodded enthusiastically, looking up the stairs, dying to see the little room again.

'Then I'll leave you to get your things organised,' Olivia clenched her hands together, as if not quite knowing what to do next. 'Just give me a call when you're ready and we'll have a cuppa before you face the study.' She bit her lip, then hurried down the hall.

Nina started up the two flights of stairs. She looked down at the oatmeal carpet, which was immaculate now that Olivia employed Marie to clean, but which had always been covered in domestic tumbleweed whilst the boys had been growing up and money had been tighter. Now, it appeared that every surface in the house was dusted and polished until it gleamed, and that carpets were vacuumed to cotton-wool cleanness. Apart from the study, it would seem.

Nina felt that, with each stair, she was stepping back into her own past. Reaching the top, she turned left and saw that the door of her old bedroom was open. She smiled as she saw the little cast-iron bed freshly dressed in a quilt of blue roses on a white background and, on the bedside table, a small jam jar exploded with handpicked flowers from the fields surrounding the mill.

There was a small dressing table by the window, and Nina walked over to it before looking out onto the river. She remembered falling asleep to the sound of it when she'd been lucky enough to escape her own home and stay at the mill overnight. It would lull her into the most delicious of sleeps, and then be the first thing she'd hear in the morning – well, if the boys didn't wake her up first.

The room was just as she remembered, with the neat little hand-painted bookcase in the corner filled with rows of orange Penguin novels, their slender spines making them look like a row of literary supermodels.

The old wardrobe at the other side of the room, like an extra from a C. S. Lewis novel, seemed to smile a welcome at her, the light bouncing off the polished wood.

After her hateful flat, the room was like a five-star hotel. The snow-white carpet was soft, the furniture unbroken and the wallpaper complete, and there wasn't a damp patch in sight.

The window had been left open and she breathed in a couple of lungfuls of fresh air before unzipping her suitcase and putting her clothes out on the bed. She'd hang them up later. Now, however, it was time to start work.

'Oh my God!' Nina started, as she looked up from the bed. A tall figure was standing in the doorway. 'Dominic!' she gasped, 'I didn't hear you. You gave me such a shock.'

'Didn't mean to,' he said, daring to venture into the room a little. 'I wanted to have this waiting for you – to cheer the room up a bit.'

'Oh?' Nina watched as he produced a small watercolour from behind his back, framed in palest gilt. 'Oh Dominic, that's lovely!' She took the picture from him and looked at the sunset view over the river and across the meadows, in pale pinks and deepest blues. 'You're so talented. I bet you're going to be in all the big London galleries before long.'

'Well, I don't know about that. I've got a show in Tombland at the end of August though.'

'Really?'

Dominic nodded. 'It's a start,' he said.

'And I'm sure it'll be a really good start, too.' She smiled at him. Little Dommie – all grown-up and making his way in the world.

'Anyway, I hope you like it,' he said, nervously watching for her response.

'I do! I *love* it. Thank you.'

'Only the room was so bare.'

'Not at all – with a view like this,' Nina said, 'and I already have half of the meadow by my bedside,' she added, nodding to the flowers. 'Aren't they lovely?'

'I'm glad you like them.'

Nina looked at Dominic. Had he picked them? She'd just assumed that Olivia had collected them for her. Suddenly, she felt embarrassed.

'Anyway, I was just going to go downstairs and make a start on your father's study,' she told him, deciding it best to be businesslike.

'Yes,' Dominic said, his eyes straying towards the bed where Nina's clothes were spilled out across the quilt. Nina saw where he was looking and realised that several pairs of lacy knickers and bras were on display and that Dominic had turned quite red.

'I saw your other paintings in the hallway,' she said quickly, trying to divert attention away from her exhibition of underwear. 'They're amazing. I don't know how you do it.'

'Well, I'm not very good at anything else,' he said, his dark eyes flickering over her face for an instant.

'Oh, I'm sure that's not true. Anyway, you should be proud. I wish I was artistic.'

Dominic grinned. 'If you can restore any kind of order to Dad's study, then you'll deserve the Turner Prize.'

They smiled at each other and Nina placed his painting on her bedside table next to the flowers.

'I suppose I'd better make a start,' she said, but noticed that Dominic's eyes had strayed to the bed again. Nina followed the pathway of his vision and saw what it was that had caught his eye.

It was her nightie – girlie pink with spaghetti straps and covered in tiny daisies.

Olivia was still clenching her hands together and looking decidedly agitated.

'So, I've been making a list of things I'd love your help with for the party arrangements, but the most important thing really is for you to help Dudley. I'm not sure what he'll need in terms of a research assistant – I'm sure he'll let you know – but – well – I'm not quite sure where you want to start,' she said, her eyes wide and apologetic. 'It's all such an awful muddle, isn't it?'

'Is Mr Milton at home today?' Nina asked.

'No – er – he's still in London, at his brother's – but he'll be back tomorrow.' Olivia looked around the room in horror. 'Probably best if I leave you to it? I don't want to get in your way.'

Nina nodded.

'Well, good luck then.' Olivia left the room and Nina turned back and looked at the tip that lay before her. It probably hadn't been a good idea to wear white.

She reached into the pocket of her cotton trousers for a hair-band and tied her bob back into a short ponytail before rolling her sleeves up. It was time for battle to commence.

After two hours of hard work, which had mainly involved shifting things from one side of the room to the other, Nina was ready to start on the paperwork. She'd managed to clear one of the desks, the one she assumed was to be hers, and had even put her own personal stamp on it: her framed photo of her little dog, Bertie, which had been homeless since they'd both left the clutches of Hilary Jackson.

'I've a feeling we're going to like it here, Bertie,' she said, smiling at the little silver frame and noticing how at home he looked on his new desk. Yes, everything was going to be just fine, she told herself.

There was only one thing that had bamboozled her that morning, and that was a little cupboard in the corner of the study behind Dudley's desk. She could see a piece of paper had been trapped in its door but, when she'd tried to tidy it up, she'd realised that the door was locked and that the key was nowhere to be seen. She'd looked around for it for a few minutes, but soon realised that she probably wasn't meant to be able to find it and so she left the cupboard alone, wondering what was hidden behind its secretive door.

After the briefest of lunch breaks, followed by another hour of tidying, Nina looked up from a sample of Dudley's scribble on the top of a particularly large mound of papers. Something had caught her eye from beyond the patio doors and, looking closer, she noticed a young woman out in the garden with dark wavy hair and a pretty face.

Nina walked across to the doors, which she'd opened earlier in the hope of alleviating some of the mustiness of the room. The young woman was half hidden in one of the borders behind a plant with leaves the size of an elephant's foot, and was wielding a large silver spade. However, she'd stopped her work and was watching something, her gaze unwavering. Nina followed the girl's gaze and saw the object of her fascination: Dominic.

He was walking across the lawn, his head inclined towards the ground, completely unaware of his female audience. And the girl was mesmerized. Nina hadn't seen anything like it outside of a movie. Her vision was one of perfect softness, as if she was looking at a divine painting; she wasn't aware of anything else around her, least of all Nina.

As Nina watched, she felt a strange tickle in her nose. It wasn't really surprising, with the amount of dust that had been trapped amongst the paperwork in Dudley's study, and her nose twitched, her face stretching and contorting. She was going to sneeze.

'Aaaachooooo!'

The dark-haired girl behind the plant almost left the ground in shock.

'Good heavens!' she cried from across the garden. 'Who are you?'

'I'm Nina Elliot, the new secretary,' Nina said, sniffing loudly as she approached her across the lawn.

'Oh,' the girl said, swallowing hard.

'And you are?' Nina smiled gently as she reached for a tissue from her pocket.

'Faye,' the girl said, her voice a little croaky until she cleared her throat. 'Darnley.'

'Hello, Faye,' Nina reached the border to shake hands and was offered a warm, dust-encrusted one.

'I was just looking—' Faye started, but bit her lip and didn't finish her sentence.

'I'm sorry I startled you,' Nina said quickly.

Faye nodded. 'It's okay. I was miles away, that's all – planning a new herbaceous border for Olivia.'

Nina nodded, not quite sure what that sort of work entailed. 'Sounds interesting,' she said.

'Oh, it is,' Faye said. 'Olivia's given me a very generous budget and it's a dream being able to plant exactly what I want, but it's quite a lot of pressure, too. This garden's so beautiful and I want to do it justice.'

'I'm sure you will,' Nina said, noticing the beautiful green lawns, the neatly clipped hedges and the arch that led to the walled garden, which was smothered with a vigorous white rose, perfuming the air with its delicious scent. When she'd babysat, much of her time had been spent indoors and she hadn't really got to know the gardens; a great shame, as they were so lovely. Perhaps she'd be able to explore them now though, she thought, imagining being able to take her tea breaks on a bench surrounded by lavender and birdsong.

'New secretary, you say?' the girl asked.

'Yes.'

'You must be brave to take Dudley on,' Faye said, tucking a dark curl behind her ear and leaving a streak of dirt across her rosy cheek.

'Oh, I don't know about that. You should have seen my last boss,' Nina grinned.

'Worse than Dudley?'

'Easily!' Nina said. 'But you've had a tough job too – although I'm guessing Olivia's an easier boss to work for than Dudley.'

Faye nodded, 'She's brilliant, but there's a lot to do. It's never really been managed before, you know? Dudley's never had time and Olivia never gets further than a few bedding plants and a couple of hanging baskets. I've been wanting to tackle the place for years and I'm finally qualified to do so. I really love it here – it's such a special place – and it's a real honour to be given so much freedom to make the garden work.'

Nina looked at the large blue eyes and instantly recognised a fellow romantic and daydreamer.

'And I'm a friend of Dominic's,' Faye added quietly, assessing Nina's response before she continued. 'An old friend.'

'Oh,' Nina said, 'I see.' She nodded, remembering Olivia mentioning the heartbroken ex-girlfriend that she was so intent on getting back with Dominic.

'But we don't really talk these days. He spends half his time trying to avoid me. In fact, I spend more time talking to his mother.'

Nina wondered if it was her place to say something, but Faye beat her to it.

'We used to go out together at sixth form,' she said, 'and we were friends for years before that. But all that stopped when university came along. Dommie stopped emailing, didn't phone and avoided seeing me whenever he was at home in the holidays and then, one day, I got this awful email from him saying that he thought we should break up.' She took a deep breath as if seeing the message before her again. 'We met up at this little pub we used to go to and I spent the entire evening trying not to cry whilst he listed all the reasons why we shouldn't be together.'

'Oh, dear,' Nina said. 'Was it a very long list?'

'He seemed to be doing a lot of talking, but I really didn't hear much after the initial, "I think we should break up".

But it mainly consisted of him wanting to make it as an artist and how he had to dedicate himself completely to it.' Faye shook her head. 'It was as though he saw me as this terrible distraction.'

'And you've been trying to get back together with him in spite of all that?' Nina asked, her head cocked to one side as she tried to understand this young girl.

'Well, kind of,' she said. 'But I really don't know what to do. Only I'm not ready to give up on what we had. Although I have tried – believe me. I've been out with other men and even signed up for some really bad blind dates, but they just left me feeling empty. I've thrown myself into this gardening business as well to try and take my mind off things, but being here really isn't helping. When Olivia offered me the job, I couldn't believe my luck. I've always loved this place so much, and I really missed it when Dommie and I broke up. I couldn't help thinking that being here might rekindle things between us.'

Nina watched Faye's face and, for an awful moment, thought she was going to cry. Her eyes looked as if they were welling up with tears and her lips started to tremble.

'I'm sorry,' Faye said at last. 'I shouldn't be dumping all this stuff on you. I don't know why that all poured out of me.'

'There's no need to apologise,' Nina said. 'Actually, do you know what I was just thinking?' she suddenly said, with as much enthusiasm as she could muster.

'What?' Faye's small voice asked.

'I was wondering if there was any ice cream in the freezer. What do you think?'

'Well, it's certainly the weather for some,' Faye said, smiling back at Nina, and they left the leafy border together and headed into the house as if they'd been friends for years.

Sure enough, the freezer was stocked with a very good choice of frozen dairy desserts and, twenty minutes later, Nina and Faye had worked their way through most of them.

'Why do we bother with men?' Faye asked with a sigh, finishing her last spoonful of raspberry ripple. 'I mean, *why*?' Her whole body shrugged and she blew out her cheeks into balloon-size proportions.

'I don't know,' Nina said honestly as she savoured the last of the double-chocolate chip.

'They either ignore you, let you down or make you fall in love with them then dump you.'

Nina looked at Faye. She was far too young and pretty to have such a cynical view about relationships.

'They're not all like that, though?' Nina tried, licking the very last trace of ice cream from her spoon.

'Well, the ones I've met have been. Take Dominic for instance – we've known each other practically forever and yet he won't even know I'm here today. God! Have I just been really unlucky in love or is it always like this? Nina?'

'What?' Nina asked, surprised at suddenly being deemed the font of all knowledge.

'What do you think?' Faye pressed on.

'Oh – sorry,' Nina said, 'I thought that was a rhetorical question.'

'No – I'd *really* like an answer.'

Nina gave a light smile. 'Well, I don't know all the answers, I'm afraid. I've just got out of a relationship, so I'm not the best judge around.'

Faye's mouth dropped open slightly. 'I always stick my foot in things. Sorry. I didn't realise. Was it awful?'

Nina bit her lip. 'If you don't want to stick your foot in it further, I wouldn't ask if I were you.'

'Oh dear,' Faye said. 'I'm sorry.'

'It's okay,' Nina said. 'I've just had my confidence shaken a bit, but—' she paused.

'You're still optimistic about the future?' Faye suggested with a little smile.

Nina nodded. It was the first time she'd really thought about it since her break-up with Matt, but Faye was right. She *was* still optimistic about her future and she hadn't given up on love. Not just yet, anyway.

'But nothing's further from my mind at the moment,' she confessed to Faye. 'In fact, I've come to the mill to try and get away from all that. For once in my life, I'm putting me first – and that means knuckling down and doing a really good job here.'

'So, what if Prince Charming turned up *right* now?' Faye asked.

'I'd tell him that his timing's awful and that he can jolly well come back later when I'm good and ready,' Nina said.

Faye grinned. 'Really?'

'Really,' Nina said with a very determined nod. And then a wonderful idea occurred to her. She might have sworn off love herself, but what if she could help bring Faye and Dominic back together again? Dominic was one of the sweetest people she'd ever met and she'd instantly warmed to Faye, too.

Nina bit her lip in contemplation. Olivia was convinced that the two youngsters should be a couple and Nina was beginning to see that, too.

Chapter Nine

Once Nina finally made it back into the study, she sat down on one of the newly excavated office chairs she had found in a corner of the room and thought of the last half hour spent in the company of Faye. She had instantly liked her and could easily see why Olivia was so attached to her. So what was Dominic's problem? Did he really have no feelings for her anymore? Had his work taken over his life to such an extent that there wasn't any room left for a girlfriend – or was there more to it than that?

Nina shook her head. She hadn't been summoned to the mill to try and work out the love lives of its inhabitants – as interesting as they may be. She had a job to do and, half an hour later, she was immersed in a pile of old receipts when she heard a car crunch to a halt on the driveway. Ziggy had definitely heard it, too, because his barks echoed around the hallway, and Nina heard Olivia open the front door.

Curious to see who the visitor was, Nina got up and walked over to the window, spotting an old red Jaguar parked as haphazardly as the other cars, although she couldn't actually see anyone in it.

She was just about to return to her desk when a man sat up in the front seat, brushing a pipe against his jacket, which he'd obviously just retrieved from the floor of the car. That, Nina thought, might very well explain the careless distribution of tobacco tendrils all over the paperwork she'd cleared that morning. Nina watched as he twitched his large white moustache and coughed before getting out of the car. It was Dudley Milton.

It was at this point that Olivia ran out from the house to greet him with a kiss. Nina smiled as she saw the two of them together: him so tall and hefty, and she so tiny and slim. Nina strained to hear them, but nothing was audible until they were both in the hallway.

'I've got a surprise for you,' Olivia was saying as she batted Ziggy away.

'Have you really?' Dudley's voice was as loud as it was deep. 'Not one of your *godawful* surprises, is it? Like another Labradoodle!'

'Oh, Dudley! It's nothing like that, but let's have a cup of tea first, shall we?' Olivia suggested quickly. 'Get *down*, Ziggy!'

'No – if you don't mind – I want to get right to it.' His voice was getting closer and Nina froze as she heard the door of the study opening.

'But I wanted to tell you—' Olivia's voice stopped as Dudley entered the room, his large mouth dropping open when his eyes took in what had once been a scene of total chaos.

'Dudley, dear—' Olivia began.

'What the HELL happened here?' He turned around to Olivia, his face now as red as his V-neck pullover. 'What's been going on?' he asked, but didn't pause for an explanation. 'I can't leave the place for the space of two days without someone interfering.'

81

'She's not interfering.'

'She? Who's *she*?' Dudley walked into the centre of the room. It was then that he clapped eyes on Nina.

'And who the hell are you?'

Dominic walked back over the fields to The Folly. As he'd left the mill, he'd seen Nina and Faye talking in the garden to each other. He couldn't hear what they were saying but Faye had that haunted look about her that made Dominic feel instantly guilty. It was a feeling that he'd tried to suppress since he'd broken up with her three years ago, but his emotions had been hovering dangerously close to the surface since she'd started working in the garden.

Why oh why had his mother employed her? He'd been able to forget about Faye whilst he'd been away at college, but seeing her here at the mill had resurrected all sorts of feelings that he thought he'd said goodbye to.

He knew what his mother had in mind, of course – that the two of them should get back together. In fact, she was doing absolutely everything she could to make it happen, short of actually booking the church, but he'd made his decision, hadn't he? He had to concentrate on his work.

All too often, he'd seen artists – good artists – throw it all away because they got involved in a relationship. Events overtook them and, before they knew it, a baby would become part of the equation and any dreams of making it as an artist flew out of the window as the parents knuckled down to a sensible job – one that was guaranteed to pay the bills. Well, Dominic was determined not to make that mistake. It was a tough decision to make and it seemed absolutely heartless, he knew that, but what choice did he have if he really wanted to make it as an artist? And yet, he couldn't help remembering the good times he'd had with Faye and how effortless everything had been with her. They'd never had to work at their relationship because they'd just been content to be with each other. Most of his friends at the time had always been in a nervous state as to what to do on a date. Which restaurant should they go to? What film should they see? But with Dominic and Faye, it had been so simple. They'd just meet up and talk. It didn't really matter what they did. They might wander into town and look around a few galleries, but they'd be equally happy to go for a walk by the river.

Dominic had fond memories of those walks. He always had his sketch book in his pocket and would secretly take it out and capture those little moments when Faye's hair was blowing back from her face or when she was running through the fallen beech leaves, her boots kicking up great heaps of them. He still had all those sketches.

He sighed. Whether sitting, walking or running, Faye had always been smiling. He missed that smile so much. He hadn't seen it for years and he had a feeling that he was partially to blame for its disappearance, but he just hadn't been ready to settle down into a cosy, full-on relationship and he knew that that was exactly what Faye had wanted from him. It had all become too serious too quickly, and he'd used the excuse of his work and his departure to college to put an end to things.

He shook his head. See! This was exactly the reason why he had to forget her – because she filled his head when he should have been focussing on more important things. He took a deep breath and tried to banish Faye from his mind.

Walking through the fields, he smiled as the first sight of The Folly greeted him, its mellow red bricks glowing in the sunlight. He never grew tired of looking at it. The Folly had stood in the grounds of The Old Mill House for over a hundred years and, as far as Dominic remembered, had never been used for anything more than storing old bits of tired machinery. It had been his idea to renovate it. So, during the Easter holidays before graduation, he'd arrived home with three mates who'd spent the holiday sleeping rough in the old building, and creating what they'd called 'a new living space' over its four compact storeys.

Olivia had been horrified. First of all, because they should have been cramming for their finals. Secondly, because she couldn't understand why her son wanted to live in a pile of old bricks that was fit only to house bales of hay and spiders, especially when he had a perfectly comfortable, spacious room at the mill. But Dominic had wanted his own space, even if it was a pretty basic set-up, with recycled furniture that had definitely seen better days.

Now, with its bare floorboards and two separate living areas joined by a salvaged wrought-iron staircase, it was the perfect den for a budding artist. The trouble was, Dominic hadn't actually sold anything since he'd taken up residence and had yet to replenish his own savings and repay his father's loan.

Not one to go running back home at the first sign of failure, Dominic was determined to make a go of it, but that meant making money – and fast. The pressure was really on for his upcoming show in Norwich, but the question was, could he really pull it off?

Dudley paced up and down the centre of the study, his words coming out in fits and starts. 'I can't believe you've gone behind my back like this!'

'Dudley! Not in front of Nina!' Olivia remonstrated.

'*Two* days!'

'Yes – that's right – we weren't expecting you back until tomorrow,' Olivia said in her defence.

'What difference does that make?' Dudley bellowed.

'I was going to tell you about it,' Olivia said.

'But the damage is already done!' Dudley grimaced at his desk.

'Damage! Oh, I've never heard such nonsense. The only damage in this room has been *you* ever since you retired and started holing yourself up in here!' Olivia shouted back at her husband. He turned around to look at her, her green eyes sparkling with fury.

'*Me?*'

'Yes, *you,* you great oaf! Ever since Teri left—'

'Don't *ever* mention her name in here!' He was pacing again and Nina stood stock-still, her ears burning as the pair of them shouted at each other.

'Ever since Teri left, you've been running around the house like a mad man, what with this crazy novel business you keep muttering about,' Olivia continued undeterred. 'You've *no* idea what you've been like to live with, and we're just not going to put up with it. For a start, I want you to move all these library books that I keep finding in strange towers all over the house, as well as all these messy bits of paper with your scribble on them. *This* is your study! I don't want you taking over the whole house. The boys will all be home soon for the summer and I refuse to have any more chaos than is absolutely necessary.'

Nina watched, hardly daring to breathe, hardly daring to move an inch from her dark corner of the room.

Dudley stopped pacing and held Olivia's gaze. It was like

a scene from a Western, with both of them waiting for the other to either back down or draw their guns. It was Dudley who decided to back down first.

'I think you'd better introduce me to our new secretary,' he said in a strangely subdued voice.

'*That's* more like it,' Olivia sighed with relief. 'Nina, you can come out now,' she said with more than a touch of humour, well aware that she had been hiding in the shadows whilst the scene had played itself out.

Nina emerged and stretched her hand out to meet Dudley's.

'Well? Don't you recognise her?' Olivia prompted.

'Recognise her?' Dudley's white eyebrows rose.

'There aren't too many Ninas about, are there?'

'Nina,' Dudley said thoughtfully. 'NINA!' he suddenly exclaimed, taking her hand again and shaking it vigorously. 'Good heavens! Young Nina – the babysitter!'

'Hello, Mr Milton,' Nina said, suppressing a sudden urge to hiccup for the first time since leaving the claws of Hilary Jackson.

'Dudley – I think you can call me Dudley.' His hand was still shaking hers, but then his face clouded with embarrassment and he withdrew it, raking it through his thick white hair.

'I should think so, too,' Olivia said, as if reading her husband's mind.

'I er—' he began, sounding very much like Dominic apologising the day before, 'I feel I should apologise for my earlier outburst.'

Nina looked down onto the rug, feeling the weight of his embarrassment.

'Really, Dudley, I don't know what got in to you. We're

only trying to help. I don't know how you think you can live in such a pigsty of a study and be able to work efficiently. You can't produce anything good in this awful mess. It just isn't conducive to a calm mind – and it's a calm mind you'll need if you're going to get this novel finished.'

'All right, all right!' Dudley raised his hands into the air in obvious defeat, but his eyes were scouring the room at the same time. 'It's just that I don't like strangers going through my things.'

'But Nina's hardly a stranger now, is she?'

'I'm sorry, Mr Milton – er – Dudley – if I've upset you in any way,' Nina said. 'My only intention was to help. I really want to help out, and I know I can. I've made a start, but—'

'But she needs *you* to be at least a little cooperative if she's to continue,' Olivia finished.

Dudley glanced at Olivia, before walking over to the table that Nina had been in the process of tidying when he'd arrived so unexpectedly. His fingers gingerly touched the receipts and papers she'd been organising into neat piles, his eyes narrowing at her work. Reaching forward, he picked up what looked like an invoice, examining it in silence. After a few moments, he turned around, holding the yellow paper.

'Ferrars, Byrne and Co.,' he said rather cryptically to Olivia.

'What?'

'The invoice I've been trying to find for the last three months,' he explained.

'What did I say?' Olivia said, giving her husband an ironic smile. 'I tell you, it's a stroke of luck that Nina came along when she did.'

Chapter Ten

Olivia had made out a list of items that she thought would make Nina's life a lot easier and had sent Dudley off into Norwich to buy them.

'There, that should keep him out of our hair for a few hours,' she said with a smile. 'I *do* apologise for his behaviour.'

'It's quite all right,' Nina assured her. 'I don't think I'd be very happy if I found a stranger in my private study. If I had a study, I mean.'

'But you're not a stranger, Nina,' Olivia said. 'You're like family to us!'

Nina smiled. It was the loveliest thing anybody had ever said to her. Growing up as an only child to parents who didn't pay her much attention and paid her even less now, she'd never really felt as if she had a family. But, with the Miltons, she really felt a connection – a deep sense of truly feeling a part of something bigger than herself.

For a moment, Olivia hovered in the door and Nina instinctively knew that she was working up to something.

'You know, Nina,' she began, 'I'm worried about you being shut away here in this office all day.'

'Oh, there's no need,' Nina said. 'I'm quite used to it.'

'Yes but a young person like yourself needs air and exercise, don't you think?'

'I guess,' Nina said warily.

Olivia nodded. 'And I have just the thing for you. Darling Ziggy!'

Nina's eyes widened in surprise. 'Ziggy?'

'I think it would be marvellous if you could find the time to give him a couple of walks a day. It would do you no end of good to get you away from that computer and I'm sure Ziggy would respond *so* much better to you than he does to me.'

'But I've never had any experience with dogs,' Nina said rather hopelessly, feeling that she'd already lost this particular battle.

'Oh, I just *know* you two will get along famously – just like you charmed our boys when you were their babysitter!' Olivia said with a winning smile.

'But dogs aren't boys,' Nina said, wondering if her rather simple statement would be enough to change Olivia's mind.

'Well, of course they aren't,' Olivia agreed. 'I hear dogs are *much* easier. Now, let me fetch you his lead. He sometimes tugs at it with his mouth, but you mustn't let him do that. And try to discourage him from jumping up and barking. It's very annoying. Oh, and don't let him anywhere near the water. He always makes for the muddiest part and he's *very* ill-mannered if you have to wash him.'

Nina swallowed hard and tried not to bolt in sheer terror.

'Okay?' Olivia said.

'Yes,' Nina said, her eyes wide with fear.

Ten minutes later, Nina was on her first ever dog walk,

her heart racing wildly at the thought of being responsible for the rather crazy animal at the end of the lead. The Labrador part of Ziggy was strong and determined, whilst the poodle part was flighty and excitable. It was a lethal combination that had Nina's right shoulder straining in its socket as he pulled her along the river bank.

She remembered having desperately wanted a dog when she was a little girl, endlessly bugging her parents with requests, but they told her that dogs were a burden and that they tied you down and would be a pain when you went away on holiday – only Nina couldn't really remember going on that many holidays. Still, perhaps she might not have been able to handle the responsibility as a youngster – at least not if she'd been bought a dog like Ziggy.

'Slow *down*!' she called, giving the lead a firm tug and stopping in her tracks. He stopped and turned around to look at her as if to say, *What's happening? Why aren't we moving forward? Forward's good!*

'Now, a little gentler,' Nina said, giving Ziggy some slack. Immediately, he tugged at full force, dragging her along the riverbank and over a particularly tussocky area, which set her off-balance and made her cry as she twisted her ankle and went flying forward, letting go of the lead as she landed in an ungainly heap on the ground. For a moment, the world seemed to tip and spin and Nina watched help-lessly as Ziggy bounded away from her, quickly losing himself through a hedgerow.

Nina sighed and, using both hands as levers, tried to push herself up from the ground.

'Ouch!' she cried as she put her full weight on the twisted ankle. 'Ziggy!' she called, but the dog was long gone, probably charging across the fields towards the next village. She shook her head. What on earth was she going to tell Olivia? She'd put her trust in Nina and now her darling dog was missing.

Hobbling forward along the riverbank, Nina tried to see through the thick hedge, desperate to catch a glimpse of Ziggy. Surely he couldn't have gone that far, she reasoned, although she knew he could probably break all land speed records if he put his mind to it.

It was then that she heard barking from further along the path. Her heart raced and she walked faster, wincing each time her right foot hit the ground, but eager to round the corner in the hope of Ziggy being there. The path moved away from the river, skirting a barley field, which moved like a gentle green sea under the summer breeze. Once again, she heard a bark, but her spirits sank when she realised that it wasn't Ziggy's bark after all.

Sure enough, from around the corner came a sleek black and white collie who, as soon as she saw Nina, started barking again, causing Nina to flatten herself up against the hedge.

'Don't show her you're afraid!' Nina told herself, but that was easier said than done when a dog was eyeing you up with a none-too-friendly expression on its face.

'Bess?' a voice called from around the corner and Nina watched as a tall, fair-haired man came striding into view. 'I'm so sorry,' he said, seeing Nina's pale face as she stood frozen to the spot. 'Heel, Bess.'

Nina watched as the collie turned and slunk back towards her master.

'Are you okay?' he asked when it was obvious that Nina had no intention of venturing out of the hedge until she was quite sure everything was under control.

'I, er—'

'Bess wouldn't harm a fly – honestly,' he continued, giving his dog a fuss and then brushing a hand through his hair as he stood back up to full height. 'She's the soppiest girl on the planet, aren't you, Bessie? Just likes a bit of a bark when she meets new people.'

'Right,' Nina said, swallowing hard and finally moving away from her hawthorn security blanket.

'She didn't mean to scare you and I'm sorry she did. She sometimes runs ahead of me.' He looked at her and Nina was suddenly gazing into a pair of bright blue eyes.

'It's okay,' she found herself saying. 'I wasn't scared.'

'No?' he said, looking amused and unconvinced.

'It's just best to be sure before you approach a strange dog, isn't it?'

'Oh, absolutely,' he said.

'*Dog!*' Nina suddenly cried.

'Pardon?'

'I've lost my dog.'

'You've got a dog?'

She nodded. 'She got away from me just before I met yours and I haven't seen her since.' Panic rose once again in Nina's chest as she stumbled along the footpath.

'You've hurt yourself,' the man said, following in her stumbling wake.

'Yes, I'm afraid I twisted my ankle when Ziggy got away from me.'

'Ziggy?'

'The dog I was walking. Do you know her?'

'I've seen her around,' the man said.

'Will you help me look for her? I mean, if you've got time.'

'Of course,' he said with a little smile. 'Anything for a fellow dog-walker.'

Nina felt the weight lift from her a little as they walked along the track by the hedgerow. A skylark was pouring its song down from a peerless blue sky and the sun was sparkling on the river in the distance, but there wasn't time to enjoy the beauty of the day.

'Ziggy!' Nina cried.

'Ziggy!' the man echoed.

The hedgerow petered out and a large expanse of field greeted them and, there in the distance, was the missing dog.

'Ziggy!' Nina called. 'Come here, boy!' She bent forward, her hands on her knees in what she hoped was an encouraging position, but Ziggy didn't appear to hear his new mistress. 'Oh, dear,' she said at last. 'I don't think we're going to get him back.'

'Don't give up so easily,' the man said. 'Mind if I give it a go?'

'Be my guest,' Nina said.

'*Come* on, Ziggy!' the man cried and Nina watched in wonder as the dog's ears immediately pricked up and his head cocked to one side as he acknowledged the man. And then something bizarre happened. Ziggy suddenly seemed to forget what he was doing in the middle of the field and tore across it at great speed, the force of his movement pushing his flappy ears behind him so that they looked like furry bunting.

'Wow! You really have a way with animals,' Nina said, impressed, as the dog lolloped towards them.

'Oh, it's nothing really,' the man said with a grin as he bent down to ruffle Ziggy's soft head as he collided into his legs.

'Well, I wish he'd listen to me like he does you,' Nina said, quickly grabbing the lead before Ziggy had a chance to run off again.

'It just takes time,' the man said, looking up at Nina as he continued to fuss Ziggy. 'So, this is your dog?' he said.

'No,' she said. 'I'm just walking him for his owner.'

'I see,' he said.

There was a pause and Nina suddenly felt awkward. 'I'm sorry to have taken up your day like this. It's the first time I've walked Ziggy and I guess I'm a little nervous.'

'There's no need to apologise,' he said, giving her a smile that she found disturbingly attractive. Now was definitely not the time to bump into a handsome man, she thought, as she looked down at her scuffed shoes and dusty jeans. She pushed her hair out of her face and hoped she hadn't just streaked that with dirt too.

'I'm Nina,' she said, remembering her manners.

'Justin,' he said, extending a large hand towards her. Nina shook it, marvelling at its warmth and strength, and gazing up into the blue eyes once more. He was, she had to admit, the most gorgeous man she'd ever seen.

'Well, I'd better get back,' she said a moment later, realising, rather embarrassingly, that she'd been staring at him for longer than was deemed polite. 'They're waiting for me,' she added.

'Sure,' he said, giving an easy-going kind of smile that made Nina's heart leap. 'Maybe I'll see you again. I often walk this way. About this time.'

'Oh,' she said, trying not to show that she was bothered either one way or another.

'I could give you some tips on how to handle Ziggy, if you like,' he added.

'Right,' Nina said.

'Yeah?'

'We'll see. I'm not sure what I'm doing,' she said and then she gave a little smile to neutralise her statement.

'Are you sure you don't need any help getting back, with your ankle?' He asked.

'Oh, it's not far. I'm just at the mill.'

He nodded. 'Well, if you're sure—'

'I'll be fine,' she assured him, quite determined not to play the weak heroine from some nineteenth-century novel.

Ziggy gave a tug on the lead and Nina knew that it was time to go.

'Don't let him take charge,' Justin said. 'If he pulls, stop walking. He'll soon learn.'

Nina nodded. Was it really as simple as that? 'Thanks,' she said.

'You're welcome. Nina.' The way he added her name at the end like that made her heart skip a beat, and his blue eyes fixed on her for a moment before he turned away, giving a low whistle that brought Bess the collie to heel immediately. She turned to go, too, willing herself not to look around as she hobbled down the footpath, but the temptation was too much for her as she reached the bend and she quickly glanced over her shoulder, watching as he walked away with his faithful collie by his side.

Justin. She didn't know his last name. In fact, she didn't know anything else about him other than he was very tall with fair hair, bright blue eyes and a smile that could warm a girl's heart on the coldest winter day. She stood there for a moment, just watching him, and then he turned around as if he'd felt her eyes on his back and gave a little wave.

Nina felt her face flame with embarrassment at being caught and she turned quickly, forgetting the tip he'd told her about not letting Ziggy be the boss in her hurry to get back to the mill.

Trying to put all sorts of handsome strangers out of her mind after giving Ziggy a quick groom and making sure he was settled in his basket, Nina got to work clearing some space on Dudley's shelves for the box files he was going to bring back from his trip into town. She'd soon have everything tidied away and then she could start to help Dudley with the research for his novel. She knew that Olivia had lots of things planned for the anniversary party that she was hoping for Nina's help with, too. It seemed she was going to be very busy.

She returned to her desk and pulled out the heavy wooden chair, dragging it over to the shelves and standing on it before grabbing a handful of the papers that were taking up an inordinate amount of space.

It was then that she noticed what she thought was a ream of paper, but which she soon discovered to be pages and pages of double-line-spaced typing.

'It's the novel!' she said triumphantly, jumping down off the chair and returning to her desk with it. Her eyes quickly scanned the first page, then the second, third and fourth and, before she knew it, it was late into the afternoon and Nina was just about to clock off after her first very long day. When she finished the last page she scoured the room for more, desperate to know how the story continued. But there was no sign of anything.

She scratched her head and frowned. She never would have thought it. When Olivia had said Dudley was writing a novel she'd thought – European spy novel, American-style thriller, perhaps even science-fiction. But nothing had prepared her for this.

Dudley Milton was writing a historical romance.

Chapter Eleven

When Nina left the study, it was with the knowledge that it was in a much better state now, but there was still a long way to go. However, she could do no more before a well-earned cup of tea, and so she took herself off to the kitchen. Dominic was there, standing over the sink, the kettle in hand and his back to the door.

'Make one for me too, please,' she said cheerfully, batting down an excitable Ziggy who had been dozing by the Aga before she'd entered the room.

Dominic turned around and gave her a warm, sunny smile that lit up his face. He was quite cute really; she could see why Faye was still so crazy about him. His hair was incredibly short at the back – in that way that encouraged girls to brush their fingers against it – but it was longer at the front, thick and very dark. His eyebrows were dark, too, and his face was slim and beautiful.

'How do you like it?' Dominic asked.

'What?' Nina asked, confused by his question.

'Your tea?'

'Oh! Milk, no sugar,' Nina said.

'Sweet enough?' Dominic suggested, a twinkle in his dark

eyes as he smiled. He bent down to find the milk in the fridge, and Nina drew a chair out and sat down.

'So, what brings you up to the house?' she began, wondering if he'd come to get a glimpse of Faye.

'Oh you know – ran out of food at my place.'

Nina nodded. 'And where is your place exactly?'

'The Folly.' He turned to look at her expectantly. 'It's one of the old buildings, don't you remember?'

'Yes! I do,' Nina was suddenly blasted by an image from her past. 'We once ended up there on a walk, didn't we? That evening when the day seemed to stretch on forever. We'd been paddling further up the river in the shallows and decided that a walk would be the best way to dry off. Remember?'

'I remember,' Dominic said with a smile. 'You were wearing that big straw hat with the red ribbon.'

'Gosh!' Nina said. 'Yes.'

'Have you still got it?'

'No. I'm afraid my boyfriend's dog ate it.'

'Your boyfriend?'

'We're no longer together,' she said quickly.

'Maybe it's just as well,' he said.

Nina looked perplexed. 'What do you mean?'

'Well, you don't want some mad dog eating its way through your wardrobe, do you?'

'Oh, I suppose,' she said. 'So, tell me about The Folly. You can't actually live in it, can you?'

'Oh, yeah! A few mates and I did it up. It's great – although I haven't spent a winter in it yet. I've got to get some money together before then so I can afford to heat the old place. You'll have to come and have a look some time. I'm sure you'd love it,' Dominic said, sloshing milk enthusiastically into the mugs and adding two sugars into his own.

'I'd love to. Thanks!' Nina took the mug he offered and watched as he screeched a chair out from under the table and sat down opposite her.

'You know,' he began, 'I was racking my brains, trying to remember the last time you babysat here.'

'Were you?' Nina grinned.

'And I couldn't think when it was.'

'Well, there were so many occasions—'

'We missed you,' he said suddenly. Nina looked up from her mug. 'Nobody could ever replace you.'

'Oh, I'm sure that's nonsense,' she said.

'No, really – you were a one-off!' his eyes widened as he spoke, making Nina feel almost uncomfortable.

'The girl Mum got in after you was a real bitch.'

'Dommie!' Nina cried, shocked at his choice of words. She still couldn't help but think of him as an innocent little boy who didn't have a bad bone or a bad word in him.

'Sorry!' he said quickly, 'but she was. She used to march us to bed and then cavort on the sofa with her boyfriend.'

'How do you know that?' Nina's eyebrows disappeared into her blonde fringe.

Dominic blushed slightly and his cheeks dimpled. 'Because Alex and I used to sneak down the stairs and watch.'

'Oh, you didn't!'

'Before you say anything, it had nothing to do with me!' He leant back in his chair and held his hands up in a gesture of innocence.

'Oh, I suppose it was all your big bad brother's idea?' Nina teased. Dominic just grinned at her.

She took a sip of tea as she tried not to imagine what exactly the young boys had witnessed in the front room. Then something occurred to her. If they had spied on one babysitter, why not another? Had they spied on her? Had she been the victim of schoolboy curiosity? Had they witnessed her as she'd nosied through the family photo albums and rifled through their parents' CD and book collections? God almighty – had they spied on her the night she'd decided to give a one-woman show to Olivia's Barbra Streisand album?

'And how do you know I didn't have boyfriends over?' she ventured. Dominic almost spluttered a mouthful of tea across the table. 'Did you spy on me, too? Dominic?'

He looked at her, his brown eyes crinkling at the edges. 'How about later then?' he said. 'Come over to The Folly this evening?"

'Dominic – you haven't answered my question!' Nina said.

'Come on – you want to see The Folly, don't you?' His face was positively rosy from trying to suppress what Nina guessed was a confession.

'Er – well . . .' she hesitated, her mind clouded with confusion.

'We could walk along the river – like we used to.'

Nina couldn't help smiling at the memory. But, back then, she had been a babysitter and Alex and Dominic had worn bright woollen hats and matching gloves, and had played hide-and-seek in the old Folly. An invitation to the now-private home of a young man, via a riverside walk, had quite different connotations – especially if he had romance in mind. That wouldn't fit in at all with Nina's plans to get him back together with Faye. Which reminded her – she really did have to get moving with that little idea.

But Nina didn't have time to answer as the front door suddenly crashed open.

'Anyone home?' a male voice cried.

Nina looked at Dominic. His mouth had dropped open and his face had set in a frown.

'Hullo there, bruv!' A tall, fair-haired young man breezed into the kitchen and gave Dominic a sound slap on the back. 'How are you? Good to see me?'

'Hello, Alex.'

'And who do we have here? Latest girl, Dom?' His eyes flicked back up to Nina as he raked a hand through his tousled hair.

'Erm, w— well—' Dominic stuttered.

'I must say, your taste's improving with age.'

Nina felt his eyes raking quickly up and down the length of her.

'No, Alex – this is Dad's new secretary. I thought you'd remember her.'

'Don't tell me!' Alex put a hand up and he looked at Nina again, his brown eyes narrowing. There was a moment's pause. 'Nina Elliot,' he said suddenly, causing her to blush. 'Didn't you think I'd remember?

'No,' she said quietly, staring into eyes that seemed to wink at her.

'Who wouldn't remember you?' He took a step closer and held his hand out. Nina reached out to shake it and gasped when he took it up to his mouth to kiss it.

'Welcome back,' he said, a grin stretching across his face, making Nina's heart somersault. It's really great to see you again.'

102

'Thanks,' she said. 'You too.'

'So, how have you been? What have you been up to all these years?'

Nina smiled. 'Nothing much, I'm afraid. A bit of this and that. A few awful jobs and a few dreadful boyfriends – you know how it goes.' She gave a nervous laugh.

'I'm sure you've been breaking hearts left, right and centre,' Alex said and Nina felt herself blushing.

'Oh, I don't know about that,' she said.

'You always were a heartbreaker,' he told her.

'What?' Nina said in surprise. 'I was not!'

'The worst sort, too,' Alex added, 'because you don't know when you're doing it.'

'Oh, Alex!' Nina said, hoping he was teasing her. There was definitely a twinkle in his eye that she seemed to remember from all those years ago. He always had been a terrible tease.

'So, what are you doing this evening?' he suddenly asked her.

'Well, I—'

'Only I thought you might like a spin in the new car – out to the Broads? Find a nice little pub by the water? What do you say?'

Nina felt that her head was nodding quite independently of any thought inside it.

'Good. Will you be ready in about an hour? That should give us plenty of time to find somewhere, shouldn't it?'

'Fine,' Nina said, her mouth strangely dry.

'Great!' Alex said, clapping his hands together. 'I have a feeling this is going to be one hell of a summer!'

*   *   *

103

Dominic was furious. Just who did Alex think he was – marching in like that and snatching Nina from right under his nose, just as they'd been getting along so well? But wasn't it absolutely typical of him? It was just the sort of behaviour he'd come to expect from his brother over the years. He'd been sure Nina would have spent the evening with him. She'd been on the verge of accepting his invitation when Alex had barged in.

Alex really was the limit when it came to women. Bring a pretty girl within a one-mile circumference of him and he'd track her down and hound her until she'd promised to go out with him. It had always been the same. Ever since they were boys, he'd had to get in there first, make an impression and prove he was the best.

Dominic sighed, knowing that if Nina was to stay the duration of the summer, he'd better warn her about Alex before it was too late.

Chapter Twelve

Nina didn't know why she felt so guilty about saying yes to going out with Alex. She'd finished work for the day and they hadn't seen each other for years. What harm would there be in having a quiet meal together and catching up on old times?

Having been just that little bit older than Dominic when she'd babysat them, she'd been able to talk to him and it would be great to catch up with him tonight.

It felt like ages since she'd been taken out to dinner but, she reasoned, this was not a date. It was nothing more than a get-together with somebody from her past whom she felt great affection for. That was all. Besides, she was curious to get to know the grown-up Alex and wanted to see the young man he'd become.

She looked in the mirror that leant against the wall, and straightened her dress. Perhaps it was because Dominic had asked her first, and she hadn't actually said yes or no before Alex had made her an offer of his own. Maybe that's what was worrying her. Anyway, she'd sort things out with Dominic another time. She only hoped that she hadn't upset him by agreeing to take off with Alex so spontaneously.

A couple of years older than Dominic, Alex had always

been the confident one. He was always pushing boundaries, whether it was to do with his school homework or their strictly imposed bedtimes.

'Oh, Neeenah!' he'd cry as if in physical agony. 'It's not fair.'

That was it with Alex – if the world didn't revolve around him all the time then it just wasn't fair. But, even though he'd tried her patience on occasion, they'd had so many happy times together. Nina remembered watching him swimming in the river, practicing his guitar in the living room and showing her the best way to make toast – if she remembered correctly, it had something to do with raspberry jam and marshmallow fluff.

'Mum makes it for us all the time,' he'd assured her when she'd expressed some concern over the sickly sweet mess he'd made.

Nina smiled. As a child, Alex had liked to get his own way and, from what she'd seen of him so far today, that hadn't changed at all. She grabbed her brush and ran it quickly through her hair, biting her lip as she wondered why it was so important to look nice. She shook her head, dismissing the thought that she was doing this for Alex, because it was time to go.

Grabbing her bag, she hurried down the stairs and stood in the hallway.

'Nina?' Alex's voice came from the living room, and he appeared in the doorway, smartly dressed in beige linen trousers and crisp white shirt, his face clean-shaven and smelling citrussy. 'Ready to go?' he asked and Nina nodded.

As they left the house, Nina gasped at the car that greeted her in the driveway.

'You've got to be kidding!' she said, looking at Alex for confirmation.

'Only the best for you!' he dismissed casually, his eyes twinkling as he shook his keys in the air.

There before her, gleaming in the bright rays of the sun, was a sleek white Alfa Romeo Spider. Nina didn't know much about cars, but she knew the difference between an old classic and an old banger and, up until now, her boyfriends had only driven the latter.

'Is this really yours?' she asked as Alex opened the door of the two-seater for her.

'Of course,' he grinned, walking around to the driver's door and lowering himself into the seat. 'Well,' he added, 'for the summer, anyway.'

Nina looked at him. 'Hired?'

'No, no. It belongs to a friend. One good turn deserves another and all that.'

'And he trusts you with it?' Nina said mischievously.

'Yes! I'm no boy-racer, you know. I can handle a car sensibly.'

'Well, I'm glad to hear it,' Nina said, as he turned the key in the ignition, wondering what kind of favour would warrant the lending of such a car for the duration of the summer.

'Got your belt on?' Alex looked at her briefly as they turned out of the lane onto the main road. She nodded. 'Okay, hold onto your hair!'

He wasn't kidding. As the car picked up speed, Nina began to wish she'd tied her hair back as it blew both horizontally and vertically behind her. It was exhilarating, thrilling and ever-so-slightly terrifying. The back lanes of Norfolk had always been on the narrow side, but Nina had never seen them at such a close range before. Being exposed to the elements in a tiny car really made her feel a part of the landscape. It was almost like flying. They were literally driving through the air. At one point, she almost stretched a hand out to touch the banks, but thought better of it as they sped by a bramble hedge.

She looked at Alex, who was sporting a grin that almost tickled his ears. She could still see the naughty little boy there, dancing around the brown eyes. He'd always been determined to have the best, and he looked as if he'd got it now.

'Happy?' he asked, as he slowed to avoid a pothole in the middle of the road.

Nina looked at him and nodded. 'Yes!' she yelled back, her voice carried far behind them as he accelerated again. 'I thought you said you weren't a boy racer?' she shouted to him.

'I lied!' he said and Nina couldn't help but laugh. His exuberance might verge on the dangerous, but it was also highly infectious.

Solitary houses, farms and churches blurred past as the Spider tunnelled further into the Norfolk countryside. Nina almost called out several times as she saw likely candidates for the pub grub they were allegedly looking for, but Alex seemed to know where he was heading.

When he finally pulled over at a small pub whose black and white flints glinted in the evening sun, Nina sat for a moment, allowing her body to adjust to the sensation of being still again.

'You look like a little haystack!' Alex laughed as he looked at her.

'Thanks a lot!' she cried, self-consciously flattening her hair with her hands.

'No – I like it!' he said quickly.

She threw him a look of disbelief. 'Well, you look like you've had electric shock treatment,' she retorted.

'That's the price you pay for a good ride,' he said, looking Nina straight in the eye and making her blush. 'Come on,' he said, getting out of the car. 'The other thing a good ride's renowned for giving you is an appetite.'

The Bittern was on one of the many broads that made Norfolk a favourite holiday destination. Its garden sloped down to the water and several bright white boats had been moored along its banks whilst the thirsty occupants drank their fill in the pub. Nina wondered if there were regulations about drinking and sailing as there were with drinking and driving. For the sake of the bitterns, and the other wildlife, she sincerely hoped there were.

She looked at the depiction of the large, rather unpleasant-looking bird on the signpost and wondered if it had just been made up. After all her years in Norfolk, she'd never seen anything that looked like that.

'You go and grab a seat and I'll get us a menu. What do you want to drink?' Alex asked.

'Just a mineral water, thanks.'

'You sure you don't want a proper drink? You're not on babysitting duty now, you know.'

'A mineral water is fine, thank you.'

'Okey-dokey,' Alex said, winking at her and disappearing into the pub, leaving Nina to enter the garden and choose a bench. She was glad she'd brought her jacket with her and she slipped it on as she chose a seat not too close to the water but with an unrivalled view of it.

As she waited for him to return, she couldn't help

thinking how strange it was to be going out for the evening with Alex. If somebody had told her the week before that she'd be back at The Old Mill House and enjoying the company of Alex and Dominic, she would never have believed them. She could see now why Olivia was so proud of her sons – Dominic with his budding career as an artist and Alex leading an exciting life in London. Olivia had said that Alex hadn't quite settled in the right job yet but he would be brilliant in whatever he set his mind to, and Nina was apt to agree with her. Alex had spark and she was quite sure that he would set the world alight once he had found his focus.

Then there was Dudley. She wouldn't exactly say that he'd made her feel at home yet – he was too wrapped up in his own world to worry much about how Nina was feeling – but there was a gentleness in his manner that she so appreciated after the way she'd been treated by her last boss, and they were beginning to work really well together, with him giving her a little bit more responsibility each day and her taking it with alacrity. She really had never felt happier in her life.

It was then that Alex appeared with the drinks and menu and sat down opposite her. They placed a quick order and Nina sipped her drink, her vision blurring somewhere over the water to the reed beds beyond.

'So, you're Father's new secretary,' Alex said, breaking the silence and claiming Nina's attention.

'Yes,' she said. 'Why – have there been many?'

Alex laughed. 'You could say that.'

'Oh dear,' Nina's mouth dropped.

'No, don't worry – I'm sure you'll last longer than the others.'

110

'I've only been here a few days but I was just beginning to feel at home,' she said, thinking of how much happier she was in her new job than she had been in any other.

'Good,' Alex smiled. 'It's nice to have you back again.'

Nina looked into his brown eyes. They were a feature he had in common with Dominic, but there was something quite different about Alex's eyes: they had a mischievous quality – a note of naughtiness.

'It's been a long time,' he said, in the kind of tone that made Nina think he was about to reach across the table to hold her hand.

'Yes,' she said simply. 'Alex – do you know what happened to Teri?'

He almost choked on his drink. 'Teri? Why? What have you heard?'

'Nothing, really. Your mother mentioned she was Dudley's last assistant and I wondered why she left.' Was it her imagination, she wondered, or had Alex's cheeks developed a rosy hue?

'Well, it was . . .' he paused, 'it got a bit much for her, working with Dad. He can be difficult at times. Not that you'll have any problems with him, I'm sure,' he quickly added.

'Is that the *only* reason she left?' Nina held his gaze, and she could almost see Alex buckling underneath her – just like when he'd been a young boy trying to convince her that he'd finished all his homework and should be allowed to watch TV for the rest of the evening. Then he cleared his throat nervously and gave a grin.

'Well,' he said, 'we might have had the *tiniest* misunderstanding.'

'Oh, really?'

He shrugged and took another sip of his drink.

'Alex?' she probed.

'Hey,' he said, 'you're not my babysitter any more. I don't have to answer to you.' There was a twinkle in his eye as he said this. 'But, if you must know, I was sort of seeing her for a little while.'

'*Sort of* seeing her? What does that mean?'

'It means that we weren't – you know – mutually exclusive.'

'Oh, right,' Nina said, clarity dawning.

'Well, Teri got really narked when she saw me with Katy. I'd invited her home for dinner and Teri had stayed late to finish something for Dad. I had no idea she'd be there but – like I said – we had an understanding.'

Nina frowned. 'It seems to me that this understanding was all on your side, Alex.'

He grinned again. 'Yeah. You might be right about that.'

Nina shook her head in despair – but she couldn't help smiling, too, because he'd grown into just the sort of cheeky, flippant young man that she'd guessed he'd become.

'I believe Mum's roped you into helping with this crazy party idea,' he said, changing the subject.

'Yes, and typing your father's novel, too,' Nina said.

Alex laughed. 'If Dad's a novelist, then I'm a monk!'

Nina looked up, surprised at his disbelief. 'Looks like you've got a change of vocation then, because I've read the first few chapters.'

Alex almost did a double take. '*Really*?'

'Yes. And it's very good,' Nina said with a hint of pride at her new employer's talent.

'What's it about?' Alex was suddenly very earnest.

'Well, I think that's a secret for the time being.'

He eyed her for a moment. 'I admire your loyalty,' he said, 'but you can tell me, can't you?'

Nina smiled and shook her head. She hadn't been at the mill long, but she already felt enormously loyal towards her new boss.

'Oh – go on!' Alex said, leaning across the table. 'Nina!'

'No!' she said.

'Please!' his voice was getting louder. 'I won't let on,' he said, standing up and moving to sit next to Nina on her side of the picnic bench.

'Alex – the bench will tip over!'

'Go on!' He pushed his head closer to her.

'I've said no!' She felt as if she were turning into the old babysitter once more.

'Tell me – tell me!' he chanted and began tickling her.

'Alex – get off!' she cried, aware that several pairs of curious eyes were looking in their direction. 'STOP IT!'

Alex sat up and stared at her, startled at her command, his face very close to hers. Nina looked at him, aware that her heart was beating ten to the dozen. For a moment, neither of them spoke.

'Cottage pie twice?' a shrill voice came from behind them, breaking the spell. Alex leapt up to move back to his side of the bench, knocking over his drink in the process, and spilling the contents onto the grass. The waitress looked on, unamused. She'd seen it all before.

'Er – better make that another cola, please,' he said. The waitress nodded and left them to their meal. 'Ooops!' Alex grinned and started to chuckle.

'You idiot!' Nina whispered, but she was giggling, too.

'Sorry about that,' he said, catching her gaze and holding it.

'We'd better eat this whilst it's hot,' Nina said.

On the drive back, Nina glanced at Alex, wondering if she dared to pry a little into family affairs.

'Alex?' she asked hesitantly.

'Yeah?'

'What exactly happened between Faye and Dominic?'

Alex's eyes narrowed but his gaze remained fixed on the road ahead. 'Why do you want to know?'

'Oh – no reason. It's just that it seems rather odd, don't you think?'

'Odd? How?'

'That she spends so much time at the mill in the hope of patching things up with Dominic when he obviously isn't interested in her anymore.'

Alex was silent. 'Faye's a lovely person,' he said as the countryside flashed behind them.

'That's why I can't understand why Dominic broke up with her,' Nina said. 'I bet they were absolutely brilliant together. They're both such lovely people, and I can't bear to see Faye so sad about it all. Do you have any ideas what might have happened? She talks to you, doesn't she?'

Alex shook his head. 'Not about Dominic.'

'Oh,' Nina said.

'I've told her that she really needs to move on, but I guess she's one of life's great romantics and just won't give up,' he said.

Nina smiled. That was sweet, she thought. Behind the facade of a typical lad, Alex really was very caring.

Suddenly, a memory from the past flashed before her

114

that reminded her that Alex had a darker side. It had been an evening just before Christmas when she'd been babysitting. She'd been making hot chocolate in the kitchen and had heard the young Alex and Dominic squabbling in the front room under the Christmas tree. She'd tiptoed towards the door, wondering if she could overhear what it was they were fighting about, and had heard their voices clearly from the hallway.

'You don't even like Anna,' Dominic was saying. 'She was my friend first.'

'But she's my friend *now*,' Alex was saying. 'She thinks you're boring and she doesn't want to be friends with you anymore.'

Dominic had got up from where he'd been sitting under the Christmas tree and had stormed out of the room, almost crashing into Nina, while Alex had sat there with a smug expression on his face.

Nina looked at him now, hoping that the past wasn't repeating itself again and that Alex wasn't somehow involved in the break-up between Dominic and Faye. She wouldn't be surprised if he was.

Chapter Thirteen

'You'll never *believe* what I've managed to pull off!' Olivia beamed from the threshold of the study the next morning.

'What?' Nina asked, looking up from the computer screen where she'd been typing Dudley's novel and trying to take her mind off the night before.

'Well,' Olivia began, making sure her husband wasn't about before entering the room, 'I've been thinking about dear Dominic and his determination to be an artist, and I've persuaded the ladies at the Country Circle to sit for their portraits!'

'Portraits?' Nina said in surprise.

'Yes! Isn't it marvellous! They're all terribly keen and terribly well-off – Dominic could more or less charge whatever he wants.' Olivia clapped her hands together like an excited schoolgirl.

Nina had a sudden image of a line of little old ladies with perms, hitting each other with their handbags in order to be the first to sit for the handsome young artist.

'I didn't know Dominic did portraits,' Nina said.

'Well of course he does – he's an artist, isn't he?'

Nina thought of his huge abstract landscapes. She'd not seen any evidence to suggest that Dominic's burning ambition was to paint Norfolk's population of retired ladies.

'He'll make a fortune! I must grab him and tell him whilst he's here! But this will involve you, too, Nina. You'll be able to help Dominic, won't you? There are over twenty women in the circle, and they'll need to be given appointments and such like. Could you diarise for Dominic? Now that you've got the study in some sort of order?'

'Well there's the anniversary party to arrange yet, and Dudley's asked me to make a start on some research for his novel,' Nina indicated the computer screen in front of her.

'Yes, I know,' Olivia's green eyes widened, 'but you can do it. I have every faith in you.'

Nina smiled hesitantly. Did she have a choice? 'Well, I suppose I can squeeze it in,' she said, wondering if Olivia Milton was just a nicer version of Hilary Jackson and that she'd still be expected to break her back at work in exchange for a sweet smile and gentle pleading.

'You're wonderful! Whatever did we do before you came?' Olivia teased, leaving the room as quickly as she'd entered it.

Nina turned her attention back to the novel and became instantly engrossed in the story of Lord Ellis Glavin and the beautiful young Caroline. Dudley had asked her to start typing up the novel as it stood, whilst he'd disappeared with his notepad to a corner of the house where he wouldn't be disturbed.

The pages of typing she'd found on clearing the study on her first day were now barely visible after Dudley's pen had scribbled his alterations in his own peculiar shorthand. Nina wished that there were prescription glasses she could get in order to decipher it all, but made do with twisting her neck and the paper at odd angles. She shook her head, forecasting eye strain and neck pain for herself in the near future. Still, she became so wrapped up in her task that she hardly heard the knocking on the French doors a few minutes later. It was Faye.

Nina sprang out of her chair and went to open the door.

'Hi!' Faye said, pushing her dark hair out of her face and smearing something green across her forehead in the process. 'I'm just taking a break after digging up a rather unruly bramble bush and wondered how you were settling in.'

'Oh, good, thanks. Just trying to work out Dudley's handwriting.'

'Rather you than me,' Faye said and then she cocked her head to one side. 'Nina?'

'Yes?'

'I heard you went out with Alex. Is that right?'

Nina looked surprised. 'How did you hear about that?'

'The mill is a very small world. Everyone knows exactly what everybody else is up to,' Faye said with a grin. 'So, how did it go?'

'We were just catching up on old times, really,' Nina said.

Faye nodded. 'Don't forget your vow.'

Nina frowned. 'My vow?'

'To avoid men,' Faye reminded her.

'But I'm not seeing Alex,' Nina said quickly.

'Well, *you* might think that but Alex probably thinks you're an item now.'

'Oh, that's ridiculous.'

Faye's eyebrows rose a fraction. 'I'd just recommend caution when it comes to Alex,' she said.

Nina chewed her lip. 'Faye?'

'Yes?'

'Has he ever made a play for you?'

'Alex?'

Nina nodded.

'Of course he has!' Faye said. 'He's Alex. He makes a play for every girl!'

Nina grinned and was just about to ask more when she heard somebody knocking on the study door. She wondered who it could be this time and realised she'd never get any work done if the daily intrusion rate was so high.

'Come in!' Nina sang. The door creaked open slowly and Dominic appeared.

'Hello,' Nina said.

He entered the room and then clocked Faye. 'Oh,' he said.

'Hello, Dom,' Faye said, her face flushing at coming face-to-face with her ex.

Nina stood between them avidly watching, the air positively crackling with awkwardness. But there was definitely something else there besides the awkwardness, she thought. If she wasn't mistaken, the blushes that coloured the cheeks of the distraught couple told of an affection that hadn't been completely forgotten. Maybe it was still there, Nina mused, bubbling away under the surface and just needing a little bit of help – a gentle push in the right direction from a well-meaning intermediary – in order for it to make a resurgence.

'Hi,' Dominic said, his voice sounding small and odd. 'You okay?'

Faye nodded. 'You?'

'Good.'

'Good,' Faye echoed.

Nina blinked at the stunted monosyllables that passed between them and wondered if she should intervene, but Faye got there first.

'I should get back,' she said. 'There's a rambling rector that desperately needs my attention.'

'A what?'

'It's a rose,' she said with a little smile, before leaving.

Nina turned back to Dominic. He was watching Faye as she crossed the lawn, a pained look on his face. She watched him for a moment and wondered what thoughts were cascading around his brain.

'Are you all right? You look a bit shell-shocked.' Nina said at last, looking at his face – as pale as a Romantic poet's – and saw the uneasy look in his dark eyes.

'I am,' he said, walking into the room properly now that Faye had gone, a scowl darkening his face. 'Mum's just told me the news about the portrait painting.' He sighed and sat down in his father's chair on the other side of the room.

'Oh – I see.'

'You know about it?' he asked, not sounding surprised.

'Yes,' Nina confessed, 'she did mention it.'

Dominic threw his head back to the ceiling and closed his eyes. Nina looked across at him, noticing the stubble on his face and under his chin. His shirt was open at the collar and she could see where he'd caught the sun.

She blinked and looked away. 'Aren't you pleased about it?'

He stretched his arms and sat up in the chair, looking across at Nina. 'It's good of Mum, I know, and I should be grateful,' he started. 'She's always doing her best to help – she really is.'

'But?'

'But – it isn't really what I want to be doing. For one thing, there's this exhibition I'm meant to be preparing for.' He shrugged his shoulders. 'And I know it sounds ungrateful but the idea of painting a succession of elderly ladies in twinsets and pearls doesn't really appeal to me.'

Nina smiled, catching his eye. He smiled back. 'I had a feeling that might be the case,' she said.

'You did?'

'Well, from what I've seen and heard about your painting.'

He nodded. 'Well, you're right.'

'But won't it be good money? Didn't you say you wanted to save a bit?'

'Oh yes, of course, but I hoped I wouldn't have to stoop to conveyor-belt art.'

'Well, we all occasionally have to do things that we'd really rather not be doing,' Nina said. 'We can't always be living the dream. I'm afraid reality steps in from time to time and makes slaves of us all.'

'You mean you'd rather not be here?' he said, looking at her from across the room, an expression of disappointment on his face.

'Oh, no!' Nina said quickly. 'I love it here! But I can't grow too fond of it because I don't think it's going to last forever.'

'Is that why you've got the local paper permanently glued to your face?' Dominic motioned to the corner of her desk.

Nina nodded. 'I'm being more select in what I choose nowadays because I've had my fill of rotten jobs, but everyone has to go through them. I know that now.'

Dominic stroked the stubble on his chin. 'I guess,' he said. 'I just wish mine wasn't in the middle of the summer holidays when I want to be in the fields with my easel, not stuck indoors with some seventy-year-old lady.'

'But it won't last forever, will it? It might even lead to other things?' she said encouragingly.

He grinned. 'You're amazing,' he said. 'There isn't an ounce of woe in you, is there?'

Nina shook her head, 'You didn't see me in my last job.'

'What happened?' Dominic leant forward in his father's chair.

'Well, in essence, I told my boss what I thought of her and walked out,' she said, smiling. It sounded quite good when she put it like that. 'I'd never done anything like that before in my life but I'd decided that enough was enough, you know?'

'Really? Wow!' Dominic looked suitably impressed. 'That's amazing. I really admire you – but I hope you don't do that to us because it looks like I'm going to need your help as much as Dad does.'

Nina looked into his brown eyes; as dark and beautiful as his brother's, although missing the naughty sparkle that Alex's had. Dominic's were more thoughtful, more soulful.

Nina bit her lip. She hadn't seen Alex since they'd got home last night, and his car hadn't been in the drive that morning.

'So how did last night go?' Dominic asked, as if reading her mind.

'Oh, it was nice,' Nina smiled, feeling herself blush.

'Where did you end up?'

'The Bittern?' she said, not knowing if Dominic knew of it.

'Right. Should have guessed,' Dominic's brow developed a very deep scowl. 'It's where he usually goes.'

'You mean it's where he takes all his women?' Nina

remarked, not sounding surprised, but feeling a little disappointed all the same.

An expression of guilt suddenly chased the scowl away from Dominic's face. 'Sorry, I shouldn't have said that.'

'Don't worry about it. It was just a friendly meal,' Nina said, trying not to think of how Alex had looked at her and how her pulse had reacted. 'Listen,' she began, 'I'm sorry I let you down like that – I mean – I should have given you an answer instead of swanning off as I did.'

'I would have liked one,' Dominic said quietly.

Nina gulped. She shouldn't have brought it up. She should have kept quiet and pretended that she'd forgotten about his invitation to The Folly, but she wasn't made like that. She felt awful about what she'd done, and she just had to apologise.

'Are you going to give me one, then?' Dominic asked.

'What?' Nina looked at his expectant face, his eyes so wide that his forehead was beginning to crinkle again.

'An answer,' he smiled, making her smile too. 'You've already had dinner with my big brother, so what about having dinner with me? I wouldn't say I'm the world's best cook, but at least I *can* cook,' he said.

Nina felt her smile widening, 'Yes. That would be nice.'

'Good!' he said, leaping out of the chair, 'Mum's cooking for us all tonight so we'd better make it tomorrow. I'll meet you here. About seven? And, if this sun holds out, we can take that walk along the river.'

Nina nodded. 'Seven o'clock,' she said to Dominic as he left the room, a sunbeam smile warming his face.

Later that morning, Dudley looked up from the neat pile of typescript that Nina had printed out for him. She had learnt that he would often lift his head in a manner suggesting that he was about to say something momentous but that he was, in fact, only in deep thought about his story.

She watched him for a moment, her eyes resting on his red lambswool V-neck. He always seemed to be wearing it, despite the heat. It was as much a part of him as his white eyebrows and gravelly voice, but she couldn't help wondering if he owned just one pullover, or if he had a drawer chock-full of identical tops.

He exhaled a deep, dragon-like breath that startled Nina, his white eyebrows shooting into the bridge of his nose.

'I'm not happy,' he said in a quiet but, nevertheless, rather frightening voice.

'No?' Nina piped. What on earth could be wrong, she panicked? Had her fingers been on the wrong keys and she'd typed a load of gobbledegook? Had she misread all his corrections and made a mockery of his story?

'No,' Dudley resonated, 'it's Caroline. There's something wrong with Caroline. She's not real. She's two-dimensional. Didn't you feel that?'

'No!' Nina said, thankful that it wasn't herself that was at fault but Dudley's romantic heroine. 'But then again, I'm no writer,' she said.

'No, but you read, don't you?' he asked, sounding like a schoolmaster who only wanted to hear answers with the word 'yes' in them.

'Yes,' Nina obliged.

'But you felt that she was real enough, did you?'

Nina bit her lip. She'd never been asked her opinion when she'd worked for Hilary Jackson and she'd had no idea that she'd been employed as a literary critic by the Miltons. She didn't know what to say. She only knew that she was no expert when it came to analysing novels; she read a novel and either enjoyed it and put it in her bookcase or hated it and gave it to the local charity shop.

'Perhaps she could be a bit more energetic,' Nina hesitated, not quite knowing where that idea had come from.

'Energetic?' Dudley asked, his eyebrows forming question marks.

'Yes,' Nina said, 'at the moment, I feel she's a bit passive – do you know what I mean? When she first arrives at Caldour, for instance. I know she's young and is stunned with her new surroundings but she seems rather . . .' Nina paused, searching desperately for the right word.

Dudley leant forward slightly, 'Rather what?'

'Wimpy,' Nina said, and then blushed. Had she been too forward? She looked at her boss who was chewing the inside of his cheeks, quite sure he would erupt at any moment.

'Yes,' he said at last, rubbing his chin in a gesture that reminded her at once of Dominic, 'you're right. She's wimpy!'

Nina gave a half-smile of relief. 'What I mean is, perhaps you could make her a little less—'

'Wimpy!' Dudley said and suddenly burst into a fit of uncontrollable laughter, which was very deep and very loud and rather contagious, because it started Nina off, too, and they probably wouldn't have stopped for a good long time if it hadn't been for a knock on the study door.

'Dudley?' It was Olivia. 'What on *earth* is going on in here?'

Dudley sniffed loudly and tried to assemble his features

into some sort of order. Nina, too, wiped her eyes and stopped laughing as she turned around.

'Nothing! Nothing!' he said quickly.

'Well,' Olivia said, 'I'm hoping you'll let me borrow Nina. Ziggy is going absolutely bonkers in the kitchen and is in dire need of a walk and I'm sure Nina could do with some time away from her desk.'

'Well, just don't monopolise her,' Dudley said with a warning snort. 'I need her here. She's a marvel – an absolute marvel.'

'Didn't I tell you that?' Olivia said, smiling at Nina as they left the room together. 'It must be *so* wonderful to be needed,' she said.

Ziggy was in fighting mood when Nina left the house with him, tugging at the lead in an attempt to be five minutes ahead of himself at any given moment. Each time he tugged, Nina stopped walking, but as soon as she started moving again Ziggy would lunge forwards as if in an attempt to make up for lost time. In the end, Nina found it easier to be dragged than to keep on stopping and starting and so flew along the river bank towards the fields. It would at least get the whole experience over and done with as quickly as possible.

It was as she was approaching the barley field that she remembered the encounter the day before with Justin and Bess. She looked at her watch. She was earlier today. Not that she was hoping to meet him or anything. She had to get back to her duties with Dudley and didn't have time to be talking to strangers on footpaths – no matter how handsome they might be.

'Heel, Ziggy,' she said, doing her best to rein the dog in as he tried to dive into a patch of brambles, nose-first.

'Come on, now,' she said, doing her best to make an effort with the out-of-control animal. 'You're going to walk *nicely*!' she told him. 'Like a polite dog who respects his human companion and not like a wild beast who's only interested in the next good sniff.'

They walked in tandem for a few minutes, Nina keeping a tight hold of the lead and stopping each time Ziggy pulled. It was frustrating and exhausting, but it did seem to be working and, after a while, Nina felt confident enough to slacken her hold on the lead. It was a mistake. Ziggy immediately felt his handler relax and took full advantage of it, springing forward with a wild look in his eye as if he'd been held captive for a decade.

'No! *Ziggy*!' Nina cried but the dog was firmly in charge now and wasn't going to relinquish that power without a struggle. Nina felt herself being dragged along, the path flying under her feet as the dog picked up speed.

If the man hadn't been walking just around the corner to stop Ziggy's progress, Nina might have been flying across the Norfolk landscape for hours. But there he was, with Bess by his side.

'Nina!'

'Justin?'

'Hey!' he said, a smile stretching across his face. 'Are you okay?'

Was she forever destined to have him ask that question of her whenever they met, she wondered?

'I'm fine,' she said, trying desperately to recover her balance whilst keeping a firm hold of Ziggy's lead.

'How's he been behaving?'

'Like a stroppy teenager,' Nina said with a laugh.

'Oh, dear,' Justin said.

'And I've been stopping and starting just like you said, only the very second I gave him some slack he—'

'Took off like a rocket?'

'Exactly!' Nina said, nodding her head enthusiastically.

'Well, he's a young dog, full of energy. You'd probably be disappointed if he *didn't* try things on every now and then.'

'Believe me – I would *not* be disappointed!' Nina said, recovering her breath.

He smiled at her and Nina looked up at him. He was over six feet tall and had a look of a movie star she'd once seen in an old black and white film. Was it Errol Flynn? And did that bode well? Probably not.

'Here,' he said, 'allow me?' He held his hand out for the lead and Nina gave it to him. 'Yep, he's strong all right,' he said a moment later, 'so it's really important you nip this behaviour in the bud because you've got to maintain control. Remember that dogs are pack animals and are used to having a leader and being told what to do. Well, you've got to be that leader. You've got to show him that you know how to control him and then he'll feel safe.'

'That's all very well,' Nina said, 'but how do I do that?' She watched as Justin walked Ziggy along the footpath, stopping whenever he tugged on the lead and starting again when he was calm.

'It's just a case of being consistent. That's all. And not just when out walking either. You've got to be the boss at home, too.'

'But it's not really my home,' Nina said.

Justin turned to look at her.

'I'm just working there over the summer. I don't really live there and Ziggy isn't my dog.'

'But you're the one I see walking him,' Justin pointed out.

128

'Yes,' Nina said with a laugh. 'That task does seem to have fallen to me.'

'So, you've got to be the boss of him.'

'Right,' she said, nodding her head with determination but still feeling hopelessly lost.

'Don't look so worried!' Justin said. 'Just focus on one or two things to get right every day and you'll make excellent progress.'

'Is it really that simple?'

'It really is,' he said.

'I'm glad you think so,' she said, taking the lead back from him. 'How did you get to be so knowledgeable anyway? Are you a dog whisperer or something?' she asked.

Justin smiled and shook his head. 'No, just a dog owner who wanted to keep his collie under control. I kind of inherited her and she was in a bit of a state when I got her.'

'Really?'

He nodded again. 'Her previous owner had mistreated her and she was terrified of men. I think she was hit or something awful, and I really thought I was fighting a losing battle. She was so painfully shy and I couldn't get near her for weeks – but time and patience won through and she's the best friend I have in the world now.'

Nina's heart melted at the confession and she watched as he stroked the soft head of the dog.

'Anyway,' he continued, 'I seem to know more about Ziggy than you at the moment.'

Nina looked surprised. 'Well, there's not much to tell,' she said.

'I don't believe that for a minute,' he said, his blue eyes bright and inquisitive.

'Really, I'm not that interesting a subject,' she said.

'Tell me anyway,' he insisted, with an encouraging smile.

Nina took a deep breath and they walked together along the sun-baked footpath, the green-gold barley field stretching to the horizon in front of them.

'I recently left my job in Norwich. I'd been there ages but, recently, I began to begrudge every single second of my time in the office and finally realised that I had to leave.'

'That sounds very brave,' he said.

'Oh, it wasn't really. It took the encouragement of a good friend and a few glasses of wine one lunchtime before I got up the nerve.'

'Still, it's good to make a decision you're happy with,' he said.

Nina nodded. 'And then I ran into Olivia – she lives at the mill.'

'Yes,' Justin said.

'You know her?'

'We've met.'

'She's lovely and I really think it's fate that we bumped into each other when we did because she offered me a job working for her husband. He's writing a novel and I'm helping him sort everything out.'

'Really?'

'You don't think I can?'

'No – I didn't mean that. I can't believe he's – Dudley's – writing a novel.'

'Oh, believe it. It's very good, too.'

'You're kidding?'

Nina nodded. 'He has a wonderful turn of phrase and there's a lot of humour in it, too. He's very funny, you know.'

Justin laughed. 'I can't quite imagine that.'

Nina smiled. 'I wouldn't have believed it either if I hadn't read it with my own eyes, but he's very talented.'

They walked on or rather they walked, stopped, walked, stopped again as Ziggy learned to do things properly.

'You know, I used to babysit for the Milton family,' Nina went on.

'You did?'

'Years ago when the two youngest boys were at school. The eldest was away at boarding school so I never got to see him but, to be honest, two young boys were quite enough to handle.'

'I bet they were, too.'

Nina smiled as she remembered the young Dominic and Alex once again.

'So, you've never met Billy?'

Nina shook her head. 'I'm sure I'll see him at the anniversary party.'

'Ah, yes, I've heard about that.'

'Are you coming?'

'I expect so.'

'Do you know the Miltons well?' Nina asked.

'Well, I've always lived around here and you tend to get to know people quite well.'

Nina nodded. 'I think half of Norfolk is coming, judging by the catering that's being laid on.'

'The Miltons never like to skimp on anything, especially when it comes to parties,' Justin said.

'It must be nice having a large family,' Nina said wistfully as she stopped in the middle of the path after Ziggy had pulled on his lead once again.

'You're not from a large family, I take it?'

131

'No,' Nina said. 'I'm an only child and I don't even see my parents much these days.'

'That all sounds rather sad.'

'Oh, I don't know. It all seems quite normal to me,' Nina said with a shrug, 'although I can't help envying families like the Miltons, who always seem so happy in each other's company, even if they're fighting, you know?'

'I know,' Justin said.

'You've got a big family, too?' she asked.

'A couple of brothers, yes,' he said.

'And you all get on?'

'Pretty much,' he said. 'We spend enough time together so as to remain friends, but enough time apart so that we don't become enemies.'

Nina laughed. 'That sounds like the perfect recipe for a happy family.'

They walked on, reaching the river once more and startling a pair of moor hens who danced across the water to the far bank, away from the prying eyes of the humans and the inquisitive noses of the dogs. The water was deeper and slower here, and not for the fainthearted swimmer. The Milton boys had been brought up along this river, though, and knew every bank and curve. Nina remembered the time that they had all swam until the last pink streaks of sky had faded into darkness and then made their way home across the fields with wet towels and happy hearts.

A light breeze picked up now and Nina's hair was blown back from her face. The sun felt delicious and the weathermen had promised a good summer for once in the UK. After the recent years of dismal grey skies and temperatures that meant the entire population was still sporting jumpers and coats throughout the school holidays, a long hot summer was just what everybody needed. Nina was so grateful that she would be spending it at the mill – even if it did mean that she had become a dog trainer as part of the bargain.

'That's it!' Justin said, breaking into her thoughts as they walked along the path. 'Excellent progress. You're looking great together. Good teamwork!'

Nina laughed at the praise.

'How does it feel?'

'Really good!' she said. 'I just have to keep it up now, don't I?'

'Oh, yes. That's the real trick. It's easy to lapse into old habits, but dogs respond well to consistency. Keep up the good work and the rewards are there.'

Suddenly, Nina's phone beeped. She retrieved it from her trouser pocket. 'Oh, dear,' she said a moment later.

'Anything wrong?'

'I'm needed back at the mill. Paperwork crisis!'

'Ah,' he said.

They looked at one another and Nina couldn't help feeling sad that the walk had come to an end already.

'I can't thank you enough for all your help.'

'Well, you're not quite there yet. There's still a long way to go.'

'Of course,' she said with a nod.

'But I'm happy to help whenever you like.'

They paused for a moment, the sweet spiralling song of a skylark cascading down upon them.

'Well, I'd better be—'

'Nina!' Justin said.

'Yes?'

'I was just wondering if you'd like a drink sometime. Or a chat. Or another walk.'

133

She smiled.

'I mean, we don't always have to talk about dogs, do we?'

'I guess not,' she said.

'It might be nice to talk about other things, too,' he said.

'Okay,' she said, her heart racing. Was he asking her out on a date? And how did she feel about that? She'd told herself that she was going to steer clear of men, but she had to admit that the idea of going out with Justin was rather exciting.

'Here,' he said, grabbing a piece of paper from his pocket and scribbling down his mobile number. 'Give me a call.'

Nina took it. It seemed wonderfully old-fashioned to be given a piece of paper with a handwritten number on it rather than somebody just ringing your phone or offering you a business card. 'Thank you,' she said, 'for everything.'

'You're welcome,' he told her.

'Okay,' she said, not quite knowing how to say goodbye, but Justin did it for her, raising his hand in a friendly wave and whistling to Bess who had her black and white nose stuffed into a tussocky piece of grass.

Nina turned with Ziggy and the two of them headed down the footpath towards the old bridge that would lead them back to the mill.

'I'm not going to look back this time,' she said. 'I'm not. I'm *not*.'

But, as soon as she reached the bridge, she sneaked a look back at the retreating figure of Justin, and couldn't help smiling when he turned around, too, and gave her a final friendly wave.

Chapter Fourteen

Nina had forgotten how much she used to enjoy eating with the Miltons. Sitting in the dining room with them now, she looked at them all in turn and couldn't help feeling a little jolt of happiness at being made so welcome. Like Faye, she thought, who was sitting between herself and Alex. They had both been made honorary members of the family.

'You know, we haven't had a proper family meal for ages,' Olivia said excitedly, her eyes darting around the table. 'Although it's such a shame that Billy couldn't make it. I think he's flying across Europe or somewhere.'

'You're probably right,' Dudley said, 'but I don't understand why he doesn't stay here with us when he finally comes back down to earth.'

'Oh, you can't expect him to do that. He'd much rather be with his friends,' Olivia said. 'Staying up late and going on pub crawls or whatever it is they get up to.'

'He can do that and still stay here,' Dudley said.

Olivia shook her head. 'It's not the same thing at all. You remember when you were young, don't you? You wouldn't want to be reporting home and answering awkward questions from your parents all the time, would you?'

'I'm not in the habit of asking awkward questions,' Dudley said, taking a sip of wine from an elegant crystal glass.

Olivia laughed. 'Of course not, darling!' she said in a sing-song, tongue-in-cheek kind of a way.

'I'm still getting over that time you asked that girlfriend of mine – what was her name?' Alex said.

'Phoebe,' Dominic prompted him, obviously knowing the story.

'Phoebe – ah, yes!' Alex continued. 'Well, I remember the time you asked her if I'd proposed to her yet.'

'And what was wrong with that?' Dudley asked. 'She was a decent girl. Good family. Intelligent.'

'Dad – it was our second date!' Alex said.

Dudley shook his head. 'Makes no difference when you know you've met the right woman,' he said. 'I knew the minute I saw your mother.'

'Oh, Dudley – you did not! I had to coax you for *months*.'

Nina exchanged looks with Dominic across the table and they grinned at one another. She loved listening to their stories and their banter, even though she couldn't help feeling that she was somehow intruding on a special family moment. But it was an honour all the same. She'd never had many family moments of her own. There wasn't really much of a chance, being an only child with a father who worked away from home for weeks at a time. In fact, the only time Nina remembered an occasion that could loosely be referred to as a family moment was a trip to Great Yarmouth when she was seven, but even that had been far from perfect.

Nina's dad had refused to pay for the car park and had then acted out a scene of outrageous disbelief, worthy of any budding Othello, when he'd got a ticket for parking in a residential area. Nina had been so embarrassed by his ranting in the middle of the street that she'd run into an arcade and hidden, only to be found and slapped sonorously on her bare legs by her mother in front of a group of highly amused teenagers. She had stung all the way back to Norwich.

Did the Miltons know how lucky they were, Nina wondered? In an age where broken families were the norm, their situation seemed unusual in the extreme.

Olivia gave a little laugh. 'Do you remember that time Billy brought home that girl who looked like a horse?'

Alex burst out laughing. 'She did, didn't she?'

Nina's eyes doubled in size. 'Really?'

Olivia nodded. 'She had this mane of hair that she kept swishing about and a long face and the most enormous teeth I've ever seen, poor girl. Billy never forgave me for pointing it out to him, but I was merely saving him from a lifetime of teasing. Perhaps that's why he never brings girls home any more. We scared him off and he now keeps his paramours away.

'Pass the butter, Nina, dear,' Olivia sang. 'We have met the most wonderful girls through our boys, haven't we, Dudley?' she continued. 'But nobody has surpassed the lovely Faye.'

Nina almost choked on a chunk of cucumber and Faye blushed to the very core of her being and, when she glanced up at Dominic, Nina could see he had done the same.

'Now, don't go embarrassing the young ones,' Dudley said, waggling his knife at Olivia in warning.

'But you have to admit I'm right,' Olivia charged on, completely undaunted. 'Our Faye is very special,' she said, leaning forward in her seat to smile at the blushing girl. 'The mill wouldn't be the same without her, would it?'

Dudley harrumphed and Alex gave a laugh as Dominic continued to blush.

'Well, I don't know about anyone else, but I can't quite believe that we have Nanny Nina in our midst,' Alex said, causing Nina to join in with the blushing competition. 'Fancy the Night Angel descending upon us again!'

Dudley spluttered into his mixed salad and Dominic's fork scratched and skated out of control on his plate.

'God! I'd forgotten we used to call her those names!' Dudley laughed.

'Don't embarrass her!' Olivia chided. 'I'm sure she had nicknames for you, too.'

'Did you?' Alex probed.

Nina cleared her throat. 'Well, er—'

'I'm sure, unlike you, Alex, that Nina is *far* too polite to divulge them,' Olivia said, giving him a warning glare.

'What were they? I can't remember you ever calling us anything,' Alex said, completely ignoring his mother.

'Well, of course she wouldn't! Did you ever call her Nanny Nina to her face?' Olivia smiled, causing Alex to blush for a change.

'Oh, come on, Nina. What did you used to call me?' Alex said, naturally assuming that he was important enough to warrant a nickname. 'You *must* have had a name for me.'

'I didn't – honestly,' Nina said, casting back in her mind to see if there really was something amusing to retrieve. No, she'd never had a nickname for Alex. Of that she was quite sure.

'Let Nina eat in peace, Alex,' Dominic complained.

Alex was quiet for a moment, but not because his brother had asked him to be. Nina watched as he eyed her every now and then, and saw as the moment of realisation as it dawned upon him. 'I've got it!' he said, triumphantly spearing a radish and holding it aloft. Nina grimaced. She believed him. 'You didn't have one for me, but you had one for Dominic, didn't you? Am I right?'

'Alex!' Olivia hushed.

'Alex!' Dominic warned with a dark glare.

Nina looked around the table, distraught at being the centre of attention. She looked down at her plate and counted her tomatoes. One. Two. Three. Four. She wished she could pick them up, one by one, and pelt Alex with them.

'I really don't know why you're making such a scene about it,' Nina said, trying to make light of the situation in the hope that it would go away.

'I'm not!' Alex remonstrated. 'But *you* certainly are!'

The whole table had suddenly grown silent and four pairs of eyes were pinned to her; Alex's, Faye's, Olivia's and even Dudley's. All except Dominic's. He was hiding under a deep scowl.

Nina could see that she would get no peace until she'd divulged her secret. She bit her lip as she looked at Dominic. She hadn't meant to embarrass him. Would he ever forgive her? But it was too late now.

'It was Dom—' she stopped, as if regretting it already.

'Yes?' Alex encouraged.

'Domino.'

Alex spluttered. '*Domino*?'

Nina nodded.

'Oh, that's so sweet! If only we'd thought of it!' Olivia giggled. 'I suppose it was because he was so small.'

'Oh, Mum!' Dominic said with a groan.

'What?' Olivia continued to giggle. 'I think it's lovely.'

'Olivia, you're embarrassing him,' Dudley growled.

'Domino!' Alex said with a hearty laugh.

'Isn't it cute?' Olivia smiled, handing the plate of bread around, oblivious to Dominic's discomfort at the far end of the table. It was then that Nina saw something that nobody else seemed to notice – a brief moment when Dominic and Faye caught each other's eyes. It was so fleeting, but tiny smiles were exchanged and Nina felt sure that there was warmth within those smiles. Warmth, under-standing – and maybe even a little regret at a love having been lost.

Simplicity was the key word, Dominic thought, as he scoured his bare cupboards for ingredients the next day. Pasta with salad would be light enough, and it would mean that he wouldn't have to go shopping, which in turn meant he could spend more time organising himself and his place. It wouldn't be quite the spread of the night before, but then, he'd never be able to compete with his mother when it came to home cooking.

For a moment, he rolled his eyes as he remembered last night's dinner. Alex had apologised afterwards in his effort-less way and Dominic had done his best to shrug it off. After dessert, which had been a very large helping of Eton Mess, Nina had helped Olivia to stack the dishwasher and Dominic had hung around the living room in the hope of talking to her at some point. He listened to her silvery laughter coming from the kitchen. She seemed so at home at the mill and it was hard to imagine a life without her there. His mother obviously adored her and his father's temper had eased ever so slightly since her arrival. Just like when she'd been a babysitter, she was working wonders on them all.

A moment later, he heard her walking down the hallway, with Ziggy by her side.

'Nina,' he'd called.

'Yes?'

'Can I talk to you?'

'Of course,' she said. 'I'm just going to give Ziggy a run in the garden.'

'I'll come with you,' he said and the two of them left the house together. The evening had cooled and a lavender sky sewn with bright stars greeted them.

'It's a beautiful evening,' she said.

Dominic nodded and wanted to tell her that she was beautiful, too, but, as ever in her presence, he had become tongue-tied and cripplingly shy.

'What was it you wanted to talk about?' she asked him, unclipping Ziggy from his lead and watching as he romped around the garden, stuffing his head in the borders, which Faye took so many hours organising.

'Well, I—'

'Gosh,' Nina suddenly interrupted him. 'I hope Alex didn't embarrass you too much at dinner. I can't apologise enough about that revelation. I shouldn't have said anything.'

'It's okay,' he assured her. He hadn't really minded. It was only Alex's chiding which had upset him. He didn't blame Nina. In fact, he'd rather liked being the focus of her attention. He'd been special enough to warrant a nickname, and that had made him smile. And, of course, it was also one up on Alex.

'I'm sorry,' she said. 'I've interrupted you. What were you going to say?'

They walked across the lawn towards a long beech hedge in which was set a wooden gate that had been painted a brilliant turquoise decades ago and was happily flaking into old age. Nina opened it and they walked through into a small walled garden.

'I love it here,' she said. 'It's so peaceful.'

'It's so messy,' Dominic said. 'Mum keeps bugging Dad to do something with it.'

'Perhaps Faye will come up with something wonderful. She's full of good ideas.'

Dominic didn't say anything.

'Dommie – what *did* happen with Faye?'

He merely shook his head. 'We drifted apart. That was all.'

Nina frowned. 'Did you two—'

'Do you mind if we don't talk about it?' Dominic said. 'It's bad enough that Mum keeps pushing her under my nose.'

'Okay,' Nina said, 'of course.' But Dominic could see that her eyes were full of curiosity and her mind was full of questions.

'I don't want to talk about Faye. I want to talk about you.'

'Oh,' Nina said in surprise.

'I wanted to make sure you're still okay for dinner tomorrow night.'

'Oh, yes, I am. Thank you, Dommie.'

He winced inwardly at her use of the name Dommie.

He wished she'd call him by his full name now. After all, he wasn't a little boy in pyjamas any more.

'Great!' he said.

'You Miltons certainly know how to keep a girl well fed,' she said, grinning up at him.

'Oh, well, we can do it another time if you prefer,' he said, feeling himself blush.

'No, no!' she said quickly. 'I was only teasing. Tomorrow would be fine,' she said, and they watched in amusement as Ziggy leapt over a scraggy box hedge and lifted his leg up against an old scarecrow.

Now, after a day of preparing canvases for his upcoming show, Dominic had a whole evening of Nina's company to look forward to. Alone. No interruptions and no Alex. But, first of all, he had to clear away some of his work. It was okay to have standing room only when he was on his own, but Nina might not appreciate having to squeeze between rows of paintings and having near-misses with easels and dirty jam jars.

He started to move his canvases until they all leant up against the same wall like some trendy art shop, and gathered up the brushes that were scattered across the floor like kindling. That was when he found them. The Faye canvases. He'd meant to get rid of them, but he just hadn't had the heart. They'd been painted at sixth form during their last few months together and the naivety of the portraits struck him now. The artist in him was desperate to be rid of them. He should paint over them with something more professional, he told himself, but the young man instinctively knew that that would be wrong.

Dominic gazed at the gentle face looking right out of

the canvas at him as if she was in the room with him there and then. Those enormous eyes of hers were so expressive, he thought. And there was that glimmer of a smile playing around her lips, perhaps at a long-forgotten shared joke.

He shook his head. He didn't have time for this. He placed them behind the small sofa and got back to work, whipping a duster over his chairs, carefully checking for signs of paint. There'd be nothing worse than if Nina sat down and got up with a burnt sienna bottom.

Finally, he stood in the middle of the room to survey the scene. The converted folly might not have been everyone's idea of the perfect property – for a start, it was about three times as tall as it was wide – but to Dominic, it was perfect. He loved the long, slender windows that allowed the extraordinary East Anglian light to illuminate his work. He adored the bare floorboards that echoed under his shoes and he loved the warmth of the red brick; soft to the eye, but wonderfully gritty to the touch.

He loved the unusual and the quirky, and he sincerely hoped that Nina would love it too.

In her bedroom at the mill, Nina was wishing that she could shake the word *date* from her mind as she got ready before Dominic arrived. It was, yet again, just a simple friendly invitation to dinner. Besides, she was quite determined not to get involved with another man. She really hadn't thought that Dominic would mention his invitation again after the embarrassing nickname revelation of the night before. Still, she couldn't dispel the way he'd looked at her as he'd reminded her of her promise in the walled garden; so earnest, so imploring, and she got the distinct feeling that the word *date* would be foremost in his mind, if not her own. But she had definitely sworn off men – that much was clear in her mind. Tonight, she was merely making amends for having been so rude to Dominic when she'd taken off to the pub with Alex, and maybe – just maybe – she'd be able to find out more about Faye. Nina had instantly warmed to Faye the moment she'd met her; she could really feel the girl's heartache and couldn't help wondering if it would be possible to bring about a reconciliation between her and Dominic. She just couldn't shake the feeling that this young couple were meant to be together.

Nina sighed. She knew herself what it was like to be so hopelessly love-struck that everything else in the world seemed trivial. She remembered the first time she'd met Matt. They'd both belonged to the same gym and there'd been a Christmas party one year. She'd seen him before, of course, but she'd always been much too shy to say hello to him and he hadn't known she'd existed before the incident with the punch. Somebody had knocked into him and he'd crashed right into her, magenta punch spilling all down the front of her dress.

It wasn't the best of introductions, and it should have been an omen that things wouldn't work out, but Nina had been lost from that first encounter and, even when she knew that he was no good for her, his hold over her had been unyielding.

For a moment, Nina caught her own gaze in the mirror, and a pair of sad hazel eyes stared back at her. They were eyes that said they still remembered. Eyes that hadn't been able to close against the truth even though she'd managed to physically run away from it. Matt had tried to contact her, leaving message after message, but Nina had deleted every single one of them, not allowing herself to listen to them after the last abusive one he'd left for her.

Nina blinked hard, dispelling thoughts of past times and emotional crimes, and turned her attention to her meagre wardrobe. She didn't have many decent dresses, but it wouldn't be seemly to wear the same dress that she'd worn when she'd gone out with Alex. So, she pulled out a long white dress splashed with vibrant poppies.

Quickly flinging off the neat shirt and cotton trousers she'd worn for work, she hummed lightly as she smoothed the dress down over her body. It felt delicious; like a second skin, but a much cooler one. She turned to the mirror and gasped. Not only did it feel like a second skin, it looked like one, too.

'Jeans and T-shirt!' she whistled through clenched teeth.

'Nina?' Dominic's voice called from downstairs. 'Are you ready?'

'Er – yes! Just a minute,' Nina called, looking desperately at the clock and noting that it was only ten to seven. Dominic was more than a little prompt.

Anyway, it was too late to change now so she grabbed a cardigan from the bottom of her bed and hid as much of her body with it as she could.

'I'll be down in a moment,' Nina shouted, flattening her hair against her head and licking her lips to remove a little of their pink gloss. She grabbed her white pumps from under the bed and flung her feet into them. That would tone the overall image down a bit, she thought.

Dominic was in the hall, standing under one of his paintings as if posing for a celebrity magazine article.

'Hello,' Nina said, noticing the smart navy shirt and black jeans.

'Hello,' he echoed, his eyes wide and full of poppies. 'I like your dress,' he smiled. Nina bit her lip. She really should have put her jeans on.

'Do you?' she asked, nervously doing up another button of her cardigan.

Dominic nodded. 'I like your pumps, too.'

'Oh?' Nina said, wishing she'd put Wellies on instead.

'Come on – let's go,' he said, opening the door for her like a true gentleman.

Leaving the house, they crossed the bridge and followed the footpath that ran alongside the river. It was a perfect summer's evening. Swallows dipped and dived along the water and the air hummed with insects. It was warm enough to walk without a cardigan, but Nina thought she'd better keep it on. She wouldn't want to give Dominic the wrong impression and, if there was a dress to give the wrong impression, then she was wearing it.

He looked nice though, she thought, as they ambled across the field, the sun low on the horizon. His eyes sparkled like dark jewels in the evening sunlight. Faye, she was quite sure, would have swooned.

Nina jolted at the thought as an idea occurred to her. She was going to have to talk to Dominic about Faye.

'I hope you like pasta,' Dominic began casually.

'Oh, yes,' Nina said, wondering how she could bring the subject of Faye up. It wasn't going to be easy, slotting the name of an ex-girlfriend into a conversation about pasta. 'Do you cook a lot?'

'When I have the time,' he said.

'Did you used to cook for Faye?' she asked. Oh dear. That wasn't terribly subtle, but it was the best she could do in the circumstances.

Dominic turned to look at Nina, his face clouded over with suspicion, as if he knew she had a hidden agenda. Honestly, she might as well have had her mission tattooed across her forehead, she thought.

'I wish she'd get a gardening project somewhere else,' Dominic said quietly. 'Mum really shouldn't be encouraging her to spend so much time here. It just isn't right.'

'But it would be a hard garden to beat. It's a lovely place,' Nina said.

'You think so?'

'Of course. Faye obviously likes it.'

Dominic frowned again. 'I can't understand why you're so interested in Faye, Nina! *Must* we always talk about her?'

Yes, Nina thought. ''Course not,' she said with a light smile, as if she didn't care one way or another.

'Come on,' he said, his stride picking up, scattering a fine cloud of insects from the tall blonde grasses at the side of the path. 'I'm starving. And I'm banning all conversations about anyone who isn't you.'

Had Nina thought of Dominic as a potential suitor rather than as an ex-ward, she would have been impressed by his attempts to set the scene for romance. As it was, she saw that he'd made a genuine effort to accommodate a guest in a rather sparsely furnished room.

The Folly had always been an impressive building from the outside, but Nina had never thought of it as having any potential as a home. It was amazing, she thought, how Dominic had transformed it, turning it into something worthy of a feature in a glossy magazine. She grinned at the stacks of canvases leaning precariously against the walls and the rows of bottles and heaps of half-squeezed-out tubes of paint on shelves made from salvaged timber.

A tiny table was set in the centre of the room. It was one of the few items of furniture in the place, and it looked as lost as a dinghy out at sea. Nina's eyes scanned the room, her homemaking gene placing a comfortable sofa here and arranging a bookcase there. Tall candlestands would look just perfect and large pottery vases filled with flowers would brighten the room.

'What do you think?' Dominic asked, his hands dug deep into his pockets, his shoulders hunched close to his body, as if nervous of her reply.

'It's lovely,' Nina said truthfully, 'but perhaps a woman's touch might help.'

'Are you offering?' His eyebrows rose suggestively and then he blushed as if he realised that that was the sort of thing Alex would say, not him.

Nina cleared her throat. 'Well, I know this is your work-space, but it could be a little more homely,' she said gently, trying to keep the conversation as neutral as possible by veering the talk towards curtains and cushions. 'You know, with some fabrics here and there. Just a few touches.'

Dominic nodded, scratching his chin. 'I'm not very good at that. Besides, after doing the place up I couldn't afford to buy a bean, let alone a beanbag.'

Nina smiled. 'If it's any consolation, I don't own one of those either. All I have is currently in my room at the mill.'

'But you're—'

'Twenty-eight – I know,' Nina said, as if she'd been found guilty of a heinous crime.

'I wasn't going to say that,' Dominic assured her.

'But you were thinking it?' she teased.

'No! I was going to say that you're not some flako artist.'

'But neither are you,' she said with a smile.

149

'Yeah – right!'

'But you're *not*!' Nina stressed. 'Everyone knows how difficult it is to make it, even when you're as talented as you are. It just takes a lot of hard work and a little bit of time.'

Dominic looked at her. 'You're marvellous!' he said.

Nina blushed. She really must make an effort not to be quite so nice to him all the time.

'I can't believe you did all these,' she said, changing the direction of the conversation as quickly as she could by admiring a group of sketches he'd hung haphazardly on the walls. 'And these are beautiful, too. Are they for your show?'

'No. The ones over there are going to the show.'

Nina looked across the room at the stack of paintings. 'Wow, you've been working so hard, Dommie.' She then took a step closer to inspect the trio of pencil sketches that had captivated her. Three women; two in profile and one gazing straight at the artist. Nina wondered who they were. They certainly weren't Faye.

'Who are they?' she asked.

Dominic joined her by his pictures. 'I cheated with those. They're not of anybody real. They're inspired by the Pre-Raphaelites.'

'They're so lovely – so serene.' Nina stared at them, their soft beauty quite captivating. From the corner of her eye, she could see Dominic staring at her.

'What is it?' she turned to look at him.

'Your mouth. I'd never noticed before, but it's just like a Rossetti.'

'Rossetti? What's that? A kind of pasta?' she said with a tiny smile.

Dominic smiled. 'No! He was a painter – from this period,' he motioned to his sketches. 'He painted beautiful women. And your mouth is just like one of his sitters.'

'Is it?' Nina's fingers flew up to touch her lips. She cleared her throat. 'Let's eat, shall we?'

Nina couldn't help noticing how different Dominic was from Alex. For a start, he didn't get up and come round to the other side of the table to tickle her. But it was more than that. He was fundamentally different. Where Alex had sped Nina along the Norfolk lanes in an Alfa Romeo Spider to a pub meal, Dominic had walked her by the riverside to a home-cooked dinner. Where Alex had teased, joked and made a thorough nuisance of himself, Dominic was quiet, calm and thoughtful.

There were several moments throughout the meal when Nina felt sure that Dominic was going to interrupt Handel's *Water Music* to say something significant, but each time he stopped himself short. His expressions had certainly seemed to indicate that there were unspoken words tumbling around in his head but, whenever she'd thought he was about to speak, he'd merely placed another fork-load of food into his mouth.

By the end of the meal, Nina was beginning to get frustrated. Had he something to say? Perhaps he really wanted to talk about Faye. After he'd silenced her by the river, Nina hadn't dared to mention her name again. But, even though she desperately wanted to help bring the two of them back together again, she wasn't one to mince words either. If he had something to say then she wanted to hear it.

'Dominic? Is there something you want to ask me?' she said, taking a sip of the wine he'd poured for her.

Dominic looked up, startled. 'What?'

'You look as if you've been trying to say something for the last half hour, and you'll end up with indigestion if you don't say it soon.'

His eyes widened at her openness. 'What makes you think I've something to say?'

'Because I know you. Well, I *used* to know you,' Nina corrected. 'And I know when you're on the verge of saying something. Like the time when you'd dropped Alex's toothbrush in the toilet and were hovering around on the landing waiting for somebody to help you, but not actually telling them what the problem was. Remember?'

'I remember,' he said with a reluctant nod.

'Well, you've got that same expression on your face now. Am I right?'

He half-smiled. 'Yes,' he said.

'And remember the time you sneaked down the stairs at half-past ten at night pretending you couldn't sleep? And really it was because you were bursting to tell me what you'd made your mum for Christmas? A tissue-box covered in celebrities cut out of old—'

'*Hello!* magazines!' Dominic finished. 'Yes. I know.'

'You scared me half to death when I saw you standing behind me in your pyjamas! And I still don't know how *Roman Holiday* ends.'

'Sorry!' he smiled, looking self-conscious at the fact that he had once been a little boy who had worn Thomas the Tank Engine pyjamas. 'Blimey Nina, I do wish you didn't remember all that babysitting stuff quite so clearly.'

'Sorry,' she said.

'It's as though you're trying to stop me from saying what I want to say.'

'So there *is* something you want to say?' Nina said. Dominic looked at her and Nina felt herself straightening in anticipation. 'What is it?'

'Well, it's not that easy,' Dominic said quietly, leaning forward slightly in his chair.

Nina began to fidget. 'You know you can tell me anything, don't you?' she encouraged.

Dominic nodded. 'I know. You're marvellous.'

'Don't be starting all that again,' Nina warned.

He pushed the remains of his pasta around on his plate. He wasn't going to eat it, but he hadn't quite finished with the cutlery yet.

'Dominic!' He looked up from the large swirl he'd created in the thin layer of sauce. 'Are you going to tell me or not?'

He put his knife and fork down and nodded. 'As long as you don't interrupt. Just listen to what I've got to say – before you say anything.'

'Okay,' Nina said, a mixture of anticipation and anxiety bubbling in her stomach.

Dominic cleared his throat to begin. But a sudden loud knocking on the door prevented his words from ever leaving his mouth.

Chapter Fifteen

'Helloooo! Anyone at home?' a cheery voice called.

It was Alex. Of course it was Alex. It was *always* Alex. Who else could arrive with such an accurate sense of timing?

'Hi, Dom! Hope I'm not interrupting anything,' he said as he barged into the room, a mischievous grin lurking in the corners of his mouth as he eyed Nina and Dominic at the table. Together. Alone.

'Well, you are actually,' Dominic began, but he might just as well have said nothing.

'I was looking for Nina,' Alex said, as if that was the most natural explanation in the world.

'Were you?' Nina met his gaze full-on and felt herself reddening.

'Yes,' Alex said, moving an artists' palette off a nearby stool and noisily drawing it up to the table. Dominic watched in amazement as his brother stretched an arm towards the centre of the table to reach the baguette.

'Mind the candle!' he warned, his voice fuelled by fury. Alex shrugged and blew it out.

'You should watch these things – dangerous, you know.'

'Only when you're around,' Dominic said under his breath.

The brothers looked at one another and Nina half-expected to see a bolt of lightning at the place where their eyes met.

'What are you eating, anyway?' Alex asked, eyeing the remains of Dominic's plate with unreserved disgust.

'Pasta salad,' Nina smiled. 'It's really good, Dominic.'

'What – Dom made it?' Alex said incredulously, as if the notion of making one's own food was preposterous. 'Sure it's not a defrosted M&S job?'

'No, it isn't,' Dominic all but growled. 'Just because your idea of food is to throw a couple of tenners across a pub counter—'

'Excuse me, bro, but my idea of food is to take a beautiful young lady out for a meal, not subject her to eating in a room that smells like a cat's weed in it.'

'It's turps. And it doesn't smell that bad,' Dominic said with a weary sigh.

'So, what was it?' Nina asked in a slightly raised voice, trying to dispel the tension that was rising between the brothers as fast as her colouring. Honestly, it was as if the last decade had slipped away and she'd reprised her old role as referee, trying to keep the warring brothers from starting a fight.

Alex eyed her leisurely as he stuffed his mouth with a portion of torn bread. He then shrugged. 'Nothing in particular. Just wanted to see you.'

'Well, we're eating,' Dominic pointed out.

'No!' Alex laughed.

'Yes!' Dominic retaliated. Nina was beginning to feel rather uncomfortable and fidgeted in her chair. But it wasn't her job to intervene any more. She couldn't tell them off and send them running to their bedrooms like she had done in the past.

'I was thinking,' Alex said, breaking the brief barrier of silence, 'we should really go swimming.'

'What?' Dominic blurted.

'Yes!' Alex cried. 'It's certainly warm enough.'

'But it's after eight o'clock,' Nina said.

'So?'

'And we're still eating,' Dominic said.

'God – you're such a killjoy, Dom,' Alex groaned, scraping his stool back from the table. 'Nina? Fancy a quick dip in the river?'

'Er—' she looked at Dominic, but his eyes were fixed firmly on his plate. 'Maybe another time?'

'Might not be another time,' Alex said, unbuttoning his shirt as he strode over to the door. 'Best to go with these things, I say.'

Nina watched in amazement as he whipped the shirt from his body and turned around to look at her. 'Sure you're not tempted?' he asked, his hand on the door.

'No, she's not,' Dominic said angrily and, for a moment, Nina thought he was about to get up from his chair and thump his brother right in the middle of his tanned chest.

'Okay!' Alex held a hand up in resignation, the twinkle in his eyes seeming to brighten.

'But thanks,' Nina said and Alex nodded before leaving and closing the door quietly behind him. For a millisecond, Nina could have sworn he'd winked at her, but it was so fast that she convinced herself she must have imagined it.

Turning her attention to Dominic, she watched as he stood up and collected her plate, piling it noisily on top of his own.

'Dommie—'

'It's Dominic, Nina. Please don't call me Dommie anymore.'

'Sorry,' she said quickly. 'I was just going to say that that was really nice. Thank you.' Again, she was fully aware that his high spirits at the start of the evening had evaporated the moment his brother had appeared.

'Dessert?' he asked, making it sound like an order instead of an offer. Nina nodded and Dominic disappeared behind a wicker screen that sectioned off his tiny kitchen.

What had he been about to say when Alex had waltzed in? Nina rested her head on her hands and sighed. That was the second time Alex had done that to Dominic. He really did have an uncanny sense of timing. Perhaps that was all part of being an older brother? But how could she find out what it was that Dominic had been about to tell her?

'Do you want a hand in there?' she asked, trying to sound as jolly as she could.

'No,' Dominic said simply and curtly.

Nina listened as he moved about the kitchen, and almost leapt from her seat when she heard a plate clatter into the sink and Dominic cursing under his breath.

No, she thought, she wouldn't find out what Dominic had wanted to tell her tonight. The moment had been lost.

Nina woke from a sleep so troubled that even the rush of the river couldn't soothe her. She leapt out of bed and shook her head vigorously, like a waterlogged dog. Her bedroom at the top of the house was hot and humid and she walked across to the window to open it, the night air warm and still, filled with the scent of honeysuckle and roses.

She took a few deep steadying breaths.

'Oh God!' she whispered, as she acknowledged what was

happening. She started to pace the room, her nightie twisting around her legs in a gauzy bondage as she moved.

'Dommie Milton has a crush on me?' she said into the empty room and, if she wasn't mistaken, she was beginning to believe that Alex was making a play for her, too. She'd done her best to block it out, but it had been quite obvious tonight and there was no running away from it any more.

She thought about the way Dominic had behaved – the little looks, the blushing, his being tongue-tied, and she thought about his fury when he'd been interrupted by Alex. She'd been so naive to think that she could just be friends with the boys.

'Oh God,' Nina groaned, wondering if it was too early in the morning to ring Janey for advice. She could just imagine what her friend would say though.

'What are you complaining about? Why not enjoy the attention? It's not every woman who has two handsome brothers running after her! You'd be mad not to make the most of something like that.'

Yes, Nina thought, Janey would probably not be the best person to advise her with something like this. Anyway, maybe it was just a rivalry thing. Maybe the two brothers were just asserting themselves, and their feelings were nothing more than a kind of game to see who could win her first.

Nina sighed. She'd thought that coming to the mill was a sure-fire way of turning the page and making a new, simpler life for herself. However, this particular page not only refused to be turned, but seemed to repeat itself on subsequent pages like some freak printing error. Was it ever possible to get away from everything, she wondered? Was it ever possible to find some peace?

She walked to the window again and stared out into the velvety darkness, glimpsing the rush of the river under the bridge in the moonlight. This was such a special place and Nina didn't want to do anything that would jeopardise her time there. She was there to work – not to get into some weird love triangle with two brothers. She had to nip this thing in the bud before it got out of control. As much as she adored the Milton boys, she could never see them through romantic eyes. It just didn't feel right, however handsome they might be.

Then there was Justin. In the busy daily life at the mill, she'd almost forgotten her new dog-walking friend and the little slip of paper he'd given her with his phone number on. He was still waiting for her to call him, wasn't he? She sighed. Nina wasn't used to so much male attention; she was used to being one man's doormat. It was a strange situation to find herself in – but not a totally unpleasant one, she had to admit. However, she had made a vow, which Faye had witnessed and seemed very keen for Nina to adhere to. She was not going to get involved with a man. It was too early. *Way* too early. So Dominic's love-struck looks, Alex's flirtatious ways and Justin's suggestion of dinner all had to be put on the backburner because she was unavailable.

A few hours later, after finally managing to get to sleep, she was awoken by a knock on her door.

'Who is it?' she asked grouchily, wondering who would have the nerve at half past seven on a Saturday morning.

'It's me – Dominic.'

Nina gasped. 'What do you want?' she asked, feeling horribly embarrassed that he was standing outside her bedroom after she'd just dreamt about him. It was almost as if she'd conjured him up.

159

'I need to talk to you.'

Nina panicked, grabbed her dressing-gown and pushed her hands quickly through her hair.

'Just a minute,' she stalled, before padding across the room with bare feet and opening the door.

Dominic was leaning against the wall. His face was pale and unshaved, and he was wearing combat pants with slashes all the way down them and a T-shirt splattered with red paint, making him look as if he'd had a horrific nosebleed.

'What is it?' she asked in concern.

'I can't believe what's happened,' he said, somewhat cryptically. 'I guess I just didn't believe it.'

'Believe what?' Nina urged impatiently.

'Mum – she's taken three portrait sittings for today!'

Nina's mouth dropped open, half in relief and half in surprise that he hadn't been about to declare his undying love for her. 'But that's good, isn't it?' she said.

'I didn't think it would happen so soon,' he said, looking totally stunned.

'Dominic – you didn't think it would happen at all, did you? You were hoping it wouldn't happen anyway – weren't you?' she said, cocking her head to one side.

He met her gaze and nodded. 'I've got this group exhibition in Norwich coming up and I really need to get organised for that, but I don't think Mum believes that we're actually going to sell anything. She thinks I'm just playing.'

'Oh, I don't think that's true.'

'But this portrait thing – that's proper money, agreed upfront. She believes in that,' Dominic said. 'But I just don't feel ready for it. Look.' He handed her a piece of paper with three names written on it.

160

'Edna Bowridge. Felicity Makepeace. Maisie Myhill,' Nina read the names and smiled.

'And that's just today's. Mum thinks I can cope with that workload each day. She's already talking about Monday's bookings.' Dominic's voice was barely audible. His dark eyes looked terrified, as if he'd been told that his life depended upon his artistic skills. 'I've never speed-painted before. It usually takes me weeks to complete a canvas.'

'Yes, but we're not talking Turner Prize stuff here, are we?' Nina kindly pointed out. 'We're just talking about a few old ladies who want something to hang on their walls. Half of them probably can't see properly anyway.'

'Oh, thanks very much!' he said, rolling his eyes at the ceiling.

'No – I didn't mean the paintings wouldn't be good,' Nina added quickly, 'I'm just saying that they won't be expecting you to create the *Mona Lisa*.'

Dominic sighed loudly and Nina watched his body slump against the wall. She hugged her dressing-gown to herself, aware that it had gaped open at the neck.

'Did I wake you?' he asked, suddenly noticing her attire.

Nina bit her lip. 'No,' she said although, in a way, he had. Or his face in her dream had – but she wasn't going to tell him that.

'What do you want, Nina?'

'Pardon?' she said.

'From life?'

'God, Dominic. You're getting rather profound for a Saturday morning, aren't you?'

'What I mean is, would you be happy doing something you really didn't want to be doing?'

Nina sighed. 'I know you'd rather be doing other things, Dommie – Dominic – but you don't have much choice at the moment, do you? And yes, I've often had to settle for second best. You just have to make the most of it by telling yourself that things will get better.'

Dominic smiled at her. 'Will you help me, then?'

'What would you like me to do?'

'I don't know – greet them, make cups of tea – that sort of thing. Moral support stuff, I suppose.'

Nina looked at this handsome boy, who seemed so unsure of himself. It was probably a very bad idea to spend any length of time with him, especially after their dinner together.

'I'd be very grateful,' he said, a small smile breaking over his unshaven face.

Nina smiled back at him. She felt a strange but pleasant feeling of warmth spreading through her body. It was, undoubtedly, the irresistible knowledge that she was needed, and that she felt truly valued by the people she was working with.

'I'd be happy to help,' she said, 'but on one condition.'

'What's that?'

'You have to stop panicking, have a shave and get yourself into some decent clothes so that these ladies you'll be painting don't think you're some kind of thug.'

'That's more than *one* condition,' he pointed out with a grin.

Nina grinned. 'I drive a hard bargain – get used to it.'

Chapter Sixteen

If gossiping were an Olympic sport then Edna Bowridge would have won a gold medal. She'd started chatting away to herself even before Nina had opened the front door.

'Lovely, aren't they?' she beamed, pointing to the terracotta pots at the front of The Old Mill House, the light bouncing off her pink-rimmed glasses.

'Mrs Bowridge?' Nina smiled.

'Edna – please,' she corrected, stepping into the hall. Nina took her heavy tweed coat from her, wondering how on earth she hadn't suffocated in the heat. Underneath, she was wearing a crisp white blouse with a pearl necklace peeping through the opening, and a dark green tartan skirt and matching waistcoat. Nina couldn't help but notice a very large safety pin on the front of the skirt. She hadn't seen anything like that for years; not since her days at Sunday school anyway, when the teacher, as old as the church itself, had sported similar hairy monstrosities that would make the children wriggle and itch if they had the misfortune to be pulled up onto her lap.

'We've got the studio upstairs,' Nina explained. 'It's a south-facing room, so it's lovely and warm.'

'This is the first time I've done anything like this,' Edna

said excitedly, 'But – gosh, all these stairs are going to make me rather red-faced for my portrait,' she puffed, her hand very firmly on the banister rail.

'I'm sure Dominic will take that into account,' Nina said, leading the way up to the second-floor bedroom, which Dominic had turned into a studio. It had been his bedroom when he'd lived at the mill and, being at the front of the house, the light was perfect.

'Pleased to meet you, Mrs Bowridge.' Dominic stepped forward to shake her hand as she entered the room. He had obviously taken Nina's advice because he was now clean-shaven, wearing a crisp denim shirt and had perfected his greeting and handshake so that he gave an instant impression of confidence and serenity.

'Please, call me Edna,' she said, somewhat out of breath.

'Can I get you a cup of tea or coffee?' Nina asked.

'A glass of water would be fine,' Edna said before turning back to Dominic. 'Right, my boy, where do you want me?'

Nina found herself spending most of the morning with Dominic and Edna. She could barely get a word in edgeways, let alone make up an excuse to leave the room. Edna rabbited non-stop and Nina felt herself going off into a trance.

She covered every subject from her neighbour's homemade apple strudel to nuclear disasters in the space of her first sitting, but it all rather amused Nina. Every now and then she glanced over at Dominic to try and catch his eye, but he seemed to have built up a sound barrier between himself and his subject – which was just as well, as Nina would probably have started laughing and not been able to stop.

'Er – Edna,' Dominic said at length, 'I'm going to have to ask you to stop talking now. I'm painting your mouth.'

'Oh, I am sorry! I'm such a chatterbox, aren't I? I know I am. You just tell me when you're ready and I'll be as quiet as a church mouse. You won't hear another word out of me.'

'I'm ready now,' Dominic said.

'Oh. Right.'

Nina smiled, chewing her lip to stop herself from giggling, her ears filling with blissful silence for the first time in two hours.

When Edna's allotted time had ended, Nina showed her out, closing the door behind her before stretching her arms high above her head and yawning loudly. She bounced back up the stairs and into the studio.

'Thank goodness that's over!'

'One down, two to go,' Dominic said with a sigh.

'But she seemed pleased with the portrait so far.'

Dominic nodded. 'If only she'd shut up for a few minutes. She could talk the legs off a millipede, never mind a donkey.'

Nina giggled. 'Can I have a look?' Nina moved to where Dominic had taken up residence for his morning's work.

He coughed nervously. 'I don't really like people seeing work that isn't—'

'Wow!'

'—finished.'

Nina was too quick for him and was stood before the canvas before Dominic had time to persuade her otherwise.

'It's wonderful!' she looked at him, mouth agape. 'I mean, *wonderful*.'

'You think so?' his voice rasped, as if all the moisture in his mouth and throat had suddenly evaporated.

'Yes, of course! I wasn't quite sure what to expect. I mean,' Nina tutted at herself, 'most portraits I've seen have been so – wrong! Do you know what I mean? It's probably not the right word. But you can almost hear her talking! It's amazing.' Nina paused and looked at the image of Edna Bowridge. There was such life, such vivacity, and yet it was so simple.

Dominic took a step closer and looked at the portrait as if he was seeing it for the first time; as if he didn't quite believe Nina.

'And you shouldn't be so shy about it. You should be proud. God, if I could paint like this, I'd shout it from the rooftops.' She turned to face him and, for a moment, saw herself reflected in Dominic's eyes: smile in full beam and eyes dancing with light.

'I talk too much,' she said quickly, casting her glance down to the floor.

'No. You don't,' Dominic said quietly. 'And it wouldn't matter if you did because I like to listen.'

'No, I shouldn't have pried,' she said, shaking her head. Not if you don't like people looking at your work in progress.'

'It's all right. I really don't mind.'

'Because I liked it?' Nina teased with a grin.

'I'm not that vain,' Dominic said with a laugh. 'I wouldn't mind if you didn't like it.'

'Really?' Nina looked at him, his dark eyes half-hidden by thick lashes. 'You really wouldn't care if I said I didn't like your painting?' she asked.

There was a moment's silence, as if Nina's question warranted some thought before answering.

'I only want you to be honest,' Dominic said at last, his voice calm but still rather grainy, as if he were on the verge of a sore throat.

'Then I love it,' Nina said, looking back at the picture. 'I can't be more honest than that.' She turned back to Dominic. He was still staring at her. 'What?' Nina squinted at him.

'Love. If you love it . . .' his voice all but disappeared, 'the portrait – you'll have to let me paint one of you some time.'

'Oh?' Nina was taken aback by the suggestion.

'Would you?' he croaked.

'I don't think I'd make a very good model,' Nina confessed. 'I fidget too much. I'm like a jack-in-the-box. You know? I get bored.'

'I see.'

'Yes,' she said, thinking it would be a very bad idea indeed to be alone in a room with Dominic with them both just staring at each other for hours on end. It was too intimate, too personal. She had to nip this in the bud once and for all. Dominic was meant to be with Faye – that much was clear to her. So, every overture he made towards her had to be stopped in its tracks.

They stood in silence and Nina wished that Edna was back in the room to fill it with her idle chatter again.

'Can I get you a sandwich? We've got just under an hour before Felicity Makepeace arrives,' Nina said, walking quickly to the windowledge and looking at the schedule she'd left there.

'Yes, please,' Dominic said, his voice returning to normal.

'Good,' she said somewhat hurriedly and left the room, her heart beating a little faster than normal at the embarrassment of Dominic's suggestion that he should paint her.

Nina looked longingly out of the landing window at the perfect blue summer sky, trying to calculate how long another two sittings would take. She thought that it would be well into the evening before she could venture outdoors. Still, she'd said she'd help Dominic, and she couldn't let him down, no matter how claustrophobic she felt with the situation now.

As she walked down the hall, she could hear someone whistling in the kitchen. It was a kind of happy, tuneless whistle that didn't seem to be going anywhere in particular, and Nina just knew it belonged to Alex.

Entering the kitchen, she saw him sat on a stool, with one leg casually crossed over the other as he waited for the kettle to boil.

'Hello there, Nina,' he said cheerily as she walked in.

'Hello,' she said, feeling as if she'd left one awkward situation only to find herself slap bang in the middle of another one.

'What you now doin'?' he said in a thick Norfolk accent that made her giggle.

'I've been helping Dominic out with his old ladies,' she told him.

'Good grief! I always knew he had a thing about older women. How many does he have, then?'

'Well, there's three today and, if you must know – he's painting them!'

'Oh, painting them, is he? What colour's he painting them?' he asked, eyebrows raised in amusement at his own joke.

Nina pulled a silly face at him by way of a reprimand.

'He's very good. You should be proud of your little brother.'

'Yeah? Has he painted you yet?'

'No,' Nina said, somewhat taken aback.

'Why not? You'd make a perfect model.'

Nina quickly busied herself with a loaf of bread and a chunk of cheese.

'I'd paint you,' Alex said, 'if I could paint, that is. But seeing as I can't, you'll just have to settle with me driving you out to the coast instead.'

'What?' Nina said as she looked up from the cheddar.

'I was thinking of going out to the Burnhams. It's a great day, and you owe me a swim. Or a paddle at least. How about it?'

Nina turned to look at him. 'Are you serious?'

'I'm *always* serious.'

Nina looked at the lopsided grin. He really was very charming and had the unnerving ability to always catch her off guard. 'But I've promised to help Dominic out today.'

'Well, *un*promise! He can cope with a few old ladies by himself, can't he? Just look outside at that sky and tell me you'd rather sit indoors smelling turps than be strolling along the sand with the sea breeze in your hair.'

'That was rather poetical,' Nina said.

'I know. But has it worked?' he asked with a grin.

Nina sighed. There was no doubt that she longed to be out of doors and she'd become increasingly uncomfortable since Dominic had asked if he could paint her – but what exactly would she say to him?

'Come on. You know you want to!' Alex beamed at her. 'Just think of the warm sun on your body and the cool sea to swim in.'

Nina was thinking about it. She was also thinking about how good it would be to escape from Dominic and from any more inappropriate suggestions he might come up with in-between portraits.

'Do you want *me* to tell Dominic?' Alex pressed her after a silence that had dragged on much too long for his liking.

'No!' Nina said. 'I'll tell him. I don't want you to cause a scene.'

'Great! So you're coming?'

Nina slapped a couple of slices of cheese in the sandwiches and let her eyes drift out into the garden. 'I guess I am,' she said. 'Just give me a few minutes.'

Nina returned upstairs with sandwiches and drinks on a tray and cautiously entered the studio.

'Oh, thanks,' Dominic said. 'You needn't have brought them up here.'

'It's no problem,' she said, guilt flooding through her at the news she had to impart.

'I thought we might sit outside. Get some air before the next old dear arrives,' Dominic said, taking a bite into the soft brown bread.

'Dominic,' Nina began, deciding to leave her sandwich until after her betrayal, 'I was thinking of going out soon.'

'Good idea,' he said between mouthfuls.

'Yes, I thought so.' Nina paused, wondering how she was going to phrase this. 'Would it be okay if I left you to it this afternoon? You're coping so well and I don't think you really need me cramping your style.'

'You're not cramping my style! I love having you around,' he said, giving her a smile.

'Thanks,' she said and, for a few moments, they sat and ate quietly together.

'Where was it you wanted to go?' Dominic asked at length.

'Out to the coast,' Nina said.

'What – on your own? I didn't know you had a car.'

'I don't. I'm going with Alex.' She spoke the words quickly, as if they might pass by without him noticing.

Dominic choked on the last of his sandwich. 'Bloody hell, Nina! You don't half know how to deliver a line.'

'Sorry,' she said.

'Yeah – and you will be if you go with Alex.' Dominic's tone changed. 'Have you any idea what he's like with women?'

'No, but I suppose I'm going to find out,' she said provocatively.

'You're joking, aren't you?' Dominic's eyes met hers, dark and serious.

'No, I'm not. For goodness' sake, Dominic, we're only going to the beach. What's the big deal?'

'I don't think Alex is going to see it quite like that. Are you so completely naive?'

'I'm not naive,' Nina almost shouted, not liking the idea of being reprimanded by somebody she used to babysit.

'Good! Then someone really should tell you about Alex. He's not right for you.'

'Dommie! We're just going to the beach – we're not eloping!'

'But I just think you should know what he's like.' Dominic ran a hand through his dark hair. 'He likes women,' he said. 'A lot of women – usually at the same time.'

Nina's eyes narrowed in consternation at the implication of Dominic's words.

'That came out wrong,' Dominic said. 'I mean, he *sees* a lot of women – usually without telling them about the others he's involved with. I think his personal record is five.'

'Dommie, I don't need to hear—'

'I just don't want you being taken in by him and getting hurt.'

'Look, I appreciate your concern, but this is just an afternoon out, okay?' She got up, grabbed her plate and crossed the room to the door. 'And even if I *did* need to know the whole sordid truth about Alex, I think I could handle it.'

'Well, if you think you can handle the truth then try this for size,' Dominic shouted after her.

Nina stopped. 'What?' She looked back at him sitting by his easel, his hair ruffled and his eyes narrowed in concentration.

'I—'

'*What?*' she repeated, staring at him.

'I – you – we . . .' Dominic stammered, his words refusing to comply with his brain. 'God, Nina!' he finally managed. 'Just go, will you?'

Chapter Seventeen

Nina stormed out of the room. She didn't appreciate being told how to behave and, in particular, that she was naive, by someone seven years her junior. Just who did Dominic think he was? And she'd made such an effort to help him that morning, when she could have been outside having fun.

She reached the kitchen and flung her plate into the sink, where it made a satisfying crash. She'd been working all week and had been pushed into helping Dominic against her will. Well, not quite against her will, but he should have remembered that it was out of the goodness of her heart that she'd offered to help him in her free time. Well, she was going out now and she was jolly well going to enjoy herself. This *was* the weekend, after all.

She left the kitchen and ran up the stairs to her bedroom where she searched through her drawers for her denim shorts and her favourite lime-green T-shirt.

Minutes later, she tied her hair back into a casual ponytail and slipped her feet into a pair of silver sandals. She was ready to hit the beach. For a moment, she wondered if she'd made the right decision in going to the beach with Alex. Hadn't she just promised herself that she wasn't going to jeopardise her position at the mill by getting involved with either of the brothers?

She shook her head. A trip to the beach was just a trip to the beach and Dominic was wrong to make anything more of it than that. Alex was no more than a friend, although she had to admit that she found him attractive. Still, even if she *was* looking to leap into another relationship, it wouldn't be with somebody like Alex. But she was quite determined to enjoy his company today. She only hoped that he didn't expect any more from her than friendship.

Who needed Malibu or Bondi Beach when the sun was shining down on the north Norfolk coast? It had been years since Nina had ventured out that way. Janey used to pester her father to take them there in the summer holidays when they were teenagers, but now that Janey had a regular dose of the Med via her father's company, Gulliver's Travels, she'd forgotten all about the beauty that lay on her own doorstep.

Alex parked the car in a grassy enclosed car park and reached behind his seat, producing a battered bottle of sun cream.

'How many ladies' limbs have been covered in that?' Nina asked with a wry smile, not really wanting to know the answer.

'Pardon?'

'Nothing,' Nina shook her head, wishing she hadn't said anything.

'No – what did you say? Has Dom being saying something?' Nina tried to avoid looking at Alex, but it was virtually impossible. 'If he's been colouring me black, I think I've a right to know.'

Nina bit her lip. If she didn't tell him, he'd probably start tickling her again, and she didn't want that. No, she really *didn't* want that, she told herself.

'He just told me not to come here with you, that's all, and he might have mentioned something about you having lots of girlfriends.'

Alex nodded. 'The trouble with Dominic is that he's a little too serious for his own good. Don't get me wrong, we're the best of mates but, if there's one thing we can't agree on, it's women. He thinks I'm a playboy and I think he's a prude.'

'And are you?'

'What? A playboy?' he asked and Nina nodded. 'Depends how you define the word.'

Nina rolled her eyes. 'Well, have you had a lot of girlfriends?'

Alex chuckled. 'I've never been asked that before.' His brown eyes glinted with mischief. 'I suppose you could say that I like women. Let's just leave it at that, shall we?'

'But Dominic obviously thinks—'

'Nina – Dominic lives in one of his paintings where the world is coloured and controlled by him and him alone. It's bloody hard work getting through to him sometimes. Rather like digging a grave with a fork. He's not in the real world, so there's no point in talking about it with him.'

Nina bit her lip. Wasn't that just a little bit severe? It made poor Dominic sound quite uncompromising, and Nina felt sure that he wasn't.

'Come on. Are we going for this walk or what?' Alex asked, opening the door.

'Will the car be all right here?'

'It's insured.'

'Nothing worries you very much, does it?' Nina remarked.

'There's no fun in worrying,' Alex shrugged his shoulders, 'is there?'

Burnham Overy Staithe was one of Nina's favourite places. The miles of golden sand felt delicious, so Nina and Alex walked barefoot, feeling the hard, cold ridges of the sand under their toes as they approached a great pool of water in-shore.

Nina shrieked as she dipped her toes into it, but was soon wading up to her knees. Alex followed her in, kicking the water as he walked and sending puddles flying through the air.

'Hey! Watch it!' she shouted.

'What?'

'You splashed me!'

'Did not!' he said indignantly.

'Well, what do you call this then?' Nina held out a piece of soaked lime green T-shirt for him to inspect.

'You've got yourself wet. You should be more careful.' His eyes seemed to wink at her.

'I *am* being careful!'

Alex just shook his head and Nina narrowed her eyes at him and continued to wade through the water.

It wasn't long before she felt another splash of water soaking into the thin material of her T-shirt.

'Hey!' she shrieked, noticing that Alex had taken his shirt off.

'What!' Alex grinned at her. 'Well, seeing as you're already wet, why not have a proper paddle?' He waded to the other side of the pool and rolled his trousers up higher. Looking up, he saw her watching and grinned.

'Last one in's a coward,' he shouted as he ran towards

the sea. Nina followed, screaming excitedly as she ran over the cool sand.

Alex was first in and began to splash his legs about in an attempt to acclimatise. Nina edged in a little more gently, laughing as her legs slowly disappeared into the icy water.

'It's cold. There's no way I'm swimming in this!' she cried.

'It's glorious.' Alex cupped his hands and let water trickle through his fingers. 'Want to get wet?' he called.

Before Nina knew what was happening, he'd dipped his hands into the water again and flung the droplets across at her.

'Hey!'

Moved into action, Nina bent down and scooped up as much water as her hands could hold and sent it showering over Alex's head. His eyes blinked in shock and amazement.

'You want a fight – you've got one!' he shouted and both of them began kicking and splashing.

Great drops of water filled the air, catching the sun before landing to soak into their clothes. Screams and cries bounced over the water as limbs fought furiously.

'No! No more!' Nina was the first to protest. Wading out of the water, she shook her arms and pulled her ponytail loose, ruffling her fingers through her damp hair. Alex didn't follow immediately but continued to send little puddles flying through the air.

'Alex – you'll get soaked!' she laughed.

'You're not my babysitter anymore,' he called back.

Nina knew she wasn't. They were two young adults and she was all too aware of the fact as he decided to leave the water and join her on the sand.

She gulped. Wasn't it usually the sexy young woman who walked semi-naked out of the sea? Not this time. She really couldn't help it, but her eyes were positively cemented to him as he raked a hand through his hair and squeezed the excess water from it. Nina tried to smile casually, as if good-looking men walked half-naked towards her every day, but it was rather difficult. He was beautiful. So strong. So tanned. So young.

So young! And he was getting closer.

Alex flung his arms out, desperate to get the warmth of the sun onto his chilled body. He couldn't help laughing as he saw the sodden figure of Nina.

'I feel horrible,' she moaned, averting her eyes and pretending to concentrate on shaking her T-shirt out. Alex landed heavily beside her, feeling the wet legs of his trousers. 'Look at me!' he laughed.

'I'm trying not to.'

'Pardon?'

'Nothing.' Nina stapled her lips together with her teeth.

'Blimey. I can't be doing with this.' He stood up and hastily unfastened the zip, pushing his trousers down his legs with one swift movement and revealing a pair of navy boxer shorts. 'That's better,' he said, as he lay the trousers flat on the sand to dry out. Nina looked at his bare legs glistening in the sun and watched as he tilted his head back and closed his eyes.

She rubbed her frozen limbs then lay back on the sand, not caring if it stuck in her hair.

'What do you suppose Dominic would say?' she asked suddenly.

'To what?'

'To us here, like this?'

'He'd probably tell you that I was the devil and that you couldn't trust me as far as you could throw me.'

'I don't think I could throw you very far,' Nina pointed out.

'Exactly,' Alex smiled at her. She was beginning to feel swamped by all of his smiles, not knowing what to do with them. But she didn't have to do anything. She just watched as he moved closer to her.

His first kiss came as no real surprise. It was warm and soft, almost as if he was testing her out. And she liked it. She felt herself sink gently into the sand as if it were a feather quilt, and she closed her eyes to experience the sensation of his mouth against hers. There wasn't anything predatory about it. It wasn't one of those tongue-chasing, teeth-clashing kisses. It was as soft as snowflakes but oh so warm.

It felt like an age since she'd last been kissed, since she'd last felt desire and been desired – at the same time. Her body had been on ice, but it was thawing wondrously fast now.

When they finally stopped, they looked into each other's eyes.

'We shouldn't have done that,' Nina whispered.

'Why not?'

'Because I'm a man-free zone at the moment.'

'*What*?' Alex said incredulously.

'Besides,' Nina continued, 'it just isn't right – me being here with you.'

'You mean you're meant to be working,' Alex tutted and sat upright, squinting out to sea. Nina sat up, too. 'You should be looking after Dominic, is that it?'

Nina sighed. 'Just what is it with you two?'

179

'Well,' Alex began, turning back to look at her, 'if you really want to know – it's you.'

'Me?'

'Yes – *you*! Dominic's always had a crush on you and I think it's got a lot worse since you came back.'

'Oh rubbish! What do you mean *always*? I've been away for over a decade!'

'Ah – but you never forget your first love.'

Nina sighed loudly. 'I don't want to hear this! I'm not his first love at all – Faye is. *Faye* is the one he should be with – not me. I'm just a—'

'What?'

'I'm just a silly crush that he's going to get over,' Nina said. 'Now, I don't want to hear any more about it, okay?'

'Well, you did ask,' Alex pointed out.

'It's just ridiculous. I mean, if I met the person I had a crush on when I was eleven, I'd probably die from embarrassment.'

'Well, our Dominic's an old romantic.'

Nina dug her heels into the sand as if she were trying to disown them. What was it with brothers? Why did Alex have to go and tell her that? And why, if he knew Dominic still had a crush on her, was he kissing her? Had Alex had a crush on her, too, all those years ago? Had he a crush on her now – or was he just trying to get one over on Dominic?

'Alex,' she said, 'romance is the last thing on my mind at the moment.'

'Okay,' he said.

Nina looked at him. She was puzzled. She'd half-expected him to put up a fight, but he was so casual that it concerned her more. It wasn't very flattering not to be fought for, especially by someone who had taken his trousers off in front of her.

'Yes,' she said firmly, trying not to look at his expanse of bare leg, 'I'm at the mill to work.'

'I know,' he said, following Nina's example and digging his heels into a cool trench in the sand.

'Good,' Nina said.

'Do you want half a Bounty?'

'What?'

'I've got a Bounty in my pocket,' he said.

'Erm, all right then. Thanks.' She took her half and ate it in bemused silence.

'Alex,' she said after a while.

'Yes?'

'Aren't your trousers dry yet?'

They let another hour pass by before they got up to walk back to the car. Nina looked up into the clouds; wispy and distant. It was strange but the kiss seemed to have been forgotten, which was a relief to Nina. Alex, she thought, was such a happy-go-lucky chap, wasn't he?

'The sky's so huge here, isn't it?' she said. Alex nodded. He hadn't said much since her declaration of independence, and she couldn't really be bothered to make conversation. If he didn't want to talk then that was fine.

'I've never met anyone quite like you, Nina,' he suddenly said.

Nina bit her lip. Oh, dear. So the kiss hadn't been forgotten. She took a deep breath. She had to play this down or she'd end up in serious trouble.

'Yeah, right!' she said, as her thoughts ping-ponged around her brain in search of a direction in which to change the conversation.

'No – really! I'm not just saying that. I really like you, Nina. I love the way you've just slotted into life at the mill like you belong there, and I love your energy and enthusiasm for everything – the way you handle Dad and Ziggy. You're not afraid of anything, are you? And the way you ate that cottage pie at the pub the other night.'

'What?' Nina had somehow lost his train of thought.

'It's such a relief to go out with a girl who doesn't pick at her food or order a salad with no dressing and nothing remotely tasty in it.'

Nina felt her colouring rising like an Oriental sun on the blank sky of her face.

'You've got summer in your face,' Alex said suddenly. Nina thought it best to ignore his comment.

Alex merely smiled, and suddenly his body was very close to hers, blocking out the sun and the breeze and the large expanse of beach. Nina could feel the warmth of his breath as his mouth inched nearer hers. He was going to kiss her again and what was she trying to do to stop it? Nothing!

'Er – Alex,' she whispered. 'I think we should be going.'

'Do you?' She nodded and they almost banged noses. 'You don't want to stay?' She shook her head. 'Okay,' he said, and she watched as he marched in the direction of the car park without saying another word.

He didn't speak at all on the way back home, either. Nina wasn't sure what was more uncomfortable; the glassy feeling of sand in between her toes or the deathly silence between her and Alex. She wanted to break it – to say something humorous to lighten the atmosphere – but couldn't think of anything to talk about.

After leaving the narrow lanes of the north Norfolk coast, the Alfa Romeo sped along the main road back to Norwich like a little bolt of white lightning, the breeze sending Nina's hair out behind her like a comet's tail, but she sat absolutely motionless, as if scared to draw attention to herself if she moved an inch.

She wasn't sure how she felt about the kiss. It had been so unexpected but, as kisses went, she couldn't deny that it had been wonderful. She'd forgotten the last time she'd been kissed like that. The last few months with Matt had been rather barren in the love department and Nina had forgotten what it felt like to be the focus of somebody's desire. But this was all very awkward. She hadn't come to the mill – or the beach – to be kissed. She'd come to work, she'd come to recover and find out what she wanted in life and a kiss was just going to get in the way of all that. She didn't feel ready for it, especially with somebody like Alex.

She remembered Dominic's warning about his brother and wondered how he was getting on with his afternoon appointments. She felt a pang of guilt at having left him to fend for himself whilst she'd been out getting kissed in the sand. But she couldn't exactly help him with the actual painting, could she? And Alex was right; he should be able to handle a few old dears by himself.

Nina bit her lip as she thought of Dominic and what Alex had told her. Could she trust Alex to tell her the truth? Did Dominic really have a crush on her? She'd have to put the idea out of her mind if she was to get on with her work successfully, and she'd much rather avoid Dominic if she could, but that wasn't going to be easy with all the portraits lined up for the length of the summer.

She could avoid him for the rest of today though, she thought, as Alex swung the car into the lane that led to The Old Mill House and, with any luck, he'd still be busy painting. She'd sneak in through the hall and creep up the stairs to her room. With any luck, by the time Monday came around, he'd have forgotten that she'd left him to go to the beach with his brother.

As Alex parked the car in the driveway, Nina saw a solitary figure sitting on the front doorstep. There was no chance of her just sneaking into the house now.

It was Faye.

Chapter Eighteen

'Hey, Faye!' Alex chorused as he got out of the car.

'Hello, Alex.'

'What are you up to?' he asked, marching over to her and ruffling her hair.

'Nothing,' Faye said, her voice limp and lifeless.

'Let me rephrase that – what's up?'

'Nothing,' she said again. 'I've been waiting for Nina.'

'Have you?' Nina said and, although she was tired, windswept, covered in sand and very hungry, she suddenly felt rather maternal towards Faye. She looked as pale and fragile as a cobweb, and her pose on the doorstep put Nina in mind of a latchkey kid.

'Are you locked out?' she asked her.

Faye nodded. 'I've been doing a few extra chores in the garden that had to be done this weekend and Olivia said she'd left my wages in the house, but nobody's answering the door.'

'Mum and Dad are in town today,' Alex explained. 'And Dominic's working.'

'But he is in the house,' Nina pointed out.

'Well, he's not answering the door,' Faye said.

'Are you hungry?' Nina asked. Faye nodded. 'Come on

then. I'll fix us some tea and we can eat it out in the garden.' She fished in her bag for her key and let them in. Alex disappeared up the stairs and Nina and Faye wandered through to the kitchen.

'Where've you two been?' Faye asked, her voice regaining a little of its usual vivacity.

'Out to the coast,' Nina said, filling the kettle.

'Oh.' Faye picked up an apple and rolled it in the palm of her hand as she eyed Nina. 'So, are you and Alex seeing each other?'

Nina turned around. 'Why do you ask that?'

'Well, why else would you go to the beach with him?' Faye asked.

'Why must everyone think something's going on?' Nina said with an exasperated sigh as she opened the fridge.

'Because you went out with Alex,' Faye said.

'Get hold of that,' Nina said, chucking a bag of mixed salad at Faye. 'I'm going to have a shower. When I come back, I expect tea to be ready.'

'Yes, ma'am!' Faye saluted, making Nina grin in spite of herself.

'You really *should* watch yourself with Alex,' Faye said later in the garden as she crunched on a stick of celery that had been liberally speared in mayonnaise.

'You don't need to tell me,' Nina said, 'because there's absolutely nothing going on.' She looked at Faye, hoping that she couldn't see the image of her and Alex kissing on the beach that was floating before her eyes. She blinked the image away, cursing herself for her foolishness. What had she been thinking? But that was the trouble – she hadn't been thinking; she'd been swept up in the moment – the sun-drenched, windswept moment.

'He's an odd one is Alex,' Faye said, interrupting her thoughts.

'Odd?' Nina asked. 'How?'

'Well,' Faye crossed a leg underneath her on the deck chair, 'he's always told me how he's desperate to find the right girl but that he seems fated to wander the earth in search of her.'

Nina started to giggle. 'That's a very lame excuse for putting it around!'

Faye smiled. 'Yeah – I know. But I kind of feel sorry for him. He is lovely. He deserves to find that special someone.'

They were silent for a moment, listening to the rich notes of a blackbird from inside the laurel hedge.

'Where's he living?' Nina asked.

'Oh, he's got a little flat in Kew not far from where he works. It's really nice, actually – it overlooks the river.'

'You been there?'

'Yes,' Faye said. 'Just the once.'

Nina looked at her quizzically.

'It's not what you think,' Faye said. 'I'd just left college and Dominic wasn't taking my calls. I think Alex took pity on me and invited me over. We just had a chat. He told me to forget Dommie and move on.'

'And he didn't make a play for you himself?' Nina asked.

Faye looked shocked for a moment, but then she sighed. 'Of course he did. He's Alex!'

Nina grinned.

'But I told him I wasn't interested and he was very sweet – he said he had to try and that Dommie wasn't worthy of me and all that.'

187

Nina nodded, trying to imagine the scene in Alex's flat.

'I wonder what Dominic's been doing all day,' Faye said, as casually as possible.

Nina looked at her and knew in her heart that this girl was still in love with him – no matter how hard she tried to protest, and no matter what Alex had told her that day about moving on.

'Olivia's got him a whole summer's work. He's been asked to paint the women in the Country Circle.'

'Really?' Faye said.

'I think Olivia's worried about him earning enough to keep himself in paints. And she's probably hoping it will open other doors for him,' Nina said.

Faye grimaced. 'That's just asking for trouble. I don't know what it is about him, but he seems to bring out the maternal instinct in older women. It's quite horrible! Have you met Felicity Makepeace?'

'No,' Nina said, 'but I left Dominic alone for his appointment with her this afternoon.'

'Oh, you didn't!' Faye exclaimed. 'Poor Dom! She'd have eaten him alive! No wonder he hasn't been able to answer the door. She's probably had her wicked way with him and left him for dead.' Faye paused to catch breath. 'You've heard of the phrase mutton dressed as lamb? Well we're talking serious killer-mutton here.'

Nina smiled, trying to imagine somebody called Makepeace in white stilettos and scarlet lipstick.

'So, he's painting portraits?' Faye asked.

Nina nodded and then, slowly, an idea began to occur to her. An idea that might just bring Dominic and Faye back together again at last.

Chapter Nineteen

Sunday morning dawned bright and clear with a sky dotted with tiny white clouds, promising hours of uninterrupted sunshine. It felt funny to have the weekends off when she was living at the mill. Nina felt as if she should still be working, but Dudley obviously had no plans of the sort because he had driven off early to his country club. Meanwhile, Olivia had downed tools and ventured into town for a music recital and lunch with Billy.

Of course, Olivia hadn't gone without one little plea.

'You will take care of Ziggy now, won't you?' she asked, her pretty eyes pleading and absolutely impossible to refuse. 'I've given him a quick run this morning so just a couple of little walks should do the trick. You know, he's *so* much calmer these days! I can see you're working your magic on him,' she added as a sweetener.

Nina hadn't minded. In fact, she was glad of a companion that day because the mill seemed spookily quiet without the family rushing about or Faye poking in and out in search of fortifying cups of tea.

She wandered around for a while, sitting with a novel in the living room with only the reassuring tick of an antique clock on the mantelpiece for company, and then she made a cup of tea, staring out of the kitchen window at the empty garden.

It was sometime after lunch that Ziggy's big brown eyes and tail thumping on the kitchen floor became too much for her and she grabbed his lead and gave him a little nod. It was all the encouragement he needed and she watched in amusement as he hightailed it out of the kitchen, skidding his way down the hall towards the front door.

Remembering not to allow Ziggy to pull, Nina kept control, smiling to herself at the progress she had managed to make in such a short space of time. She'd been practising in the house too with commands for 'sit', 'stay' and 'down'. He really was a very bright dog; one only had to channel that intelligence in the right direction. Something, Nina reasoned, Olivia had neither the time nor the patience to do.

Together, they headed along the river, pausing to watch the swallows skimming along the shallows as the water wound its way through the meadows. They walked by a row of weeping willows, whose long green branches trailed in the water as if caressing it.

It felt good to be out of doors, but Nina couldn't help missing a bit of company and her thoughts turned inevitably to Justin. She always looked out for him each time she walked Ziggy now, and it seemed strange not to see him on the footpath. She pulled the piece of paper out of her skirt pocket and looked down at it. There was his phone number and the words: *Justin – call me!*

'Should I?' she asked Ziggy. 'Should I call him?'

Ziggy's eyes were bright as he looked up at the sound of her voice, but he wasn't very forthcoming with advice.

Nina bit her lip. It seemed so forward just to ring him out of the blue, but he'd told her to do exactly that and she had agreed. But what about her vow to steer clear of men? That's what had been putting her off calling him. She wanted some time out from all that relationship stuff, didn't she?

But you like him, don't you? Vow or no vow – you've been thinking about him.

It was true. It might have been Alex who had kissed her but, although rather wonderful, the kiss had meant nothing to Nina. She liked Alex, of course, but she didn't think of him as a potential partner. But Justin . . . there was just something about him that she couldn't shake from her mind and she knew she wanted to know more about him.

Nina sighed. Try as she might to focus on being a man-free zone, she couldn't help thinking about the handsome dog-walker who had been so sweet and patient with her and Ziggy. And those piercing blue eyes and heart-melting smile were pretty hard to banish from her mind, too. Besides, it would just be plain rude not to give him a call, and Nina wasn't the sort to be rude, was she?

Clearing her throat, she got her phone out and called the number. The line was crackly when Justin answered it and there was background noise of traffic.

'It's Nina!' she hollered when he couldn't make out who it was.

'Oh, Nina!' he cried. 'How are you?'

'I'm good.'

'How's Ziggy?'

'He's right here. We're by the river and just wondering if you and Bess are around.'

'I'm just heading out of Norwich,' he said. 'It shouldn't take me too long to reach you. How about I meet you at the oak tree?'

'Okay then. I'll see you there,' Nina said, her heart racing as she hung up. There, she thought, that hadn't been too hard.

The oak tree was quite famous in the county. Thought to be at least five hundred years old, its girth was as thick as the back of a double-decker bus and it was still producing a good crop of acorns each year. It had numerous hearts and initials carved into its bark and, on the summer solstice, parties of dancers and musicians would congregate, tying ribbons to the branches and drinking punch until the early hours.

Nina walked towards it now, marvelling at its size and beauty, stretching out a hand to touch its roughened, reptilian-like bark and gazing up into its emerald leaves, which provided a dappled shade on the ground beneath by the river bank.

Looking down into the water, Nina had a sudden rush of temptation and, still trying to keep hold of Ziggy, she was slipping her feet out of her shoes before she could think of a reason not to, letting the river wash over her toes as she sat on the bank. The water was cold and chilled her body, but the rhythm of it soothed her.

Taking advantage of the warm afternoon, she realised she couldn't remember the last time she'd dipped her toes into the River Yare. They'd been teenage toes for sure. She looked out across the broad stretch of navy river and on towards the fields to where The Folly stood. It looked unusually tall against the horizontal landscape. Briefly, she wondered what Dominic was doing. Probably something brilliant, she thought, sighing in contentment. How lucky she was to be there. After working for Hilary Jackson in the city, being at the mill made her feel as if she'd been transported into a fairytale world. It was truly idyllic.

She tilted her head back and took in the enormity of the blue sky, stretching luxuriously before throwing her arms up into the air and laying back on the grass. She closed her eyes and listened to the uninterrupted flow of the water, her ankle-length linen skirt making a satisfactory blanket underneath her. Ziggy watched her for a moment and then decided to join her, flopping on the grass beside her, his tongue lolling out of his mouth as he panted in the heat.

'It's too hot to do anything else, isn't it?' she said, patting his head gently and gazing into the river. Maybe she and Justin could go for a paddle together later – or was that improper at this stage in their relationship, she wondered?

She thought of her day at the beach with Alex and grimaced. She should never have gone. Dominic had been right to warn her and Faye had been right to reprimand her. But, it was done now and there was nothing she could do but try to make sure it never happened again.

For a moment, she closed her eyes against the bright sun, her lids dancing with myriad colours and her skin slowly cooling in the shade of the oak tree. It was only when she felt the gentle pressure of Ziggy on the end of his lead that she realised she had fallen asleep and, on opening her eyes, she saw Bess, her glossy black and white coat darting in and out of the tall grasses that lined the footpath. She gave a hearty bark when she spied Nina and ran over to her and Ziggy.

'Hello, Bess!' Nina cried, pulling her feet out of the water. The dog instantly flopped down on the ground as if all the air had been sucked out of her and her tongue popped out of her mouth so that she became a matching bookend to Ziggy. 'Where's your lord and master, then?'

It didn't take long before Justin came into view. He was

wearing a pair of beige cotton trousers and a white shirt, which looked ridiculously crisp on such a sunny day but immensely attractive, for he had unbuttoned it at the throat and rolled the sleeves up to reveal arms that were tanned and toned.

'Hello,' he said cheerily as he spotted Nina under the tree with the two dogs. 'You all look very comfortable. May I join you?'

'Of course,' Nina said. 'Pick the least dusty spot and sit down.'

'It was good to hear from you,' he said, sitting on the warm earth beside her.

'I hope you didn't mind me ringing you,' she said anxiously.

'Why should I mind? I was hoping you would ring me.'

'You were?'

'Of course! I did ask you to, didn't I?' His blue eyes sparkled in the dappled sunlight and Nina felt herself blushing. 'In fact, if you hadn't have rung me, I would have called you.'

'But I didn't give you my number,' Nina said.

'But I know where you're staying,' he said with a smile. 'Anyway, why *didn't* you give me your number?'

Nina bit her lip. 'Well, we're still getting to know each other,' she said.

'But we can't get to know each other very well if I don't have your phone number and can't call you,' he said with a lopsided smile.

Nina nodded. 'I know. I'm sorry. It's just—' she paused, 'I guess I'm being a bit careful these days.'

Justin's eyebrows rose a fraction. 'Trouble before?'

Nina nodded. 'But that's all in the past now.'

194

'Good,' he said.

'You know,' she said, 'we really don't know anything about each other. I don't even know your full name, I don't know what you do for a living, I'm not even sure—'

'Stop!' he said lightly, a hand raised in the air. 'Do we really need to know all that stuff? I mean, tell me it all matters. Tell me that it would really make a difference if I told you that my name was – I don't know – Milton, for example.'

'But that's the name of the family I'm working for,' Nina said.

'I know. But does it matter? If my name is Milton or Jones or Fortesque-Walpole?'

Nina laughed. 'I guess not.'

'And I don't need to know yours. All I need to know is that you like me enough to spend time with me and that Bess likes you, too. That's always a good sign.'

'Doesn't she always like everybody?'

'Oh, no,' Justin said. 'She wouldn't have a thing to do with one of my exes. Used to slink away into a corner with her tail between her legs.'

'Oh, dear,' Nina said.

'I should have ended things there and then, but it took me eight whole months to realise that she was seeing one of my colleagues behind my back.'

Nina blinked in surprise. 'That's awful.'

'And Bess knew about it all the time, didn't you, girl?'

'You don't really believe that, do you?' Nina asked.

Justin smiled and stroked his dog's sun-warmed head. 'No,' he said with a smile, 'but I pay more attention to who she trusts these days.'

'Animals are a good judge of character, aren't they?' Nina said.

195

'I think so,' Justin said with a little nod. 'Have you any of your own?'

Nina shook her head. 'My parents said that animals shouldn't be kept in a house and that they made mess everywhere,' she said with a shrug. 'I bugged them for years for a rabbit or a guinea pig or a hamster, but they wouldn't be persuaded.'

'That's too bad,' he said. 'We were never without them growing up. Cats, dogs, rabbits – there was always some animal in the house causing chaos.'

Nina laughed. 'I remember one evening when I was babysitting for the Miltons and their pet rat escaped. He was an enormous thing and had somehow got trapped behind a radiator.'

Justin laughed, too. 'What on earth did you do?'

'The boys were frantic with worry and so was I. I don't particularly like rats but Hank was very endearing in his own ratty way and I didn't want to see him get hurt. Alex was going through a real Norwich City football club phase and was wearing his yellow and green scarf and it suddenly dawned on me that we could use it to rescue Hank, so we lowered it behind the radiator, making a little hammock underneath him, and then hauled him out.'

'That was very innovative of you!' Justin said with a grin.

'Us babysitters have to be resourceful, you know,' she said, smiling at the memory.

They sat quietly for a moment, watching a pair of swifts chasing each other across the barley field, their high-pitched calls piercing the air.

'So, how's the novel-writing business going?' Justin asked at last.

'Dudley doesn't work at the weekends. I think Olivia

insists that he takes proper time off. Either that or she just likes to get him out of the house for a few hours.'

'But it's all going well?'

'Oh, yes,' Nina said.

'And what's he going to do with it when it's all finished?'

Nina looked thoughtful. 'I don't really know,' she said. 'He's never talked about it.'

'You think he'll try to find a publisher?'

'I don't see why not,' she said. 'Why write otherwise? I can't imagine he's doing it just to pass the time.'

Justin shook his head. 'Imagine – Dudley Milton, a novelist!'

'I know!' Nina said. 'I couldn't believe it when I first saw the novel, but it's really very good. I hope it is published.'

Justin took a deep breath. 'Nina,' he said, 'I would love to take you out sometime. I really think we should stop meeting on dusty footpaths and have a sit down somewhere with chairs, don't you?'

'Oh, I don't know,' she said with a smile, 'I rather like dusty old footpaths.'

'I'd suggest dinner, but I've just had a mammoth lunch and I've got to head back to London this evening.'

'Oh,' she said. 'For work?'

'Afraid so.'

Nina didn't ask what he did and he didn't volunteer. It didn't seem to matter on such a sunny Sunday. Who wanted to talk about work when the skylarks were singing and a warm breeze was caressing your face?

'Well, why don't you come back to the mill for a cup of tea? There's some ginger cake left too. We could eat in the garden – there are real chairs there.'

'Oh, no,' Justin said quickly. 'I'd hate to intrude.'

'You wouldn't be,' Nina assured him, taking a quick look at her watch. 'Everybody's out and they won't be back for hours yet. Dominic's in town at his gallery, Dudley's at his club and Olivia's having lunch with Billy and then going on to do some shopping before heading to a music recital.'

He looked a little unsure. 'Well, I'm not—'

'Go on! You'll *love* the mill! It's got one of those gorgeous country kitchens with a big bright Aga in the middle of it and a slate floor and . . . ginger cake!'

Justin smiled. 'Okay, you've sold it to me.'

'Good,' Nina said, and the two of them stood up and brushed themselves down. The dogs were up in an instant, too, and the four of them walked amiably together towards the mill.

Olivia had told Nina that she could have friends over, but she still felt a little odd inviting this particular new friend to the mill. There was something about Justin that made her feel intensely comfortable though, as if they had known each other for much longer than just a few days. Perhaps it was the connection that they'd made with their dogs. After all, who couldn't like a man who had a dog? Nina felt that it would be virtually impossible that such a man could harbour any nasty secrets. Still, she couldn't help wanting to know a little more about him.

'Where is it you live?' she asked him as they crossed the bridge.

'West Carleton,' he said. 'I'm staying with friends, but I'd like to get a place of my own out this way. I've got a little flat I rent in London, too, for when I'm working there, but I try to get out to Norfolk whenever I can.'

'You were brought up here?'

He nodded.

'And you have family here?'

'All my family's in Norfolk,' he said.

They'd reached the blue front door and Nina fished the key out of her pocket.

'You can let Bess off her lead if you like. I'll just make us some tea and we can have it out in the garden.'

Nina trotted off to the kitchen with Ziggy by her side. She gave him a dog chew and he settled happily in his basket as Nina made the tea and cut two generous slices of ginger cake, which she placed on pretty china plates covered in bright yellow sunflowers.

'Nearly ready,' she called down the hallway and, when there was no answer, she went in search of Justin. He wasn't in the living room so she tried the dining room and was just entering as he was closing one of the drawers of a mahogany sideboard.

'Everything all right?' Nina asked.

'Yes,' he said, turning around and looking a little flustered. 'Just admiring the furniture. Beautiful wood, isn't it?'

'I suppose it is,' Nina said, looking at it properly for the first time. 'They have some lovely antique pieces.'

He nodded.

'Ready for tea and cake?'

'Always,' he said with a smile and they left the room together, followed by Bess.

The ornate white metal table and chairs in the garden were in partial shade by late afternoon, but it was still pleasantly warm by the rose borders and Justin seemed very taken with it.

'It's a beautiful house, isn't it?' he said. 'I always forget how lovely it is.'

Nina looked across the table at him, his blue eyes dreamy as he took in his surroundings.

'I still can't believe I'm here,' Nina said. 'I keep thinking I'm going to wake up in my horrible little flat and have to go to work at that horrible little office. This all feels like a dream.'

'And you're here for how long?' he asked her.

She sighed. 'I don't like to remember, but it was agreed that I'd stay just for the length of the summer.'

'Then let's hope that this one is a particularly long summer,' he said and they smiled at one another.

'Yes,' Nina said. 'I really do hope it is.'

'They're very lucky to have you – the Miltons,' he said.

'No, I'm the lucky one.'

He shook his head. 'They're not the easiest family to get along with. I mean, that's what I've heard.'

'What exactly have you heard?' Nina said, frowning in curiosity.

'Oh, just that Dudley has a bit of a temper and Olivia can be – what's the right word – scatty!'

'She's a total sweetheart,' Nina said, 'and Dudley's an angel once you've got him sorted out. And as long as you know what he needs before he knows himself!'

Justin grinned. 'And how about Alex and Dominic?'

Nina took a sip of her tea before answering with a half lie. 'I don't see them too often. Dominic's busy with his paintings and Alex comes and goes.'

'But they must have tried to—' he paused.

'What?' Nina asked.

Justin shook his head. 'I mean, a pretty girl like you turning up – it must have ruffled some feathers.'

'I don't know what you mean!' Nina said with a blush.

'I think you know exactly what I mean,' Justin said, his eyes glinting in a knowing sort of way. 'They always were competitive, those two. I hope they're not making your life difficult.'

'Not at all,' Nina said, casting her eyes down to the ground and hoping that Justin wouldn't notice her fast-rising colouring.

'Listen,' he said, looking at his watch again. 'I'd really better be making a move.'

'Already?' she said and then she bit her lip as she realised how very ardent she sounded. 'I mean, it's early.'

It was then that they heard a car horn in the lane.

'Oh, it's Dudley!' Nina said. 'He's back much earlier than I expected.'

Suddenly, Justin was on his feet and Bess was up and alert. 'Blimey,' he said. 'I've really got to fly.'

'Oh, don't worry!' Nina said with a reassuring smile. 'Stop and say hello. I'm sure he'd love to see you.'

But Justin had virtually sprinted to the little gate in the wall of the garden that led out into the lane.

'No, no,' he called back. 'I'd hate to intrude.'

'You're not intru—'

'I'll give you a call,' he cried and Nina watched, perplexed, as he hurried over the bridge with Bess.

'Extraordinary!' she said to herself, cursing herself for feeling disappointed when he didn't turn back to wave at her. She couldn't help wondering if she'd ever see him again.

Chapter Twenty

It turned out that Dudley *had* been working on Sunday – getting up very early in the morning before he went out to his club – because he'd left a whole pile of notes, ready to be typed up on Monday. So without further ado, Nina made a start.

She was always surprised at how quickly time flew when she was typing. Even the laborious task of reading Dudley's scrawl didn't stop the clock racing, and it was with some surprise that the doorbell disturbed her trance at eleven o'clock. She hit the print icon and the ink-jet kickstarted into life.

She was glad of the distraction of work because her mind was still reeling over the events of Sunday afternoon when Justin had made his comedy sketch departure from the mill. Sitting at her desk now, she found it hard to believe that she'd felt she'd had a connection with this man. One minute, they'd been happily drinking tea and chatting like old friends and then, the next minute, he'd been hightailing it out of the garden with a very sorry explanation.

Nina shook her head feeling a mixture of bemusement and rejection. Was she never destined to meet a nice *normal* man? She was going to have to try and put him out of her mind, she decided. It was the only way.

The sound of the doorbell brought her back to the present and she paused a moment, waiting to see if anybody was going to answer it. She got up from her chair and peered out at the driveway. There was a cherry bright Metro in the driveway that she didn't recognise.

The bell went again and Nina left the study to answer it.

To say that the sight that greeted her was shocking was an understatement, for there on the doorstep of the mill was a Joan Collins lookalike, sporting dark sunglasses, a pale headscarf, a white knee-length coat, and smoking a very long cigarette.

'Hello,' Nina said hesitantly, her eyes taking in the extraordinary person who must surely have taken the wrong flight out of LA. 'Can I help you?'

'Ah!' she said, stubbing out the very long cigarette on the doorstep and pushing past Nina. 'Dominic,' she said, without giving any further information.

'Yes?' Nina said, pretending that she didn't understand her abruptness.

The woman surveyed her through the smoky lenses of her glasses. 'I'm here to see Dominic,' she said, enunciating each word as though Nina were stupid.

'Oh, I see,' Nina said, keeping a smile in check. 'Is he expecting you?'

This time, the woman removed her glasses. 'Well, of course he's expecting me! What else would I be doing here?'

'I'll show you upstairs then.' Nina led the way upstairs, the words *stuck-up cow* teetering dangerously on the tip of her tongue.

She knocked on Dominic's door, not quite sure of the reception she'd receive after their last meeting.

'Come in,' his voice called from inside and Nina opened the door to see him standing in the middle of the room, a red shirt unbuttoned at the throat and a pair of black jeans on.

The Joan Collins lookalike pushed past Nina in her haste to get into the room. 'Ah, Dominic! I told this young lady that you were expecting me but she didn't seem to understand me.' She looked back at Nina and her perfectly made-up face scowled severely at her.

'Well, of course I'm expecting you, Mrs Makepeace,' Dominic said, all politeness and smiles.

Nina registered the name, her eyes widening. So this was Felicity Makepeace. Faye had been right about the killer-mutton dressed as lamb. She'd never seen anyone like her. She didn't think that ladies really dressed like that after a certain age. It just didn't seem right. But, if Felicity Makepeace's flirty-girl shoes and film-star sunglasses had surprised Nina, that was nothing compared to what she was about to reveal.

As Dominic set the easel up, Mrs Makepeace unbuttoned the pale coat to reveal the sort of dress Nina would have thought twice about wearing at night, let alone during the day. It was a low-cut thigh-skimming number in blue silk, which embraced her body like a second skin. Nina was conscious that her mouth had dropped open and quickly snapped it shut before anybody could notice.

She watched, mesmerised, as Mrs Makepeace sat down on a velvet chair that Dominic had brought from downstairs. As she made herself comfortable, the dress crept its way up another couple of inches. Nina looked across at

Dominic, who was setting up his paints and brushes, not really paying attention to the display of flesh in front of him.

'Do you need any help, Dominic?' Nina asked, not really wishing to spend any more time in the room, but feeling bad about having let Dominic down before.

'No, I can cope, thanks. But how about seeing you at lunch?'

'Oh,' Nina said, surprised. 'Okay.'

'One o'clock?'

Nina nodded and gave him a half-smile, hoping that he'd forgiven and forgotten her escapade with Alex.

'See you later, then,' he said quietly, returning her smile and making her feel a lot happier.

At a quarter to one, Nina heard the front door open and close. She walked over to the window in time to see Felicity Makepeace climbing into her car, without a thought about the amount of leg on display for all to see.

Nina ambled through to the kitchen and was greeted by Olivia.

'Are you getting on all right?' she asked cheerily, a plate of sandwiches in her hands, which she was about to take through to the front room. 'And what are you typing today? Would it be the scene where Caroline and Ellis are stargazing from the tower?'

Nina looked stunned for a moment. 'Er – yes.'

Olivia laughed. 'Don't worry, I won't let on. I'm not meant to have any idea what Dudley's writing about, but he does tend to leave the papers all over the bed and then fall asleep. I just can't resist having a peek at what he's been up to.' She laughed coquettishly. 'It's good though, isn't it?'

Nina looked at her, surprised by her question. 'Yes. I think so.'

'Oh, I've just remembered,' Olivia said. 'Alex is going to pop along to Party Parade. It's on the outskirts of Norwich. It's the most *marvellous* place and I've got a big list of things for him to get but – well – you know what men are like with these things. If I put "purple balloons" and they don't have any, he'd be likely to pick up pink ones instead and that just won't do. Do you think you could go along with him? Supervise things for me?'

Nina chewed her lip. The idea of another trip in close proximity with Alex didn't really appeal to her at all after the disaster at the beach, but organising the anniversary party was part of her job description so she couldn't very well say no, could she?

'Of course,' she said with a smile. 'Just let me know when.'

Olivia nodded and they both turned around as Dominic waltzed into the room. 'Hi, Nina. Hi, Mum.'

'DOMINIC!' she yelled, making Nina jump. 'What's that on your cheek?' Olivia's expression of horror crinkled her whole face.

Dominic searched quickly for a mirror, consternation clouding his face, but Olivia had started to laugh.

'What is it? Get it off – whatever it is!' Dominic cried.

It was then that Nina saw the magenta streak of lipstick right across his cheek. She reached into the pocket of her trousers for a clean tissue.

'Here, let me,' she said, stepping forward. Dominic bent down obediently and Nina wiped the worst of the lipstick off. 'Blimey – this stuff's like emulsion!' she exclaimed, as she doubled her tissue over and wiped the smear that was fast turning Dominic's cheek into a Hawaiian sunset.

Dominic chuckled.

'I suppose this was Madam Makepeace marking her territory?' Nina enquired, causing Dominic to start.

'She's a bit over-friendly, that's all,' he explained.

'I hope she pays extra for the privilege,' Olivia said, leaving the room.

'Actually, I think that's her idea of a tip,' Dominic smiled.

'Well, next time she goes for a grope, I think you should tell her you'd prefer ready money,' Nina suggested with a laugh.

'Yes,' Dominic said, lifting his head, 'thanks.'

Nina threw the now-pink tissue into the bin. 'Right, lunch.'

'So, how are the portraits going?' Nina asked once they'd sat down at the table.

'Fine,' Dominic said, nodding as he munched. 'I've worked out that each client will need about three sittings, so the workload should be quite manageable after all. I have to say that it's all a bit of a surprise. I'm actually quite enjoying it. I think I was just a bit nervous at first because I wasn't sure what I was letting myself in for, but it's not bad as jobs go.'

'That's great, Dommie,' Nina said with a smile. 'You'll be raking it in then?'

'It'll make a nice change.'

'Yes,' Nina said, 'and I know how you can make a few extra pounds on top.'

'Yeah?'

Nina nodded. 'I'd like to have a portrait done,' she said.

Dominic looked at her incredulously. 'Really?' he said, his brown eyes wide with joy.

'Could you set that up for me?' she asked. 'Perhaps at The Folly?'

He nodded. 'When were you thinking of?' he asked.

'Well, let me check some other things first and I'll give you a call, okay?'

Dominic nodded, and the sweet smile that crossed his face made Nina feel just a little bit guilty at what she was plotting.

Chapter Twenty-One

It was shortly after lunch that Dudley made a surprise appearance. Nina hadn't expected him back as he'd said he was going to the library and then onto a museum. He was studying costumes from the time when his novel was set but, from the look on his face, things hadn't gone well.

'I can't seem to find what I'm after at all,' he told Nina as he paced up and down the study. She watched him for a moment, wondering if it was her place to interject and ask him if there was anything she could do to help. Would he appreciate that or would it upset him? She didn't know much about writers, but weren't they solitary beings who hid away with their muse and hated interruptions? Perhaps Teri had offered some such help and had ignited Dudley's artistic temperament. Well, that was something Nina certainly didn't want to do.

'Well?' he said, turning to look at her, his face red with either exertion or anger.

'Is there something I can do?' Nina dared to ask.

'I wish you would. I wish you would!' he said.

'Okay,' Nina said. 'What do you need to know?'

Dudley fished around in his jacket pocket, brought out

209

a tatty piece of paper covered in his scrawl and handed it to Nina. She looked down at the strange list.

Fashion of the 1860s.

What was Charles Darwin doing?

Would Caroline have been religious? Would she have read Darwin?

Look up popular names for girls.

What novels were being published?

Was sugar readily available?

Look up astronomy – what was known in Victorian times?

The list went on and on in his maddening handwriting, with lines crossing out some of the scribbles and asterisks marking others. It really was a terrible jumble of unregulated thoughts.

'Well?' Dudley said again.

'Would you like me to look these things up for you?' Nina asked. 'They should be quite straightforward on the internet.'

Dudley made a derisive noise in his throat. 'The internet!' he said.

Nina tried to stop herself from smiling. So her employer obviously wasn't a silver surfer.

'It's amazing what you can find out on the internet – it's a brilliant tool for a writer. Really – I'd recommend it. Perhaps I could give you a crash course.'

Dudley flopped down in his chair and surveyed the mass of papers in front of him whilst Nina looked on and made a tentative start on Dudley's long list. It was just a couple of minutes later when she called him over to her desk. He peered closely at the screen.

'What have you got there?' he asked.

'It's a database of names that were popular in the 1860s.'

Dudley dragged his chair from across the room and sat down next to Nina.

'Good heavens!' he said. 'How on earth did you find that?'

'It was very easy. I just used a search engine.' He frowned at her. 'You really must let me give you a few lessons sometime. You'll fly through some of this research.'

He made another dismissive noise but then gave a great cry of joy that made Nina jump out of her chair in surprise.

'Look at that!' he said and Nina looked. 'Lissy!'

Nina looked at the name on the screen. 'Lissy?' she said.

'Just the sort of name I was after. Perfect for the niece, don't you think?'

'The one that comes in during the dinner?'

'The very one!'

Nina nodded.

'Write it down!' he barked. 'Before we forget it. And that one, too. I like that!'

'Which one?'

'Evadne. You just see if I can't shoehorn an Evadne in there somehow.'

They turned to look at each other and Nina saw the look of complete delight on Dudley's face. She laughed as he took hold of the mouse.

'What do I do?' he asked.

Nina couldn't quite believe that, so far, Dudley had only used his computer as a very sophisticated word processor and had done no more than sent the occasional email from his last workplace. It was hard to believe that he hadn't actually used the internet for research purposes before.

'Click on that link there. That's right,' Nina said, watching as her boss cautiously surfed the net.

'Bless my soul. Bless my soul!' he sang. 'I predict many *many* lost hours of writing now I've discovered this. Why I let Teri have all the fun with my research, I don't know!'

Nina smiled to herself and vowed not to mention the world of social media just yet. Not until they'd completed the first draft of his novel, anyway.

It was only half an hour later when the eruption began. Nina was in the kitchen making coffee when she heard a long string of expletives coming from the study.

'Dudley?' she cried, dropping her teaspoon and running back along the hall as quickly as she could.

'WHAT THE BLAZES IS GOING ON HERE?' Dudley yelled as Nina entered the room. His face was a startling red and his eyes looked as if they were about to pop out of his head.

'What's happened?' Nina asked, looking around the room as if a fire might have started somewhere.

'It's gone! It's all gone!' Dudley said, gesticulating at the computer.

'*What's* all gone?'

'I had this page up and was making notes and it just *DISAPPEARED!*'

'Let me see.' Nina nudged him gently to one side as she took control of the mouse. 'There you go,' she said a moment later.

'WHAT? Where the *hell* did that go?'

'You must have clicked this little button at the top – see?'

Dudley squinted at the screen. 'Bloody hell!' he said, shaking his head. 'I never saw that. It nearly gave me a heart attack.'

'It nearly gave me one, too!' Nina said. 'But that button shrinks the page down. It doesn't mean you've lost it.'

Dudley shook his head and stared at Nina in wordless wonder. 'Well, I erm—'

'You're welcome,' Nina said with a tiny smile. The crisis had been diverted and Dudley was, once again, in control of his temper.

After an afternoon spent at the keyboard tutoring Dudley in the ways of the web, Nina made a much-needed cup of tea and walked out into the garden, stopping to dip her nose into a large burgundy-coloured rose whose perfume was deeply intoxicating. Ziggy had followed her outside and the two of them ventured into the walled garden where Faye was working with a fork.

She stood up to full height when she saw Nina approaching.

'That looks like hard work,' Nina said, feeling guilty that she did nothing more strenuous than a spot of typing.

'You know they call gardening the "green gym"?' Faye said, pushing her dark hair out of her face. 'You can definitely feel the benefits when digging. I'm going to have iron-strong muscles if I work my way round this place over the summer.'

Nina smiled. 'So, Olivia's agreed to turn this into a vegetable garden?'

Faye nodded. 'I told her how much money she could save on her shopping bill if she just planted a few rows of salad and potatoes and she told me to get started. It's going to be so beautiful. I've been looking into heritage varieties because it would be so nice to have them growing here. They're really lovely to look at, too. I think Olivia's been put off growing vegetables because – well – they aren't flowers, but I've slowly been changing her mind and introducing her to varieties that taste good and look good, too.'

Nina looked around in admiration. The walled garden was going to be fabulous and she so admired what Faye was doing, but she mustn't let it distract her now from her mission; the mission that she'd had in mind ever since she'd seen the way Faye had looked at Dominic, and the way she'd seen him looking at her, too.

'I was talking to Dominic before,' Nina said as casually as possible.

'Oh, yes?' Faye said, looking up from her work once again, her eyes softening at the mention of his name.

'You know he's doing these portraits?'

'Yes. How is he getting on?'

'Oh, fine,' Nina said. 'I mean, I don't think it's what he really wants to be doing.'

'Of course not,' Faye said. 'He shouldn't be wasting his talent on a bunch of vain women who have nothing better to do with their time. He should be out there,' she said, pointing across the garden to the countryside beyond, 'painting great big East Anglian skies and fields like Constable and Gainsborough – not stuck in a room doing portraits.'

'Actually, there is *one* portrait he really wants to paint.'

'Is there?' Faye said with a frown.

Nina nodded. 'Yours,' she said.

There was a pause and Faye seemed to be weighing up the possibility that that was true.

'Really? He said that?' she asked.

Nina swallowed hard. This wasn't going to work, was it? She wasn't at all sure she was doing the right thing here

214

and she felt certain that she was going to be found out and struck down by lightning for her wickedness. But she couldn't bear to see this sweet young couple torn apart when they were so obviously right for each other. She had to give this a try.

'He just didn't know how to ask you,' Nina went on. There was no going back now, she thought.

'But he hasn't spoken to me for months – not properly, anyway. Why would he suddenly want to paint me?' Faye didn't look convinced.

'Why don't you go along to The Folly and find out?' Nina said. 'What harm can it do?' She bit her lip, trying desperately not to hiccup at such a vital moment. She felt quite sure that it was just a case of getting Faye and Dominic back in the same room together, really talking, without the distraction of a family meal or interruptions from the likes of Alex to get in their way.

'Goodness,' Faye said with a little laugh. 'You think he wants to see me again? I mean – *really* see me?'

'I think you should find out, don't you? Even if it turns out he doesn't want to paint you, I think you should talk,' Nina said, thinking it best that she should cover herself.

Faye nodded. 'What exactly did he say to you?' she asked.

Nina gave a little shrug. 'Oh, just that—' she paused. What exactly was she going to say? 'Just that – well, you know how much he loves painting.'

Faye nodded vaguely.

'And you're so – well – so paintable.'

'He said that?'

'Not exactly,' Nina confessed, 'but I just know he was thinking it.' She swallowed down a hiccup and looked at Faye. How could a painter *not* want to paint that face, she thought? With her large expressive eyes and rosy skin and her long shiny locks, she was picture-perfect and Nina was quite sure that Dominic would see that if only he had the opportunity to look at her uninterrupted.

'Gosh, Nina,' Faye said. 'I'm really not sure about this.'

'What do you mean?' Nina asked in panic. She'd thought Faye would down tools and run to The Folly at a moment's notice.

'It feels strange, you know?'

'But I thought you still liked him,' Nina said.

Faye looked at Nina for a moment. 'Of course I do,' she said. 'I haven't been out with anyone else – not seriously anyway – since we broke up, and I can't imagine a future without Dommie in it.'

'Then go to The Folly,' Nina said gently, trying desperately not to sound too pushy. 'What have you got to lose?'

Faye wiped her hands on the front of her pale cut-off jeans and started fiddling with her hair. 'Right now?'

'Well, I think he'd be happy to wait until you're ready,' Nina said with a little smile. 'Shall I ring him and find out for you?'

Faye nodded, seemingly having lost the power of speech.

'Great,' Nina said, 'I'll give him a quick call. Wait right there.'

Faye wasn't going anywhere and, as Nina ran back to the house with Ziggy in tow, she hoped with all her heart that she was doing the right thing.

Once back in the privacy of Dudley's study, she took a deep breath and rang Dominic.

'Hi Dominic,' she said cheerily. 'I'm ringing about the portrait. Would you be free this evening?'

* * *

216

Nina was just trying to decipher a scene that Dudley had scribbled on the back of an envelope. He'd said it was very important to the plot development, but Nina really couldn't make out a single word. She was just putting it to one side to query later when Olivia knocked on the door and entered.

'Oh, Nina – look!' she said in triumph. 'We've been sent canapés!'

Nina looked at the enormous box that Olivia was holding. It was tied with a silky ribbon and looked delicious enough to eat itself.

'Do come and help me test them. We have a score card and have to choose at least half a dozen!'

Well, if that wasn't a good enough excuse to take a break, Nina didn't know what was.

They went through to the living room and began the onerous task of munching their way through twenty delicious canapés. There were sweet potato wedges, leek and Gruyère tarts, mini summer pasties, baby cheese straws – everything that was summery, savoury and delicious and could be popped into the mouth whilst still chatting.

'Oh, I'm in *such* a muddle now,' Olivia said after twenty minutes of munching. 'They're *all* so good!'

'I think we should definitely have a cheesy one,' Nina said.

'Yes but which cheesy one? We can't have too many of the same.'

'The mini cheese straws are gorgeous. I'd go with them,' Nina said, taking another one and popping it in her mouth just to make sure.

Olivia nodded and put another tick on the score card. Slowly but surely, they came up with their choices.

'Well, that was a good day's work,' Olivia said, 'and I doubt if I'll have any room for dinner after that little lot!'

Nina was just helping tidy things away when a car pulled up on the gravel outside and, by the screeching, sliding halt it made, she didn't need to look out of the window to know who it was.

'Oh, Alex!' Olivia cried, rushing to the door to greet him. Nina hovered anxiously in the living room, hoping that she could avoid him.

'Hello, Mum!' he said as he entered the hallway.

'You've just missed the great canapé testing session, I'm afraid,' Olivia said.

'Oh, right,' he said. 'I thought you said something about Party Parade.'

'Oh, yesh!' Olivia said as she stuffed the very last canapé into her mouth. 'Nina – I don't suppose you've got a couple of hours to spare now, have you?'

'Of course,' she said.

'Good, I'm sure Dudley wouldn't mind as it's all in aid of the celebrations. Now, Alex – you'll take care of Nina, won't you? I don't want you speeding through red traffic lights and driving across roundabouts.'

Nina looked startled for a moment.

'It was only the *one* roundabout,' he told her with a little grin.

'Yes, that great big grassy one,' Olivia said. 'You can still see your tyre marks across it. Anyway, no messing about. Parties are a serious business and I want you concentrating. Nina's got a copy of the list.'

'Okay, okay,' he said. 'Ready, Nina?'

'I'll just grab my bag.'

She met him in the hallway by the door and smiled

hesitantly at him. She hadn't seen or heard from him since their doomed trip to the coast and she really didn't know what to say to him now.

The white Alfa Romeo Spider sat gleaming on the driveway and they both got inside and, knowing that his mother was probably watching from the living-room window, Alex didn't do his usual wheel-spin take-off and didn't hit the gas before the mill was out of sight.

'How are you getting on?' he cried as the wind tore through their hair. 'How's the old man's novel coming along?'

'Good!' Nina shouted back as Alex took the bend far too quickly for her liking. She just hoped that there weren't too many grassy roundabouts between the mill and the party store.

Thankfully, they got there in one piece and entered what could only be described as a warehouse. Alex grabbed a trolley and Nina took out Olivia's list from her pocket. There were a lot of things to get and they were soon marching up and down the aisles, pulling out napkins, balloons and tea lights all in pretty shades of silver and purple, although Nina did have to keep her eye on Alex.

'I don't think your mother will want balloons with faces on,' she told him when he pulled out a packet of ferocious-looking monster balloons.

It was an amazing place and Nina was dazzled by the goodies on offer, from the rows of petal confetti from palest pink to deepest red, to the irresistible table diamonds, which came in every colour from purest ice to richest violet. It was a perfect Aladdin's cave for the eyes. It would have been so easy to get carried away and pile a heap of pretty candle lanterns into the trolley even though they weren't on Olivia's list, but Nina was very disciplined and stuck to her employer's wishes.

She was just admiring a rather gorgeous chair sash in a pretty shade of lilac when her phone beeped. She took it out of her pocket and saw a text from Justin.

Haven't heard from you since Sunday. Forgive my hasty departure. J.

Nina looked at the screen for a moment but decided not to reply. A second later, her phone beeped again. It was another message from Justin.

Bess sends her love.

Nina smiled as she saw the accompanying photo of the collie waving a hairy paw in the air. She shook her head.

'Who's that from?' Alex said, trying to peer at the screen.

'Just a friend,' Nina said.

'Boyfriend?'

'No,' she said.

'Are you seeing anyone?' he asked her.

She looked at him. 'It's none of your business.'

'Oh, really?'

'Really,' she said.

'I love it when you go all strict on me,' Alex said, his eyes sparkling in that naughty way of his. 'You sound just like my babysitter again.'

Nina frowned. How did he make that sound so utterly filthy, she wondered?

Her phone beeped again and, this time, there was a photo of Bess rolling on her back, her fluffy white belly exposed to the world.

The message *How's Ziggy?* accompanying it.

She quickly texted back a reply.

Ziggy mad as ever.

A few seconds later Justin's reply came.

Hope you're not mad at me.

Nina sighed. She was mad at him, but she couldn't help admitting that she missed him too. She took a deep breath and tapped her reply.

V mad.

A sad face was his response followed by:

I'll make it up to you. x

Nina blinked. Was that a kiss? Had he sent her a kiss?

'Nina!' A voice broke into her turmoil. 'You're not listening to a word I'm saying, are you?'

'Sorry, Alex. What?'

'What do you think of this?' He was holding up an obscenely short French maid's outfit.

'I think you've got the wrong kind of party, there.'

'What a shame,' he said. 'I think you'd look great in it.'

She gave him her best withering look. 'Put it back.'

'Don't you think you should try it on?'

'No, I don't.'

Alex gave a hearty sigh. It was funny, Nina thought, but he hadn't once mentioned their trip to the beach. She'd been half-expecting him to make another move on her, especially in the relatively dark confines of the party warehouse aisles, but he had surprised her. Perhaps he'd forgotten about the whole thing. She could easily believe that the incident meant absolutely nothing to him and that she was just another mild flirtation in a long line of flirtations that week. But how did that make her feel? Relieved, mostly, she had to admit. She really didn't want to get into a relationship with Alex Milton, however cute he was. The Milton boys were off-limits, not only because of the position she had once held as their babysitter, but because of

221

the position she found herself in now – one of responsibility and trust. She did not want to let her new employers down, or repeat Teri's mistake of getting embroiled with one of the sons and having it all end disastrously. She knew better than that and she realised that she was onto a good thing with her new job.

They spent the next half hour working their way through Olivia's list, laughing and joking as they discovered all manner of things in the warehouse. Alex really was good company, Nina thought, and he'd make some girl very happy one day – if only he could settle down with just the one, that was.

After paying for their goods, they drove back to the mill and were greeted by a cacophony of barks as Ziggy greeted them in the hallway.

'Back to your basket, Ziggy,' Nina said, pointing before following him through to the kitchen and putting the kettle on.

'Wow! You've worked wonders on him,' Alex observed. 'But then again – you work wonders on everyone.'

Nina bit her lip. This sounded as if it was heading in a dangerous direction.

'Cup of tea?' she said in as neutral a voice as possible.

'Thanks,' he said. 'I love the way you make it.' Nina turned her back on him to avoid any more flirtation. She didn't know how he did it but he managed to turn absolutely everything he said into an innuendo.

'I'll let you do your own milk and sugar,' she told him, thinking she might manage to swerve the 'sweet enough' line that he was bound to deliver.

'I'd better get back to your father,' she said as she took a sip of tea a moment later.

'Oh, don't go yet,' he said. 'I want to talk to you.'

'What about?'

Alex raked a hand through his hair and sighed before perching himself on a breakfast stool. 'The truth is, I haven't been able to stop thinking about you,' he said, his expression serious all of a sudden.

'Alex – please—'

'No – *listen* to me,' he said, holding his hand in the air to stop Nina's interruption. 'I don't think I've ever met anyone like you. You're really special.' He grinned. 'And I think what makes you special is that you don't even know you are.'

'But I'm not,' Nina said.

'There you go, you see?' He laughed.

'Alex—'

'No, let me finish,' he said and Nina sighed in resignation, knowing she wasn't going to be able to get a word in edgeways until he'd said his piece.

'Ever since you've come back here, things have changed. You've been like a breath of fresh air, Nina. You're so – so – *you*!'

She looked at his face and, although the words that were coming out of his mouth sounded horribly clichéd, he looked totally sincere.

'There's a real connection between us, Nina!' Alex went on, his face earnest and pleading. For a moment, Nina was tempted to tell him that he probably felt a connection to half of the girls in East Anglia, but she kept quiet, handing him his cup of tea and taking a fortifying sip from her own. 'And I know you felt it, too, at the beach.'

'Alex – the beach was a mistake. I shouldn't have—'

'How can you say that?' he said, his face full of anxiety.

'It was wrong of me to go there with you,' Nina said.

'Why? Give me *one* good reason.'

Nina looked at him pleadingly. She just wished he'd accept things rather than asking her to go into detail. 'Because I used to be your babysitter,' she said, deciding that directness was the best option.

'But that's an advantage, isn't it?' he said.

'How on earth can it be an advantage?'

'Because you know me so well and you know how to handle me,' he said, giving her a wink.

She shook her head again. 'Look,' she said, 'this really isn't going to work. We're just not right for each other.'

'Well, what about today?'

'What about it?' she said.

'We had a great time, didn't we?'

'Of course we did. You're a great guy, Alex. I think you'd get on with anybody. But that doesn't mean we should be together.'

'But we could have so much fun together,' he said, tipping his head to one side and managing to look both devastatingly handsome and just like the young boy she'd once taken care of. Maybe that was part of the problem. She could never be romantically involved with him because she would always see him as a child – no matter how old he was.

'Alex – I can't. I just can't.'

A heavy silence hung between them as if he'd understood her at last.

'And that's it? You're not even going to give us a chance?' he said.

'Drink your tea, Alex,' Nina said, sounding very much like the babysitter she had once been. 'It's getting cold.'

'I don't want this bloody cup of tea!' he said. 'I want *you*!'

Nina sighed. 'Alex – you're going to go right out there and find someone else in the blink of an eye.'

'You're wrong about that,' he said.

'I'm not,' Nina said, shaking her head. 'You're just the sort of guy who has no problem finding a girl and, one day, it'll be the right girl. Just believe me – I'm not the right girl for you.'

'How can you be so sure of that?'

She looked at him for a moment, taking in the handsome sulky face, and for a split second, she really wondered if she was making a huge mistake.

'Because I've met somebody,' she said at last, the confession surprising herself.

'Who?' Alex said, the word exiting his mouth faster than a bullet.

'You don't know him,' Nina said, thinking it best to be vague.

'Is that what all that texting was about in the warehouse?' he asked and Nina nodded. 'I thought so. You had a silly big grin on your face.'

'I did not!' Nina protested.

'You did,' he told her. 'When did you meet him?'

'Not long ago,' she said.

'So it's not serious, then?' Alex said optimistically.

'Alex—'

'Okay!' he said, raising his hands in defeat. 'I get the message.'

They stared at one another, their eyes duelling.

'I'm sorry,' Nina said at last. 'I really hope we can be friends.' She bit her lip, truly meaning what she said. Alex was a wonderful guy and she sincerely hoped that she could have him in her life, just not in any romantic sense.

'Friends isn't exactly what I had in mind,' he said and with that, he left the kitchen and marched down the hallway. The front door slammed a second later and the whole of the mill seemed to shake. Ziggy barked and Olivia yelped from the front room.

'Everything all right?' she asked, joining Nina in the kitchen a moment later.

Nina nodded. 'I've got to get back to work,' she said.

Dudley was sitting at his computer, his neck jutting forward at an odd angle as he guffawed to himself.

'How's the research going?' she asked him. 'What have you found out about clothes from the 1860s?'

'What?' he barked. 'Oh, never mind about that. Come and see this – it's absolutely brilliant!'

Nina approached his desk and cringed as she saw the site that Dudley had only recently discovered. It was YouTube.

'Just look at that dog! Isn't it the funniest thing you've ever seen?'

Nina watched as Dudley replayed the video of a Labradoodle jumping onto a bouncy castle and instantly deflating it.

'Hah!' Dudley laughed. 'Just like Ziggy, eh? Did you know there are *hundreds* of these dog videos – thousands, probably.'

'Yes,' Nina said with a pained expression, wondering if introducing Dudley to the World Wide Web had been a wise decision.

Just then, her phone beeped. She looked down at it in

the hope of another message from Justin, but it was Janey who'd texted.

How are you? x

Nina messaged back quickly, forwarding one of the photos of Bess that Justin had sent her. She'd had a few chats on the phone with Janey, who was in awe of the amount of attention she'd been getting since arriving at the mill. Now, the message that came back from her friend was:

Very cute, but send pic of the GUY. What's he look like?

Nina sighed. She didn't have a photo of Justin and, if she didn't see him again soon, she'd be in danger of completely forgetting what he looked like. She thought, once again, about his last message and the solitary kiss that had accompanied it. Perhaps it was a typo, she thought. She texted Janey back.

He's tall, fair-haired and handsome. And completely unpredictable. Help!

This was it, Dominic thought. This was Nina's way of saying she'd made a mistake going out with Alex and that it was really him she wanted to be with. But he had to play it cool this time. He had to be in control of things and not behave like the tongue-tied idiot he'd been on Nina's last visit to The Folly.

He'd taken a shower and had changed into a clean shirt – a dark collarless one with long sleeves that had slightly less paint on it than the others. He'd even combed his hair, although it didn't seem to make any difference. He still looked like a slightly surprised scarecrow.

Finally, to calm his nerves, he had half a glass of white

wine, but barely tasted the cold, crisp liquid as he drank it down. At least Alex wasn't around to interrupt this time, he thought. He'd left Norfolk that afternoon and, as far as Dominic was aware, wasn't coming back for a while. So, it would just be him and Nina, with only a canvas to come between them.

Resisting the urge to top up his glass for fear that he wouldn't be able to hold his paintbrush straight, he left the tiny kitchen and darted around the room at the top of The Folly that he used as his studio. He'd brought up a large wooden chair, which his mother had found at a car boot sale. It was beautiful enough to warrant painting, but not posh enough to worry about paint being splattered on it.

He grabbed a couple of cushions and placed them on the chair, angling them so that they looked aesthetically pleasing, remembering his mother's words. 'Don't just have cushions on a chair in a slumpy lump. Make them sit up, straight as soldiers.'

Well, they were straight now, Dominic thought, looking around the rest of the room quickly for anything else to straighten. Women liked straight things, didn't they?

'Okay, okay,' he told himself once he was quite sure everything was as perfect as a very messy artist could ever hope for. He returned downstairs and looked at the little clock on the wall next to a print of Monet's garden at Giverny. It was about time. Sure enough, a couple of minutes later, there was a knock on the door. Dominic ran a hand through his hair and, hoping for the best, opened the door. But it wasn't Nina who was standing there, but Faye.

'Hello,' she said in a small voice, her large eyes gazing up at him.

'Faye?' he said, his surprise evident in his voice.

'This is strange, isn't it?' she said.

'Yes,' he said. 'What are you doing here?'

Faye grinned. 'As forgetful as ever, are you? I'm here for the portrait,' she said, stepping into the room and gasping. 'Oh, Dom! You've worked wonders on this place.'

'The portrait?'

'It's so beautiful. I just love how you've left some of this flint bare.' She ran her fingers over the knobbly black and white stone.

'What portrait?' Dominic asked.

'Nina told me that you wanted to paint me,' she said, not at all surprised at being questioned about her being there. Dominic had always lived in a world of his own and was apt to forget things.

Dominic watched as his former girlfriend moved around the room, looking and touching everything, and his mind worked overtime as he tried to fathom what was going on. Either there'd been some terrible misunderstanding or this was Nina's strange way of going about matchmaking him with Faye. Either way, he didn't have the heart to tell Faye.

Dominic closed his eyes and took a deep, steadying breath. What was it with people forever pushing him and Faye together? They'd broken up. They'd proved that they weren't meant to be together. It was over, and that was all there was to it. Although he had to grudgingly admit that he'd found himself thinking of her more and more during the past few weeks. But that wasn't strange really when you came to think about it, as it was impossible to avoid her when she was working at the mill.

'I love this,' Faye said, bending to examine a large canvas he'd painted the previous month of the barley field, its brilliant green ears fresh and luminous under the enormous dome of the East Anglian sky. 'And this, too,' she said, gazing in wonder at a smaller painting of a nearby wood from across a golden meadow of buttercups.

'Faye?' he began, clearing his throat. He'd better get this over and done with as quickly as possible, he thought.

'Yes?' She turned towards him and, once again, he was at the mercy of her clear gaze.

'Shall we begin?'

Faye really was the most infuriating model. She wouldn't keep still for a minute and couldn't have held a decent pose even if he'd been paying her. The whole thing was a big mistake, Dominic thought, looking over his easel towards her as she sat rigidly in the wooden chair, her eyes staring somewhere over his right shoulder. As much as he wanted to confront Nina about the whole thing, he just couldn't bring himself to tell Faye what was going on – but the reality of having his ex in his studio was taking its toll on him and his mind kept spiralling back to the past.

'Dominic – you'll be partnering Faye,' his drama teacher, Mrs Fenton, had barked during a Year Eight lesson. 'Come on, now! Get into places.'

It had been one of those silly warm-up sessions where you had to place the palms of your hands against your partner's and mirror their actions. Faye had moved her hands and Dominic had mirrored them. They'd smiled, giggled and . . . what? Fallen in love? Had it really happened so suddenly and simply?

Dominic had hated drama lessons, always wishing himself back in the art room with the quiet companionship of paper and paint. But something had happened that day in the wreck of the drama studio with its peeling walls and scuffed floor, and Dominic and Faye had been inseparable ever since. Well, until he'd gone to university.

It wasn't that he'd met anybody else there and it wasn't that he'd forgotten Faye. He didn't even make an attempt to put her out of his thoughts, but his mind had slowly become filled with other things. He'd fully immersed himself in his work. He'd become obsessed by it – by the idea of making it as an artist. Every waking hour was filled with pushing himself forward, and many of his dreaming hours, too. He simply hadn't had time for anything else.

His mother had been baffled and heartbroken when he'd told her they had split. 'You *can't* do that, Dommie,' she'd cried at him. 'You two were just so right for each other!'

But he hadn't listened. He'd done his best to try to forget Faye after he'd broken up with her and as he'd become more and more engrossed in his work. He hadn't replied to her emails or her texts, he'd dodged her phone calls, and he'd always managed to be out of the house whenever she called during the holidays.

Why? Why had he done that? What had he been so afraid of? He really couldn't explain it, unless it was just the normal fear of a young man moving towards the inevitability of making a commitment to one person.

He looked at her now and it wasn't the artist's eye that gazed at her, but that of the boy who had mirrored those hand actions in the drama studio all those years ago. His mouth had gone quite dry as he mixed his white paint with a scrape of crimson alizarin and lemon yellow before running the knife through the mixture. He wouldn't think about their time together – of trips to the north Norfolk coast where they would play hide and seek in the sand dunes. Nor would he think about those sweet Christmas kisses under the enormous bunches of misletoe that his mother hung in the hallway each December.

All those moments, all those memories, now seemed to belong to a different period in his life altogether. No, he wouldn't think of them as his eyes moved across her face, over the hollow of her throat and down the plane of her chest. Faye. His sweet, loving Faye.

He shook his head and looked back up to her face. This was going to be a long session. A very long session indeed.

Chapter Twenty-Two

Back at the mill, Nina was reading an H. E. Bates novel in her room when her mobile beeped. She picked it up. It was a text from Justin.

You haven't replied. See you soon? J x

There was a kiss again. That solitary little 'x' that was causing her all sorts of concern. She stared at it until her eyes hurt.

Busy at work she texted back.

It was a few minutes later when his reply came.

Not too busy for dinner? x

She bit her lip.

We'll see she replied, not putting a kiss.

What was it she wanted from him, she wondered? He was making all the right noises and she genuinely liked him, and yet she was still holding back. Was it because she felt so raw and wounded from her relationship with Matt? Or was it the odd way he had left her in the garden that day? Something hadn't quite seemed right about that and, if there was one thing she was sensitive to now, it was strange behaviour in men.

When she thought of the brief time they'd spent together

and the laughter they'd shared, she couldn't help smiling and hoping that they would see each other again. But, the more she thought about it, perhaps it would be best if they kept things casual. Dinner, she thought, might be getting a bit too serious too quickly. Perhaps they should share a few more dog walks first.

And, thinking of dog walks, Nina ventured downstairs, whistling for Ziggy who came belting out of the kitchen, skidding to a neat halt by her feet.

'Is that you, Nina?' Olivia's voice called from the living room where she was watching a costume drama on TV.

'Yes,' Nina replied. 'I'm just taking Ziggy out.'

'Oh, thank you! I'm absolutely *glued* to the TV and just *have* to know if this young servant girl is pregnant!'

Dudley, who was sitting in his favourite armchair behind the *Financial Times*, grunted something.

'Now, don't you be so condescending. You want to find out *just* as much as me, I know you do!'

Nina grinned and left them to it. She opened the front door and headed out over the bridge into the fields, looking back over her shoulder at The Old Mill House. How beautiful it looked, in the evening sunshine, its white facade as bright as a pearl amongst the deep greens of the countryside. She felt as if she had been there forever and yet it had only been a few weeks. Even with the trouble she'd had with the two brothers, Nina couldn't help feeling as if she'd really been accepted into the Milton family, something she had never felt before, even within her own small family.

Thinking back to her own parents, she tried to imagine them sitting amiably in the same room together and just couldn't. Her mother was far too volatile to sit contentedly in a chair in front of a costume drama, and her father

– Nina stopped. She didn't actually know anything much about her father. He'd always worked hard at his job as a salesman but, beyond that, she really didn't know anything about him. The time he spent at home was chiefly spent alone in his study with his books and his computer, but Nina had no idea what he did in there for all those hours, and her mother had never seemed that interested, either.

Nina had often wondered why they'd had a child, because neither of them spent any time with her and they certainly never knew her growing up. If it hadn't been for Janey, Nina might well have gone out of her mind, but her best friend had always helped her to laugh through the odd and awkward times at home.

'Nobody gets on with their parents, anyway,' Janey had told her, but Nina knew that wasn't true – her times babysitting for the Miltons had taught her that. She'd watched them all together in what she called the happy tumble of family life. They genuinely seemed to like each other and Nina had found that so strange and wonderful that she couldn't help but want to be a part of it, and now here she was once again – back with the Miltons.

She stopped for a moment – not because Ziggy had been pulling on his lead, but to watch a ghostly barn owl crossing the field beside her, its white wings silent. She loved it there and was dreading, absolutely dreading, having to leave at the end of the summer.

It was then that her phone beeped. It was Justin again.

Have to return to London. See you at the weekend? Love to Ziggy. J x

She looked along the path, the knowledge that Justin and Bess wouldn't be appearing around the corner at any second saddening her.

'Come on, Ziggy,' she said, and the two of them walked towards the misty-blue banks of the river.

It was dusk by the time Dominic had finished. It had been the strangest few hours of his life, with thoughts and memories flying through his brain and getting in the way of his work. Like the time he and Faye had visited London and had wandered around The National Gallery together, marvelling at the masterpieces by Monet, Tuner and Van Gogh.

'You're going to be a great painter one day,' Faye had told him, squeezing his hand as they had gazed into the joyous faces of Gainsborough's daughters.

'And you'll be my famous model,' he'd told her and she'd laughed.

'I'll hold you to that,' she'd said, and here she was now in his room, sitting for him as if the years in between had melted away and they'd never been apart. As if he'd never ended things so abruptly.

Finally, Dominic decided enough was enough and put his brushes down.

'Can I see it?' Faye asked, stretching her arms high above her head as she moved towards the easel.

'Do you mind if you don't? It's early stages at the moment. It'll only disappoint.'

'I'm sure it won't,' she said.

'Please,' he said, their eyes meeting. Dominic could feel a blush heating his face at her close scrutiny.

'Okay,' Faye said with a little smile.

They left the studio and went downstairs towards the door. He wasn't going to offer a drink. They'd taken a five-minute break during the painting session and Dominic had

236

felt uncomfortable – an awkward apology hovering on his lips for his behaviour in the past, but he just couldn't heave the words out and so he'd fiddled about with his brushes, knocking into his easel at one point and then spilling tea down his trouser leg. He'd been relieved to get back to work.

'Where's your car?' he asked.

'At the mill.'

He nodded. 'Do you want me to walk you back?'

'It's okay. I'll be fine,' she said, her eyes meeting his again. He looked away quickly. He couldn't bear the intensity of her gaze.

'So—' she began.

'I'll call you,' he said and she nodded. He watched as Faye walked down the little path, her feet kicking through the daisies, until she was out of sight.

Shutting the door, Dominic breathed a sigh of relief and went back up to the studio to view the evening's work. There she was, with that sweet, gentle face, her eyes edged with anxiety and the lips seemingly poised to say something. They'd both been on the verge of saying something all evening, hadn't they? And yet both had remained silent, getting on with the job in hand.

As he tidied his paint things away, washing his brushes with the green soap that smelled wonderfully of peppermint, his mind jumped back into the past, when he'd first tried to paint Faye.

'You've made me look like an ogre!' she'd screamed, slapping his arm playfully.

'You're a fidget!' he'd told her. 'You can't sit still for a minute.'

'But I don't look like *that* even when I'm fidgeting!'

They'd laughed and kissed and laughed some more. That had pretty much been the pattern of their relationship. So much laughter. He hadn't realised until now how much he'd missed that. But Nina had still overstepped the mark with her little matchmaking scheme and he was going to confront her about it. She had no business to meddle in his affairs, no matter how good her intentions were.

When he turned up at the mill the next day, charging into his father's study, Nina was standing on tiptoes, trying to reach a file on the top shelf of the bookcase.

'Dommie!' she exclaimed. 'Whatever's the matter?'

'Nina,' he began, 'last night—'

'Yes, how did the portrait go?' she asked.

He stared at her for a moment as if she was quite mad. 'I thought I was going to be painting *you*!'

'Me?' Nina said, returning to her computer with the retrieved file. 'Whatever would I want my portrait painted for?'

'You said—'

'What?'

'I thought you said you wanted a portrait painting.'

'I did. But not mine. I meant I wanted you to paint Faye.'

'Nina?' he said, his dark eyes narrowed in consternation. 'Why would you do that to me?'

'Is it going well?'

'That's not really the point, is it?' Dominic said.

'Isn't it?'

'No, it isn't! You set me up, didn't you?' Dominic said. 'Nina! Please look at me when I'm talking to you.'

Nina forsook the keyboard, turning around in surprise

238

at the tone of his voice and he saw a faint blush creep over her cheeks.

'Why did you do that?' he asked her, his voice quieter now.

Nina bit her lip. 'I thought you'd want to paint Faye, that's all.'

'That's rubbish and you know it. You're trying to push us back together again, aren't you? Just like Mum's been trying to do. Have you and Faye been talking about it – plotting behind my back?'

'No!' Nina cried. 'Nothing like that.'

'Really? Why don't I believe you?'

'Well, it doesn't matter what you believe, really,' Nina said, 'because it's not true.'

Dominic stood silent and brooding for a moment whilst Nina's fingers began tap-tapping at her keyboard again.

'Nina,' he began.

'Yes,' she said, only giving him half her attention.

'I think you should know something.'

'Yes?'

'It would help if you looked at me when I'm talking.'

Once again, Nina turned around. 'What is it?'

Dominic took a deep breath. 'Look – it's not Faye I'm interested in. It's you!'

Nina shook her head. 'Don't say that.'

'Why not? It's about time I said it,' Dominic said. 'Every time I've been going to say it, I've been interrupted by Alex or Faye—'

'Listen!' Nina said. 'You really mustn't say things like that.'

'Why not when I feel them?' Dominic answered hopelessly.

'Because I don't feel that way about you,' she said and there was a dreadful pause between them.

'You don't?' Dominic said.

'I don't think I ever could,' Nina added.

'Is it because of the whole babysitting thing?' he asked after a moment.

Nina nodded, her hazel eyes filled with remorse. 'I'm sorry,' she said, feeling a horrible sense of déjà vu after her conversation with Alex just the day before.

Dominic walked across the room and flopped down in his father's office chair. 'Just bad timing, then?' he said, berating the fact that the universe had played a spectacularly bad joke on him. 'That seems so unfair.'

'I'm sorry,' Nina repeated.

'But what if we'd just met. I mean – *now*. What if—'

'I guess we'll never know,' Nina said gently.

Dominic looked at her from across the room. Her face was soft and filled with compassion. 'You're just saying that out of kindness, aren't you?'

'Oh, Dommie—'

'It's Dominic, Nina.'

There was another pause as they both let things settle between them for a moment.

'I'm really sorry – Dominic. I think you're a terrific person – I really do. You're bright and talented and sweet and kind—'

'All the qualities people highlight when they're not interested in you romantically.' He gave the tiniest of smiles. 'And it's not because of Alex, is it?' he added.

'No!' Nina said, shaking her head.

'You're not – you know – in love with him?'

'Whatever gave you that idea?' she said, her eyes wide.

'Well, you seem to be spending a lot of time with him.'

'That was a mistake,' Nina said. 'I shouldn't have gone to the beach with him. I just thought it would be fun – that's all.'

Dominic nodded, seemingly satisfied with her answer.

'Dominic,' she began again, 'You will finish Faye's portrait, won't you?'

He stood up and was silent for a moment. 'Well, I can't not finish the portrait, can I? It's impossible. It wouldn't be right. I always have to finish a painting, even if I'm not enjoying it or even when I know it's not working.'

'But this one's working, isn't it?' Nina asked.

He nodded again. 'It's actually very good.'

Nina smiled. 'You're happy with it?'

Dominic looked across the room at Nina. 'I don't mean I'm happy with the situation,' he said, 'but the painting's not bad.'

'Good,' Nina said. 'I knew this would all work out.'

Dominic sighed and shook his head. 'Sometimes, you sound scarily like Mum!'

Chapter Twenty-Three

'You are a *very* bad friend!' Janey chided as Nina entered her living room and flopped down onto a mass of very pink cushions. 'What have you been doing all these weeks? And don't say you've texted me, because that doesn't count!'

Nina took the cup of tea she was handed and smiled apologetically at her friend. 'I'm so sorry, Janey. I meant to call you so many times. I just don't know where the time's gone.'

'That's a sorry excuse,' Janey said, tutting and sitting down next to her before taking a sip of tea. 'I've been worried sick.'

'No you haven't!' Nina cried. 'You've been off gallivanting around the Italian coast.'

'That's important research for our new Mediterranean brochure,' she said seriously.

'You mean you didn't enjoy yourself?'

'Oh, it was wonderful! And I met the most amazing guy called Renato! He's only twenty-six, but he owns his own company and has this incredible villa on the Amalfi coast.'

'I thought holiday romances were frowned upon at Gulliver's Travels,' Nina said.

'Well, they are for the other members of staff, but I'm a company director now. Dad's promoted me!'

'Oh, that's wonderful,' Nina said. 'Congratulations, Janey.'

'So, I can have as many holiday romances as I like now.'

Nina grinned. 'And I'm sure you will.'

'So, tell me what's been happening with you at the mill!' Janey said, elbowing her friend in impatience.

All of a sudden, the light went out of Nina's eyes and her face crumpled into a frown. 'Oh Janey, I was so looking forward to being back there. It's the most perfect place. Olivia's made me so welcome and Dudley's been brilliant to work with – despite the warnings about his temper.'

'But? I can definitely hear a *but* coming.'

Nina nodded. 'I'm afraid I seem to have caused nothing but trouble since I arrived,' she said with a sigh. 'I've upset Alex by telling him there's no chance of a relationship ever developing between us. And Dominic's furious with me for setting him up with Faye. And to top it all, I've no idea what's going on with Justin.'

Janey looked perplexed. 'Do you want to start again, because I've absolutely no idea who half of these people are!'

Nina filled her in on what had been going on over the past few weeks and, when she came to the end of her tale, Janey stared at her in wide-eyed wonder.

'So, let me see if I've got this straight. Dominic's got a huge crush on you, but Faye has a huge crush on him and you think they should be back together. You've kissed Alex and he's in love with you, too, but you reckon you don't fancy him – but you might fancy a bloke called Justin whose dog you keep texting me pictures of, but you don't know

243

anything about him, and you're not even sure if you'll ever see him again.'

'That's about the size of it,' Nina said hopelessly.

'Gosh, I think we're going to need more than a cup of tea to get you through this mess.'

After eating their way through a defrosted lasagne and at least three glasses of wine each, the conversation turned back to men.

'You like this Justin, don't you?' Janey said.

'I really don't know that much about him,' Nina confessed.

'Except that he's handsome and charming and kind to waifs and strays,' Janey said with a grin.

Nina nodded. 'Oh yes, he's all those things, and I keep telling myself that no man who is so brilliant with animals could be a bad person. You should see him with Bess and Ziggy. It's really amazing. He's so patient and kind and he always knows exactly how to handle them.'

'So, what's the problem?'

Nina poured herself some more wine and took a thoughtful sip. 'I just can't help thinking that he's hiding something.'

'Like what? A girlfriend? A wife?'

'I really don't know.'

Janey chewed her lip. 'Renato's married,' she said.

'Your Italian?'

She nodded. 'But he's split up from her and she's living in New York.'

'Says Renato,' Nina said.

'What do you mean?' Janey said, her eyes narrowing.

'Are you sure he's telling you the truth?' Nina said.

'Of *course* he's telling me the truth!' Janey said defiantly.

'Anyway, I don't suppose it matters as I doubt I'll see him again.'

Nina rolled her eyes. It was ever thus with her friend – a new country and a new man. That was how she lived. 'One of the perks of the job,' she used to say.

'But I get the feeling you'd like to see this Justin again. Am I right?' They left the table together, taking their glasses and the second bottle of wine across to the sofa.

'But the way he ran off after we last met,' Nina said. 'It was so odd – as if he really didn't want to see Dudley. What was all that about?'

Janey shrugged. 'I don't know. Maybe he had a run-in with Dudley when he was a kid. You said he knew the Milton boys. Perhaps he was friends with them and got into trouble with their dad.'

'But he's a grown man now. Surely he wouldn't still be scared of Dudley,' Nina said.

'But you said he *was* pretty scary,' Janey pointed out.

'Well, to begin with,' Nina said. 'I suppose he was.'

'There you go, then. It's probably something simple like that. We all have some scary adult we remember from our childhood, don't we? I'd rather not meet that science teacher, Mr Gipps, again. Not after what I did to his Bunsen burner!'

Nina sighed. 'I want to trust him, I really do.'

'Then why don't you?' Janey said. 'Honestly, Nina. It's not as if you're planning a big romance or anything. I thought you said you wanted a break from all that after he-who-shall-not-be-mentioned. So why not just take things one step at a time and enjoy a bit of summer fun?'

Nina looked at her friend's smiling face across the table

and couldn't help thinking she was right. What was she making such a big fuss about, anyway? She probably wouldn't even see Justin again.

'Okay,' she said at last. 'I'll try not to worry so much. Now, what's for dessert?'

Nina got a taxi back to The Old Mill House that night. It was late, but the hallway light had been left on for her, casting a warm glow and lighting her way to the kitchen where Ziggy was sleeping.

She knelt down to stroke his head as he opened an eye and thumped his tail on the quarry tile floor.

'Have you been out, boy?' she whispered to him and his head sunk back down into his cushion, which Nina took as a yes. It was then that footsteps were heard on the stairs and it wasn't long before Olivia entered the kitchen, her red hair tousled and her face cloudy with sleep.

'Oh, I'm so sorry – I didn't mean to disturb you,' Nina said.

'You didn't, my dear!' Olivia assured her. 'I'm a light sleeper and Dudley's been snoring away tonight. I thought it best to get up. Did you have a nice evening with your friend?'

'Yes, thank you,' Nina said, standing up and walking across to the sink to fill a glass with water.

Olivia nodded. 'I used to have so many lovely nights out with my girlfriends before the boys arrived. It's not the same afterwards, you mark my words. Everyone says they'll keep in touch and that they won't let families change them, but it's all nonsense, of course.'

Nina smiled. 'Did I miss anything here?' she asked.

Olivia's eyes suddenly lit up. 'You most certainly did!

And I'm sorry you were out because you'll never guess who dropped by.'

'Who?'

'Billy! It was such a lovely surprise. I wasn't expecting him at all. Thought he'd gone away.'

Nina laughed. 'We keep missing each other, don't we?' she said.

'Not to worry. I've told him that he's going to be your partner for the anniversary party.'

'You have?' Nina said in surprise.

Olivia nodded excitedly. 'You'll make *such* a handsome couple!' she said, and Nina sighed inwardly. Was this Olivia matchmaking again? 'Although,' she continued, 'I got the distinct impression that there might be a girl on the scene.'

'Really?' Nina said.

Olivia nodded. 'He didn't say too much, of course. He never does. Always one to play his cards close to his chest when it comes to women, our Billy, but there was something about him this evening – a certain glow.'

Nina looked at Olivia's happy face and knew that, in her mind, she was choosing flowers for the church in time for an autumn wedding.

'Then perhaps I shouldn't be partnering him at the party,' she said.

'Oh, nonsense!' Olivia said. 'Better safe than sorry when it comes to partners. This other girl might just be passing through.'

Nina smiled. 'Well, it's been a long day,' she said at last and Olivia nodded.

Once in bed, Nina thought about Janey's words of advice. 'Enjoy a bit of summer fun,' she'd told her. Why did

Nina find that so hard to do? Why couldn't she flirt happily with Dominic and Alex and enjoy the uncomplicated attention of Justin and allow herself to be matchmade with Billy?

'Because I'm not made like that,' she whispered into the darkness. She couldn't help it, but she wanted the big romance – the romance that was definitely going somewhere and had a future rather than a fade out.

Nina turned over in bed. After her experience with Matt, it was surprising to have such feelings once again. The heart was a truly incredible thing, she couldn't help thinking, but she also remembered that it could get you into a lot of trouble, too.

Chapter Twenty-Four

Days slipped by and weeks passed as Nina continued her duties at the mill. It was an early afternoon in late July and Nina had just finished typing a pile of notes that Dudley had produced the night before. She'd never seen anyone so prolific. They were making good progress on *The Solitary Neighbour* and Nina imagined that it wouldn't be long before she typed those two magical words: The End.

After almost two months at the mill, Nina had fallen into a very satisfying routine with Dudley and felt comfortable with his funny little ways and occasional bursts of temper. They didn't scare her anymore; she merely worked around them, giving him some space when he needed to be alone and taking charge of situations that he was finding hard to cope with, such as navigating certain websites.

She was relieved that his earlier addiction to Labradoodle videos on YouTube had waned and he was now, once again, fully immersed in his novel. Nina was kept busy typing up the previous day's scribbles as well as continuing to research important facts and figures for his book, which she found both challenging and enjoyable.

It was after Nina had made them both a cup of tea that

she decided to ask him something that she hadn't yet dared to. But, before she could broach the subject, he spoke.

'I hope you don't mind, but I've revised the latest chapter of the novel completely,' he said, walking across the study towards her. 'I've made it much tighter. Anyway, see what you think of it and let me know.'

'I will,' she said. She loved the way he trusted her opinion so much now with the novel.

'Dudley?' she asked.

He looked up from his computer, his white eyebrows hovering over his eyes. 'What?' he barked – it was a bark that Nina had come to be rather fond of.

'I was just wondering what your plans are for when you finish the novel.'

Dudley looked confused for a moment, as if he had never even tried to imagine such a time. 'Well, I—' he paused. 'I guess I'll write another.'

'But what will you do with this one?'

He stroked his chin and looked thoughtful.

'I mean, are you going to try and get it published?' Nina added.

He didn't answer for a moment, but stared out of the French doors into the garden beyond. 'What do you think?' he asked her at last.

Nina's mouth dropped open in surprise. What did *she* think? He was asking her opinion on what was a pretty important decision to make. She felt a swell of pride at being so trusted by him. It was something she had never experienced in the workplace and it made her feel so happy.

'I think,' she began, 'that you should definitely send it to a publisher or an agent. I believe that's what writers do.'

'Is it?'

She nodded. 'I've done a little bit of research on the internet about it all. You can even self-publish. It's very easy these days.'

'You've been thinking about this for a while, have you?'

Nina bit her lip, hoping that he wouldn't think she'd overstepped the mark. 'I think the novel deserves to be read,' she told him. 'It's a wonderful story and it would be so sad to think that we're the only people who will ever read it.'

Dudley picked up his pipe, but didn't light it. He just tapped it into the palm of his left hand as he thought things through.

'What do you think?' Nina prompted him a moment later.

His eyebrows were dangerously close to the brow of his nose now, but then a tiny smile broke across his face. 'I think I should very much like to see my little book published. Look into it some more for me, will you?'

Nina beamed him a smile. 'I certainly will,' she said, making a mental note to make a good long list of agents and publishers whom she hoped would like what she was fast becoming to think of as *their* novel.

'But this business is just between you and me, right?'

'Right!' Nina said.

'And we still keep everything under lock and key. There aren't many things in this house that are mine, but this book is mine and, until it's finished, *nobody* sees it but you and me!'

Nina immediately thought of Olivia's confession to reading it and wondered how many others had seen the manuscript. Poor Dudley, she thought. There was very little privacy to be had at the mill. He had recently insisted that he and Nina kept the study door locked whenever they left the room. It seemed rather a ridiculous set-up, particularly if you were just going down the hall to make a cup of tea in the kitchen. But, Dudley assured her, those were the precise moments when one could be taken advantage of.

It was as though he were researching a cure to the common cold rather than scribbling a historical romance that would probably never see the light of day, but it was Nina's job to oblige him. Although, perhaps she should warn him not to read any more of his novel in bed and then fall asleep – leaving his chapters in the clutches of Olivia.

She smiled. She rather liked being Dudley's trusted assistant with honoured access to his most private novel. It was a true privilege, and one she had never been afforded before.

Along with her progress on Dudley's novel, Nina had been given another list of things to organise for the wedding anniversary party. Olivia had ordered the marquee that was to be erected in the back garden, but had left Nina in charge of most of the other things. That meant that there was a long list of people to coordinate.

That afternoon had been set aside for a progress report.

'Have we got the final number of guests now?' Olivia asked as she placed a tray with tea and homemade cherry scones on the table in the front room.

'Out of the eighty invited, there have been only five so far who can't make it.'

'Excellent!' Olivia enthused.

'So I've informed the caterers.'

'And they've got the number of vegetarians and other dietary requirements?'

Nina nodded. 'I've also been in touch with the rental company and have given them a final number for chairs and tables.'

Olivia smiled as she poured the tea. 'And how are the decorations coming on? What about all these marvellous balloons?'

'No problems there. We've got the twenty-five large silver balloons to launch at the end of the evening and we've also got a mix of silver and purple for inside the marquee.'

'It's like getting married all over again!' Olivia laughed. 'I'm so excited!'

Nina smiled. She was looking forward to the party almost as much as Olivia, and had been formally invited to sit at the table with the Miltons.

'The florist is going to erect two stands of flowers and trailing foliage at the entrance, and a rope of ivy and silver ribbon around the marquee.'

'And have you been in touch with the band?'

'Yes. They're booked and raring to go, too,' Nina told her.

'It isn't a real party without real music and dancing, is it?'

'Livvy?' a voice called from the hall.

'We're in here, Dud.'

'Did I hear dancing mentioned?' Dudley asked, breezing into the room and whisking Olivia out of her seat. She giggled as Dudley spun her around the room. Nina watched, mesmerised. She'd never seen Dudley in such a good mood. Wow, she thought; twenty-five years of marriage and they still wanted to dance together. Now that was something to aim for.

'Stop, stop!' Olivia pleaded after a moment.

'You'll need more practice than that before the big day.'

'I know, but the champagne will fuel me. OH, CHAMPAGNE!'

'All in hand,' Nina assured her.

'This girl,' Olivia started, short of breath after her waltz around the living room, 'is an absolute gem.'

'Don't I know it,' Dudley agreed, causing Nina to blush.

As well as the party arrangements, there was Nina's dog-walking duties with Ziggy. Whilst it had been a job that had been forced upon her without much in the way of consultation, it was one she couldn't imagine living without now.

'You're *so* good with him!' Olivia had told her one evening over a glass of wine.

'I am?' Nina had said in surprise.

'I've seen how he is around you. You just have the knack. Honestly, I wish I had half your talent with him. He'd be a much calmer dog, I'm sure!'

Nina knew that Olivia was just buttering her up and would do and say almost anything to get Ziggy off her hands. Still, she had come to love her time with Ziggy, getting to know the footpaths across the fields and through the woods and learning the different moods of the river. It was such a far cry from her previous job, but Nina was all too aware that her time at the mill was fast drawing to a close.

On one particularly beautiful July evening, Nina and Ziggy were emerging from a little wood and heading down to the river. The sky was slowly turning from a duck-egg blue to a rich apricot streaked with violet clouds, and a cool breeze had encouraged Nina to do up the buttons on her yellow cotton cardigan. She was going to miss these walks, she thought. How easy it was to just leave the mill and immediately find oneself in the middle of some of

Norfolk's loveliest countryside. She often wondered if she would have discovered it herself if it hadn't been for her dog-walking duties. She certainly wouldn't have met Justin if it hadn't been for Ziggy.

She still hadn't seen him since his strange departure from the mill all those weeks ago, but they had swapped innumerable texts since then, with photos of Bess and Ziggy flying between their phones and silly snippets of news. It was a funny kind of relationship, but it brightened many of Nina's solitary hours at the computer.

She was just watching a deer dancing across a field when she saw him.

'Justin?' she called.

'Nina!' he said. 'I was just going to text you.'

'I didn't know you were back in Norfolk.'

'No. I didn't know myself until a couple of hours ago. Got some unexpected time off. Have to go back first thing tomorrow, though.'

'Oh,' she said, unable to disguise her disappointment. 'Where's Bess?'

'Got her nose stuck in a rabbit hole,' he said, bending down to stroke Ziggy's head. 'This one's looking a lot calmer, these days.'

'Oh, he's still a Labradoodle and can be a bit of a wild child when he wants to be.'

'Can't we all?' Justin said, his eyes twinkling. 'And how are you?'

'Good,' she said. 'You?' She cringed at the awkwardness of the conversation. It was strange; she felt like she knew this man but realised that there was so much about him that she didn't know. It felt like a long time since she'd last seen him.

'Yes, pretty good,' he said. 'And how's the novel coming along?'

'Really well. I don't think it'll be long until it's finished.'

'Wow!' Justin said. 'That's pretty impressive.'

Nina nodded. 'I never thought I'd get the chance to be involved in something so exciting,' she said. 'I got so used to working in that awful office with the boss from hell, and I kind of just imagined the rest of my life would be like that with no hope of reprieve!'

'And then you found this place.'

'Yes,' she said. 'It's so special to me. I've really been made welcome here and I feel—' she paused. 'I feel as if I'm beginning to find myself. Olivia and Dudley have trusted me with so much and have given me the space and time to do things my way. They're very special people.'

'Yes,' Justin said. 'They are.'

Suddenly, Nina got excited. 'Why don't you come back to the mill and say hello to them? I'm sure they'd love to see you.'

'No, no,' he said. 'Another time. It's getting late now.'

Nina looked at the last streaks of light in the sky and nodded. 'I suppose I should be getting back, otherwise I won't be able to see where I'm going.'

Justin nodded. 'That's what I miss most about the coun-tryside – the all-enveloping darkness.'

'You miss that?'

'Why yes!' he said.

Nina laughed. 'It seems like a strange thing to miss.'

'Not at all. Not when you have street lamps, neon signs and security lights all battling to keep you awake at night. I really miss the comforting depths of the countryside's darkness.'

'Well, I don't want to be scrambling about in this night's particular darkness,' Nina said.

'Let me walk you back,' Justin said, whistling for Bess who soon joined them.

'But then you'll have to walk home in the dark,' Nina pointed out.

'Yes, but I like it and I'm used to it. And I also have a torch.'

'Ah!' Nina said as they walked along the riverside footpath with the stars high above them.

'Nina,' he said after a moment. 'Have you thought about what you're going to do after the summer?'

She sighed. 'I've been half-heartedly looking out for other jobs – I was kind of hoping that Dudley would have said something by now about keeping me on, but he hasn't. He's mentioned starting another book, but I don't know how serious he is about it and if he even needs me for it.'

'What will you do?'

'Brood a lot!' Nina said with a laugh that only went some way towards masking her insecurity. 'Look for another Milton family?' she suggested.

'That won't be easy to find,' he said.

'I know,' she said.

They'd reached the bridge and the sound of the rushing water filled their ears.

'You'd better head back,' she said, bending to stroke Bess.

He nodded. 'I wish I— I wish we had longer,' he said. 'I always seem to be rushing back to London.'

Nina gave a little smile. 'Yes,' she said and then he did something that took her completely by surprise – he bent forward and kissed her cheek.

'Good night,' he said and turned to leave before she had

257

the chance to say anything, leaving Nina to watch his tall figure become engulfed in the darkness of the Norfolk countryside.

She turned and walked across the bridge. 'Did that really happen?' she asked Ziggy, but Ziggy didn't have time to concern himself about kisses. He wanted some supper, and pulled at the lead in order to reach the front door faster.

'Is that you, Nina?' Dudley shouted from the study as Nina closed the front door behind her and unclipped Ziggy's lead.

'Hello,' she said, joining him in the study. 'You okay?'

'My pipe!' he complained, searching his desk like a madman. 'Nina! Have you seen it?'

She shook her head. 'No,' she said. 'I'm afraid not.'

Dudley charged out of the room to frantically search elsewhere when Nina's phone beeped. It was a text from Justin.

Really sorry not to have more time with you. J x.

Not to worry, Nina texted back. *Dudley's in the middle of a pipe crisis. Can't find it!* She pressed send.

Try the bowl on the dresser Justin replied.

Without thinking, Nina walked through to the kitchen and, sure enough, there was the lost pipe in the bowl on the old oak dresser.

'Dudley?' she cried down the hallway. 'I've found your pipe.'

He charged down the hall towards her. 'What on *earth* is it doing there?' he asked in bemusement, picking up the pipe and shaking his head in despair as if somebody had played an awful trick on him.

Nina looked down at her phone and typed the following message to Justin.

How on earth did you know where it was?

But there was no reply from him.

'Whatever happened to that lovely young lady your mother was always talking about?' Edna Bowridge asked, the necessity to talk after a whole hour of silence proving too much for her. 'Now what was her name? I've quite forgotten.'

Dominic pressed his lips together and pretended not to hear as he got on with the portrait that seemed to be taking him an absolute age.

'Kate, was it? No. May? No. That wasn't it either. Oh dear, my memory's fading like a photograph in the sun. Don't grow old, Dominic.'

'I'll try not to,' Dominic grinned.

'FAYE!' she shouted suddenly, making Dominic jump. 'Am I right?'

Dominic nodded.

'Whatever happened to her?'

'We broke up.' Dominic heard his own voice but barely recognised it. It sounded hard and cold and he didn't like it.

'Oh.' For a moment, Edna was quiet once more. 'Well, that's a shame, I must say. Your mother always liked Faye.'

'She still does, Mrs Bowridge.'

'But you don't see her anymore?'

'Well, I see her all the time,' Dominic said. 'She's never away from the mill.'

'Oh? What, you mean you're still friends?'

'Er, no – not exactly.'

259

Edna's eyebrows rose a fraction. 'Then she's seeing Alex?'

Dominic almost dropped his paintbrush.

'Sorry, dear. I must let you concentrate.'

Dominic took a deep breath. 'I'm almost finished.'

Edna nodded. 'I'm afraid not, Dominic. As far as romantic complications are concerned, you've only just begun.'

Dominic couldn't help dwelling on Edna's words as he walked the short distance from the mill to The Folly later that afternoon. It was a week after his first painting session with Faye and he'd since spent hours looking at the image he'd painted. It was really coming along, and Faye hadn't been quite such a fidget during their second session together.

Catching his first glimpse of his beloved folly as he turned the corner, he thought about those last two hours they'd spent together. She'd arrived with her dark hair scraped back after a day's gardening and her cheeks had been flushed.

'Faye!' Dominic had cried. 'Your colouring's way too high. We'll have to let it calm down before we can begin. And do something with your hair. You can't have it up like that.'

She'd nodded and apologised profusely, saying she'd lost track of time whilst staking Olivia's roses.

'They're looking glorious right now,' she'd told him. 'You must come and see them. There's this fabulous pink one called "The Ingenious Mr Fairchild". Isn't that a brilliant name?'

Dominic had nodded and said something vague whilst Faye had babbled on about other roses with equally bizarre names. Then he'd remembered that she always babbled

260

when she was nervous. The first time he'd brought her home to the mill, she'd chattered her way through the whole of dinner. It was a wonder that she'd managed to eat anything at all because she'd filled the room with her inane prattle until Olivia had gently placed her hand on hers and calmed her down.

'I've never really been obsessed with roses until I came to the mill,' she'd continued, 'but they really are the most terrific—'

'Faye!' Dominic had said.

'Yes?'

Dominic didn't say anything, only held her gaze for a moment.

'Oh,' she said at last. 'I'm babbling, aren't I?'

He'd given the tiniest of nods and then watched as she let her hair loose, allowing it to fall about her face in dark waves. For a moment he'd felt utterly lost, as if he'd spiralled back in time to the day when he'd first seen her do that during a trip to the Broads.

They'd been walking through Wroxham and had stopped on the bridge, peering down at the boats below. The sun had come out and a light breeze had tickled their faces, and Faye had reached around and untied her hair, letting it blow around her face.

'Dominic?' she'd said. 'Is this all right?'

He'd been jolted back into the present, the vision of the teenage Faye being replaced by the real-life one before him.

'Yes,' he said. 'Sit down.'

He'd painted for just over two hours, with a break in the middle in which she drank coffee and he'd paced around, staring at the floorboards and absent-mindedly sorting through tubes of paint.

'Are you okay? You look tired,' she told him, when she sat back down.

'Do I?' he'd said, surprised by her attention. He wasn't used to somebody caring about him in that way anymore.

She'd nodded. 'You shouldn't work so hard,' she'd said. 'I bet you're pushing yourself with this upcoming show as well as all these portraits your mum's set up for you. You should take things easier.'

'I'm fine,' he'd told her, suddenly realising that his eyes were actually quite sore.

'I could come over some time and make you a meal,' she'd said.

'I don't need you to mother me, Faye,' he'd said, biting his tongue as he realised how blunt he'd sounded. She'd only been trying to help, after all. He'd looked at her pale moonshiny face. 'Sorry,' he'd said.

'It's okay,' she'd said and he'd felt absolutely wretched. Why was he always so mean to Faye? And why was she so sweet in spite of that meanness?

'Let's just get this session done,' he'd said, distancing himself from her further by placing himself behind the canvas.

When Faye had left later that evening, he'd stared at himself in the studio mirror.

'What's happening to you?' he'd asked his reflection. 'Why are you behaving like this?'

The face that stared back at him was pale and blank, like one of his unpainted canvases and, as he stared into his dark eyes, one word formed itself slowly but surely on his lips.

'Faye.'

Chapter Twenty-Five

It was a gloriously sunny morning at the beginning of August and Nina's desk was covered with the morning mail. She was just in the process of opening it whilst Dudley was out at the city library when she realised she'd made a mistake. One of the envelopes had been addressed to Mr D. Milton and Nina had assumed it was to Dudley but, on opening it, she saw that it was actually addressed to Dominic.

To read or not to read – that was the question. Seeing that it was from a gallery in London, Nina hesitated for a moment, but her curiosity soon got the better of her.

Dear Mr Milton, it began. *Thank you for your letter and for coming to visit us last week.*

Nina blinked. Dominic had kept very quiet about going to London, hadn't he?

It was a pleasure to view your work and, although we were unable to take your paintings for this autumn's group exhibition, we would be keen to exhibit your work in our spring show.

She gasped. Dominic was going to exhibit at a gallery in London and, judging by the address, it was a pretty good one, too. This was big news, she thought, and he'd no doubt want to hear it straight away.

'Olivia!' she called, leaving her desk with the letter hastily stuffed back into its envelope. 'I'm just popping to The Folly. I've got a letter for Dominic.'

'Okay!' Olivia called back from the kitchen where she was elbow deep in jam-making. 'Tell him to get himself over here for a decent meal. He doesn't look as if he's eating enough by half.'

Nina smiled. Always the mother, she thought.

It felt funny leaving the mill without Ziggy in tow, but she'd walk him later. Right now, she had to get to The Folly as quickly as possible. A London gallery, she thought, wondering what Dominic would think about it all. It had been hard not to blurt the news to Olivia, but it was Dominic's news – not hers.

This could really change things for him. Perhaps he'd want to move to London, Nina thought, her legs slicing through the long grass along the footpath. How would Olivia feel if that happened? There was a special bond between her and Dominic and it would break Olivia's heart if her youngest left for the big city. Billy was already there and Alex came and went like a whirling dervish. Sure, they popped by for the occasional weekend or Sunday lunch, but it was never the same as living nearby, was it?

Then again, Nina really couldn't imagine Dominic living anywhere near the capital. It might well suit Billy and Alex, but Dominic's home was in the gentle Norfolk countryside. Then there was The Folly. He'd poured himself into converting the place and it was very unlikely that he'd ever be able to afford a four-storey Victorian folly within the M25.

Nina gazed up at the mellow red-bricked home as she turned the corner. It rose up out of the trees like something out of a poem by Alfred Lord Tennyson. No, she thought. Dominic wouldn't be leaving here for a good while yet.

There was no answer when she rang the old-fashioned bell that Dominic had hung up outside the large wooden front door. She waited a moment, realising that it would take a good while for someone on the top floor to reach the ground floor, but she was still waiting a couple of minutes and two more bell pulls later. There was no letterbox; all of Dominic's mail went to the mill. Nina took a couple of steps back and gazed up into the air at the windows high above her.

'Dommie!' she called. 'Dominic?'

There was no reply so, not wanting to return with the letter, she tried the front door. It was unlocked.

'Hello?' she cried, opening the door and entering the front room. 'Dominic? Are you there?' She walked forward and peered up the staircase that led up the tower. 'I've got some post for you.'

She could have just left the post on the dining table and returned to the mill but, for the second time that day, curiosity got the better of Nina and she found herself walking up the stairs, her feet clanging musically on the spiral metal steps.

Up and up she went, but there was no Dominic, and Nina soon found herself on the top floor with the large picture window framing the barley field and the woods beyond so perfectly. She stood looking out at the view for a moment, noticing the curve of the river and the oak tree where she'd sat with Justin. She smiled, thinking of the ease of their conversation and wondering if she'd ever see him again. He hadn't been back to Norfolk since that night when he'd kissed her on the bridge and, although they'd been swapping the occasional text, it wasn't the same as face-to-face conversation, was it? And a text kiss just wasn't the same as the real thing, Nina couldn't help thinking.

She'd replayed that scene on the bridge a hundred times, each time wondering what he'd been thinking. Why hadn't he kissed her on the mouth? There was a part of her that was a little irked by his gentlemanliness and she couldn't help imagining what it would have been like if he'd kissed her properly in the inky darkness of a summer night, the sound of the rushing water beneath them. But had she really wanted that? Nina's mind was still reeling between her vow not to get involved with another man for a good long while and Janey's advice to let go and have some fun.

She shook her head and wondered what Justin was doing now and where was he doing it? His texts were always so short and vague and gave little away.

Can't make it back this weekend.

Got to go away again.

Last-minute booking. So sorry.

What did it all mean, she wondered? He was always talking about going away and last-minute bookings. Was he some sort of secret agent or just an estate agent? Nina sighed. She realized now that it hadn't been such a great idea to tell each other so little about themselves although, on reflection, he knew a lot more about her than she did him.

Putting Justin out of her mind once again, Nina turned back into the room. It was quite hot up there, but two of the smaller windows had been left open to allow the movement of air and to combat the ever-present smell of turps.

Her feet creaked over the bare floorboards. The walls of the room seemed to be closing in on themselves as there were canvases stacked up against them, and jars and brushes littered every available surface. Nina smiled. It was quite beautiful as messes went, she had to admit.

She walked into the centre of the room, looking around at the family of canvases that greeted her there. It wouldn't do any harm to have a little peep – just to see what Dominic had been up to over the last few weeks. He wouldn't mind, would he?

She crossed the room to the most promising-looking pile of canvases, wondering what she'd find there. There were far more paintings than he'd had sitters, but perhaps he made more than one painting of each lady, as Dudley wrote at least three different versions of each chapter of his novel. There was only one way to find out.

She blinked and turned to look through the neat row of canvases behind her. There was Edna Bowridge looking sweet in her pearls; Felicity Makepeace in her sexy silk number, and then there was another lady with friendly eyes and a pretty smile who must have been Maisie Myhill, but whom Nina hadn't met. Dominic had certainly been kept busy over the summer.

Next to them were a series of sketch-like paintings on hardboard. They were all of scenes around The Folly painted at different times of day, from the early morning summer mist to deeply burning sunsets. Each one was jewel-like in its beauty.

A little table stood against the wall in this part of the room and there was a sketch book on it. Nina's fingers trailed over it for a moment before opening it up, and what she saw made her gasp. Page after page, sketch after sketch.

'Faye!' she cried, her eyes widening in wonder at the beautiful drawings which, Nina guessed, must have been done from imagination rather than from life – for here was Faye dancing in the barley field, her arms stretching high above her, and here she was, sitting in the walled garden in what looked like a ballgown.

She smiled. Faye was not the sort of girl who you'd see in a dress unless it was a very special occasion, so it was very telling that Dominic had chosen to picture her wearing one.

She closed the sketch book and walked over to the easel and that's when she saw the painting of Faye that Dominic had been working on. Nina knew she shouldn't be there; shouldn't be looking at it, but – like with the sketch book – she just couldn't help herself. Her eyes scanned the dark hair, the childlike stare of the eyes and the pale pink skin. Faye was truly beautiful and Nina couldn't help but gasp at the vision that met her eyes. She knew at once that the artist who had painted such a picture and had filled such a sketch book must surely be in love with the subject. It wasn't just her imagination and it wasn't just wishful thinking. Dominic was falling in love with Faye all over again – she truly believed that.

Goodness, Nina thought with a smile. Had her little matchmaking plan really worked its magic?

Chapter Twenty-Six

It wasn't the response she'd expected. July had turned into August and things were moving ever-closer towards the anniversary party. Olivia was sitting, looking down at the tablecloth, a scowl threatening to wrinkle her immaculate make-up. She was in serious danger of being displeased with Dudley. It didn't happen very often, but she felt that it was about to happen right now.

'I'm not having Harry Barclay sitting anywhere near us,' Dudley growled, his face flaming red.

'Oh, for goodness' sake,' Olivia summoned up the courage to speak her piece, 'he used to be your best friend.'

'That was before he groped your bottom at our wedding reception.'

'Dudley – that was twenty-five years ago, and you know he'd had a few too many glasses of champagne. It must have gone to his head.'

'My fists should have gone to his head, too,' Dudley said, his face threatening to split like an overripe tomato.

'Well, he's been invited now. We can't *un*invite him.'

Dudley looked down at the printed list of guests, ready to assemble into neat little groups that wouldn't upset or offend anyone. Olivia watched as he surveyed the names, a smile replacing her frown as she thought of how Dudley had leapt to her honour at their wedding reception all those years ago. He could be so demonstrative sometimes. She wondered, briefly, if there might be a repeat performance at their anniversary party, but soon thought better of it. If Harry Barclay's hands strayed a second time, it would be the last for sure. Dudley wasn't a violent man, but Olivia shuddered to think what might happen if Harry raised Dudley's hackles again. No, she'd better listen to him.

'I suppose we could sit him near Aunt Harriet. Harry and Harriet might make a nice pairing,' Olivia said with a little laugh.

Dudley looked up from the paper. 'I'm not sitting my aunt near the marquee door.'

'Dudley – nobody's sitting near the marquee door.'

'Then where do you propose we put Harry?'

'Give that here,' Olivia said, snatching the sketch of the marquee Dominic had drawn for them. 'Look!' Olivia pointed with one of her pink talons.

Dudley harrumphed. 'I'll still have to look at him.'

'You'll have to look at everyone, Dud, that's the point of having a top table.'

'I still don't see why you invited him.'

'Because he's your oldest friend,' Olivia stressed.

'That's no excuse,' Dudley retorted. 'I didn't invite Hannah Forbes, did I?'

Olivia's eyes shot wide open. 'That's different.'

'Nothing different, as far as I can see.'

'Oh, Dudley. She practically ravished you! How could you expect me to want to invite *her*?' Olivia looked across at her husband, astonished that he'd even suggest such a

270

thing. 'You're laughing!' Olivia suddenly noticed that Dudley was chuckling to himself. 'What's so funny? 'Cause there's absolutely nothing funny about Hannah Forbes. I could smell her cheap perfume on you for *weeks* afterwards. I was surprised she even needed that mistletoe as an excuse. She'd been dying to get her claws into you for years.'

'But she was your chief bridesmaid,' Dudley said, still smiling.

'Yes, well, that was an error in judgement on my part,' Olivia conceded and then she sighed. Planning the party was supposed to be as much fun as the party itself, but this was awful. She wondered why she was so anxious for her sons to marry. Did she really didn't want to go through this charade three more times?

'So, what are we going to do about Harry Barclay? Dudley said.

'Oh, if it's really bothering you that much,' Olivia began, 'stick one of the floral displays in front of him so you don't have to look at each other.'

Dominic had opened the large picture window in the studio and the evening breeze had cooled the room. He could hear the sound of swallows wheeling over the field and the soothing rustle of the poplar leaves. All was calm. Apart from Faye.

'I feel so stiff,' she complained, rolling her shoulders back and stretching her neck from side to side.

'You're working too hard in the garden,' he said. 'Mum's taking advantage of you. You should tell her you're not up to all that manual work. She should have got a man in to do all that digging you've been doing.'

'Oh, you're so old-fashioned, Dom!' Faye said with a

giggle. 'I can manage perfectly well. I don't need a man. I can handle a spade as well as any man can.'

'Yes, but you're overdoing things,' he said, his face full of concern.

Faye stared at him, seeing a look in his face that she hadn't seen for years.

He cleared his throat and looked away. 'We can do this another time,' he continued, 'if you want.'

'No, no!' Faye said quickly. 'I want to do it now. It's just—' she rolled her shoulders again and, before he could stop himself, Dominic had crossed the room and was gently massaging her.

'You're all knotted up,' he said. 'It's like you've got rocks under your skin.'

Faye sighed. 'Oh – right there,' she said. 'Just – *there!*'

Dominic continued to massage, his long fingers finding the tender places between her shoulder blades. 'I think you need to see a professional and then give Mum the bill.'

'No – I'm fine,' Faye said.

'I don't think you're being paid enough to do this sort of damage to yourself.'

Faye turned around and Dominic's hands dropped to his side. His dark eyes looked anxious.

'It's nothing,' she said. 'I might just have been overdoing things a bit – that's all.'

'Yes, well, you don't want to do yourself in completely,' Dominic said and they gazed at each other for a moment longer than was necessary; as if totally aware that this was the first proper conversation they'd had in years and that it might be leading somewhere.

Faye blinked hard and Dominic cleared his throat again and turned away. 'Let's make a start, shall we?'

Faye didn't fidget that much during the session. She seemed to be more relaxed now and Dominic had picked up speed with the painting. The dreadful awkwardness that had hung so heavily between them when she'd first arrived at The Folly seemed to have disappeared. They were finally comfortable in one another's presence and yet, perversely, Dominic couldn't help feeling uncomfortable *because* of that. Sitting just a few feet in front of him was his first love and one of the best friends he had ever had – and he had thrown that all away. Discarded it, as if it had been a piece of cheap rubbish.

He shook his head. He couldn't be thinking about all that now. He had to finish the portrait. But it was too late. Faye had been watching him.

'Dom?' she said. 'Are you okay?'

He pursed his lips together. 'I'm fine,' he said, holding it all back.

'Do you want to talk about something?' Faye said, moving forward in her chair ever so slightly.

'Don't move!' he shouted.

'Sorry,' Faye said, inching back. 'It's just, I thought you looked like you were trying to say something.'

'What could I possibly have to say?' he said, his abrupt tone shocking even himself.

Faye blushed and Dominic silently cursed himself, because her colouring had changed, just as he was about to apply the finishing touches.

It was half an hour later that he put his brushes down and Faye stood up, stretching her arms above her head and yawning.

'Is it finished?'

Dominic nodded. 'As much as it can be,' he said.

'Can I see it?'

He nodded. 'Sure.'

Faye walked towards the easel. 'I'm actually quite nervous,' she said, inching closer to the canvas and to Dominic, who was hovering behind it like an anxious parent. 'Oh,' she said a moment later, the word dropping out of her mouth suddenly and almost silently.

'What?' Dominic sounded panic-stricken. 'You don't like it?'

'No,' Faye said.

'Oh God!' Dominic said.

'No – *no!*' Faye said. 'I didn't mean, "No, I don't like it". I meant "No, I don't *not* like it".'

'*What?*'

She turned to look at him. 'I love it!' she said, her eyes shining in the half-dark of the room.

'You do?'

'It's – I've never seen myself like that before,' she said. 'Do I really look like that?'

'You really look like that,' Dominic said. 'I've even managed to catch that fidget of yours.'

'Yes,' Faye said. 'I can see.' She stared at the portrait a moment longer. 'It's amazing. It's like looking in a really weird mirror that's reflecting back more than the image itself.'

Dominic smiled. 'That's a very good way of putting it.'

'You've captured – *something.*' Faye laughed. 'I'm finding it hard to explain.'

'You're explaining it perfectly well,' he said.

'Well, I must pay you,' she said, reaching for the handbag that she'd left at the side of the chair.

'No, Faye, you don't need to pay.'

'But I must pay you – it's hours of your time,' she insisted.

'No,' he said. 'You don't owe me anything.'

'But I really think I should pay you something,' Faye said.

Dominic shook his head. 'I owe you, Faye. I really do.'

Their eyes darted towards each other, meeting briefly before darting away again.

'Thank you,' Faye said at last.

'You're welcome,' Dominic replied.

Faye shrugged herself into her light denim jacket and placed a daisy-embroidered scarf around her neck. She took one last sweeping look around the room as if she knew she would never be invited back again.

'Well, I'd better get going,' she said, making towards the top of the spiral staircase.

'I'll walk you back,' Dominic said, following her down the stairs.

'There's no need,' Faye told him, but he left The Folly with her all the same and she didn't try to protest again.

The evening air was cool after the heat of the day and they walked towards the mill through the dusky fields, a pair of deer startling them as they bounded across the field towards the wood. The sky was a milky violet and the pale beginnings of a moon broke through the clouds.

Dominic inhaled deeply. He loved summer – he loved all the seasons – but summer was very special to him; its long luxurious hours meaning he could spend even more time than usual behind his easel in the surrounding fields. Winter was always so depressing for a plein air painter who relied on the great outdoors for inspiration and so he always worked long hours during the summer, painting until the sunset and the evening breeze chased him indoors.

'There's a gallery in London that wants to show my work,' he suddenly said, deciding to share his piece of news with Faye.

'Oh, that's marvellous, Dom! I'm so pleased for you,' she said, turning to look at him.

They continued walking side by side and then changed to one behind the other as the path narrowed, their feet soft on the hard-baked earth, which had recently cracked from lack of rain.

'You won't be moving there, will you?' Faye suddenly asked, anxiety in her voice.

'Why would I want to do that?' he said, startled by her question.

'Well, I thought you might be tempted – if that's where your future lies.'

'It's just a few paintings – probably only half a dozen a year,' he said. 'I'll get the train and be back home to paint the fields by evening.'

Faye smiled at the image he created. 'I couldn't live anywhere else – not ever,' she said. 'Could you?'

'No,' he said simply. 'I think I'll be tied to this place all my life.'

'Well, it's a very good place to be tied to,' she said. Suddenly, she giggled, a delicious sound that seemed to bubble out of the very centre of her.

'What?' Dominic said.

'I was just thinking about how miserable I was when I first left home for college. I *hated* it! I was so homesick all the time. I once even pretended to be ill just so I could come home in the middle of term.'

'I didn't know,' Dominic said.

'No,' Faye said, quite sure that Dominic was blushing in

the twilight. It had been about the time that he'd stopped communicating with her. 'Anyway, I knew then that I could never live anywhere else. I really thought I'd be more adventurous when I left school and would want to see something of the world, but I'm just happy being here. Does that sound really dull and boring?'

'No!' Dominic said. 'It sounds honest and—' he paused.

'What?'

'Very you. You always were happiest at home with your family and your garden. Are you still at Meads Cottage?'

'Oh, yes,' Faye said. 'Mum and Dad will never move, either. I'm betting they'll be there forever.'

'And you and Harry, too?'

Faye laughed. 'No, Harry left last year. He's got a little flat near Carrow Road now.'

'Oh, right,' Dominic said, thinking of Faye's older brother. 'And everyone's well?'

They'd reached the bridge in front of the mill and there was a warm glow of lamplight from the living room, but Dominic and Faye were still hidden in the shadows. They stopped walking for a minute, the cool night air wrapping around them.

'Everyone's fine, thank you.' Faye nodded. 'Dominic?'

'Yes?'

'Why all these questions?'

'What do you mean?' he asked.

'I mean, you haven't done more than grunt at me for the last three years – why all the interest now?' She looked up at him in the darkness, the faintest glimmer of moonlight on his face.

'I was just being—'

'Don't say polite,' Faye said. '*Please* don't say you were just being polite!'

'Faye—'

'Because I couldn't stand that. I couldn't bear you to be making light conversation if this wasn't going somewhere.' Her voice sounded strained, as if she was holding back tears.

'Faye!' Dominic cried.

'What?' she said.

But how could he say it? How could he heave his heart up into his mouth and tell her how he felt about her? It was such a surprising, wondrous feeling, one that had been sneaking up on him for a while now. He shook his head. He'd been so convinced that he was falling in love with Nina, but that had been nothing more than a passing crush – some kind of summer madness, perhaps. But all the time, the *real* thing had been staring him in the face.

He swallowed hard. 'You're not making things very easy!' he said. 'I'm not just being polite! I'm trying to—'

'What?' Faye said, her voice quiet now, but no less desperate.

'I'm trying to—'

'Dominic?' A voice suddenly called from the door of the mill house. Olivia's voice. 'Is that you?'

'It's just us, Mum!' Dominic shouted back.

'Have you got Faye with you?' Olivia called, desperate to be heard above the rush of water.

'I'm here, Mrs Milton!' Faye cried.

'We were getting worried about you!' Olivia said, stepping out into the night in her ballet pump-style slippers. 'We saw your car was still here and thought you might have collapsed under the rhubarb bush or something. We sent

278

Ziggy out into the garden to find you, but he only came back with a disgusting old bone he'd dug up from somewhere.'

A little giggle escaped Faye, and Dominic couldn't help but smile as the two of them left the sanctuary of the bridge and walked towards the driveway, where Faye's little car waited to take her home.

'Well, I'll leave you two to it,' Olivia said as they were illuminated by the light streaming out of the front door.

Faye walked over to her car and fished around in her handbag for her keys. 'I'd better get going,' she said, opening the door.

'Faye?' Dominic said.

'Yes?' She paused, half in, half out of the car.

'I had a nice evening,' he said.

'Me too,' she said, their eyes meeting, wondering. 'Dominic?'

'Yes?'

'Were you going to say anything – on the bridge?'

'On the bridge?'

'Yes – before your mum opened the door.'

He paused for a moment before answering. 'No,' he said at last. 'It was nothing.'

'Really?' Faye said, not bothering to hide her disappointment.

Dominic nodded and watched as she got into her car and drove off into the night.

That night, Olivia was sitting up in bed, folding and unfolding the arms of her reading glasses whilst chewing her lip. Her mind was a tempest of activity as she went over the events of that evening, seeing – once again – the image of her son and Faye standing on the bridge together. What had they been doing, she wondered? What exactly had she interrupted?

'Livvy!' Dudley's voice came from somewhere underneath the duvet.

'What, darling? I thought you were asleep,' she said.

'I'm trying to bloody sleep but you're keeping me awake with your infernal twitching! Now put those glasses down and get some rest.'

Olivia sighed and looked at the little clock on her bedside table. It was after midnight, but she knew her mind was too full for it to invite sleep in. Still, she placed her reading glasses by her book and switched off the lamp, snuggling down into bed.

'Dudley,' she whispered a moment later. 'DUDLEY!'

'Whaaaaat?' Dudley groaned, rolling over in bed to face his wife. 'For heavens' sake, Livvy – get some sleep.'

'I can't!' she replied, 'and I don't know how you can, either.'

Dudley made a sound as if he was deflating. Perhaps he realised he wasn't going to get any sleep until he'd fully participated in a midnight conversation.

'What's going on?' he asked under sufferance.

Olivia propped herself up on an elbow and sighed into the darkness. 'This evening, I was getting worried about Faye. Her car was still in our driveway, you see, but she'd finished work hours before. I was keeping an eye on it, thinking she might have gone for a walk or something, but it wasn't until late that she turned up – with Dominic.'

'Right,' Dudley said.

'So, what were they doing?' Olivia asked in exasperation.

'What do you mean?'

'I mean, what where they doing out there on the bridge in the middle of the night?'

'I have absolutely no idea,' Dudley said with a weary sigh.

'Put it this way – I *don't* think they were discussing my herbaceous border. But what puzzles me is that I thought Dommie had a crush on Nina.'

'Nina? Our Dom?'

'Yes!' she said. 'He's so tongue-tied and bashful around her.'

'Is he?'

'Yes, he is,' she said. 'What do you think's going on? I really have to find out.'

'Livvy – you can't expect to know what's going on all the time.'

'Why not?' she asked.

'Because our boys have to have some privacy. They're grown men now. You have to let them have a bit of personal space.'

'Personal space?' Olivia said the words as if they were quite foreign to her.

'Yes – let them get on with things and don't be worrying about them every five minutes.'

She sighed. It wasn't the same for fathers was it?, she thought. Dudley had stopped worrying about his sons almost as soon as they were upright and walking, but a mother continued to worry – it never went away. It was also obvious to her that Dudley didn't really care what was going on right under his nose. It didn't matter whom his sons were seeing or not seeing. Well, *she* cared, and she was quite determined to find out what was going on.

'I definitely interrupted something,' she said. 'If only I

hadn't opened the door and charged out into the night like that. I feel quite sure something was going on. What if he'd been about to kiss her? Or propose to her – and I ruined it?'

'You're letting that imagination of yours get carried away again. They were probably just talking about—'

'What? *What* on earth could they have been talking about in the middle of the night?'

Dudley made another deflating sort of noise.

'And then there's this business with Nina and Alex,' Olivia went on.

'What business?' Dudley said, suddenly very much awake again at the mention of his secretary.

'I'm absolutely *positive* something's going on there. Has she said anything to you?'

'About Alex?' Dudley said.

'*Yes*, about Alex.'

'No,' Dudley said, wrestling with his pillow. 'Why would she say anything to me? What's been going on?'

'Well, that's what I'm trying to find out. Something's going on between them.'

'Livvy – you've really got to rein in that imagination of yours. It'll all come to no good.'

'Oh, stop being so melodramatic. I have a right to know what's going on under my own roof.'

'Well, probably nothing much. You're more than likely imagining the whole thing.'

'You think so?'

'I know so,' Dudley said. 'Our sons only have to drop a girl's name into a casual conversation and you're planning what to wear to their first-born's christening.'

'That's *so* untrue!' Olivia said.

'Oh no it's not and you know it!' he said and he sighed again. 'Really, you've just got to let them get on with things in their own time. You can't keep building things up in your own mind and then being disappointed. Now,' he said, 'I'm going to sleep and I suggest you do the same.'

Olivia shook her head. She was quite determined to find out what was going on – and if that meant cross-questioning Nina about it then so be it. She wasn't building things up in her own mind. *Some*thing was going on, she was sure of it, and Dudley would jolly well apologise to her when she proved him wrong.

Chapter Twenty-Seven

'Don't forget that I've booked you for tomorrow,' Olivia said, popping her head round the study door just as Dudley was in full dictation mode.

'Booked me?' Nina said, looking up in surprise.

'Yes,' Olivia said, eyes bright. 'We're off to London for a spot of shopping – just the two of us.' She held Nina's gaze for a moment. 'Don't say you've forgotten!'

Nina's mind somersaulted back over the last few days. Not once had Olivia said anything about a trip to London. She would definitely have remembered if she had. She looked across the room at Dudley, who simply shrugged in resignation. He obviously wasn't going to put up a fight. A man could never beat a woman when it came to shopping, it seemed.

'We'll be leaving first thing in the morning,' Olivia added.

'Fine,' Nina said. 'I'm looking forward to it.' But she wasn't. Not really. For a while now, Olivia had been a little cool towards her. Nina thought it dated back to when Alex had stormed out after telling her how he felt about her. Did Olivia know what had been going on between her and her sons? Or did she at least suspect?

Was this confrontation time?

She sighed and got back to the job in hand. Dudley had recently started to dictate passages of his book directly to Nina. It was a new way of working for them and showed an incredible amount of trust on the part of Dudley; he obviously felt comfortable enough with Nina to work that way with her – to be in the first creative flush and have her transcribe his thoughts straight from his imagination. For Nina, it was absolutely fascinating. Not only did she bypass the stage of having to decipher Dudley's appalling handwriting, but she also gained an insight into the creative process. The only trouble was trying to keep up with him. She was a pretty fast typist, but Dudley in full flow was something to behold.

'How much have we got?' he barked across the room as soon as Olivia had gone.

'Three pages,' Nina told him.

'What do you think of the ending? Enough of a cliff-hanger for that chapter?'

'Oh, I think so,' she told him honestly. '*I'd* want to read on.'

'Nina,' he said, looking thoughtful, his fingertips together below his chin.

'Yes?'

'I can't tell you what a great help you've been. All this would have taken me – well – I can't think how long it would have taken me. I would probably still have been writing this book after our *fiftieth* wedding anniversary.'

'I'm sure you would have found a way,' she told him.

'But not such a pleasant one,' he said.

Nina swallowed hard. Ever since she had begun work at the mill, she had been aware that her time there was limited, and hearing Dudley now almost brought tears to her eyes. She had never worked in a place where she had felt so valued – but he wasn't going to say the words that she so longed to hear, was he?

Stay, Nina. Stay on as my permanent assistant. I can't think of continuing without you.

No, he didn't say those words, and so Nina did her best to enjoy the moment and not think about the uncertain future that lay ahead.

Olivia made sure that they made an early start to London, but they hadn't even made it to Thetford before she brought up the subject of her sons. It started innocently enough. Nina was sitting as quietly as possible in the passenger seat of Olivia's Volvo when she sighed.

'Don't ever become a mother, Nina,' she said. 'Or, at least, a mother of three boys.' She drummed her burgundy nails on the steering wheel. 'Why would anyone want to have three boys?' She took her eyes off the road briefly to look at Nina, a hint of humour taking the edge off her question. 'I swear they're more trouble than girls. What do you think?' Olivia asked.

Nina cleared her throat. 'Well – er – I wouldn't know.'

'Do you have brothers?'

'No. I'm an only child,' she said.

'Oh, yes. Sorry, I'd forgotten,' Olivia smiled an apology. 'But you're lucky in a way. I was one of four and it was nothing but fight, fight, fight. We all get along screamingly now, of course, but that's because we don't have to share a house, clothes and the same bath water.'

'But the boys get on okay, don't they?' Nina said, surprised that she, too, was referring to them as boys, despite having somehow become romantically involved with two of them.

'I'm not sure,' she said through gritted teeth. 'I sense there's a bit of tension at the moment. Whenever Alex and Dommie are together, they always seem to be fighting with one another and that's not normal. Of course, they've always teased one another – that's what brothers do – but it's more than that this time, and I need to know what's going on!'

Oh, dear, Nina thought. They weren't terribly far from Grime's Graves and Nina had a vision of Olivia throwing her down one of the Neolithic flint mines if she were to confess being the root cause of tension between Alex and Dominic. Or, at the very least, she could be thrown out of her job at the mill.

'I haven't heard from Alex for an absolute age,' Olivia said. 'Not since—' she paused. Was she expecting Nina to fill in the gaps?

'But he'll be back for the party, won't he?' Nina said, anxious that she might have driven him away at such an important time.

'Oh yes – no doubt – but it would be nice to see a bit more of him. But I expect he's keeping himself busy in London. We might even see him today!' Olivia sounded cheerful at the thought.

Nina fidgeted in her seat. The last thing she wanted was to run into Alex when she was with his mother. That would be really awkward.

'So, where are we going to start shopping?' Nina asked, eager to change the subject.

'Why not be really ambitious and make for Knightsbridge?'

'Harrods?'

'Start at the top and work your way down! That's what I always say,' Olivia smiled. 'I want something devastatingly elegant for the party in silver. But Dudley won't know if I've spent fifty pounds or five-hundred pounds. So we can keep this little treat just between the two of us. Plus, we must get something for you, too.'

'Me?' Nina asked in surprise.

'Of course! You're one of our special guests, Nina. I think a beautiful shade of raspberry for you. Blondes always look stunning in red. I'm sure my boys won't be able to resist you.'

Nina's eyes widened at Olivia's words. Were they deliberately provocative? Was she expecting a confession from her on this outing? Was that the real reason behind it?

'I know the perfect place to leave the car. We can catch the tube in – much easier. I always love the excitement of the tube, don't you?'

When they reached London, Olivia parked the car in a leafy, suburban avenue that she knew from her days as a student. The tube station wasn't far and they were soon moling about on the underground; dodging and dancing around commuters and consumers. Nina couldn't help feeling nervous at the experience, even though it wasn't her first time on the tube. She'd always been a little claustrophobic, but tried not to think how far below ground they were as they stood at the top of an escalator.

'Isn't this fun?' Olivia enthused. Nina nodded back, her face white with fear.

They reached the bottom and Nina would have fallen over her own feet if Olivia hadn't caught her by the shoulders.

'Are you all right, Nina, dear?'

'Erm – I'm fine,' Nina said quietly. 'It's just that I get a bit nervous underground.'

'Well, don't worry. Stick close by me,' Olivia said, 'and just think of it as an adventure.'

Nina smiled hesitantly, unable to shake the thought that Olivia hadn't quite finished her cross-questioning of her yet.

The evening dresses in Harrods could not be described as anything other than elegant. One in particular that caught Olivia's eye was a streamlined, silver backless number, as fine as gossamer. Unfortunately, the price wasn't streamlined. Olivia picked up the price tag and dropped it as if it had burnt her fingers.

'Can I help you?' a leggy assistant with palomino-blonde hair approached them.

'We'll let you know when you can, thank you,' Olivia smiled. The young assistant looked down her aquiline nose and clicked her tongue before walking over to a more promising-looking customer.

'Who does she think she is?' Nina said, infuriated.

'Nina – she's a shop assistant. Just remember that. We're the customers – the ones with the money to spend here.'

'Not enough though, I fear,' Nina said, picking up another price tag at random and grimacing at it.

'I know,' Olivia sighed, 'but she doesn't know that, does she? Just stick your nose in the air and keep saying the word "haughty" to yourself.'

Nina giggled, but still couldn't help feeling that the assistant knew exactly how much money they didn't have in their handbags.

'Come on – let's get out of here,' Olivia said, after

looking at another price tag with more figures than a phone number.

Three hours later, they left the changing rooms of a shop on Bond Street with two perfectly beautiful gowns at a fraction of the price, yet still with a carrier bag worthy of having driven all the way to London.

Olivia had found her dress in a skin-like silver fabric and Nina had opted for a simple cocktail dress in a dark crimson. Olivia had thrown a piece of plastic over the counter and insisted that Nina thought nothing of it.

After an overpriced sandwich and cup of coffee in a cafe off Oxford Street, they headed towards the tube before the rush hour. Nina was just beginning to breathe easily after having managed to dodge Alex all day when Olivia suddenly shouted his name as they were crossing the road.

'Where?' Nina said aghast, her eyes scanning the length of the street.

'No – I was just thinking – this is where Alex had his first job after leaving college. See that building there, with all the dark glass?'

Nina peered up at the windows, anxious that Alex might be glaring down at her.

'Come on,' Olivia said, sighing heavily, 'let's go home.'

Thankfully, it didn't take them long to leave the great metropolis behind them and find their way back to the leafy avenue where they'd left the car.

'Mission accomplished!' Olivia declared as they got in the car. 'Well, almost.'

Nina looked at her. 'Have you forgotten something?'

'No, not exactly,' Olivia said.

'What is it?' she asked her.

Olivia turned her eyes to her passenger. 'Nina, you know I think of you almost as a daughter,' she paused.

'But?' Nina suggested, her heart hammering in her chest. Had the moment for the confrontation come at last?

'Yes, there is a but,' Olivia admitted. 'We all love having you at the mill and we'd hate to lose you before the end of the summer, but I do realise that it might be necessary.'

Nina frowned. What could Olivia mean? 'I don't understand,' she said.

'I think you do,' Olivia said quietly. 'I have an idea of what's been going on – between you and Dominic. I mean, I've seen the way he looks at you.'

Nina quickly shook her head. 'Oh, no – Olivia! Nothing's going on.'

Olivia frowned as if she couldn't quite believe she might have got things wrong. 'Nothing?' she blurted. 'Are you sure?'

Nina was surprised by the question. 'Of course I'm sure. I'm absolutely positive. There is nothing going on between me and Dominic, I promise you.'

'But he's always hanging around, he's always asking questions about you and I've seen the way he looks at you. Don't deny it. You must know how he feels about you!'

Nina sighed. 'Olivia, trust me, nothing is going on. I admit, at first, Dominic might have had a bit of a crush on me, but I told him I didn't feel the same way.'

'You did?' She took her eyes off the road for a moment and looked at Nina.

'I don't think I could ever be involved with Dominic, even though he's one of the sweetest boys – men – I've ever met.' Nina gave a little laugh. 'You see – I still think of him as that little boy I used to babysit, and no amount of growing up will ever be able to shake that image from my mind.'

Olivia nodded. 'Well I'm very glad to hear it, because you know I'm hoping he'll see the light and get back together with Faye sometime soon and I'd hate for anything to happen to prevent that. They really are meant to be together, don't you think?'

Nina nodded. 'I do,' she said. 'In fact, I've been encouraging that myself.'

Olivia gasped in surprise at this news. 'You have?'

Nina smiled. 'Faye would take him back tomorrow – we both know that.'

'Yes!' Olivia said.

'So, I kind of set them up. I told Faye that Dominic wanted to paint her.'

'And that's why she was coming back from The Folly the other night?' Olivia said.

'I expect so,' Nina said.

'Then you might be onto something,' Olivia said. 'I saw them together on the bridge in the dark and I'm certain Dominic was almost about to kiss her.'

'Really?' Nina said. 'Then why did you think he was interested in me?'

Olivia shook her head. 'Oh, this is all so confusing. I really don't know what on earth is going on with you young ones!'

'But I can assure you that nothing is going on between me and Dominic,' Nina said again.

Olivia took a deep breath. 'So, what's going on with you and Alex, then? I presume something *is* going on there?'

Nina bit her lip. She was on the verge of hiccups but managed to suppress them. She'd never been interrogated like this before and couldn't help feeling horribly guilty, even though she was quite sure that she had nothing to feel guilty about.

'Have you been seeing Alex?' Olivia continued.

'No,' Nina said. 'Not really. We went out a couple of times. I really shouldn't have, but he's hard to say no to.'

'Yes,' Olivia said knowingly. 'I know a lot of girls who have had trouble saying no to our Alex.'

'But it's over now. I mean, it never really began,' Nina said, wincing at how she must be coming across to Olivia.

'So, Dominic was in love with you, but—'

'I wouldn't say in love,' Nina interrupted. 'Not really.'

Olivia nodded. 'Well, a massive crush, then? Is that what we're calling it?'

Nina didn't know what to say and so said nothing.

'And I suspect that Alex declared his undying love for you in the kitchen that day, didn't he?' Olivia went on.

'Oh, I wouldn't put it like that,' Nina said.

'No?' Olivia took her eyes off the road again. 'How would you put it?'

Nina stared at Olivia in dismay. What on earth could she possibly say? She knew she'd brought this situation on herself and she felt truly awful about it, but she couldn't seem to find the words to explain her way out of the terrible muddle she now found herself in.

'I'm so sorry, Olivia,' she said at last. 'I never meant to cause any trouble.'

'My darling Nina – you are *just* the sort of girl I would pick out for one of my boys. You really are.' Her voice seemed gentler now and Nina hoped that Olivia was in the process of forgiving her. 'But my boys are – well, my boys, and I can't bear to see them unhappy.'

'And I wouldn't want to make them unhappy – really I wouldn't. They still mean the world to me.'

'Do they?' Olivia asked.

'Of course they do. Your whole family is so precious to me and I'd never do anything to hurt any of you.'

Olivia sighed. 'I know you wouldn't, Nina,' she said.

'But, if you think ill of me, I'll perfectly understand if you want to find a replacement secretary for Dudley,' Nina said, blinking back tears that were threatening to spill at the thought of leaving The Old Mill House even earlier than anticipated.

'Leave? Are you *mad*? I don't want you to leave!' she cried, much to Nina's relief. 'We all *adore* having you at the mill. It's just that I've been trying to find out what on earth's been going on. Nobody tells me anything – not when it comes to matters of the heart, anyway, and I do like to be kept informed about these sorts of things.'

Nina gave a little smile. 'Then we're friends?'

'Of *course* we're friends. The very best of friends, in fact. Anyone who can handle my Dudley is right up there in my books, and anyone who can handle Ziggy deserves a medal. Anyway, you can't possibly think of leaving just yet – because I want to see you in that gorgeous party dress!'

Nina laughed in relief. She was staying. For the time being at least.

Chapter Twenty-Eight

It was a week after her trip to London with Olivia and, after a morning of typing up Dudley's notes for a rather convoluted in-depth plot synopsis for his novel, Nina's eyes felt sore. She needed a break and the best place for that was the garden.

As she opened the back door and stepped out into the sunshine, she realised that she was fast becoming dependent on being able to do this – to work quietly in a beautiful Georgian house with a boss who pretty much let her get on with things, and being able to wander freely around the gardens when she wanted. Gardens that she had now fallen in love with. There was the warm wooden bench with the flaking blue paint that she liked to sit on mid-morning when it received the full glory of the sunshine, and there was the ornate white metal bench under the beech tree, which was lovely in the afternoon when it provided a dappled shade to cool sun-warmed limbs.

The Old Mill House was going to be a very hard place to leave, Nina realised. It was the thought that was occupying more and more of her mind as summer rolled on towards the day when she would no longer be needed there. August had seemed an age away when Nina had arrived at the mill but, now that the party was just a few days away and Dudley's novel was drawing to a close, where would that leave her? Back at the recruitment agency? Back at Mr Briggs' flat? Back to being on her own again?

She'd got used to being a part of the mad, chaotic world of the mill. What would she do without Olivia and Ziggy? How would she survive without Dudley's daily dictation of romance?

She felt she'd really grown since she'd left the wicked clutches of Hilary Jackson. Janey had been right. There'd been more to Nina than taking orders from a bad-tempered battleaxe whose idea of being a good boss was letting her employees go home only half an hour late. Her post at the mill might only have been short-term, but it had let her redefine herself. It had shown Nina that she could be paid for a job and be appreciated at the same time, and she would miss that if she left.

Walking across the velvet-soft grass, she pulled out her mobile from the pocket of her jeans, but there was only a message from Janey.

Any news, stranger? x

Nope! x Nina texted back. And it was true. She hadn't heard from Justin for three days now. They had been sending each other the usual little texts about day-to-day life and Nina had been keeping him up to date with Ziggy's antics and the progress of Dudley's novel. But she couldn't help feeling disappointed that she hadn't actually seen him recently.

Everything's up in the air at work he'd told her. *I can't get back to Norfolk. Miss you. x*

Nina didn't know what to think and, the longer she went without seeing him, the more she felt sure that nothing was going to happen between them – a thought that made her sad.

She looked down at her phone now and the last message she'd received from him.

Miss you. x

She'd texted him back. *Miss you, too* and her finger had hovered over the 'x' for a good long time before she sent the message without it.

It was just as she was putting her phone away that she spied Faye bent double over a clump of some kind of flower Nina couldn't ever hope of recognising. It felt like an age since she'd last had a good chat with her, and Nina was desperate to find out what had been happening with her and Dominic.

'They're all falling over,' Faye said as she saw Nina approach. 'I'll have to stake them.'

'They're lovely,' Nina said, admiring the enormous scarlet blooms.

'High maintenance, though,' Faye said.

'A lot of beautiful things are,' Nina said.

Faye laughed. 'Like one of my old school friends that I met up with last night. She couldn't stop looking at my grubby fingernails,' Faye said. 'Look!' She held out her small hands for Nina to examine. The nails were short and neatly rounded, but there was a fair amount of dirt underneath them. 'This is just from this morning. I did clean them last night but Sara wouldn't believe me. She kept showing me hers, which she'd just had done, and insisted that I went along to see her girl. "She's an absolute wonder!" she kept saying, but Sara's nails look like some kind of medieval torture that you'd threaten traitors with at the Tower of London.'

Nina laughed, surreptitiously looking down at her own short but neat nails. They were practical rather than pretty, serving her well for her hours at the keyboard.

She watched as Faye crouched down to remove some weeds.

'How's the portrait-sitting going?' Nina asked, desperate to know what had been going on since she'd set up the rendezvous between the ex-lovebirds.

'Oh, that's all over,' Faye said and there was a hint of disappointment in her voice.

'All over?' Nina said, feeling her friend's disappointment and unable to disguise her own, too.

Faye nodded and wiped her dusty hands down the front of her trousers. 'It all happened so quickly. It was only three sessions and I had to fit it around Dominic's Country Circle portraits and his preparations for his show in Norwich.'

'So—' Nina paused. What was she going to say? 'You're not seeing him again?'

The two women exchanged looks.

'He didn't say anything,' Faye said. 'I kept thinking he was on the verge of saying something, you know?'

Nina nodded.

'If only we'd had more time. If only—' Faye stopped.

'What?'

She shook her head. 'It's useless,' she said. 'There's never going to be a Dominic and me. I think our relationship is doomed.'

'Don't say that!' Nina said.

'But it is. I never really believed we'd get back together – didn't even think I wanted to – but, when I was with him at The Folly, I couldn't help but wonder what it would be like. I mean, I know Olivia's always trying to push us back together, but I don't want to push him, too. That's probably how I lost him in the first place. I was always on at him to email me, text me, phone me.'

'But that's only natural when you care about someone,' Nina said.

'But I think I pushed him away,' Faye said, shaking her head, 'and I'm never going to make that mistake again.' She picked up the large silver garden fork that had been standing up in the flower bed beside her and thrust it into the dry soil. 'I'm being philosophical about this,' she continued. 'I'm going to leave things alone. If they're meant to be, then it'll happen – but I'm not pushing. I'm not going to try and force things.'

Nina watched in awe as she stabbed the earth repeatedly with the fork and, as much as she couldn't help wanting to meddle and to – well – push, she decided that she couldn't really argue with a girl who had such command over her garden tools.

Chapter Twenty-Nine

'It's these last few chapters. I can't seem to get them right.' Dudley stopped pacing the length of the study and banged his empty pipe on his desk. 'I've got to make them more exciting.' He cleared his throat. 'At the moment, they're about as gripping as a dead hand.'

Nina looked up from her computer, but her eyes were so blurry that she couldn't quite focus on him. It was the end of the day and they'd been working so hard that she felt sure she could no longer type straight.

'This whole thing is ridiculous. Who am I trying to fool? It's all a waste of time,' Dudley said in the sort of way that begged for somebody to contradict him. But Nina didn't even hear him. 'Nina?' He looked across at her. 'Are you all right?'

'I'm fine,' she said, managing a weak smile for a second, but Dudley wasn't taken in by it. He pinched his great white moustache and stood up, after having only just sat down.

'Tell you what,' he said, clearing his throat, 'it's gone five o'clock. Why don't we break for today and come back fresh to it first thing tomorrow? I have to go into town anyway.' He got up and left the room without further explanation.

Nina remained seated, staring at her computer screen, blinking every now and then and wincing at the tightness of her eyelids.

Dudley must have given himself the deadline of the anniversary party by which to finish his novel, because Nina spent the next two days typing solidly. The pace of his story had picked up considerably as the end came into sight and Nina found the task enjoyable, if a little exhausting on the eyes, wrists and shoulders. It was a wonder her fingers didn't bleed from the speed at which they ran over the keyboard, particularly when Dudley stood over her, dictating great chunks of dialogue that moved faster than a Quentin Tarantino movie – only a little less violent. This *was* a romance he was writing, after all.

But at last, Nina got to type the two words she'd never had the pleasure of typing before: The End. An immense satisfaction filled her as she stretched her arms high above her head and blinked several times to clear the fog that had developed over her eyes from looking at the white screen for so long.

Dudley crashed down into his chair at the other side of the study and lit his pipe. Nina had got accustomed to the scent. He tried not to smoke too much when he was in the room, and would often stride around the garden when he needed a puff, his smoke drifting hazily to mingle with the honeysuckle, but he looked as if a walk in the garden might just finish him off after the day's exertion.

'Will it do?' Dudley asked, in an uncharacteristically anxious voice.

'Yes,' Nina said, nodding. 'It's wonderful. Congratulations.' She smiled, a feeling of intense pride filling her at having been part of such an exciting journey. 'It's a really wonderful story and I'm sure you're going to get it published and make thousands of readers very happy.'

Dudley shook his head in astonishment. 'Readers!' he said. 'I can't ever imagine that my little book will ever be read by anyone who isn't in this very room!'

Nina smiled as he shook his head in bewilderment. 'I know we've not heard back from anyone we've sent your opening chapters to yet, but I truly think it's only a matter of time before somebody snaps it up.'

'Do you?' Dudley looked genuinely surprised by this declaration.

Nina nodded. 'They'd be mad not to.'

She spent the rest of the day tidying around. There were odd bits of paperwork lying about that had been overlooked in Dudley's haste to finish his novel. Nina remembered with affection the first time she'd seen the study. Now, there wasn't an untidy work surface in sight. Everything had a home. It was just a pity, Nina thought, that it wasn't to be hers for much longer.

That evening, the air was cool but felt delicious after the unrelenting heat of the day, and Nina felt invigorated by it as she walked along the riverbank with Ziggy by her side. She walked like she'd never walked before; sucking in great lungfuls of air; swinging her arms as if she were on an army march, her legs slicing through the grass. She listened to the wind playing its strange melody through the trees, and watched the swallows dancing in the dusk.

She turned back to look at the house. It looked picture-perfect from across the river. Everything about it suggested peace – and yet her brief time there had been anything but peaceful. She'd managed to upset Dominic by not returning his affections, she'd failed in bringing him and Faye back together again, she'd annoyed Alex and unwittingly sent him packing and she'd made Olivia suspicious of her motives, causing the awfully embarrassing scene between them on the way back from London.

Perhaps it would be better if she just left, Nina thought, closing her eyes on the scene before her. It would be best to go before the party too. Then the Miltons could all get back to their lives without Nina's own special brand of chaos ruining everything.

'At least I didn't upset you, Ziggy!' she said, bending down to stroke his curly-haired head, her heart aching at the thought of having to leave her furry ward behind, too. What would she do without her daily dog walks? She smiled as she remembered her horror at the thought of being in charge of the mad Labradoodle, but how quickly she had bonded with him. They were true friends and the thought of not seeing him again was more than she could bear.

Blinking the tears from her eyes, Nina walked back to the house, letting Ziggy off his lead when he was in the hallway and inhaling the familiar scent of the house that she'd got so used to over the last three months. A wonderful mix of old wood, furniture polish, Olivia's flowers picked fresh from the garden and the scent of her ever-present perfume, as well as Dudley's earthy tobacco.

'Is that you, Nina?' Olivia called from the living room. 'Come and have a drink. We have Pimms!'

Nina smiled. For tonight, at least, she was still very much a part of the family.

Chapter Thirty

Simon Hudson was taking a look at the paintings Dominic had delivered to the gallery they were hiring together in Tombland for their group exhibition at the end of the month.

'Blimey, Dom – these are seriously good,' he said.

'You think?' Dominic said, seeming genuinely surprised.

'Sure,' Simon replied, 'don't you?'

Dominic shrugged. 'I can't see them any more to judge them.'

Simon gave a laugh. 'Take it from me – they're good.' He lifted one up from the floor and took it over to the large window, which looked out onto a cobbled street. The painting was a view along the river from The Folly, captured earlier in the year when the cow parsley had frothed its way along the bank.

'Nobody paints landscapes like you,' Simon said. 'You've just got a way of capturing the light that I've never seen before.'

Dominic gave a self-deprecating sort of a smile.

'Why can't I paint like you?' he asked.

'Because you paint like *you*,' Dominic said. Simon's style was abstract. He favoured bold colours and angular shapes, even if there weren't any directly in front of him. Dominic often thought that that was a wonderful way to see the world. He'd painted like that for as long as Dominic had known him. They'd met on a day course in plein air painting, which had taken place on a farm out towards the coast. Dominic's paintings had been representative and lucid; Simon's had been abstract and heady.

'I bet you're going to sell out,' Simon said.

'Would be nice,' Dominic said. 'Although I'd settle for getting noticed.'

Simon nodded. 'I've still got a massive student loan to pay off,' he said.

'Well, I've notified all the newspapers and magazines, and the mailing list was pretty extensive,' Dominic said. 'We just have to keep our fingers crossed that the show's a success. I'm hoping the other gallery owners I got in touch with show an interest.'

'And go on to represent our work and take us to the top?'

'Something like that,' Dominic said with a grin.

They talked about the perils of being a poor artist for a while, wondering if they should have studied something sensible like law or medicine, when Simon suddenly said, 'Isn't that Faye?'

'Where?' Dominic asked.

'Just outside,' Simon said, looking out of the window onto the cobbled street. 'She's heading up there.'

Before he knew what he was doing, Dominic put down the painting he was holding and was out of the door before he could explain himself, running in the direction in which Simon had pointed.

The streets were maze-like in this part of town and there

were any number of places she could have dived into but Dominic was determined to find her – even if he wasn't actually sure what he was going to say if he did catch up with her. He only knew that he *had* to speak to her.

Ever since that night walking back from The Folly in the half-darkness, he'd known that he'd made a dreadful mistake in breaking up with Faye. What had he thought he was doing, for goodness' sake? All those years he'd wasted apart from her. It was crazy when he thought about it, and even crazier still because everybody around him knew how mad he was. His mother had always been going on about Faye.

'She's the best thing to ever happen to you,' she'd repeatedly told her son. 'If you think life gets any better than Faye then you're going to be sorely disappointed.'

Even Nina had seen right through to the truth of things and she'd only been around for a few months. So how come it had taken him this long to find out for himself?

Dominic cursed himself as he ran on through the streets. He had to find her – right now. He'd wasted too much time already but, as he ran up and down each street in turn, he realised that the big confession wasn't going to happen today and so he slowly retraced his steps back to the gallery, feeling defeated and deflated.

'No luck?' Simon asked when he walked through the door.

'You sure it was her?' Dominic said.

'Pretty sure,' he said, looking at his friend quizzically. 'Why don't you give her a call?'

Dominic gave a half-smile. 'Because what I have to say really can't be said over the phone.'

* * *

It was one of those wonderfully long summer evenings when the sun seemed reluctant to set and the long tall shadows stretched across the lawn slowly and imperceptibly. Nina had spent the day tidying up around Dudley's study, filing his notes and photos and preparing email enquiries he was planning on sending to publishers. He'd been out for the day and, although Nina had been able to go about her job unchecked, she couldn't help but miss his jovial company. She didn't even mind his temper tantrums anymore. They no longer scared her, because she knew they would blow themselves out in a moment and he would be back to laughing once again. But she couldn't help feeling weighed down by the knowledge that she'd probably not be around to witness any more of those amazing tantrums because the novel was complete, the study was all in good order and everything was prepared for the anniversary party. Nina's job was done.

There was only one person she could turn to at such a time and so, sitting herself down on a wrought-iron bench beside a border stuffed with towering hollyhocks, she rang her friend.

'Nina!' Janey's cheery voice cried down the phone a moment later.

'Hi, Janey.'

'You've been hiding away from me again,' Janey said. 'What's been going on? I've left you about a thousand voicemails!'

'No you haven't,' Nina told her. 'You've left two and then you flew off to Corsica.'

'Oh, yes,' Janey said, 'and I met this amazing guy from Edinburgh who was researching a book on wildflowers.'

Nina smiled. 'What happened to the Italian you met on your last trip?'

'Who?' Janey said. 'Oh, *him*!' she said a moment later, once clarity dawned. 'We kind of lost touch. You know how it is.'

'I certainly do,' Nina said, thinking of the mysterious Justin and then going on to tell Janey about his disappearance off the face of the earth – or Norfolk at least.

'You don't know when you're going to see him again?'

'Well, I'm not really expecting to,' Nina said with a sigh that threatened to topple a nearby hollyhock.

'Oh, right!' Janey said, obviously not believing her friend.

'No, *really*, I can't see it happening. It was just one of those brief encounters,' she said wistfully.

'God, you're such a hopeless romantic, Nina! It wasn't even a fling! You could at least have had a proper fling with him, instead of a quick peck on the cheek.'

'It wasn't like that,' Nina said.

'What was it like, then?' Janey said.

She took a moment before answering, trying to work it out in her own head first. 'It wasn't like anything really. At least, not like anything I've ever known. It was just—' she paused, 'really *easy*. Like we weren't planning anything. We just enjoyed being in the moment. Does that makes sense?'

'Not really,' Janey said. 'Didn't you want to – *you know*?'

Nina couldn't help laughing. 'Well, he was certainly handsome.'

'Blimey – if I'd been you, I would have had a mad passionate affair.'

'What, on the river bank in front of the dogs?'

'Definitely!'

Nina laughed, feeling herself blush at the mere thought. 'It wasn't like that,' she said again.

'But it could be – if you give him a call,' Janey said. 'You've got his number, haven't you? Why don't you have a good long chat instead of all these silly texts flying about?'

Nina took a deep breath. 'I don't want to chase him. I just don't have that in me.'

'Oh heavens!' Janey chided. 'Men *love* to be chased! I'm sure he'd fall all over you if you gave him a call. It would be red roses and chocolates at dawn, I'm sure.'

'Anyway, it doesn't matter, because I don't think I'll ever see him again. He's probably forgotten all about me.'

'Like you've forgotten all about him?' Janey said astutely. For all her flippancy, she did have the ability to hit the nail on the head every so often.

Nina closed her eyes. 'I'm leaving here first thing on Saturday,' she said.

'But I thought the party was on Saturday afternoon,' Janey said.

'It is,' Nina said.

'You're not staying for it?' Janey sounded surprised.

'I can't,' Nina said. 'I have to go. I don't want to make a big fuss so I thought it would be easier to slip away before everything kicks off.'

'But that's *crazy*! You've virtually organised it all yourself. You should stay and have some fun!' Janey said.

Nina had spent the last few days thinking long and hard about this very issue. 'It would just be too sad knowing that I have to leave afterwards, and I'd probably only make everyone else miserable if I was down,' she reasoned. 'I *have* to go before that. It's the best thing I can do. Really it is.'

'And where exactly are you going?' Janey asked.

'Ah,' Nina said, suddenly feeling a little shy. 'Is your futon free?'

'Not exactly,' Janey said.

'Oh,' Nina said, realising that her friend had a life beyond her own needs.

'I mean, there's this stray cat that seems to have made his home on it.'

Nina laughed. 'Oh, Janey! You *hate* cats.'

'I know!'

'And you're always going away. You can't possibly look after an animal.'

'He's kind of shared by everyone in our street, I hear, but he is rather partial to my futon. Still, if you don't mind sharing.'

Nina breathed a sigh of relief at not being homeless. 'I won't mind a bit!'

Chapter Thirty-One

Saturday morning dawned bright and clear, promising the sort of day associated with ice cream, straw hats and burnt shoulder-blades. Marie the cleaner was doing her best to keep everything in order as endless lines of people marched through the garden carrying tables, chairs, crates of champagne, balloons, napkins, tablecloths, musical instruments and flowers. Poor Benji didn't quite know where to put himself, and seemed to be under somebody's feet wherever he chose to play.

'Come on, Benji. Looks like neither of us is wanted anymore,' Nina said, taking pity on him and inviting him into the study. There wasn't a lot for him to do in there, but at least he'd be out of the way, and he was company.

If Nina was honest, she felt at a bit of a loose end, too. Alex had arrived home late the night before and seemed to have taken charge of coordinating the marquee whilst Olivia and Dudley were busy coordinating themselves. So she sat in the study watching Benji dismantle one of Dominic's old Transformers, watching the clock tick round and wondering when she should quietly slip away.

She'd spent half of the night before writing a letter to Olivia and Dudley, thanking them for welcoming her to their home and for making her time there so wonderful. She told them that it was the best job she'd ever had and that she would miss them enormously. It had been a good job she'd written the piece with a Biro, too, because, had she used her favourite fountain pen, it would have ended up a terrible blotchy mess with the tears she had shed over it. She was going to leave the letter on Dudley's desk and would slip out of the house with her suitcase once the coast was clear.

Janey thought Nina was mad to miss the party and it seemed a shame that she'd never get to wear the beautiful dress that Olivia had bought her. She couldn't help feeling a bit like Cinderella before her fairy godmother makes a timely appearance. It was hard not to feel sorry for herself as she sat in the study, listening to all the to-ing and fro-ing outside in the hallway – the laughter, the shouting and the general chaos that always seemed to surround the Milton family. How she would miss it all, but Nina kept having to remind herself that she wasn't part of this family. She was just the hired help and she was no longer needed and, as ungrateful as it might seem to the Miltons that she was running away before the party, she just couldn't bear to stay – being a part of the fun and the games only to have to leave afterwards; it was just too cruel a fate.

Needing someone to confide in, she'd even texted Justin that morning about her decision.

It's all too much she'd written.

But you can't leave! he'd texted back immediately.

But I can't stay she'd said.

Are you sure they don't want to keep you on?

Nothing's been said she'd told him.

Talk to them, Nina! x

312

But she couldn't put her own selfish worries first. This was Dudley and Olivia's special day and she didn't want to spoil it with talk of employment.

'Do you fancy going out into the garden, Benji?' Nina asked, suddenly in need of some fresh air. The little boy looked up from his home on the carpet. 'We could see if we can find any snails behind the greenhouse.' Nina wasn't particularly fond of molluscs, but she thought it would be an incentive for Benji. Nina saw that she was right as he sprang up off the carpet, his toy forgotten.

They walked across the lawn together, careful to avoid the staff who were setting up in the marquee. Olivia had been most disappointed to find out that marquees only came in white, and that it hadn't been possible to have one in silver or purple to match her colour scheme. Nevertheless, it had caused great excitement as it was erected on the lawn at the back of the mill house on Friday morning.

Nina hadn't been quite sure what to expect, but was surprised when she saw an army of five men set it up. She'd taken several trips into the garden throughout the course of the morning to check on the progress. She'd never been in a marquee before, other than the tiny, tatty ones at the local fete, and she tried to imagine what it would look like once the furniture and decorations were in place. As she walked past with Benji, she attempted to get a glimpse inside the vast tent, seeing only a floating mountain of balloons in purple and silver, and a towering flower display filled with gigantic lilies that looked as if they had been carved from marble. The champagne, wine and glasses had all been delivered the day before, too. It was going to be a wonderful party.

'Come on!' Benji cried, catching hold of Nina's hand. 'Snails!'

'I don't think they will have gone anywhere,' she told him, smiling at his youthful impatience to see everything immediately, and following him as he pulled her towards the walled garden.

'Are you sure this looks okay?' Dominic asked his mother in a bedroom that was used as a dressing room these days. 'Because I feel like an idiot.'

'Well, you don't look like one,' Olivia said. 'A quick trip to the hairdressers and a half-hour session with a nailbrush to remove all that paint, and you're now the smartest young man in East Anglia,' Olivia said, brushing invisible dust off his jacket.

'I feel like a chump,' he said, shaking his head.

'Once every so often, one has to step out of one's comfort zone for the pleasure of others,' Olivia told him. 'Doesn't it feel nice to be out of those scruffy old clothes of yours?'

'No, it doesn't,' Dominic said. 'They're comfortable and they're practical.'

'But it's so nice to see you in something smart. The girls will swoon.'

Dominic sighed. There was only one girl he wanted to swoon and he wasn't even sure if she was coming to the party.

'Faye won't recognise you,' Olivia went on.

'She's coming?' Dominic said.

'Of *course* she's coming. Although she keeps telling me she won't.'

'Does she?'

Olivia nodded. 'Have you said something to upset her again?'

'No!' Dominic said.

'Because I won't have Faye upset, Dominic. You understand?'

'Mum, I'm not going to upset Faye.'

'Well, you seem to be doing nothing else these last few years,' Olivia said.

'Hey – that's not fair!'

'No? It's true though, isn't it?'

'Mum, I know it's your anniversary today, but you're not going to get away with picking on me.'

'These things need saying – whether it's an anniversary or not,' Olivia pointed out, her face unusually grave.

Dominic ran a hand through his dark hair and took a deep breath. 'Look,' he said, 'you don't need to worry about me and Faye anymore.'

Olivia's bright eyes widened at this declaration. 'Really?' she said.

'Now, don't go getting excited,' Dominic said quickly, but he could already see that it was too late. 'I'm just going to talk to her. I think—' he paused. 'I think I might have made a mistake when I split up with her.'

Possibly for the first time in her life, Olivia was speechless.

'Well, say something!' Dominic prompted her.

Olivia nodded. 'She's here now.'

'Faye?'

'Of course *Faye*!'

'In the garden?'

His mother nodded again. 'I told her to come to the party, but I didn't tell her to work in the garden – not with the party and everything – but she seemed quite determined to finish putting in a row of obelisks for the roses.'

'She's in the rose garden?'

'Yes!' Olivia said.

'Okay,' Dominic said, his eyes darting from side to side as he tried to gather his thoughts. 'She's in the rose garden.'

'Well, go on then!' Olivia said and, needing no more encouragement than that, Dominic shot out of the room, still wearing his suit.

Faye was waist-deep in roses when he saw her, wielding a hoe with feminine menace. She didn't see him approaching at first and he took a moment just to look at her. Her dark hair swung about her face and her bare arms were the colour of dark honey. She was smiling as she worked and Dominic couldn't help smiling, too, as he watched her – and that's when she saw him.

For a moment, they just stood there staring at one another – him in his smart trousers, white shirt and jacket and her in a pair of blackberry-stained denim dungarees.

'Hi,' she said at last, resting her weight against her hoe.

'Hello,' he said.

'You look—' she paused, biting her lip, her head cocked to one side, 'nice.'

He shrugged, embarrassed that he was still wearing the ridiculous clothes.

'Thanks,' he said. 'So do you.'

Faye laughed and Dominic couldn't help but laugh, too, but he hastily cleared his throat and suddenly looked very serious.

'Faye,' he said, but it was no good. The words just wouldn't come. Indeed, did any words actually exist that were up to the job of telling Faye exactly how he felt at that moment? He didn't think so, and so he had no choice but to show her how he felt instead, moving towards her and finding her lips with his in the dappled shade of the rose bed.

They didn't see the jay swooping low over the lawn to their left, nor did they notice the blackbird that hopped across the path behind them. The world had concentrated into the tiny space that they occupied and nothing else seemed to matter.

'Goodness!' Faye said a moment later. 'I wasn't expecting that!'

'No?' Dominic said.

She shook her head. 'I mean, I've been hoping for it. *So* much!'

Dominic stroked her cheek and they gazed at each other for the longest of moments, as if nothing else in the world existed. 'I'd better go,' Faye said at last.

'Don't go,' Dominic said.

'But I've got to get ready for the party. I can't very well turn up looking like this.'

'Why not?' he asked. 'You look absolutely perfect.'

Faye laughed. 'But I still have to go.'

'Listen,' Dominic said, grabbing her small hand in his before she disappeared. He swallowed hard and looked down into her gentle face and wondered how he had spent so many years without her in his life. 'I need to say sorry.' He felt her squeeze his hand in response.

'It's okay,' she told him.

'No,' he said. 'It's not okay. I treated you appallingly and I can't ever forgive myself. I don't know what happened to me. I left home and I became a different person,' he said, raking a hand through his dark hair and leaving it sticking up, so that Faye's own hand came up to flatten it back down.

'It's okay – *really*,' she told him again.

'No,' he insisted. 'It's not.' Dominic shook his head. 'I think I just got so focussed on my work and of my own sense of importance. I don't think I was a very nice person.'

'Of course you're a nice person,' Faye said. 'You were just working so hard.'

'It's no excuse,' he said. 'How could I shut you out like that? How could I think my work was more important?' He gave a funny sort of laugh. 'Because, the truth is, it means absolutely nothing without you.'

They stared at one another for what seemed like an eternity, and then Dominic took a deep breath. 'I hope you can forgive me,' he said. 'I hope – I hope we can—'

'Try again?' Faye said.

Dominic gave a nervous little laugh. 'Yes,' he said. 'I think I'd like that.'

'I would, too,' Faye said, squeezing his hand again and sealing the deal with another kiss.

Olivia was standing by the dining-room window when the two of them walked by hand in hand a moment later and her hand flew to her mouth in order to stop her scream of delight. Since her son had run out of the house, she hadn't been able to keep still and had been pacing back and forth in front of various different windows around the mill in the hope of catching a glimpse of Dominic and Faye and to find out exactly what was going on.

He'd made a mistake. He'd actually admitted to making a mistake, Olivia thought. After all those years of her trying to tell him that Faye wasn't the sort of girl to pass by, it had finally sunk in.

Olivia could hardly believe it – Dominic and Faye were a couple again – on her and Dudley's twenty-fifth wedding anniversary. She couldn't have asked for a better present.

Chapter Thirty-Two

After a manic morning of people falling over each other and dogs and children being screamed at, everything was in place for the guests' arrival and a strange quietness fell upon the mill. Nina stood looking out at the billowing white palace of the marquee. It looked glorious, as did the cheery bunting that had been threaded through the trees. Weeks of panic and preparation, and shopping and shouting had resulted in this and, for the Miltons, the party was just about to begin. That meant one thing for Nina – it was time to leave.

It didn't take long to pack. She'd only acquired two more possessions since she'd arrived at the mill: the dress Olivia had bought her and the painting Dominic had given her. It would be a shame not to wear the dress, but ungrateful to give it back, so she folded it neatly, and gently laid it on the top of her suitcase.

Nina looked at Dominic's painting. A sunset. The perfect metaphor for an ending. She felt as if she should leave it in the room – that it wasn't hers to keep, but she couldn't bear to part with it, so she slid it into a large paper bag and placed it under the red dress.

She felt a small stab of pain, which spread, adrenaline-like, through her body. For a moment, she couldn't move. She stood perfectly still in the centre of the room, her suitcase in her hand.

Opening her bedroom door for the last time, she walked down the stairs, placing her things in the hallway and leaving the letter she'd written on the table by the door before venturing into the living room where Olivia was painting her nails with silver polish.

'Ah, Nina!' she said, turning her head, which was full of curlers, and proffering an immaculate hand towards her. 'What do you think?' She indicated the finished hand.

'Very nice,' Nina said, admiring the silver-tipped hands.

'You're welcome to use it, too, if you like.'

'Oh. Thanks,' Nina half-smiled, not quite seeing herself with silver nails.

'Have you seen the painting Dommie's given us as an anniversary present?' she asked. 'It's a portrait of Dudley and I from one of my favourite photos of us. It's simply wonderful!'

'I shall have to take a look,' Nina said, blinking back the tears and doing her best to avoid having to lie. 'Listen,' she said, 'I just wanted to say thank you for everything.'

'Oh, you don't need to thank me! It's us who should be thanking *you*!' Olivia said.

'But I wanted to make sure you know how grateful I am for everything you've done for me – before the chaos of the party and everything.'

Olivia shook her head. 'You are the sweetest girl!' she said. 'Has Dudley had a word with you yet?'

Nina shook her head, knowing that it would be easier if she slipped away without seeing her boss again. She didn't think she could bear it.

'Well, make sure you—' Olivia was cut short by the telephone and Nina took the opportunity to leave.

She headed out of the mill without any real direction in mind. She supposed she should make her way to Janey's, where the futon lay in wait, until she found a place of her own.

It was hard not to slip into self-pity, but Nina refused to feel down. She'd had the most amazing summer. She'd just have to go and create an equally amazing autumn for herself somewhere new.

The driveway was beginning to fill as the first of the guests arrived and Nina squeezed through with her suitcase, taking surreptitious glances up at the windows to make sure nobody had seen her leaving.

She turned around to take a last look at the mill. Its windows winked at her in the bright afternoon sun, almost as if it were bidding her to stay. *Oh go on*, it seemed to be saying, *how can you leave me?*

'Don't make this any harder than it already is,' she said out loud. But the universe didn't appear to be listening to her, for there in the driveway stood Alex.

'Hey!' he said, a grin brightening his face. 'Where are you going?'

'Home. I mean, to a friend's,' Nina said.

'You're leaving?'

Nina nodded.

'You're not staying for the party?' he asked, a deep frown on his face.

'I can't,' she said.

Alex looked at her as if she was quite mad. 'You'll be missed,' he said.

'Everyone will be having much too good a time to miss me,' she said.

Alex laughed and shook his head. 'You're funny,' he said, shaking his head.

'What?' Nina said.

'You have absolutely no idea of your own worth, do you?'

Nina stared at him for a moment, not knowing what to say.

'I wish you'd stay,' he said. 'I'd like you to meet Amy.'

'Amy?'

'Yeah,' he said, 'or was it Amber?' His eyes were bright and mischievous.

Nina smiled. Alex would never change, would he? She had been right to believe that he had never really been in love with her, and she now feared for poor Amy. Or Amber, even. 'Maybe I'll meet her another time,' she told him. 'Whatever her name is.'

He grinned at her and then he sighed. For more than a moment, they stood looking at each other, brief memories of their shared time together floating through their minds. 'I'll be seeing you, then,' Alex said at last with a light smile, and Nina nodded.

'Bye,' she said, watching as he walked towards the house before turning for the long walk down the track that led out onto the road. The hedgerows had reached skyscraper proportions and looked like enormous green waterfalls and the fields beyond were golden under the summer sunshine. It had been a truly glorious summer, Nina thought again, and she would lock it away in her heart and never forget it.

'Blast it!' Dudley said with a grunt.

Olivia turned around from her dressing table, a curler still lodged in her hair.

'What's the matter?'

'This bloody tie. I – can't – seem – to – get – it – right,' Dudley puffed in frustration.

'Come here,' Olivia got up from her chair and crossed the room. 'You always were all fingers and thumbs on important occasions. I even had to straighten your tie at our wedding – remember?'

Dudley looked down at Olivia and their focus softened into each other so that, for a moment, Olivia forgot all about the tie.

'I can't believe that was twenty-five years ago,' Dudley said.

'We've been lucky, haven't we?' Olivia smiled a contented, wistful smile. 'Three fine boys.'

'With not a marriage in sight,' Dudley said with a chuckle.

'They'll make it,' Olivia said in defence. 'Now that Dominic and Faye are back together again and Alex is seeing that girl. Amy, wasn't it?'

'Amy? I thought he was seeing somebody called Melody,' Dudley said.

Olivia looked surprised for a moment but then sighed. 'Alex will settle down one day, I'm quite sure of it.'

'Well, he's certainly got good role models,' Dudley said, lifting his chin an inch, as if suddenly very proud of himself. Olivia smiled up at him.

'I suppose you're right. Not everyone's lasted the course though, have they?' Olivia said, patting her husband's perfect tie. 'John and Fiona. Tony and Sara. Anna and Michael.' She shook her head, thinking of the broken shards of marriages that lay around them.

'Harry Barclay and Emma, Kath and Madeleine.'

'Oh, Dudley – don't be cruel.'

'I wasn't being cruel, I was being generous – that was only the list of his wives. I didn't even include his girlfriends.'

'He's been unlucky, that's all.' Olivia brushed a speck of invisible fluff from Dudley's jacket and he gave her a wink.

'What's that for, then?' she asked.

'Can't a man wink at his wife without him being up to something?'

'No, he jolly well can't!'

Dudley chuckled. 'Oh, all right then. I've had some good news. A publisher wants to publish my book.'

'You're joking!' Olivia squealed.

'I'm not.'

'But I didn't know you'd been submitting your book for publication!' Olivia said.

'Now, don't get too excited. It's just a small imprint and it's not going to make us our fortune, but it does mean one thing.'

'What?'

'We can keep Nina on – because the publishers want me to crack on with a second book right away!'

'Really? Gosh, Dudley – that's *wonderful*! Does Nina know? Did you tell her when you gave her our little thank-you present?' she asked, thinking of the sweet gold chain they'd chosen for her.

'No, no. Not yet,' he said. 'I just got the email from them yesterday and thought I'd wait to tell her the news today.'

'Won't she be surprised!' Olivia was practically jumping up and down.

'We won't get the chance to surprise her if we don't hurry up and get ready.' Dudley looked at his watch and buttoned up his jacket before combing through his wildly white hair. 'Well, that's me ready,' he said a moment later, looking at his rather distinguished profile in the mirror. 'But I think *you* need a bit of extra work.' He stretched his hand out towards Olivia and teased out the final sleeping curler before kissing her on the nose.

Olivia felt herself blushing in a way that she hadn't for years; suddenly feeling very young again. She put her arms around Dudley and leant her head against his shirt. He smelt as if he'd just leapt down from the washing line. It was slightly strange; there wasn't a single trace of tobacco on him.

She felt his breath in her hair as he murmured something, but, with one ear pressed against his chest, she didn't quite hear what he said. But she knew what it was all the same and she whispered it back to him.

It was then that Alex entered the room. 'Have you seen Amber?' he asked.

'Amber? I thought you were seeing Amy?'

'No, it's definitely Amber,' he said. 'I'm almost a hundred per cent sure.'

'Well, no, darling!' Olivia said. 'I haven't seen her. Have you checked the kitchen? I heard Ziggy barking before and thought some poor stranger must have entered his lair and been set upon. You'd better rescue her before she's licked to death.'

'Right,' he said, making to leave the room.

'Talking of missing people,' Olivia called after him, 'have you seen Nina?'

'Yes – just a few minutes ago. She was just leaving,' Alex told her.

'What do you mean, *she was just leaving*?' Olivia said, a frown wrinkling its way across her forehead.

'Leaving,' Alex said, 'as in walking away with a suitcase in hand towards the bus stop.'

Olivia stared at her son in horror and then turned to glare at her husband.

'Did you know about this? Have you talked to her? Does she know? What's going on? Oh, Dudley!'

Dudley raised his hands in the air as if trying to shield himself from so many questions all at once. 'I haven't seen her all morning,' Dudley said. 'I caught sight of her briefly once, but she was heading out into the garden with Benji.'

'Well, go and get her!' Olivia all but screamed.

Dudley sprang into action, racing out of the room and the front door and sprinting across the driveway to his car. A moment later, he was honking his horn because one of the guest cars had parked him in, but then he was tearing down the driveway towards the bus stop, hoping to high heaven that he wasn't too late.

Nina was sitting on her suitcase at the bus stop like a waif, wondering if there was indeed a bus due before Monday morning or if she'd have to walk the eight miles to Janey's. She'd watched more of the guests turn down the little lane towards The Old Mill House and envied them the happy hours ahead, but knew that she had no place there now.

Reaching into her pocket, she pulled out her phone. There was a message waiting for her from Justin.

Where are you? x

At bus stop she texted back.

Think you're making a big mistake! x

Can't stay she texted back. *Would break my heart to leave after the party.*

What did Dudley say?

I sneaked away like a coward she confessed,
so didn't really tell him.

Nina!!!

Before she had a chance to reply, something strange
happened. A red Jaguar came to a screeching halt at the
end of the lane opposite the bus stop and an angst-ridden
Dudley leapt out of the car.

'Nina! What on earth are you doing?' he bellowed as he
ran across the road.

Nina gulped as she got off her suitcase. So, she'd been
found out. Her quiet exit wasn't going to be allowed.

'Oh, I'm so sorry, Mr Milton,' she said, feeling it was
proper to use his formal name now that she was no longer
in his employment. 'I wanted to say goodbye properly, but
I really couldn't bear to.'

'But you *can't* leave!' Dudley said, towering over her as
he reached her side. 'This whole place would fall apart
without you!'

'Oh, I don't think so,' Nina said, blushing furiously.

'Well, maybe I exaggerate. But *I* would certainly fall
apart.' He smiled at her. 'I couldn't go back to a pre-Nina
way of existence. It would be terrible! I'd never get anything
written. And that brings me nicely to my news. You'll never
guess what's happened,' he said, clapping his great hands
together.

'What?' Nina said, quite sure that Dudley was going to
burst with excitement.

'I've had the most incredible news.'

'Really?' Nina said.

'A book deal! I've been offered a book deal!'

'Your novel?' Nina said with an excited laugh. '*The Solitary Neighbour*?'

Dudley nodded. 'It's been accepted for a new imprint from one of those publishers you sent it to. I got an email yesterday and have been dying to tell you, but thought I'd wait until today as part of the celebrations. Anyway, don't get too excited – it's not much money, but it does mean I can keep you on. If you'll stay?' Dudley's white eyebrows shot into his forehead.

'If I'll stay?'

He nodded. 'Please say you'll stay, Nina! Stay with me whilst I write this next book and the next one and maybe even the one after that! I need a research assistant as well as a secretary and you've been invaluable to me as a sounding-board too. You're the only one I trust to read through my novel during early draft form.' Dudley gave a big warm-hearted chuckle, but there was a touch of the vulnerable school boy about him and Nina's heart melted.

'Oh, Mr Milton,' Nina said, tears sparkling in her eyes. 'Dudley! I'd *love* to stay!'

'You would? I mean, *you will*?'

Nina nodded and laughed as he clapped his great hands together. 'Yes!' she said. 'Yes *please*!'

'Come along then,' he said, grabbing her suitcase.

Nina could hardly contain her excitement as they bumped down the track towards The Old Mill House again. She'd truly believed that she'd never see it again and yet here she was with an open invitation to stay for as long as Dudley had ideas for stories. She must buy him some inspirational books about writing to make sure that he never ran out of ideas, she thought to herself.

'Hurry up, now!' Dudley yelled as he parked across a piece of immaculate lawn. Forgetting her suitcase for a moment, she ran across the driveway in an attempt to keep up with him.

'Livvy?' he shouted as he opened the front door. 'I've got her!'

Nina laughed. He made it sound as if she was some wonderful prize.

'Oh, Neeenah!' Olivia cried, entering the room in a cloud of perfume and silver chiffon. The rollers were long gone and her pretty red hair bounced around her flushed face. 'I was so worried that we'd lost you! How silly of us not to tell you sooner. Dudley's told you the news, hasn't he?'

'Yes, he has,' Nina said. 'It's wonderful – really wonderful!'

'I'm going to be married to a bestseller!' Olivia said, giving a little girlish laugh.

'Now, Livvy – it's just a little romance. Don't go getting too excited.'

'It's going to be a *huge* bestseller! I just know it!' she said.

Nina nodded. She thought so, too.

'Come with me,' he said a moment later and Nina followed him into the study where he produced a key from out of his desk drawer before opening the cupboard at the far end of the study – the cupboard he'd always kept under lock and key. The one place Nina had never been allowed to tidy.

Now, as the door opened, Nina gasped as she looked at the contents. There were heaps of papers in there; note-books and leaflets and all sorts of paraphernalia, including what looked very much like a Cavalier's hat.

'What on earth is all that?' she dared to ask.

He cleared his throat. 'Just a few bits and bobs I've collected for the next novel,' he said. 'I think I might need some help with it.'

Nina looked at the heap of stuff and then looked at Dudley.

'You might be here some time,' he told her.

'That suits me just fine,' she said with an enormous grin.

Chapter Thirty-Three

Nina stood dumbfounded in her old bedroom a few minutes later, a huge smile on her face as she took it all in. She was staying. She was *really* staying! She let out a little laugh, her eyes shining with joy at the thought of not having to leave The Old Mill House.

She caught sight of her reflection in the mirror on the dressing table and couldn't help but smile as if she was sharing a wonderful secret with her other self.

You are staying, her reflection seemed to say. *You are needed.*

And that meant something else. She could go to the party.

Opening up her suitcase – which Dudley had carried upstairs for her, telling her it must not leave the house again without his express permission – Nina carefully took out the red dress that she and Olivia had chosen in London, laying it out on her bed and admiring its feminine lines and pretty detailing. And then she fired herself up, flitting around like a mad thing as she got ready for the party.

Finally, when she was reasonably happy with her appearance, she left her room and went downstairs, finding Olivia in the dining room.

'Oh, Nina!' Olivia said with a gasp as she entered. 'You look gorgeous! Truly gorgeous!'

'And you do, too,' Nina said, taking in the vision in silver before her. As usual, Olivia was elegant and beautiful and her rosy perfume wafted around Nina in a heavenly cloud.

'Have you seen Alex and Amy?' Olivia said, nodding towards the window. 'I mean Amber. Don't they make the *perfect* couple?'

Nina followed her gaze and saw Alex walking with a pretty raven-haired girl who was wearing a floral-patterned dress. They were laughing and holding hands.

'Oh, she looks lovely,' Nina said.

'You know, he *is* naughty!' Olivia said. 'He rang me up a couple of nights ago and said, "Mum, I'm bringing Amy – Amber – to the party." And I said, "Who's Amber? Should I book the church?" and he just laughed after all. Apparently, they met at some talk in London by a man who'd just walked across the Atlas Mountains – and now they're going to do it, too!'

'Really?'

Olivia nodded. 'He never fails to surprise me, our Alex, and I fear he'll never settle down, but at least he's found somebody to be unsettled with. For the time being, at least.'

Nina smiled at Olivia's cheerfulness. It was good to see Alex happy. Nina had known that he wouldn't take long to fall in love again, and she sincerely hoped that he'd found the real thing this time.

'I don't suppose you've seen Dudley's pocket watch,' Olivia asked. 'He doesn't often wear it but he wanted to have it with him today and he can't find it.'

'No,' Nina said, 'I've not seen it.'

Olivia moved around the room opening drawers. 'Who on earth put this photo frame in here?' she asked, turning around with a silver frame, which housed a photo of her three sons. 'It should be on the sideboard here.'

'Let me see,' Nina said, walking towards her and taking the frame in her hands.

Olivia sighed in pleasure, her fingers stroking the glass. 'My boys,' she said, and Nina looked at the three faces in turn. Alex on the left, Dominic in the middle and—

'Billy?' she asked in a very quiet voice.

'Of course!' Olivia said. 'Isn't he handsome? Well, I think he is, but I suppose a mother will always be biased.'

'Oh, no,' Nina said, looking at the tall fair-haired man in the picture, 'you're right – he's very handsome.'

Olivia nodded, happy to acknowledge the fact that she was right. 'If *only* he would settle down. He's a pilot, you know, so he spends most of his time up in the air and flying off to all sorts of interesting places. I'm sure he meets all sorts of wonderful girls, but he hasn't brought one home for months. He did say he was seeing someone a few weeks ago, although I don't think anything came of it.' She sighed and Nina swallowed hard. 'But,' she went on, 'I thought it would be absolutely marvellous if you two kept each other company at the party. It seems absolutely absurd that you haven't actually met Billy yet. After all, you're practically family now. Anyway, he's waiting for you in the living room.'

Nina nodded. 'Right,' she said.

'Are you okay, Nina?' Olivia asked. 'You look quite strange all of a sudden.'

'No, I'm fine,' she said but Olivia was right – she suddenly felt very floaty, as if the world had tilted and she along with it.

She left the dining room and crossed the hall to the living room, taking a deep breath because she knew whom she would find in there. For it wasn't Billy who was waiting for her. It was Justin.

Chapter Thirty-Four

Justin had his back to Nina as she walked into the room, but turned around to face her when he heard her footsteps. He was wearing a sky-blue shirt, which made his blue eyes seem even brighter than normal, but his smile was hesitant.

'Hello, Nina,' he said. 'I guess my little secret is out now.'

Nina stared at him, feeling as if she couldn't breathe, let alone speak. It just seemed so strange to see him standing there in the living room at the mill and – this time – he wasn't going to run away.

'I don't understand,' she said at last.

'No,' he said. 'I think I've got some explaining to do.'

Nina nodded. 'Yes, I think you have.'

Justin took a deep breath, his hands clasped together in front of him as if he was praying. 'I'm Billy,' he began. 'Justin William Milton. Dad wanted to call me Justin, you see, and Mum wanted to call me William. Then William became Billy.'

'I'm still trying to get my head around this,' Nina said. '*You're* Billy?'

He nodded. 'But I stopped using that name when I started work. I seemed to be more of a Justin in the workplace. Billy just didn't fit me there. Does that make sense?'

Nina sighed. 'Right now, I'm not sure that *anything* makes any sense,' she said.

They stared at one another for what seemed like an eternity and then something occurred to Nina. Why hadn't she noticed the photos of Billy – Justin – that were around the room? She looked at a collection of them now on a mahogany table. They were mostly group photographs of him with his brothers where they were laughing and messing around. In one, he was wearing a cap; in another, he was wearing a pair of sunglasses. Another showed him in profile. It wouldn't have been immediately obvious to Nina, even if she had studied them closely, that this boy, Billy, was the same man she knew as Justin. Except for one photograph. The one of him with his brothers in which he'd been looking directly at the camera. The one that Olivia had found in the drawer.

'You hid that photograph in the drawer that day, didn't you? When you came back here for tea?' Nina said. She'd never really noticed that photograph before, but she obviously would have clicked if she had.

Justin nodded. 'I'm so sorry, Nina. I just wanted to get to know you away from the family. They can be pretty intense sometimes. I'm sure you know that by now. I've seen dozens of girlfriends bulldozed over by them and I wanted things to be different between us. I didn't want you feeling under any pressure – I know what Mum can be like. As soon as you mention a girl's name, she's off making lists for the engagement party. I'm sure you've seen that side of her whilst you've been working here.'

Nina had, of course, but it didn't make her feel any more comfortable about the situation she now found herself in. 'But you lied to me,' she said, her eyes narrowing in dismay.

He shook his head. 'I didn't. I *promise*. I just didn't tell you the complete truth all the time.'

'Isn't that the same thing?' she asked.

'I'd *never* lie to you, Nina. You're too special to me.'

She looked into his eyes and felt quite sure that he was telling the truth, but how could she be sure? How could she really know?

'That evening you came round to the mill for dinner – you knew I'd be out, didn't you?' she said to him, remembering the evening she'd spent with Janey and how disappointed Olivia had been that she'd missed her son.

He nodded. 'I'm sorry,' he said. 'I so wanted to see you, but you can imagine what it would be have been like if Mum had realised we were seeing each other. She would have been marching you around bridal shops before dessert had been served.'

Nina smiled in spite of herself, because she could picture the scene perfectly. Olivia would be absolutely thrilled to know that her eldest son was seeing somebody. She'd already told Nina that she had her suspicions and now Nina realised that the mysterious girl Olivia had been referring to had been her.

'Your mother says you're a pilot,' she said.

'Yes,' he said.

'So, that day when you left the garden in such a hurry and you said you had to fly – you really *did* have to fly, didn't you?'

It was Justin's turn to smile. 'I did, yes, but I didn't want to be caught by Dad, either. Honestly Nina, I really just wanted to have you to myself for a while.'

'And when you told me things were "up in the air" at work – they literally were, weren't they?'

338

Justin shook his head. 'A dreadful pun,' he said. 'It was as close to telling you the total truth as I dared at the time.'

She looked at him, his face as open and honest as she remembered it during their all-too-brief encounters, and it was impossible not to believe him. Besides, she wanted to, she really wanted to.

'Although I thought I'd given everything away with that text about Dad's pipe,' he said.

Nina nodded, realisation dawning on her. 'Ah!' she said. 'That did make me wonder. You're lucky I've been too busy to dwell on that for long or I might have worked it out.'

He shook his head. 'I've been such a fool,' he said. 'I should have just been honest with you from the start.'

'I wish you had been,' she said.

'And I'm so sorry I've not been able to see you more,' he said. 'It's been killing me, really it has. But work's been crazy and it's been impossible to get away.'

They stood silently for a moment, the grand old clock on the mantelpiece sounding the seconds between them.

'I'll understand, you know, if you don't want to see me again,' he said. 'There won't be any hard feelings.' He gave the tiniest of smiles – a smile that seemed to say that he sincerely hoped she wouldn't turn away from him now; that she'd forgive him and allow them to start again.

But Nina didn't get time to answer him because Olivia came bustling into the room.

'Ah, Nina, Billy – do hurry along now. Dudley and I have got to greet the guests. They're all arriving and it's absolute chaos! Oh, and can you possibly check on Ziggy? He's been absolutely bonkers for hours, knowing that something's going on and that he's not involved.'

Olivia left the room and Justin looked at Nina. 'Well, I'd better see to that dog,' he said.

'I'll come with you,' Nina said.

They walked down the hallway to the kitchen together, opened the door and Ziggy sprang into action, spinning around in some mad dog circles and then jumping up to stick his cold, wet nose as close to Justin's face as he could get it.

'Hey!' Justin shouted above the barking. 'I thought you'd trained this dog!'

'Don't blame *me*!' Nina said with a little laugh at the dog's antics.

'Come on, down boy!' Justin said, turning his back on Ziggy for a moment to allow him to calm down.

'How's Bess?' Nina asked.

'Oh, she's great,' Justin said, bending to fuss Ziggy now that he was a tad calmer. 'Although not enjoying the hot weather too much.'

'Who looks after her when you're away?'

'Friends here in Norfolk,' he said. 'The next village. It's where I escape to whenever I can. It's not ideal, of course. I hate not having her with me all the time, but it's the best thing for her really. I couldn't keep her in my flat in London and, until I sort myself out with a permanent place in the country, it's the only solution.'

'Why can't you keep her here?' Nina asked.

'With Ziggy?' he asked. 'You *have* seen the way my mother spoils Ziggy, haven't you? Well, Bess would be like him in no time, too.'

Nina smiled. 'I guess.'

They caught one another's eye and realised that they were

back to the people they'd been on the riverbank – talking happily and naturally about the two dogs.

'Nina—'

'Listen—'

They both spoke in unison and then laughed.

'I just wanted to say that I really like you,' Justin said. 'From the first day I saw you with Ziggy, stumbling along the footpath behind him.'

Nina bit her lip. 'I liked you, too. And Bess,' she said.

'Well, of course. Who couldn't like Bess?' he said, his smile returning like a glorious sunbeam. 'I missed you,' he said a moment later. 'I really missed you.'

'Perhaps we should only ever meet on riverbanks or – at least – with a dog present,' Nina said.

Justin laughed at that. 'I'm not sure that would work out – long term, I mean.'

'Long term?' Nina asked.

'I still want to take you to dinner, remember?'

'Well, aren't you meant to be escorting me to one right now?' she said.

He nodded. 'You're absolutely right,' he said, offering Nina his arm, which she happily linked.

Leaving the mill together, they walked across the lawn towards the marquee.

'Is that Faye with Dominic?' Nina asked as she saw the young couple walking out of the walled garden together.

'It certainly looks like it,' Justin said.

'They're back together again?' Nina asked.

'Apparently,' Justin said.

Nina grinned, but then stopped as a runaway Benji collided into her.

'Benji – NO!' Alex's voice suddenly cried from some-where behind them. 'You're not to go near those balloons!'

Nina and Justin watched in helpless wonder as the young boy tore across the lawn, with Ziggy in pursuit.

'What's going on?' Nina asked. 'Did Benji let Ziggy out?'

Thinking it a great game, Ziggy galloped after Benji who, by this stage, had managed to untie the net securing the balloons.

'Oh, no!' Nina cried. 'That's not meant to happen just yet, is it?'

'Quick! The balloons are off!' Alex shouted into the marquee and Nina and Justin watched as eighty red-faced guests piled out onto the lawn.

'Oh, *Benji*!' Marie shouted, emerging from the crowd, a look of horror on her face at her son's misconduct as he and Ziggy did a wild sort of dance together on the lawn.

'It's all right,' Olivia assured her, patting her arm. 'Look, Dudley! Aren't they beautiful?'

Nina and Justin watched as twenty-five silver balloons floated over The Old Mill House into the cloudless blue sky. Alex and Amber laughed together and Dominic and Faye exchanged a little look that seemed to speak of a future twenty-fifth wedding anniversary. It was a look that didn't go unnoticed by Olivia.

When the excitement was all over and the guests had returned to the marquee where the band had started to play, Nina turned to Justin. He was shielding his eyes as he watched the last of the balloons, but then he turned to look at Nina.

'What is it?' he asked her.

She placed her hands on her hips and shook her head.

'You know, I *still* don't know what to call you,' she told him.

'Well, it seems like you're practically one of the family now,' he said, taking her hand in his, 'so perhaps you'd better call me Billy.'

She watched as he leaned forward to kiss her. It was a moment she'd been trying to imagine since the evening on the bridge and it was definitely a moment worth waiting for.

When they finally parted, Nina couldn't help but smile.

'*Billy*,' she said. 'It might take me a little while to get used to that.'

'That's okay,' he said, 'because I think we're all counting on you being around for a good long while yet.'

Sun, sea and secrets . . .

A heart-warming and escapist read for fans of
Katie Fforde and Alexandra Potter.